PRAISE FOR KIM LAW

"*Montana Cherries* is a heartwarming yet heart-wrenching story of the heroine's struggle to accept the truth about her mother's death—and life."

—RT Book Reviews, 4 stars

"An entertaining romance with a well-developed plot and believable characters. The chemistry between Vega and JP is explosive and will have you rooting for the couple's success. Readers will definitely look forward to more works by this author."

—RT Book Reviews, 4 stars (HOT) on *Caught on Camera*

"Kim Law pens a sexy, fast-paced romance."

—*New York Times* bestselling author Lori Wilde
on *Caught on Camera*

"A solid combination of sexy fun."

—*New York Times* bestselling author Carly Phillips
on *Ex on the Beach*

"*Sugar Springs* is a deeply emotional story about family ties and second chances. If you love heartwarming small towns, this is one place you'll definitely want to visit."

—*USA Today* bestselling author Hope Ramsay

"Filled with engaging characters, *Sugar Springs* is the typical everyone-knows-everyone's-business small town. Law skillfully portrays heroine Lee Ann's doubts and fears, as well as hero Cody's struggle to be a better person than he believes he can be. And Lee Ann's young nieces are a delight."

—RT Book Reviews, 4 stars

Montana
MORNINGS

Montana
M O R N I N G S

Kim Law

Montlake
Romance

Text copyright © 2017 Kim Law
All rights reserved.

Published by Montlake Romance, Seattle

www.apub.com

Amazon, the Amazon logo, and Montlake Romance are trademarks of Amazon.com, Inc., or its affiliates.

ISBN-13: 9781503943117
ISBN-10: 1503943119

Cover design by Shasti O'Leary Soudant

Printed in the United States of America

To the Huntsville, Alabama Lunch and Learn Romance Book Club. What a great group of women! Thank you for being so welcoming each time I've visited, and for making those trips a truly enjoyable experience. And thanks for all the great ideas tossed out during our chats! I wish I lived closer, and I'd absolutely join you every month.

Prologue

This was the beginning of his and his daughter's new lives.

Gabe Wilde stood alone in the middle of the Birch Bay High School classroom, hands on hips and satisfaction overflowing, as he took in the details he'd spent the last week putting effort into. Whiteboard cleaned and waiting for the year's first assignment, periodic table gracing the back wall. Every feature of the room had been gone over with a fine-tooth comb, and he was ready for his first group of students to walk through the door. He was a high school science teacher now. And this space was all his.

Or it would be when school started the following month.

At thirty-three, a total career change might seem drastic to some, but for Gabe, at this moment in his life, it felt exactly right. And it had to be done in his hometown in Montana. Not in California, where he'd allowed his soon-to-be ex to convince him to live since leaving the family cherry orchard.

The door to the room opened with a soft whoosh, and Gabe's sister poked her head in. "Did you pick up Jenna's teacher assignment yet?"

Dani waved the piece of paper in her hand. Room assignments were being handed out in the elementary school across the street.

"I'm heading that way as soon as I leave here." Gabe made one last sweep of the room. Everything needed to be perfect. "I take it you got Haley's?"

"I did."

He looked back at his sister. "And?"

The light disappeared from her face. "They're not in the same room."

His chest ached at the words. Dani's stepdaughter, Haley, and Gabe's daughter, Jenna, were not only the same age, they were best friends. Additionally, given the issues Jenna had been through with her mother over the years—with everything escalating since he'd filed for divorce—Haley was the only person Jenna came close to being her normal self around. With everyone else, she was rude and hurtful, or she simply ignored them. In many ways, very similar to her mother. Therefore, getting Jenna and Haley into the same second-grade classroom was imperative.

"I'll talk to Colin," Gabe said. He didn't like being "that guy." The one who called in favors with the school's principal just because the two of them had gone to high school together. But for his kid? He'd do whatever it took.

"That's a good idea."

Dani slid fully into the room as Gabe remained standing in the middle of the rows of chairs, and he watched as she surveyed the space he'd been anxious to get his hands on. He didn't miss the pride that flashed through her eyes as they roamed over each detail. As she took in the nameplate he'd proudly set at the front of his desk. Though only eleven months older than him, she was still his big sister, and he had to admit that seeing her admiration for what he'd accomplished filled him with warmth.

"Teaching," she murmured when she brought her gaze back to his. "I still can't believe that's where you ended up. Who would have guessed?"

He chuckled. "Caught me off guard, too."

When he'd moved to California two years before, his one goal, other than saving his marriage, had been to figure out what he truly wanted out of life. After running the family orchard for years—a position he'd taken on solely because it had always been assumed he would—he'd decided to see if he had any real hopes and dreams of his own, and throughout his soul-searching, he'd discovered his thoughts continually turning to his freshman science teacher. The man had not only taught Gabe to appreciate the sciences, but he'd been there when Gabe had needed someone the most. Recalling that period in his life had given *him* the desire to provide the same kind of support for others. It was his time to give back. Therefore, high school teacher had seemed the obvious solution.

He'd spent the last two years getting his teaching certification and adding enough classes to his undergraduate degree to earn a chemistry major, all while working multiple jobs around his class schedule to support his wife and daughter. It had been a hard two years, but it had also been worth it. Except now he was divorced. Or about to be.

"You're going to be great at teaching." The love shining from his sister's eyes almost had him wrapping an arm around her. He wasn't much of a hugger, though, so he went another route. He lowered his gaze to her stomach instead. "And you're going to be great with a baby. You ever going to start showing, though?"

"I am!" A warm glow lit Dani's cheeks as she tugged both sides of her shirt back and pressed the material to her body. "See my bump?" She beamed up at him. "I'm at five months today."

He *could* see it, and he couldn't be more proud. The two of them—as well as their other four brothers—had come far since their family had nearly ruptured two years before, and the fact that Dani was not only happily married to Gabe's best friend and that she was the stepmother to a sweetheart of a kid thrilled him, but now she and Ben were bringing new life into their family as well. The world could be a good place sometimes.

"*Maybe* I can see it," he grudgingly admitted, and at the wide smile that suddenly covered Dani's face, Gabe couldn't help but drop an arm around her shoulders. "Come on, dumbass, let's go. Gloria is using the smoker to make barbecue tonight, and I've already been warned that if I don't get home in time to help, then I don't eat."

"You decided to stay with Dad and Gloria for good, then?" Dani asked as Gabe held the classroom door open for her. Gloria was their stepmother of eighteen months.

"Actually . . . *no.*" He and Jenna had been staying at the farm since coming home the month before, letting everyone assume that's where they would remain. But at the same time, he'd been keeping a big secret. He cut a glance down at Dani. Now seemed the time to share it. "I put in an offer on a house today."

This time it was relief that filled his sister's eyes. As well as tears. "Oh, Gabe," she whispered. Then she threw both arms around him. "Does that mean you're really staying, then? That you and Michelle aren't . . ."

He pried Dani away from him. She'd been worrying that he and Michelle might get back together? "I filed for divorce, Dani." He stared down at her. "*Months* ago."

"I know, but"—she bit her lip—"sometimes people change their minds. And you've never really talked about what happened or anything."

He hadn't talked because not everything was his family's business.

"And the divorce *isn't* final yet," she added hesitantly.

"It will be soon enough." He had a court date in Los Angeles scheduled for the day before school started. "And though a judge has yet to make it official, it's final to me. Michelle is out of our lives. For good."

His sister hugged him once more, and he again found himself staring at the top of her head.

"Really?" He gave a good-natured sigh. "Now that you're pregnant, do you plan to use hormones as an excuse to be hugging me all the damned time?"

"I might." She slapped his arm as she pulled away and then wiped at the tears once again filling her eyes. Then she gave him a tremulous smile. "I'm glad you're home, moron."

Chapter One

One month later

His daughter waited up ahead, her gaze trained on the oversize red doors in front of her, and her blonde hair pulled high on her head. She wore the yellow dress and red sequined shoes she'd picked out special for that day, with her pink PAW Patrol backpack fitted snugly over her shoulders. The sight of her brought a relieved smile to Gabe's face. The tension that had been coursing through his body for the last several days finally began to ease.

And then her small hands clenched nervously at her sides.

He cursed under his breath and picked up speed. He had *not* wanted to be late. Not for this. And to top it off, the judge hadn't even signed the divorce papers.

Gloria caught sight of him as he closed the final few feet, and she touched a hand to Jenna's shoulder. When Jenna looked up, her grandmother nodded toward Gabe.

Jenna whirled. *"Daddy."*

"Hey, kiddo." Gabe stooped and opened his arms. "I missed you."

"I missed you, too." Her words were no more than a whisper before she got them all out, and as Gabe's arms closed around the slim body, his eyes shut. He'd been gone only two days, but he'd hated having to leave at all. Not when his daughter needed him. And though she often leaned more toward pain in the ass these days than the sweet little girl he'd always known, that didn't mean she didn't need him.

"School's already started, Daddy." Worry filled Jenna's eyes. "Will I be in trouble?"

"Absolutely not." He knuckled the top of her head. "I've already talked to your new principal about it. In fact"—he dug his cell out of his pocket—"I have an e-mail from him right here that says that it's perfectly fine if you're late this morning. He also told us who your new teacher is."

He'd gotten Jenna reassigned to be in the same classroom with Haley, but then their teacher had gone on early maternity leave, leaving the school scrambling to find a last-minute replacement. They'd only finalized the plans over the weekend.

"Let me see." At Jenna's request, Gabe handed the phone over, then he looked at Gloria.

"Everything okay?" he asked.

She gave a sage nod. "One minute she's excited to meet everyone and make new friends, and the next"—she gave a tiny shrug—"we end up waiting on the front stoop, well after the bell has rung."

"I'm sorry I was late." He looked beyond the elementary school to the sprawling high school off to the right, and farther to the empty football field. Jenna wasn't alone with her nerves today. Because teaching was no longer the *only* new adventure he'd taken on for the coming year.

"It couldn't be helped," Gloria assured him. "You can't control traffic."

Nor could he have gotten back any earlier. His case hadn't been heard until the end of the day, and then there'd been a long break as it had become apparent that vital paperwork from his ex's side had been missing. Given the late hour and the fact that too many balls had to be juggled to push the divorce through in that small window of time, the proceedings had been set aside until the following month. He'd ended up catching one of the few flights still heading to Montana, which had put him in Billings around midnight.

Even six hours away by rental car, he should have been able to make it in time, but he'd gotten stuck behind an accident about an hour out. He'd called to assure Jenna that he'd stop by her classroom to see her the minute he arrived back in town, but clearly she'd instigated a different plan.

She handed the phone back to him. "I've decided that I don't like Ms. Bird."

Gabe's heart sunk. "You haven't even met her, sweetheart. Don't you think you should see what she's like first?"

"My friend Leslie met her yesterday, and she didn't like her. So I don't, either."

"That's not what Leslie said," Gloria interjected. Lines bunched between her graying brows as her gaze shifted between Jenna and Gabe. "We ran into Leslie and her family at the supermarket last night. She said Ms. Bird was nice."

Jenna shook her head. "She only said that because the grown-ups were listening, but she whispered and told me the truth. Ms. Bird isn't a nice woman. She won't like me, so I don't like her, either."

The pulse point at the side of Gabe's neck began to pound. Jenna's personality had changed so much since the divorce proceedings had begun. "How about you give her a chance before you make a decision like that?" He understood far too well the reason for the personality shift and exactly why she'd be scared to set her hopes on *any* new woman in her life. "And if you'll do that—really give Ms. Bird a chance—then I promise I won't try to change your mind if you don't like her. How about that?"

Jenna studied him with more shrewdness than a seven-year-old should possess. "But can I get a new teacher if I don't like her?"

"I'm afraid not. Ms. Bird *is* your new teacher. They won't move you again."

Once again, his daughter locked her gaze onto his. Her jawline showed her stubbornness, but the insecurity swirling in the blue starbursts around her pupils spoke the real truth. "Leslie says she's only a temporary teacher, anyway." Her chin lifted. "So there's no reason I *should* like her. She's gonna leave soon."

The air left Gabe's chest. He'd worried about that exact thing. Ms. Bird would be there for eight weeks only, at which point Mrs. Watts would return. He hadn't liked the idea of Jenna not having one teacher for the duration of the school year, but the choice had come down to either having her in a classroom with Haley *and* a temporary teacher, or *not* having her in a classroom with Haley at all. And though it had become a daily routine of his to question each and every decision he made for his daughter, in the end he'd taken the path he had so many other times over the last seven months. He'd gone with his gut.

Having Ms. Bird as her teacher would be the right move for Jenna. It had to be.

"Even though she'll have to leave"—he took his daughter's hand and gave her an encouraging smile—"it's possible that she'll be the most fun teacher *ever* until she goes." He angled his head toward the closed doors, knowing they had to move past this point and at least enter the school. "What do you say? Shouldn't we go in and find out?"

Jenna's feet remained rooted to the ground.

"You have to go in, Jenna." Gloria's soft voice drifted from the other side of him.

"But I don't *wanna*." Tears suddenly appeared in Jenna's eyes, and though Gabe had the urge to scoop his daughter up and take her immediately away from there, he didn't let himself. She had to go to class . . . and so did he.

Jenna's bottom lip trembled as silent tears slipped from the corners of her eyes, but the second Gabe stooped in front of her, she swiped at them and took a step back.

"Fine," she muttered. Her bottom lip protruded. "I'll go in. But I want to come to your room when school is over." Fear suddenly filled her gaze. "Can I do that, Daddy? Can Hannah bring me to your room?"

Hannah was the college student Gabe had hired to be his daughter's after-school babysitter. "Absolutely. But you know you won't be able to stay. I have football practice after school."

An unfortunate turn of events for the school district had left the high school without a coach only three weeks before, and deciding to call upon yet another favor, Gabe had presented the option of giving *him* a chance. Being coach to teen boys would provide more opportunity to become the mentor he wanted to be. And, after all, it wasn't as if he didn't know the system. He'd spent years volunteering with the high school's football program before moving out of the state.

The powers that be hadn't been sold on the idea at first, but when no viable candidates had surfaced, they'd been left with little choice. They'd offered him a one-year contract. With no guarantee of renewal.

"You know Pops and I would be glad to take care of her," Gloria told him softly. "She could come to our house in the afternoons if she wanted to."

"I don't want to!" Jenna shouted, all emotions now directed solely at Gloria.

Gloria's mouth snapped shut, and Gabe stared at his daughter. "Enough." He said the word calmly. "You need to apologize for yelling, and then you need to calm down." He looked at Gloria. "And I know you would. Thank you. But we're good. Jenna and I can do this."

Being on his own had been one of his personal requirements when he'd moved back to town. The home he'd grown up in had plenty of spare rooms, and staying with his dad and Gloria would definitely have made things like child care easier. But he'd found himself unable to stomach the idea. He needed to do this by himself.

"Jenna," he said, adding a warning to his tone since she had yet to apologize.

More tears squeezed out. "I'm sorry!" she wailed. And suddenly she was in Gloria's arms, and the woman was soothing her in a way Gabe knew he had yet to figure out.

He'd tried. He'd been trying for years. But there seemed to be something about a woman's touch that meant more to little girls than a dad's.

Uncomfortable, Gabe stood and took the steps needed to put him at the door, and the second Jenna had herself back under control he cleared his throat. Both ladies looked over at him.

"We have to go in, kiddo. Ms. Bird is waiting. And I've got to go meet my students, too." He wasn't officially late to class yet, due to the first hour at the high school being his free period. "Can you tell Gloria good-bye and walk me to your room?"

Jenna sniffed. "I don't know where it is." She remained in Gloria's arms.

"Then maybe you and I can find it together. What do you say?"

After a long beat, she finally nodded. Then she turned to Gloria. "Thank you for bringing me to school, Gramma," she whispered. She and Haley had taken to calling Gloria "Gramma" lately. "I'm a big girl now," Jenna continued. "I won't cry anymore."

Gloria winked at his daughter and gave her a final peck on the cheek. "You're always a big girl, sweetheart. And even big girls get scared sometimes."

She set Jenna on her feet, and Gabe watched both of them as they each sucked in a steadying breath, wiped at their eyes—he hadn't even realized Gloria had teared up—then straightened their shoulders.

And then Jenna repositioned her little purse in her right hand and lifted her left to his. "Let's do this, Daddy. We'll be okay."

Only twenty-five minutes into the morning, and Erica Bird had asked herself three times if she'd made the right decision in moving to Birch Bay. She'd never been an impulsive kind of girl, yet she'd quit her tenured job without a moment's hesitation only one week before, and until this morning she hadn't once looked back. But as she stood in front of a classroom full of anxious, excited, and some bored little faces, she thought about the unconventional apartment she'd rented in town—sight unseen—about the job she'd loved and that she'd never again have back, and about how the last few nights had been the first time in her life that she'd ever truly lived on her own. Thirty-three years old, and she was finally fully independent. And she already wanted to run back home.

Truth be told, she hadn't *wanted* to leave any of it. Not two days ago nor nearly two years before. But control of her life had been abruptly stripped from her on that late-fall day two years ago, and up until last week she'd honestly thought she'd gotten it all back under control. Only, she'd been kidding herself. She was gullible—*she was a sucker*—and she'd been on the verge of becoming someone she never wanted to be.

Her ex was her ex for a reason. She had to remember that. And she would *not* let him be in her life anymore.

She eyed the drawer where her cell phone rested. No matter how many times he texted.

A noise at the door had twenty small heads turning along with hers. No one uttered a sound as the door inched open, and as Erica rose to greet the newcomer, she glanced at the roster lying on her desk. Nerves teased at the nape of her neck. She'd been told one particular student might be late this morning, and though she was unsure of the reason for the tardiness, she did have a pretty good idea of whom that child might belong to.

She smiled at the little girl who stepped around the door in a lemon-yellow sundress, and one glance at her eyes confirmed that if this wasn't Gabe Wilde's daughter, then it had to be a family member. Erica had met his entire family while in college, and each and every one of them shared the same blue eyes now peering back at her.

She lifted her gaze to find Gabe standing behind the girl, and the shocked look on his face confirmed another suspicion. He hadn't known who *she* was.

"Erica?" he blurted out.

"It's Ms. Bird," she replied, mindful of the watching children. "And it's good to see you, Gabe."

"Good to see you, too," he muttered absentmindedly as he continued to stare at her. "But what are you doing here?"

She couldn't help the chuckle. "I live in Birch Bay now." She could've said more—she knew he was asking for more—but now was neither the time nor the place. The facts were simple. She lived there now. At least for the next two months.

And after that? She gulped. Who knew where she'd end up next.

She glanced behind Gabe, expecting to find Jenna's mother, but was surprised to see that he'd come alone. And since neither he nor Jenna had yet to step more than one foot inside the door, she went to them.

When she reached their side, she ignored the man and gave Jenna her best teacher smile. Now wasn't the time for catching up. "Welcome to the class, Jenna." When the little girl continued to study her without uttering a word, Erica tilted her head and did the same. There was a mixture of nervousness, petulance, and sheer terror in the child's eyes. The combination pulled at Erica's heartstrings. "We saved you a seat over by the window. I hope that's o—"

Erica stopped talking when Jenna shot to the opposite side of the room. Another girl had given her a finger wave, and that was all Jenna had needed.

"Jenna," Gabe spoke up. "Mrs. Bird said your seat was by the window. You can see Haley la—"

"I want to sit here," Jenna announced. Her chin quivered with the words.

"But there's no empty seat there."

Erica touched a hand to Gabe's forearm, hoping to forestall the outburst she could see building in the second grader. "She'll be fine," she said under her breath. "And it's *Ms.* Bird." At his glance, she added, "Not Mrs."

Before either of them could say more, the entire class sprang to life. Everyone began to either talk or move in their seats, which only seemed to up Jenna's stubbornness, and from Erica's viewpoint at the front of the class, she caught the lift of the child's chin as well as her unsure step back. She positioned herself slightly behind Haley's chair. Haley had taken hold of Jenna's hand when she'd reached her side, and Jenna now gripped it like a lifeline.

Erica turned to Gabe. "We'll be fine," she repeated, this time more strongly. "I'll take good care of her." When Gabe finally pulled his gaze from his daughter, Erica nodded toward the door. "You'll see her after school?" she prompted.

His eyes, so similar to Jenna's, narrowed the slightest bit, but he didn't argue. Instead, he turned back to his daughter. "I'll see you in my classroom this afternoon, Jenna. Be good."

Jenna didn't acknowledge her father's words, but Erica's eyes widened at them. In his classroom? Since when had the man become a teacher? And did that mean that he no longer managed his family's cherry orchard?

No. She answered her own question. He'd never give that up. He had to be doing both. Because that had been the one thing she'd known for certain about Gabriel Wilde back when they'd dated. He would never move away from Birch Bay. Never *not* take care of the family farm first. Hadn't that been the crux of why they'd begun to fall apart?

He would return to Birch Bay after graduation, and she'd always seen herself going home.

To her high school sweetheart, as it turned out.

Gabe was watching her again, as if to plumb the thoughts running through her head. But he was out of luck. She'd mastered masking all emotions years before. It had been key to becoming an excellent elementary school teacher. Never show fear. Never let the kids think they have the upper hand.

As it turned out, her skills had transferred to her personal life, as well. How would she have coped the last two years if they hadn't?

Anger flared as she realized she'd let her mind go to her ex yet again, and Gabe's brows lifted as if in question. The move had Erica wondering if she'd let something show, but before she could give it further thought, the noise level behind her rose even higher. Gabe backed out of the room, and with a tiny finger salute, he was gone. And Erica was left standing in front of a room of now-rowdy kids, one of whom Erica could see would *not* be sitting anywhere but beside her friend.

Erica didn't like to give in to children who simply wanted to get their way. That didn't foster respect between teacher and child, and she maintained that mutual respect had been key in the two statewide teacher-of-the-year awards she'd earned. But in this instance, she got the distinct impression that Jenna wasn't merely trying to get her way. She *needed* to sit with her friend. At least for now.

Erica glanced at the seating chart she'd made as she'd taken roll. "Nikki or Brody"—she said to the two children sitting on either side of Haley—"would one of you like to sit in Jenna's seat for now? Whoever offers can be the first one to lead us to the lunchroom today, and can do it for the rest of the week."

Both kids immediately raised their hands. "I'll do it," they shouted in unison.

"Thank you." Erica nodded and gave both a bright smile. "What great helpers you two are." She looked at the girl. "How about if we let Nikki take Jenna's seat this week, and she can lead the line to the lunchroom for us, and then Brody can sit by the window next week, and then *he* can lead the line?"

And maybe by then Jenna will be ready to sit in her own seat.

"Yes, Ms. Bird," Nikki replied. Brody looked slightly crestfallen but didn't express his disappointment audibly, while Nikki hurried to gather her notebook and pencils.

As the girl made her way across the room, the idea trickled through Erica's mind that with this position being so temporary, she could just "let it go" this one time. Let Jenna—or heck, let everyone—sit wherever they wanted. Why not?

The thought was immediately replaced by irritation. She might be a failure in her personal life, but she'd never given less than her all in her career, and she wouldn't start now.

No matter how frustrated she was with the fact that something completely out of her control had cost her her home and job, there would be no giving up on her part. Not on teaching these children, and certainly not on a seven-year-old whose entire demeanor pulled at Erica's attention.

When Nikki settled into her new seat, Erica thanked her before turning back to the now-empty chair. "Jenna, please have a seat, and we'll continue class."

Jenna didn't budge.

Instead, her gaze locked on Erica's, and the two began a centuries-old battle of wills between teacher and student. A battle that usually didn't rear its head so fervently at such a young age, but one that Erica was not unaccustomed to. She was the oldest with three much younger siblings. She'd faced belligerence her entire life.

"Jenna," Erica began again, being sure to keep her voice calm and understanding. "You may sit beside Haley this week and next. Until the end of next Friday afternoon. That's nine days. Then I'll ask you again to take the seat you've been assigned. Doesn't that seem like a fair compromise?"

Jenna's chin wobbled, and her eyes darted to the window seat. Her throat moved with a small gulp as she looked back at Haley, and Erica caught a slight nod of encouragement coming from Jenna's friend.

Finally, and without looking at Erica, Jenna sat. Erica breathed a small sigh of relief.

But her relief was short-lived when Jenna hunched her shoulders and tucked her feet up under her chair. Erica felt that she got a peek inside the little girl in that span of a few seconds. This wasn't a child wanting her way; this was a child who'd lost her way.

Chapter Two

And that, ladies and gentlemen, is what—"

The bell sounded, cutting Gabe off midsentence, and his gaze darted to the wall clock. The day was over already? Chairs screeched as they were pushed away from desks, and he took a step backward, making room for the students to file out.

"See you tomorrow, Mr. Wilde."

"Catch you outside, Coach."

Additional comments were tossed his way as the group of mostly freshmen filed past, and as the room emptied, pleasure filled Gabe's chest. He'd done well for his first day on his own. His five classes contained a mix of upper- and lowerclassmen, with subjects ranging from intermediate through the advanced sciences. The course load would make for a tough year, but he was up for it.

The door closed behind the last student, insulating Gabe from the clamor of the hallway. He could hear footsteps and chatter just outside the door, even hoots and laughter coming from farther down the hall. But inside his classroom, silence prevailed. Though only for a moment.

The door opened, and two seniors from the football team strolled in. "Hey, Coach. How was your first day?"

Gabe appreciated the question. The team had been practicing together for a week now, and several of the guys had picked up on Gabe's abundance of excitement for his new career. They'd teased him about it for days.

"Couldn't have been better," he answered. "How were yours?"

A broad grin split the ginger-haired boy's face. The look could be one of only two things coming from Chase. Something involving a girl or . . .

"I heard from Boise State."

Or football. Gabe's heart thudded for the kid. "Good news?"

Chase was a running back, six two, and as strong as an ox. And he was *good*. He'd moved to Montana from a little-known town in the middle of Oklahoma last spring when his parents had divorced and had already shown himself to be one of the best on the team. "They're watching me, Coach," Chase said now. "They're coming to a game."

"Dude!" Caleb, the other student who'd come in, thumped Chase on the back. "You didn't tell me that."

Chase's grin grew even wider. "I was saving it for Coach. He put in the word for me."

"I doubt my word did anything." Especially considering this was his first year of coaching. Yet, the speed with which Chase had heard from the school was impressive. "Your video spoke for itself," he told the boy. "As well as your talent."

"Well, I'm giving you credit. I wouldn't have sent in the video without your help."

"I only held the camera." They'd stayed late a couple of days the week before, pulling in a handful of underclassmen to help with the drills to highlight the senior's moves. "They say which game they're coming to?"

Chase's chest expanded with a deep pull of air. "All I was told is 'soon.'"

Their first game was Friday night. "Then we'd better make every minute of practice count."

The door opened, and several more players poured in, no one seeming in a hurry to dress for practice. They draped themselves over anything and everything other than an actual chair, and began talking as if Gabe weren't in the room. After Chase filled them in on his news, another mentioned the full-ride last year's quarterback had gotten at Boise, as well as a couple of other seniors up in Kalispell who'd already signed with other colleges. Football was big in Montana.

Long fingers of nerves crept slowly around Gabe's windpipe as he listened, the true stakes of his job crystallizing in a way they hadn't before. His ability to be an effective coach was so much bigger than whether he'd be able to maintain his own position in the coming years. He had to get his contract renewed, *and* he had to get that scholarship for Chase.

He had to take the team to state.

He moved through the room as the boys continued talking, tidying up for the following day and trying not to let the pressure of the task he'd been given weigh down on him. He'd secured the teaching position at the beginning of summer, as soon as he'd finished his student teaching in California. And honestly, a teaching position and coming back home was all he'd been looking for. But when the previous coach had been unexpectedly fired for taking college bribes, a flame had begun to burn in Gabe's belly. Though his volunteering with the team before had started more as a means of escaping a bad situation at home, he'd quickly grown to love it, and he'd missed it since giving it up.

Within minutes of hearing the news of the open position, he'd understood that he now wanted more. He wanted the chance to prove himself. The problem with hiring him, however, lay in the fact that even though he'd been around the system for years, *he'd* never actually played football in high school.

His younger brother Cord had, and Cord had ridden a scholarship into premed.

But Gabe? Not even for one season.

Though he'd been a star player in junior high, their mother had tied Gabe to the sidelines his freshman year. She'd been a stereotypical narcissist. Life had been all about her. So when Gabe had begun getting a lot of attention, she'd made sure to put a stop to it. She'd claimed a falling-out with the coach, and had announced that her firstborn son couldn't possibly play for someone like that.

Of course, the same hadn't applied to his brother. Cord had come along the following year, and not a word had been said about him quitting. She'd also never attended any of Cord's games.

Disgust enveloped him. She'd never cared for him, no matter how she'd acted. Just like she hadn't cared for his five siblings. And damn, but he'd known it, even back then.

His mother had treated him differently than his brothers and sister for the most part, and though no one had ever called her on it—or diagnosed her disease until after she'd died—he'd known that at times he'd been held up as the favored one. And the thing was, he'd silently enjoyed it. He'd even gone along with the majority of her decisions—no matter how irrational—because he didn't want to lose that favoritism.

But he sure as hell hadn't understood at the time how her actions were affecting him.

He pushed away thoughts of his mom and checked his watch. Jenna should have been there by now. Hannah was supposed to pick her up at her school and immediately bring her over.

So then, where were they? And should he go look for them?

I'll take good care of her.

Erica's words from that morning echoed in his head—as well as the casual way she'd dismissed him from her room. He ground his teeth together. He didn't need or want anyone else "taking good care" of his daughter. That was his job.

But also, what in the world was Erica Yarbrough doing in Birch Bay? *Bird. She was Erica Bird now.*

Only, she wasn't married anymore.

The classroom door opened once again, and this time when Gabe swung his gaze in that direction, the first thing he saw was blonde hair, now slightly drooping from its original perch.

"Daddy." The word came out more a sigh of relief than an expression of excitement as Jenna ran to him. She was halfway up his body, the tension in her limbs holding her in place, before his arms could close around her. He glanced at Hannah, and the worry darkening the other girl's eyes only added to his.

"How was school?" He drew back, taking in the pinched corners of his daughter's mouth.

"Fine."

At the shortened, one-word answer, he looked at her babysitter again but continued speaking to Jenna. "Did you have any trouble finding Miss Hannah after the bell rang?"

"No." Jenna peered over his shoulder. The players had gone quiet behind him, as if waiting their turn for Jenna's attention. Some of the older guys remembered his daughter from when he'd helped with the team before, while the others had met her when she and Hannah had stopped by practice a couple of times the week before. Several of them had become her instant buddies.

She giggled at something one of them must have done behind him.

"Jenna," Gabe said, attempting to snag his daughter's attention, but she ignored him. "Tell me about your day." Had something gone wrong? The tension still running through her body worried him. "How did you like Ms. Bird?"

"Can I go talk to Chase?" With this, she finally looked at Gabe. Her eyes had gone flat, and Gabe held in his sigh. He couldn't tell if there had been a real problem with school or if Jenna was simply freezing him out. They went back and forth from her seeming to be on his side, the two of them against the world together, to her wanting nothing to do with him.

"Sure you can," he answered, and she immediately wriggled out of his arms. "But only for a minute. The guys have to get out to the field before their big bad coach shows up."

He didn't get the laugh he'd wanted from his daughter, but several of the guys snickered under their breaths. Chase reached out a hand for Jenna. "Come hang out with us, Pigtails. We've been waiting for you."

Gabe watched as the guys in his classroom came together, all of them focusing their attention on his daughter, and he couldn't miss the way her eyes lit up.

Turning back to Hannah, he spoke in a low tone. "What happened today?"

She shrugged. "Nothing that she told me about. But she didn't want to leave when I got there. She wouldn't even consider it until Dani showed up. And *then* she wanted to go home with Dani and Haley."

"She threw a fit?"

"An impressive one."

Gabe eyed his daughter again. Hannah had been working for them for the last couple of weeks to help get Jenna acclimated to a routine, so she wasn't unaware of the tantrums Jenna could throw when she put her mind to it. It was yet another change to Jenna's personality that had taken place since last Christmas.

"In fact," Hannah continued, "it was her teacher who finally convinced her to come with me."

Gabe frowned. "Erica?"

Hannah's brows went up at his use of Erica's first name. "Ms. Bird, yeah. But it wasn't just that she convinced her to go with me, but how easily she diffused the situation. It was effortless." Hannah watched Jenna, and Gabe didn't miss the fondness on the girl's face for his daughter—nor the awe in her voice for Jenna's teacher. Hannah planned to graduate with an elementary education degree from U of M in Missoula. "Ms. Bird was impressive." She turned back to Gabe. "Did you know she's won teacher of the year twice?"

He rocked back on his heels. He'd had no idea. "She told you that?"

"No, but I looked her up after you sent me her name. Impressive. You're lucky to have her here for Jenna."

"She's only staying for a couple of months." He frowned at the unintended shortness to his words and ignored the curious glance Hannah shot his way. She hadn't meant to imply that *he* couldn't handle Jenna on his own, he knew that. And the fact was, she was right. A multi-winning teacher of the year . . . Jenna was lucky to have Erica. No matter how temporary.

"Well, I hope she sticks around after Mrs. Watts returns," Hannah added. "Even if it's only as a substitute. With any luck, a position will open up next year, and we can keep her."

Gabe didn't reply. Instead, his mind chose that moment to rewind to the day he and Erica had broken up. He'd dumped her the night he'd returned from spring break his senior year. After spending the week in LA with his now-brother-in-law, Ben. And with Michelle.

He'd met Jenna's mother that week, and man, he'd been smitten. They'd done little more than hang out. And flirt, of course. Heavy flirting. Yet, it was almost as if Gabe *had* to be with her after that. Not that he'd told Erica any of that, of course.

Instead, he'd taken her out to dinner that night, prepared to give her the we've-grown-apart speech. She'd been living an hour from campus at that point, putting in her semester of student teaching, and they'd been growing more distant since Christmas. But he'd barely gotten to his practiced speech before she'd nodded in agreement. It had been time to part ways.

Then he thought about the day he'd first met her. And he wondered how he could have ever chosen Michelle over Erica.

"Come on, Jenna." Hannah interrupted his thoughts, pulling him back to the present. Several of the guys had already left the room, and it was time for Hannah and Jenna to head home.

"I don't want to," Jenna replied. She didn't even look their way. Remaining at Chase's side, she took a step closer to the boy, and Chase's ears pinkened when she wrapped an arm around his leg.

"I've"—Chase gulped nervously—"got to go change for practice, Jenna."

"Then I'll come watch you practice."

"You can't stay today," Gabe interjected.

"But, Dad." She still didn't look at him.

"No buts. We have a very important practice this afternoon. Our first game is Friday night, and we need to be prepared." He glanced at Chase and nudged his chin toward the door. "Go on. She'll be fine."

"Why can't I stay?" Jenna whirled on him.

Gabe crossed to his daughter and squatted to be on the same level with her, but he waited until the last of the players had left the room before speaking. "This is why Miss Hannah is here, remember?" He gave his daughter an encouraging smile. "She'll keep you company after school so you won't get lonely until I get home."

"But I won't be lonely at practice." Jenna's eyes flashed hot. "I won't be any trouble, either, so why can't I stay? I don't want to go home." Her voice rose, and Gabe caught movement out of the corner of his eye as Hannah neared. But before either of them could say anything else, Jenna sprinted across the room. "I'll be good," she shouted. "I promise. I won't even talk to nobody. Just let me stay, Daddy. Please!"

Guilt squeezed his chest as his daughter literally huddled in the far corner of the room. The poor kid blamed herself for the divorce. For Michelle not loving her enough.

Or so her counselor said.

But her counselor had also made it clear that one of the best things for her was having a schedule. Loving support, of course, but also defined rules. And that meant that sitting on the sidelines every day, waiting on her father, wasn't in the plans.

When silent tears began to spill over her cheeks, Gabe sighed. He stood and held both arms out to his sides in defeat. "Fine." Jenna's sobs immediately ceased. "You can stay. But only for today." He looked at Hannah, ignoring the inner voice asking if he'd just been played. "You're good with sticking around here today?"

The teen nodded, but he saw the flash of disapproval before her gaze dropped.

When Jenna marched to Hannah's side without another word and took her hand, smiling brazenly up at the girl, Gabe suspected Hannah's disapproval might be well placed. He shouldn't have given in.

But how was he supposed to watch his daughter cry and not do anything about it?

Chapter Three

The glowing red numbers of the scoreboard read 1:06 remaining in the fourth quarter, the score 49–7. Birch Bay was *not* in the lead.

Gabe ran his hand over the back of his neck as he studied the defensive setup on the field. Everything had gone so well during practices.

The other team punted . . . and the quarterback took a knee. And Gabe blew out a relieved breath. They were putting Gabe and his guys out of their misery. Between the time provided between each play, and the number of punts remaining before turning the ball over, the clock would run down to zero. Thank goodness. It was one thing to be outplayed, but entirely another to be outcoached, and Gabe had no doubt where blame lay for tonight's massacre. He also wasn't entirely sure another week of practice would change enough before the next game.

What had he been thinking to ask for the job? He could single-handedly destroy every one of these boys' chances to play at a higher level. And for what? To prove he was worth something?

The sour burn of bile lined the back of his throat as he crossed his arms over his chest and waited for the visiting team to let the seconds tick down, then he took part in the end-of-game ritual of shaking the other team's hands. The cherry on top of the night came when the opposing coach slapped Gabe on the back in an I-feel-for-you kind of way.

The guys headed for the locker room, their long faces showcasing matching disgust with the night, and Gabe hung back, giving them time to hash it out among themselves before he and his assistant coach followed. There was no need to hurry. What was he going to say to them, anyway? That with any luck the school board would fire him before the next game?

The negative talk ticked him off as badly as the embarrassing loss had. What he needed to be doing was focusing on how to fix the situation, not on beating himself up. His skills needed work. *Quick.* And he could do with a new assistant, as well—or three. The entire coaching staff had been fired along with the head coach, and only one had been hired along with Gabe. And though the other man had experience at the junior high level, he'd seemed as out of his element as Gabe had tonight.

Gabe stooped to retrieve a water bottle that had fallen between the benches, and when he stood he forced himself to take in the reality facing him on the other side of the football field. There were embarrassingly few residents making their way off the bleachers. Most of them had gone home long ago.

Birch Bay had a reputation for a high-quality team, and the entire town made a habit of coming out to cheer them on. Rarely did anyone leave before the clock ticked down to zero.

He spit out a curse. Common sense had him following the curse word, however, with silent thanks that the Boise recruiter hadn't chosen tonight to come out. Had he, Chase's chances of a scholarship from his top pick would have been blown.

Gabe tossed the water bottle to the team manager as the lanky sophomore finished gathering the scattered equipment, then stood, his gaze on the dispersing crowd, and thought about the fact that he hadn't seen one particular new resident of the town at tonight's game. Which had surprised him. Erica had enjoyed the sport in college. They'd gone to every home game while they'd been dating and some of the away ones. She'd even been a cheerleader in high school.

So then, why hadn't she come out tonight? Surely she'd known there was a game. It was hard to miss in a town the size of Birch Bay.

The more pressing question, though, was why had he caught himself searching the faces of the crowd for her? Whether Erica took part in town gatherings or not, it mattered nothing to him. She was his daughter's teacher.

Temporary teacher.

And that was her importance in his life at this point.

His cell vibrated, bringing him back to the moment at hand, and he realized the bleachers were now completely empty. The concession stand had closed up, and his assistant coach waited for him off to the side of the stands. Enough stalling. It was time to put the first game behind them.

Turning for the locker room, Gabe pulled his phone out to find a text from Cord.

Tough one tonight. Want to go over it tomorrow?

Cord was one year younger than Gabe, an up-and-coming doctor in a high-profile clinic in Billings, and was way too busy to worry with helping his older brother out simply because Gabe had gotten in over his head. Gabe thumbed out a reply.

Definitely. Need to watch the video first, and we're moving into the new place in the morning. Call you tomorrow night?

Sounds good. Good luck with the new house.

He tucked the phone away, nodded to his assistant, and together they made their way in to join the team. It was one game. Gabe wasn't ready to throw in the towel just yet.

Week one was in the books, and everything at school had gone exactly as planned. The principal had been pleased with her efforts, the majority of the kids were fully engaged in learning, and Erica had even planted the seeds of friendships with a couple of the other teachers. In the span of a few days, she'd already accomplished exactly what she'd set out to do when she'd moved there. Same teacher, same teaching style. Same Erica.

Yet all the "rightness" aside, she found herself hesitating on calling the week a resounding success. Something seemed off.

Or heck, possibly everything was off. She simply didn't know.

She chewed the inside of her lip as she tapped the brake pedal, motioning for the oncoming car to turn off the highway in front of her, then followed along behind it, heading for her rental on the dead-end street. She wound through the late-afternoon shadows of the pines, cracking the window to take in the smells, and as sunlight flickered across her windshield, a different emotion settled around her. A kind of calmness she'd never expected to find there. She might feel out of sorts in her new position, but she couldn't say that her unease had anything to do with the town itself. She liked Birch Bay.

She'd just spent her Saturday morning exploring the region, checking out the shops and small eateries she'd found along the drive around the twenty-seven-mile-long lake. Time had then stretched into afternoon as she'd run errands in town before spending another hour exploring the local shops. And not once had she encountered anything about the place that she didn't like.

So what, then, had her tied in knots? Was it merely the lack of having family nearby?

Possibly. Other than college, she'd never lived anywhere but Silver Creek. And granted, she was only three hours from home now. She could go for a visit anytime she wanted.

But living in Silver Creek and being only three hours away were still two totally different things.

Could her issue, then, be *guilt* for leaving her family?

She pursed her lips at that. Guilt had taken up permanent residence inside her, but her current worries didn't seem to stem from that.

It could be from fear of what would come next, though. She had absolutely nothing lined up for after she finished her contract here, and not having a plan—or a full-time job—was not something she was comfortable with. Heck, quitting her secure position with little more than twenty-four hours' thought and moving away from all she'd ever known wasn't something she was comfortable with. Yet none of those possibilities gave voice to the nagging sensation that seemed to be sitting just out of her reach.

She rounded the final curve, catching the flash of Flathead Lake up ahead, and sucked in a deep breath as if she could inhale the peace of the water. The lake was one of the best things about being a resident here. A person didn't have to go far to catch glistening water winking between the many trees. The diamond-like sparkle had a soothing effect, and she'd found herself more than once in her first week on the job taking in the last minutes of daylight from a weather-worn bench at the edge of the lake. Her hometown or not, Birch Bay was a beautiful little place.

As she pulled to a stop in front of the old fire hall that had been converted into an apartment, she glanced across the street at the two-story, stucco-and-stone home. There'd been a "For Sale" sign in the yard all week, but the sign had disappeared, and a four-door all-wheel-drive truck now sat out front.

She took her time gathering up her purchases, trying to catch a peek of her new neighbors, then jumped as if she'd been caught when her phone rang. Laughing at herself, she dug out her cell, and pleasure filled her when she saw that the caller was her youngest sister. Giving up on the idea of snooping, she pushed open her car door at the same time that she connected the call.

"E!!!" Bree squealed the second she appeared on the screen. As usual, Erica's sister was FaceTiming. "How are you? How's the new school?" Bree leaned into the phone so that her brown eyes and long lashes filled the screen. "And *ohmygoodness*, how awesome is it to live in a freaking fire hall?"

More laughter spilled from Erica at her baby sister's parade of words. "Which question should I start with?"

"All of them!" Bree shouted. She readjusted the phone, pulling back enough that Erica caught sight of a café sign written in French behind the twenty-one-year-old. "Let's start with school," Bree said. "How's the new teaching gig?"

"It's great."

"That's it?" The question brimmed with disappointment.

"Well, what else should I say? I like the school. I like the other teachers." She lifted her shoulders in a shrug. "Everything is great."

Bree sat back in her chair, her pink-tipped hair shifting around her shoulders, and shot Erica a haughty look. "You quit your job, Erica Alexandra. You quit your job, grabbed the first one offered to you—leaving all of us with nothing but speculations as to why, I might add—and *then* you moved several hours away from home. All within one week. And all you can say about your new life is that it's *great*?" The corners of her lips turned down. "Come on. That's the same as calling it 'fine.' You need *more* than fine for once in your life."

Erica didn't let herself get riled over Bree's dramatics. "Fine works perfectly for me," she replied calmly. "And anyway, you're wrong. Great *is* better than fine. Much better."

Bree's eyes sparkled with mischief. "Great is as boring as you had back home."

Erica didn't respond to the jab. "Tell me what you're doing in France yet again," she said instead, and as Bree launched into a laundry list of details on her latest excursions, Erica let herself wonder, not for the first time, why her sister hadn't had to follow the rules the rest of them had.

Yarbroughs went to college. Then Yarbroughs returned home. It was the family tradition.

They grew up to hold steady and respectable jobs like teachers, accountants, and town sheriffs. And if the females wanted to veer slightly off path—assuming they had the looks for it—they competed for beauty titles *before* settling into their respectable jobs and mother-hood. Her grandmother had actually won Miss Montana back in the day, and her mother had made it to the state competition before having to pull out due to an unexpected pregnancy—which had turned out to be Erica. Annalise, their other sister, was the cream of the crop, though. She could have swept Miss USA, hands down, if she hadn't decided not to wait to enroll in medical school. She'd had that much going for her.

But even once Annalise finished her residency, she'd return to Silver Creek. Her fiancé had bought into a veterinarian practice there about a year ago, and Annalise already had a job lined up with the local oncology group.

Yet Bree. *Sigh.* Little Bree, who was tiny but also had the beauty queen looks, was more of a dreamer than anyone in their family had ever thought about being. She was an artist, often using a variety of unconventional techniques, and she maintained the absolute belief that her muse could be found *anywhere* but at home. She'd skipped college altogether, took odd jobs whenever she needed money, and she'd spent more of the last three years outside of the country than in it.

Erica was happy for her. Really, she was. She was thrilled that her baby sister got to follow her dreams, and Erica very much hoped success would someday come her way.

But she was also jealous as heck.

"You're not even listening to me, are you?"

Bree's words reached Erica, and Erica made a face. "Sorry. I was—"

"I know what you were doing." Bree huffed out a breath. "Daydreaming again." Her sister gave an exaggerated eye roll to go with the sigh. "And they say *I'm* the one with ADHD."

Erica dropped her packages onto the chair on the front porch so she could dig out her keys. "I'm not even close to ADHD, and you know it. I just let my mind wander once in a while."

"Right. Because you're bored out of your skull."

"I'm not *bored*. I'm—"

"E. Stop it. Look at yourself. You're living Mom and Dad's life. Not yours. I've watched this for years. You merely exist. You don't *live*."

"I don't have to travel the world to *live*."

"But *thankfully*"—Bree didn't so much as pause at Erica's words—"you have the opportunity to change all of that now. And dang, you've started out right. You rented a fire hall, for crying out loud. Now show it to me, will you? I'm dying to see it."

Anger flared to life at her sister's criticism. Bree had a way of getting right up under her skin when she wanted to. "Is that the real reason you called?" Erica bit out. "And not because you were curious about how my week went? About how *I'm* doing?"

"Didn't I ask how your week went?" Bree returned. "How you're doing? They were first things out of my mouth."

They stared at each other, both stubborn, and neither backing down. Bree had always been the one to push back, and it ticked Erica off every time. *She* was the older sister.

The ridiculousness of the argument knocked the air out of her, and Erica lowered her gaze. She should apologize. Bree *had* called to check on her, and she knew that. Her baby sister was her own personal cheerleader.

Yet she didn't apologize.

Instead, she opened the door to her place and took Bree inside the fire hall. Bree had come to mind the moment Erica laid eyes on the place. She'd known her dreamer of a sister would love this apartment. So without another word, she entered the bottom floor of the small two-story structure and immediately tapped the screen so her sister could see exactly what *she* saw upon entering the room.

Flipping on the overhead light, Erica smiled when Bree gasped.

"You have a pole."

Erica bit the inside of her lip at Bree's blunt statement. Yes. She had a pole. It separated the living room from the kitchen. "I was surprised to find they hadn't removed it when they'd renovated the place. It's not like I can decorate it or even spruce it up. It's actually more of an eyesore than anything." She moved to the pole and pointed the camera up. "But it does connect to my bedroom."

"E! That is absolutely the coolest thing ever. Please tell me you slide down that thing every day. Oh!" She gasped again. "And pole dancing. You *are* pole dancing, right?"

"No!" Erica flipped the screen around so that Bree once again faced her. "Of course I'm not pole dancing. Why in the world would I do that?"

"Why in the world *wouldn't* you? You have a freaking pole."

"That doesn't mean I need to strip down and start gyrating around it."

Bree shot her a knowing look. "You cannot convince me you haven't thought about it. There's a *pole* right there, for crying out loud. *And*, you dance every morning."

"I dance because it's excellent exercise."

"So is pole dancing."

They had another staring standoff, and this time Erica caved first. She glanced away, her heart pounding as she allowed one small concession to her baby sister. "It's too big," she muttered. Because, yes, she'd thought about it. She loved dance of all kinds. She'd taken classes as a kid, and the love for it had never left her.

So of course she'd considered it. But mostly it had crossed her mind because every once in a while, she found that she *wanted* to be the type of woman who gyrated around a pole.

The corners of Bree's mouth slowly quirked up when Erica finally looked back at her, but she didn't say anything. She just smiled in the annoying way a baby sister could.

"What?" Erica snapped when Bree remained silent.

Bree gave a casual shrug. "I'm just thinking about other things that can . . . *seem* . . . too big on occasion."

"*Bree.*"

"Hey. Sometimes having something big in your life is a good thing." When Erica didn't rise to the bait, Bree added, "I'm just saying."

"We both know what you're just saying." Erica pulled out her teacher voice. She didn't want to talk about fire hall poles or any other "big" items. She'd sworn off such things. "Now did you want to see the rest of this place or not?"

"Yes, Ms. Bird."

Erica gritted her teeth at her sister's mocking tone. "I could just hang up on you."

"But you won't. You love me too much." They had another small stare-off, and then Bree sighed and the bratty-sister routine fell. "*Please* don't hang up on me. I really do want to see the rest of it. Show it to me? Please?" she wheedled. "I promise I'll behave from here on out."

"You'd better," Erica grumbled. "I've had a long week, and I'm not in the mood for this."

Before Erica could begin the tour of the rental, Bree asked, "What happened?" Erica could see the worry on her sister's face. "I thought you said your week was fine."

The problem Erica had been trying to put a name to finally dawned on her. And it came in the form of one small child. "Jenna Wilde," she said.

"Who?"

"Jenna Wilde. She's in my class. She's been difficult this week."

"How so?"

"Typical acting-out stuff. Stubbornness, talking back, refusing to do as she's asked. Only"—Erica paused as she pictured the little girl—"her eyes, Bree. That child is so sad. Or adrift might be a better word. She seems to have no anchor." She shook her head. "I'm not sure. But she has terribly tall walls for a seven-year-old. She worries me."

That was it. It wasn't the trouble that Jenna had caused throughout the week. It was the worry Erica held for her.

"What's her home life like? That's what you always mention first. Have you met her parents yet?"

Bree's questions had Erica taking a good long look at her sister. She hadn't realized Bree had ever paid that much attention to anything she'd said. Sure, they talked on a regular basis and always had. And with the twelve-year age gap between them, Erica had been fully into teaching long before Bree left town, so she'd heard Erica discuss methods of dealing with different problems over the years. But Erica had never realized that her sister had soaked any of it in.

"I know her dad," Erica admitted. "Or I once did. We went to college together. But I haven't met her mom yet. Gabe brought her to school the first day, and I haven't seen either of them since."

And that bothered her, too, she realized. Since she and Gabe had once meant something to each other, she supposed she'd been expecting to hear from him over the course of the week. Especially given that he was also a new teacher in the district. She'd looked him up in the directory and found that he wasn't in the same building as she was. However, the high school was only across the street. He could have stopped by.

She'd also looked up the Wilde orchard. Just to make sure it remained in business.

The website had seemed up to date, and when she'd passed by it on her drive today, the orchard appeared to still be open.

"If you know her dad," Bree said, bringing Erica back to the present, "then maybe you should . . ." Bree's brows pulled together then. "Wait. Did you say her dad's name is Gabe? And Jenna's last name is Wilde? Wasn't that"—she blinked—"is that the guy you dated in college?"

Erica forced herself not to react. She should have known Bree would remember Gabe.

"Her *dad* is the guy you dated?"

"That's not important, Bree."

"Well, it could be!"

"But it's *not*. We broke up back then. He got married. I got married. I haven't seen him since." Which wasn't completely true. She'd run into him a few years ago in Missoula. She'd turned the corner of an aisle in a bulk-goods store, and there he'd been. It had been good to see him. "I once knew him—that's all. Now he's my student's father."

"Okay." Bree nodded slowly, as if still not believing there was nothing more to the story. "But what a coincidence, right?" Then she sucked in a breath, and her eyes went wide. "Is *that* why you took the job there?"

"*Bree*. Stop it. He has nothing to do with why I'm here. Plus, he's married." The only way Gabe had played into her decision was that, due to him, she'd been to Birch Bay before. Therefore, moving there hadn't totally seemed like an unknown. "Now can we please focus on Jenna? She's the issue. Not Gabe."

"Sure." Bree continued to eyeball her, though, and Erica wondered if she was remembering how Gabe used to tease her any time he'd visit Erica at the house. At nine years old, Bree had been completely smitten with Gabriel Wilde—and Erica had been able to say the same thing. "Is he *still* married?" Bree suddenly asked.

"Jenna." Erica reminded her. "That's who we're talking about." And as far as she knew, Gabe *was* still married. But she'd wondered that very thing when there'd been no sign of his wife all week.

"Fine." Bree made a face. "We'll talk about Jenna. So what are you going to do?"

"I'm only here for a short time," Erica said halfheartedly. "Maybe I shouldn't even worry about it."

Bree snorted. "Like you could do that. I've known you my whole life, remember? You'll get involved."

Which was true. But only because she cared. In fact, after only four days with this new group of kids, she already cared too much. It would be hard to walk away from them in only seven more weeks.

She opened her mouth to reply, to try to explain how for the first time in her life she almost didn't want to get that invested in her students. That she wanted to protect her heart. But the sound of tires crunching on loose gravel caught her attention.

"What is it?" Bree asked when Erica turned her head.

She moved to stand by the side of the window. "Someone pulled up next door."

"And . . . ?" Her sister drew the word out when Erica didn't explain the significance.

"And that house has been empty until today."

"New neighbors? Cool. Let me see."

Erica chuckled at her sister's never-ending exuberance and reversed the view so Bree could participate in Erica's nosiness. Then she sucked in a sharp breath.

"Who is it?" Bree asked.

The front door of the house had opened at the same time as the SUV's doors. "It's *them*," Erica muttered in shock. She took a half step back, careful not to be spotted through the open blinds. Gabe Wilde was her new neighbor?

"Them who?"

He moved farther out onto the small covered porch, the fray of his jeans dragging the concrete beneath his bare feet, while his daughter hopped down from the backseat of the vehicle. Haley dropped from the other side, an enormous dog following her, and Dani Denton slid from behind the steering wheel. Her cute little belly seemed to poke out even more today than when Erica had seen her at the school the afternoon before.

"Erica?" Bree prodded when Erica remained mute.

"It's *him*," she stressed. *"Gabe."* She angled the camera toward the little girl. "And his daughter."

But where was his wife?

Her gaze went back to Gabe. Or more specifically, to his hair. It had been tamed and so teacher-ish when she'd seen him earlier that week. But now it stood out in random hunks, dark and a little wild, and clearly not as closely cropped as she'd previously assumed.

She let her gaze trail down over him, and his snug T-shirt and ripped jeans made her think of the nineteen-year-old she'd temporarily lost her mind over so many years ago. That first semester with him . . . good Lord, they'd been unable to keep their hands to themselves. It'd just been sex. At first.

She tugged at the collar of her polo and swallowed as she remembered.

She'd finally accepted that her high school boyfriend didn't want her anymore now that he was in college—and she'd gotten mad.

She'd also been hurt, but more mad than anything.

So after watching her stew in their room for weeks, claiming more interest in studying than in boys, Erica's roommate had finally declared Erica's period of mourning over and talked her into dating again. Which had not been the success Lindsey had hoped. Erica either hadn't been interested in each guy from the get-go, or she'd quickly found a reason not to go out a second or third time. But Lindsey had been persistent. She'd dragged her out night after night, flirting with random guys, talking them into "giving Erica a shot" when they learned that Lindsey was in a committed relationship herself. And then Lindsey had talked her into going to the frat party.

And Erica hadn't known what hit her.

"You think that's his wife?" Bree asked. "She looks pregnant."

"That's his sister. And she is." And Erica suddenly felt very guilty if it turned out that Gabe *was* still married. Because he was as good-looking today as he had been back then. And her thoughts were currently anything but teacher-parent.

She and Bree both fell silent as they watched the action across the street. Jenna and Haley darted inside the house, the dog following close behind, and Dani met Gabe on the porch. She handed over a small purple suitcase as Gabe said something, then nodded and smiled, one hand going to her belly. Erica couldn't miss the new-mom glow of happiness. She and Dani had chatted after school a couple of times when Dani stopped by to pick up Haley, and Erica had learned that the pregnancy was her first.

"Why hasn't his wife come out?" Bree spoke again.

"I don't know."

Jenna and Haley reappeared, a smaller, more spaniel-looking dog joining them, and ran around to the backyard. The dogs loped along behind the girls, tongues lolling.

"He's very good-looking."

"He can't help it," Erica replied without thinking. "All of the Wilde boys are." She recalled that key detail from spending time at Gabe's house over a decade ago. Her gaze swung back to Dani. "As well as their sister."

"And you dumped *him* to get back together with JC?"

She shook her head. Not that Bree could see it. "He dumped me." And she hadn't officially started dating JC again until he'd graduated from Stanford and come back home.

A few more words were exchanged on the porch before Gabe called for the girls. Dani leaned down and hugged Jenna, and then Dani, Haley, and the monster dog climbed back into the SUV and pulled away. And as if aware that Erica had been standing there all along, Gabe turned his head to look at her.

"Busted," her sister murmured from the phone.

He lifted a hand in greeting, and Erica's first thought was to drop below the window and hide. She was spying on the man, after all. And she'd clearly been caught. But being the mature adult that she was, she turned her back to him instead. "About that tour of the place," she blurted out. She moved into the middle of the room and flashed the phone around for her sister to see.

"Does he have on a wedding ring?"

Erica stopped. "What?"

"Gabe. Is he wearing a wedding ring?"

"I have no idea. Why would I know that?"

"Because you're a freaking woman, E. And because that man is hot!"

"He's not that hot." At least, she hadn't noticed it when she'd seen him in her classroom. How had she missed that?

She glanced over her shoulder, groaning when she saw him still looking her way.

"He's every bit that hot," Bree argued. "Now tell me when I can come for a visit."

Erica flipped the screen back around. "Why, *exactly*, do you want to come for a visit?"

"To see where you live, of course." Bree gave her a *duh* look, and Erica let out a soft *"Oh."*

"*And* to check out your hot neighbor."

"You are not coming here to check out my hot neighbor," Erica hissed. "And anyway, you're out of the country." And he *wasn't* that hot. He couldn't be.

Because he might just be married.

She slipped around the partial wall, blocking her from view of the front picture window.

"You do know they invented these things called airplanes, right?" Bree quipped. "They take you places by flying through the air, and they get you there *really fast*. They can even go from one country to another."

As Bree rattled on, Erica pressed herself to the kitchen wall.

"Come on, E," Bree groaned. "Quit ignoring me. I need to see your place up close, not through a phone. I'll help you put your stamp on it."

Erica wasn't sure she had a stamp.

Nor was she sure why her heart was pounding a mile a minute and she was skulking through her own apartment. She edged toward the window over the sink.

"Labor Day?" Bree said. "Unless you're going home?"

"Not on your life." Leaning to the left, she reached the window and tried to covertly see across the street. "The last thing I'm in the mood for is more pretending that everything is hunky-dory with my traitorous ex and his oh-so-perfect girlfriend. That ship has sailed."

Bree briefly paused, and when she spoke again, her words had gentled. "Then I'll come to you. We'll make it a fun day, just the two of us, okay? I have an appointment with a gallery here Friday morning, but I can hop a flight soon after. With the time difference, I should be in Montana by Saturday afternoon at the latest."

Gabe and Jenna no longer stood outside their home. Heaving out a sigh of relief, Erica straightened from where she'd ended in a half crouch. The coast was clear.

Then she realized what Bree had just suggested, and she replayed the last few minutes through her head. Was her sister offering to come to Birch Bay because she felt sorry for her? Was that what this was about?

"You don't have to do that," she told Bree. Labor Day had always been a big deal for both the Yarbroughs and the Birds in Silver Creek. "I'll be fine here by myself."

"I'm not *doing* anything. I want to come. I want to see you."

Or maybe she wanted to grill her on what had happened to cause Erica to give up her security and everything she'd ever known in the span of a few days.

Erica swallowed around the sudden lump. She'd been living with her parents since her divorce but had left town before they'd returned from their annual national park vacation. They were teachers, as well, and always picked a park or two to visit each summer before the school year started. "There's no need to spend your money because of me," she told her sister. "A last-minute trip like that would be pricey."

"I have plenty of money to spend, big sister. And I'll spend it however I want."

Erica started to argue further, because she very much doubted that Bree had so much money that throwing away a chunk of it on an unexpected international flight was not a big deal. But the truth was, she'd love to see her sister. Very much. It had been months since they'd been in the same city together. And even though the age gap between the two of them was the greatest, she'd always felt closer to Bree than to either their other sister or their brother.

"Fine." She nodded at the phone. "Yes. Please. Come see me. I'd love it. But I'll pay you back for the flight."

Bree rolled her eyes.

"No arguing," Erica demanded. She strode through the house, stopping for a minute to look up the length of the pole. "But keep in mind that I only have one bed, so it'll be you on the couch. With the pole."

A soft knock sounded, and without thinking, Erica turned for the door.

"I get to sleep with the pole?" Bree sighed in an overly wanton way. Her voice rose from the palm of Erica's hand as dark-fringed eyes met Erica's across the threshold of the now-open door. "I can't wait," Bree breathed out.

Gabe's gaze slipped over Erica's shoulder to the pole.

"I'll even teach you how to dance with it," her sister continued, laughing wickedly. "No matter how *big* it is. My much older, far wiser sister might just learn a thing or two from little old me."

Gabe's low chuckle silenced Bree, but only for a second.

"He's there?" she squeaked. "E! Why didn't you tell me?"

Erica lowered her hand, trying desperately to remove her sister from the moment.

"Gabriel Wilde?" Bree squawked from beside Erica's thigh. "Is that you? Let me see you. We were just talking about you."

Gabe's brows hitched. He snagged Erica's wrist before she could pull farther away, and as he lifted her phone, the same smirk that had first captured her attention over thirteen years before appeared on his wide lips. And this time, in addition to the smirk, Erica also noticed one other pertinent detail. His ring finger was most decidedly bare.

He positioned the phone in front of him, then he tilted his head and studied Bree as if the name behind the girl with the pink hair would ever be in question.

Finally, he spoke. "If it isn't little Breedom Yarbrough."

Bree groaned at the nickname.

"You were talking about me, you say?"

"She's lying." Erica freed her hand and tapped the "End" button, cutting off her sister's protest midyelp, and silence fell as Erica stared blankly up at Gabe. She didn't speak, because, really, what could she say? He'd just overheard them talking about pole dancing. About *big* things. And all after he'd caught her spying on him.

She gulped.

45

And he wasn't married.

Or maybe he simply didn't wear a wedding ring. Not everyone did. Prince William didn't wear one, and everyone knew their marriage was solid. It meant nothing these days.

She didn't want it to mean anything to her, either.

But dang if she didn't suddenly hear her nineteen-year-old voice taunting her to make a move on the man now standing two feet in front of her. Same as she'd done the first night she'd laid eyes on him.

Chapter Four

Gabe couldn't soak her in enough. He'd just seen Erica a few days before, yet he'd been so caught off guard that morning at the school that he'd done little more than stare in shock. But today he had the pleasure of time. And the previous knowledge that he'd find her here—rumors of where "the new teacher" had rented had been circling. So he *took* the time, and he looked his fill. And he'd swear there wasn't a thing about her that had changed since the night they'd first met.

Brown hair captured in a single thick braid running down the middle of her back, easy girl-next-door looks with an overwide mouth—still glistening with the same shade of pink he remembered—and the most fascinating hazel eyes he'd ever come across. In a second's understanding, he knew he could once again make a hobby of trying to pick out the individual hues of greens and browns trapped inside the rich perimeters of olive.

He finally made himself speak. "Hello, neighbor."

"Hello," she murmured. Soft exhalations of air matched the rise and fall of her chest.

"So you and Bree were talking about me?"

She shook her head, pulling a look of disgust. "Just that you'd apparently moved in next door. Other than that, my baby sister was simply being my baby sister."

He chuckled at that. He had no doubt Bree had been antagonizing Erica. She hadn't even made it to her teen years when he and Erica had dated, yet within one meeting it had become clear that if anyone were to change the face of the Silver Creek Yarbrough clan, it would be baby-of-the-family Bree. With her current look, he'd say that she was well on her way.

He relaxed with the memories and leaned a shoulder against Erica's door. "I came over to say hi to *you*, and I got to see the always-entertaining Breedom, as well. What a treat."

"Tell me about it." Erica shot him a smirk. "Bree's certainly one of a kind."

He had the urge to tell her that she was a close second, but she'd turned her focus from him. She stood on tiptoe and peeked over his shoulder, so he followed her gaze. Jenna had taken Mike to the fenced backyard, and though there was no sight of her, Mike's occasional bark made it across the street.

"She's playing with her dog," Gabe explained.

Erica shifted her gaze back to his then, and he had the urge to fidget like a schoolboy. After several long seconds of the silent treatment, she shocked him with her next words. "Your daughter is floundering, and I doubt it's happening only while in school. It's as if she doesn't know where she fits in."

Gabe's heart ached at the truth of the statement. "She's going through a rough patch."

"Problems at home?"

He blinked. "You get right to the point."

"I'm her teacher"—she shrugged unapologetically—"and there's something going on with one of my students that worries me. I'd been hoping to run into you so we could try to get to the bottom of it, but probably I should have already sought you out."

"And you can see this in her after only four days in class?"

Another shrug. "I'm a good teacher. Why wait when I see a storm brewing?" Her gaze flicked to his house. "Her mother around? There's no need to set a later appointment if you both have a few minutes now."

Irritation flared. Erica didn't know anything about his daughter.

"We just moved in today," he explained, his words short. "So as you can probably guess, we have quite a few things we need to see to at the moment. Maybe a meeting between my wife and me could wait?"

His words seemed to pain her, but she nodded without argument. "She's your child." Then she cleared the censure from her face and offered him a fake smile—while at the same time taking a step back and reaching for the door. "Thanks for stopping by, Gabe. I'll let you get back to your unpacking."

"Wait." His hand shot out, stopping her before she could close the door. "I'm sorry. That was rude. *I* was rude." He shook his head, irritation gone, now replaced with annoyance at himself. "I shouldn't have been a jerk. You just . . ." She'd hit a button. He sighed. "I appreciate your concern for Jenna. I swear. And I didn't come over for any reason other than to be neighborly." He forced himself to once again relax. "I wanted to say hi. To officially welcome you to town. It really is good to see you. But to tell you the truth, you're the last person I would have ever expected to find here."

"You mean here in Birch Bay"—she cast her gaze around the room—"or here in a fire hall?"

He laughed at that. "Both." He'd run into her a few years back, and it had seemed as if she'd had her life completely on track. Yet, now she was *Ms.* Bird. "What in the world brought you to my neck of the woods? I figured you'd be on kid number two by now, at least. If not three." He glanced at the car sitting in the driveway. "Maybe driving a minivan instead of compact."

"I like my compact." The reply came quickly. Then she eyed the small four-door parked in front of the building as if willing herself to believe her own words.

Gabe watched her without speaking, trying to read her thoughts. He'd once been able to decipher most anything that had passed through her mind. Anyone had been able to. But that didn't seem to be so easily done these days. She'd closed herself off.

The realization saddened him.

"You okay?" He didn't know why he voiced the question. Her issues weren't his business.

Yet his words seemed to change her.

Her shoulders eased, and her chest expanded with a deep breath. Then finally, she pulled her gaze back to his. The shell around her suddenly had a crack in it, and he could see the Erica he'd once dated. "Life happens." She gave him a tight smile. "And sometimes that means you quit your job and move to another city."

Her hurt sliced him in two. "I'm sorry," he murmured. "For whatever went wrong."

"Plans change, that's all. I've adapted."

The quick dip of her eyelids signaled that she'd said enough and her walls were coming back, but since she'd given a small piece of herself, he decided to share something of him, as well. "I'm divorced." When her eyes shot back to his, he added, "Or, I soon will be. Michelle stayed in California instead of moving back here with us, so there won't be any meeting with the two of us."

"*Back* here with you? Are you saying that you left Birch Bay?"

That's the one thing he'd told her he would never do. "Two years ago."

"Why?"

He swallowed his reply. Telling of a pending divorce was one thing, but going into the details . . . He'd keep those to himself. Instead, he offered another insight. "Once I settled into LA, I began to reevaluate my life. I remembered this science teacher I once had."

"Mr. Childers?"

Warm surprise filled him. "You remember that?"

Pink spots appeared high on her cheeks. "You mentioned him a couple of times. He made an impact on you."

"He did." Gabe let his thoughts roll back to when he'd first met Mr. Childers. It had been right after his mother forced him to quit football. Without that steadying influence in his life, Gabe wasn't sure where he'd be today. "I'd like to give people the same kind of support he gave me," he confessed. "To make an impact on a student or two. So I went back to school and got my teaching certification."

Erica nodded her head, the movement so small he almost didn't see it. "Teaching suits you, though I'll admit, as well, that that was the last thing *I* expected to find when I moved here, too. But it fits. You're that type of guy."

Jenna's laughter filtered through the tree branches on the other side of the road, and both of them turned to look. There was still no sign of her, but they could hear her talking to Mike now. The dog barked in the gaps of her words, as if actively taking part in the conversation, and Gabe momentarily closed his eyes as he took in the sounds. She laughed so infrequently these days.

"I'm sorry about your divorce," Erica said softly.

He lifted his lids. "Thank you. It's been tough for both of us."

"You got custody?"

"I did."

Questions crossed Erica's face when he said no more, but she didn't voice them, and Gabe worked hard not to show his utter disgust for his ex's actions. Custody had been by default, though he'd have gone to his death to ensure he'd gotten it.

Not wanting to stand there in the middle of a Saturday afternoon and talk about the woman he preferred neither he nor his daughter ever laid eyes on again, he steered them back to safer territory. "Along with teaching, I'm also the football coach."

The way Erica's jaw dropped open made him laugh out loud.

"I know." He drew the word out. "Who would give someone like me that chance, right?"

"Not at all. I just . . ." Her words faded before a look of genuine pleasure crossed her face. "I'm happy for you, Gabe. Truly. I never would have imagined those changes, but I'm thrilled for you. So how's the team doing?"

It was his turn for his cheeks to heat. "Not good," he admitted. "Our first game was last night. Don't look up the score."

She giggled at that, and the sound made him smile. He leaned in toward her.

"You need to come to Friday night's game, Ms. Bird." His voice dropped to a conspiratorial whisper. "Everyone in town shows up for the games. If you aren't there, they'll all wonder why not."

"I didn't go last night."

"And you can bet they're already talking. Wondering what you have against football."

"I have nothing against football. I just don't care for it."

Gabe straightened. "Who do you think you're kidding? I know what town you're from. And aside from Birch Bay, they're best in the state."

"They *are* the best."

Her cheeks deepened with color once again when she realized what her words had given away.

"Not a fan, huh?" He looked her up and down one more time. "I'd be willing to bet that if someone handed you a cheerleading outfit right now you'd be right back on the sidelines."

She crossed her arms over her chest and gave him her best teacher look. "My cheerleading days are over, Gabriel Wilde." Then a twinkle appeared in her eyes. "No matter how good I might still look in a cheer uniform."

The blood suddenly left his brain. She'd had her high school uniform tucked away in her closet back in the day, and there'd been a time when he could talk her into that outfit on a regular basis.

Of course, she'd had no intention of appearing at football games while wearing it. Most cheerleaders didn't take the field sporting no underwear.

"Erica," he began, his voice having dropped to a growl while at the same time he had no idea what he intended to say.

She said nothing, herself. Just looked back at him. And Gabe could see that her thoughts had followed his. Her breaths came deeper now—and the green in her eyes darkened.

Then the sound of much-closer barking reverberated through the air, and Gabe forced himself to tuck his memories away. He pulled back from Erica as Mike let out another, closer, woof, and Gabe found his daughter standing with her dog just on the other side of the road. Her brow had drawn into a frown, her full attention directed at Erica.

"Hey, Jenna," Erica said. "How are you today?"

Jenna didn't reply.

"Come over here," Gabe said. After making sure no cars were coming down the road, he held out a hand toward his daughter. "Say hello to Ms. Bird. She's our next-door neighbor now."

His daughter turned an accusing glare on him. "Why do we have to have a neighbor?"

"Don't be rude, Jenna." He nudged his head toward Erica. "Come say hello."

She crossed her arms over her chest and stuck out her chin.

"She doesn't have to," Erica murmured beside Gabe.

"She'll be fine," he murmured back. *"Jenna,"* he warned.

Mike whined and dropped to a sitting position at his master's feet, but still, Gabe got nothing from his daughter. He hated when she acted like this.

"Be polite to Ms. Bird," he forced out, trying to maintain his own politeness, "and if you do, we'll go into town after unpacking your bedroom, and you can pick out whatever candy you want."

Jenna immediately looked at Erica. "Hello, Ms. Bird."

The words came out saccharine sweet, but as soon as they passed her lips she returned a glare to Gabe. Then with an air of superiority that was far too reminiscent of her mother, she turned with a haughty swirl and stalked toward the house. Mike trotted along behind her, while Gabe bit his tongue, embarrassed to his core. He looked like a damned fool, but he couldn't very well stalk away like Jenna had. He had an audience. He turned back to Erica, intending to apologize on behalf of his daughter, but was taken aback at the scowl directed his way.

"You just offered your daughter candy to be polite to me?"

"Yeah. Because it works."

"Right." Her expression remained incredulous. "Because that was the epitome of nice."

"Come on. Give me a break." He groaned then, unable to stop himself, and dragged a hand down over his face. "I do what I have to do, okay? She used to be such a sweet kid, but lately, she's so . . ."

He sighed. She was so her mother.

"She's *still* a sweet kid." Erica touched her fingers to his arm. "She just needs time. Divorce doesn't only affect the parents."

"Trust me, I'm fully aware of that." Irritation held Gabe's jaw tight as he looked back at the house. Jenna and Mike had disappeared inside, the front door slamming behind them, and Gabe blew out a breath. He wished like hell that his daughter's *sweetness* wasn't currently trapped beneath a layer of hurt.

"Anyway," he mumbled. He moved toward the road. It was time to go. "It was good catching up. Let me know if you need anything," he tossed out, not looking back. "I may be new to the school, but I know the town. I can provide names to who or whatever you might need."

"Thank you. That's a good resource to have." Her words grew quieter as he moved farther away, and as his foot landed on his porch, she added, "Take care of yourself, Gabe."

He slipped inside his new house without responding, and leaned back against the closed door. He *would* take care of himself. As well as Jenna. He'd pull her through this period of her life, he'd make her happy again, and somehow—some way—they would both turn out okay.

Erica came out of her back room the following Friday afternoon, her hands dusty from the cleaning she'd been doing in the storage area. The regular teacher kept the space decently organized, but after all the kids had disappeared for the day, Erica had decided to add to Mrs. Watts's efforts.

And no, her decision had nothing to do with the fact that the entire world seemed to have plans for the weekend, while she had what? A button to sew onto a blouse? A new exercise routine to try out?

She dusted her hands off on her khakis and headed for the shelves running the length of the back wall. There'd been a faculty meeting after school, and as the group of teachers chatted, it had hit her that she was one of the few without plans for the holiday weekend. After everyone attended the football game tonight, each and every one of them would kick the long weekend off with either a fun family trip or a quick adrenaline rush. Given the many outdoor activities offered in the state, adrenaline rushes weren't hard to come by. And with beautiful weather in the forecast, Erica couldn't blame them.

But she also hadn't been able to stop herself from being jealous.

She had her sister coming, sure. And that was a far cry better than sitting home alone. But the fact was, she and Bree would probably *still* sit home alone.

Additionally, she hadn't been able to keep from wondering what her ex and *Lindsey* might be up to that weekend. Because she knew how JC liked to pack the days with excitement. The Bird family sponsored an annual community picnic on Labor Day itself, but JC had never been one to sit around and do nothing during the Saturday and Sunday preceding the holiday. Erica had tagged along with him and his friends once upon a time, trying to keep up. Until she could no longer work up the pretense. She'd rather spend her weekends at home. Preferably with a good book.

But not Lindsey.

Erica's college roommate had always been up for an adventure. Especially if it involved ones that allowed her to steal another woman's husband.

Her cell dinged at the front of the room, and she shot upright from her squatting position in front of shelves. Her heart raced. It wouldn't seriously be JC texting her again, would it? She hadn't heard from him since the first day of school when he'd "simply wanted to see how the first day of her new job had gone." She hadn't replied to his text, so she'd hoped he'd gotten the message to leave her alone.

Of course, it could just as easily be Bree. She checked in with her regularly.

Only, JC was the one who'd always liked to reach out on Friday nights.

Sourness turned her stomach as she thought about the woman she'd let herself become over the summer.

Almost become.

The cell dinged again, a reminder when she didn't clear it in time, and she rose and crossed the classroom with a determined stride. No point hiding from a text message. How ridiculous would that be? But when she snatched up her phone, instead of anxiety wracking her body, relief washed through it. It was neither JC nor Bree. It was from a number she didn't recognize, but one she thought she might know the owner of.

Tonight's game? Yes? You'll be there?

Was the message really from Gabe? Several of the other teachers had asked if she planned to go tonight. It could be one of them reaching out. Another message came in.

This is Gabe, btw. I got your number from the paperwork in Jenna's backpack.

Erica bit her lip as she punched out a quick reply.

That is *not* the reason I shared my phone number.

Worked out in my favor, though, didn't it?

A smile broke out. He could be very arrogant when he wanted to be; she remembered that well about him. But she still wouldn't be going to the game.

Sorry. I can't make it tonight.

There was that button she needed to sew on.

Of course you "can" make it. The question is "will" you?

She started to type out a reply, but stopped, thumbs hovering, when a feeling of being watched swept over her. She looked up to find a dark-haired, very teacher-ish-looking Gabriel Wilde standing on the other side of her door, his face peering in through the window at her.

He pushed open the door. "*Will* you, Erica? You know you don't want to be the only person in town not there."

She wanted to say yes if for no other reason than that he'd asked her. But she hadn't been to a football game in two years. Intentionally.

JC had been the star quarterback in high school, while she'd cheered him on from the sidelines. They'd always been at games together. Heck, they'd *met* at a football game years before they'd ever started dating, and after they'd married, it had been assumed that Mr. and Mrs. James Christopher Bird the third would not only attend all home games together, but they'd be front and center in the crowd. After all, going to high school football was tradition in their town. Just as it was here.

Only, two seasons ago JC had changed all that.

Gabe crossed to her desk and peered down at her. He shot her a pleading look. "Be there so if I blow this game, too, I'll know I have a least one person in the stands *not* wanting my head on a platter?"

That made her laugh. "Gossip about last week's game *has* been pretty rough."

"Tell me about it. It was a bloodbath." He shuddered. "Mortifying."

When his hip landed on the corner of her desk, Erica's gaze dropped, hanging on the medium-washed jeans he wore. They looked fairly new, and were definitely in far better shape than the frayed pair he'd been wearing Saturday afternoon. His hair was also better tamed.

He dipped his head and caught her gaze. "You can't go home and grade papers on a Friday night, Ms. Bird," he chided. "That's not allowed in Birch Bay."

Grading papers was first on her list after she'd taken care of that button.

"How about if I promise to listen to it on the radio?" she asked. "Then I'll be able to both join the gossip around school next week, as well as be there for you if everyone else in town is ready to burn you at the stake." She soaked in his blue gaze. "All you'll have to do is walk across the street."

He seemed to contemplate the suggestion—while she imagined him with his Wilde-boy swagger walking across the road toward her.

"Or you could just be in the crowd," he suggested again.

A gust of desire suddenly filled her, but not solely for Gabe. More like for living. She was tired of sitting at home by herself every night. Tired of not being able to call up a friend just to hang out.

But she didn't go to football games anymore. JC got that in the divorce, as well.

"I really am sorry."

He sat up straighter then, a look of defeat on his face, as well as a hint of disappointment. "Your loss, Ms. Bird." He stood and moved from her desk. "The whole town will be talking about you, and there won't be a thing I can do to stop them."

It wouldn't be the first time she'd been talked about.

She eyed him as he crossed the room, the idea of watching Gabe in the position of coach stirring up a funny feeling inside her. She could picture him on the sidelines being the man in charge. And she liked that picture.

When she realized where he was headed, she stood and followed. "She doesn't sit there anymore."

Gabe looked back at her.

"The kids got to pick new seats today," Erica explained. She pointed out Jenna's desk for the coming week. "They picked in order of who had the most check marks for helpful behavior."

His eyes went to the whiteboard at the side of the room. There was a list on the board encompassing each of the students' names. Beside his daughter's was one single check mark, and Erica couldn't miss the way his chest deflated as he scanned over the remainder of the list.

"She's still giving you problems?" he asked.

"Not as much. She actually *got* a check mark this week. That's better than last week. And she's talked a bit more, participated in class a couple of times."

"What was the one check mark for?" He moved to Jenna's new desk.

"For writing out Tuesday's math assignment on the board." She showed him where his daughter's carefully printed words remained.

Gabe pulled a red folder from the desk, keeping his gaze downcast as he dug through the other items crammed into Jenna's personal space. "I shouldn't have pushed back at you last weekend," he said. "But she and I talked about it afterward. About her trying harder in class." He glanced up. "About her being nicer. She sees a counselor twice a week. I set that up when she first started acting out. Months ago. What I'm saying is that I'm trying. That *she's* trying." He blew out a frustrated breath. "At least most of the time she is. Other times"—he shook his head—"she can just be a jerk."

He'd finished in a mumble, and Erica nodded in understanding. "It sounds like she's on the right track. But keep in mind that sometimes she simply *needs* to be a jerk. And that's okay. She's going through a lot, and she has to be able to push back once in a while. I'm an easy target."

He quit sorting through Jenna's books, and the lost look on his face pulled at Erica. "But no one should have to be a target."

The way he said the words had her wondering if there was even more to the story.

She crossed to him and pulled out the math book that went with the red folder. Jenna might have conceded to being helpful by writing the homework assignment on the board, but she'd held her ground when she'd refused to take that very assignment home with her. "It doesn't change the fact that I am," she told him. "And *that's* okay, too. Don't push her too hard, Gabe. She needs time."

"I'm giving her time." He waved Jenna's book in the air. "I don't plan to chew her out for this trick, and given what you just told me, you and I both know she left it here on purpose."

"I know she did. I watched her do it." She pictured father and daughter in front of her house last weekend, facing off across the street.

She understood the type of anger inside Jenna. The need to have control of *something* in her life. Erica had felt for the little girl in that moment.

Gabe's jaw hardened as he looked at her. "Are you telling me that you saw my daughter leaving her assignment here, on purpose, yet you didn't correct the situation?"

"That's exactly what I'm telling you."

"Why would you do that?" He looked at her as if she'd grown two heads.

"Because taking home her assignment was her decision to make. And one *you* should let her make," she added, her voice dipping dangerously close to rude.

Gabe shoved everything else back into Jenna's desk, his movements jerky, then he once again picked up the math book. Anger brewed in his hard glare, and Erica couldn't help but be a little taken aback at the severity of it. "You're her teacher," he ground out. "It's your *job* to see that she takes her work home with her."

She stood her ground. "And you're her dad. It's your job to do what's best for her."

Fire rolled from his ears. "Are you saying I don't do what's best for my daughter?"

She'd realized her misstep the second the words left her mouth. She shouldn't talk to any parent that way, even if she had once dated him. "No, Gabe. I'm sorry. I didn't mean that at all. I'm just cranky because it's been a long week." And because she had a pitifully boring existence. "I do things a bit different from you, that's all I'm saying. And I shouldn't have implied—"

"I've put my daughter's education into your hands," he interrupted, his voice unnaturally calm. "And you seem to have no concern for it whatsoever."

"Now that's not true at all." Erica held her hands up in front of her. She really did feel like a heel for her comment. She'd never talk to another parent that way. But heel or not, she wouldn't let anyone stand there and call her out on something that wasn't true. "I care for your daughter's education, Gabe. More than you realize. Kids mean the world me. But I don't feel it's helpful to take away their right to make their own decisions. That's all I'm saying."

He scowled at her, a muscle ticking at his jawline, and after several seconds he simply turned and headed for the door. The door slammed against the wall as he yanked it open, and he left without saying a word. After watching until he'd disappeared, Erica slowly returned to her desk. Her mind whirled as she retraced through the argument. She'd messed up, she knew that. She had no right to talk to any parent that way.

But at the same time, she was pretty sure she'd just been given an insight into her angry young student. Her daddy didn't let her mess up. And clearly, he didn't let her make her own decisions. Which would totally play into her poor attitude.

Her phone dinged with another text, and this time she was even more afraid to look.

But it wasn't from Gabe.

Hey, Erica, this is Dani Denton. I meant to invite you to a cookout when I saw you today, but I forgot. I'll blame it on pregnancy brain. Anyway, it should be fun, at Nick's house on Monday, family and friends both, starting around five. Please come? Our whole family would love to see you, and I know Haley would be thrilled. She talks about you all the time.

Too many thoughts fought to be heard as she read through the message a second time. Plans for the holiday beckoned. But that meant she'd have to see Gabe—who no doubt would *not* want to see her after the argument they'd just had.

Although, if she went, she could apologize more sincerely.

And she knew Bree would be thrilled to see him.

Only . . . She chewed on her lip as she considered her next question. Could going to the cookout make things worse with Jenna? Or maybe it would give Erica the opportunity to close the gap between them a bit.

She sighed. Why couldn't life just be simple?

She tapped out a reply.

Thanks for the invite, but my sister is coming into town.

Then you have to come! We'd love to meet your sister. And you can't have her in town for the holiday with nothing to do. Please say yes.

Would Gabe run her out the second she walked in?

She made a face at the thought. Did she really care if he tried? It wasn't him inviting her. Nor would it be at his house.

Nick was one of Gabe's younger brothers— a twin. Dani had mentioned in passing that he'd gotten married in the last year and had a charming little house in a neighborhood next to the lake. Hanging out there Monday evening sounded pretty perfect to her, and the more she thought about it, the more she sensed this would give Jenna the chance to see Erica as something other than an authority figure. And bonus, Erica really liked Dani. She remembered Gabe's sister from the time she and he had dated, and since Dani picked Haley up at school most days, the two of them had talked quite a few times over the last two weeks.

Therefore . . . decision made. She sent a quick text.

Yes.

As far as she was concerned, Gabe wasn't a factor in the cookout.

Chapter Five

*G*abe wasn't a factor in the cookout.

Erica had told herself that at least fifty times in the last twenty-four hours. It didn't matter that he wouldn't want her there. Bree was excited to go, and Erica looked forward to seeing Gabe's family again. So what Gabe may or may not want didn't matter. He wasn't a factor.

Only, he totally *would* be a factor. Because she had to apologize to him.

She still couldn't believe she'd so bluntly tossed out insults to a student's parent. What had she been thinking?

"I can't tell you how excited I am to see this place," Bree said from the passenger seat of the car.

Erica pulled to a stop in front of her apartment and shifted into park, then both of them leaned forward at the same time to stare out at the two-story building. She'd picked her sister up at the airport a couple of hours ago, and they'd grabbed a late lunch before driving here. And now, Erica found herself as excited to show the place to Bree as Bree was to see it.

"You're going to love it," Erica told her sister.

"I already love it. I did the instant you told me you'd rented the place."

Erica didn't even try to hide her smile. Though she still couldn't say why she'd chosen the unique little living space, she'd grown quite fond of it in the short time she'd been there. She headed for the red front door while Bree grabbed her bag out of the car, and with a dramatic swoop of her arm, Erica ushered her sister inside.

Bree's luggage thumped to the ground just inside the door.

"What an entrance." Bree's head turned in every direction, as if trying to take in each detail all at once. "I mean, I know you showed me this view over the phone, but, E, this place is *stunning*."

"They did a great job, didn't they?" Erica shrugged out of her cardigan. "You only noticed the pole the first time I showed it to you."

"The pole is hard to miss," Bree acknowledged. The infamous pole stood fifteen feet in front of them, and Bree immediately headed for it. She put a hand to its smooth surface, stroking her fingers along its curves as she continued to take in the rest of the space. Then she turned back toward Erica, and her eyes combed over the front wall of the house. She looked straight up, taking in what she could see in Erica's bedroom above, trailed her eyes back down over the vintage-style pendant lights hanging throughout the open floor plan, then lowered her gaze to the polished concrete floors they stood on. "This place is perfect."

Erica nodded. "I'm infatuated with it. Come on, let's start in the kitchen."

The place was a mix of contemporary and vintage, while also maintaining the integrity of the original brick, now exposed along the length of the living room wall, and the oversize garage door, off to the right. They stepped into the kitchen where cabinets lined the front wall of the house, and opposite that, a curved island looked out over the first floor.

"E"—Bree sighed as she trailed a hand along the granite—"please say you cook here."

"You know I like to cook." Erica slid her own palm over the cool stone, same as Bree. "This place makes me wish I knew enough people locally to entertain. I'd throw parties simply because of this room."

"You should totally throw parties."

If she ever did, they'd be quiet events, Erica thought. Not the neighborhood block parties that had been her ex-husband's idea of a casual get-together.

They moved into the dining area, which was laid out on the other side of the kitchen. The still-functioning garage door framed the front of the room, while a set of French doors outlined the back. The space wasn't huge, but it was long. It held a narrow square-legged dining table that could easily seat eight, as well as two small bistro tables positioned farther back in the room, and when Erica tapped the door opener, as well as the light switch next to it, the space transformed from renovated fire hall into quaint little Italian villa.

As the outside came in, she threw open the French doors. Small twinkle lights now dotted the interior walls and extended to the private courtyard outside, and with another flick of a switch, the main overheads went out, and romance saturated the air. All they needed was a roving violinist and a hot dinner date or two.

"Ohymygod, E. Tell me you'll live here forever."

Erica laughed at her sister. "I've only got it rented for the rest of the year." Though her contract with the school was for only two months, it had been made clear that she'd be welcome to stay on as an as-needed substitute for any length of time she wished. With that in mind, she'd signed a longer lease just in case she found nothing else. She couldn't very well hold no job whatsoever.

"Then buy the place when your lease is up." Bree continued to gawk in every direction. "And I'm not joking. Buy it for a vacation home if nothing else."

"I do love it." And it *was* also for sale. The owner had shared that information when Erica had e-mailed back the signed rental agreement. And *she'd* shared it with Bree.

But buy it?

That was so not something she'd normally do. Even if she did have a small nest egg thanks to the settlement from her divorce.

As her sister wandered through the courtyard, taking the time to circle one of the decades-old sequoia trees, Erica pointed out the almost-hidden path that led down to the lake and the little bench she enjoyed watching the sunsets from.

"Go check it out," Erica told her. "I'm going to run upstairs and change."

Bree passed a glance over Erica's tweed pants and sleeveless blouse. "Please do. You've made me feel like I should raise my hand to speak to you ever since you picked me up."

Erica scowled. "What's wrong with it? I like to look nice when I go out."

"You *like* to look like an elementary school teacher."

"Well . . ." She peered down at herself. "That's what I am."

"Yep." Bree found the speakers hidden in the flowers, and ran a finger over the mesh front. "But it doesn't mean you have to look the part twenty-four seven."

The words stung, but Erica shrugged them off. Bree's style was more eclectic—bohemian chic one day, short-shorts and knee-high boots the next. And the girl had never come close to holding down a regular nine-to-five. So Erica got that she didn't understand the need to maintain a look. But still . . .

She glanced at her outfit once more as she hurried up to her bedroom. She looked nice, but she knew what Bree had been implying with her words. She looked *boring*.

Which wasn't a shocker.

After hanging up the trousers and blouse she'd had on only long enough to run to the airport, she pulled out a pair of yoga pants and a black cami, then added the crop top she'd run across while shopping the weekend before. Though she'd bought the top to wear only while there by herself, she knew Bree would appreciate her ability to be a bit more than teacherly, even if only in her own home.

Jogging back down the stairs, she closed the garage door and turned off the indoor twinkle lights, leaving only a couple of the pendant lights to burn. Then she uncorked a bottle of wine while she waited for Bree's return. The path down to the lake was only one-fourth of a mile, but the view at the end was stunning. Erica had taken several sips of the Pinot Noir by the time her sister returned, and when Erica handed over the other glass, Bree let out a low wolf whistle.

"Now *that's* a cute top."

Erica twirled in place, showing off the keyhole back and the crocheted lace detail. "I saw this in a boutique here in town and just had to have it. They have a lot of cute things." She turned back to Bree. "I'll take you by there if you stay long enough."

Bree hadn't committed to staying any length of time, as she so rarely did. Nor did she now. "Turn back around," she said instead.

Confused, Erica faced the other way.

"That's what I thought. Your shirt isn't the only cute thing you've got going on. Your ass is on fire."

"Oh, good grief." Erica frowned at her sister. "Grow up."

"Really. You keep that thing so tucked away, I had no idea. Put it on display a bit."

"There's no need to put it on display." Though she did know it was in tip-top shape. She glanced over her shoulder at the top curve of her rear and thought about the years of dancing she'd put in since childhood. She'd continued to take classes in college, and had even taught a kids' dance class after school for a while. "And anyway, *where* would I display it?"

"At this cookout we're going to, for one."

She couldn't very well waltz around in front of Gabe's family showcasing her rear. "I think I'll pass."

"It's your call." Bree topped off her wine and moved to the couch. "But I'm telling you, *that* outfit would be a far better choice for a cookout than Bermudas and a pullover." She took a long swallow of her wine as her gaze strayed around the room. "And I'm also telling you that Mom and Dad are going to *die* when I tell them about this place. Maybe knowing you're set up so well here will lessen their worries."

Erica lowered to the other end of the couch. "You've talked to them?"

"About you?" Bree shook her head. "Not in so many words, but they are Mom and Dad. You know they're worried as well as I do."

Erica nodded. "I hated the timing of everything."

And she was aware of their worry. Her mom had called the instant they'd returned from vacation, panicked at the idea of Erica walking away from her job. Before Erica could say much more than that she'd needed a change, her dad had come on the line to assure her that he'd just spoken with the superintendent and that she could have her job back. They hadn't filled it yet. She'd made halfhearted excuses and gotten off the phone. And then she'd thrown herself across her bed and cried. She hated disappointing her parents.

Unable to stomach the guilt, she'd avoided their calls since.

"I'm going to go out on a very short limb here," her sister said now, "and guess that you being *here* has something to do with your jackass of an ex still being back *there*. Though I can't imagine what he could have possibly done at this point to make matters worse."

Erica took in the venom lacing Bree's words. She'd never been one to beat around the bush, and Bree had never cared for JC at all.

"I slept with him," Erica suddenly blurted out. Then she cringed. "More than once."

She sucked in a gulp of air, as if she hadn't been able to breathe without getting the words out, while Bree took her time taking another sip of her wine. She watched Erica as she swallowed the liquid, then casually leaned forward, reaching out to the trunk that served as a coffee table, and set down her glass.

"I take it to mean that you slept with him *recently*?"

Erica could no longer bring herself to look at her sister. Nor was she about to tell her that JC had texted her *again* just that morning—and that she'd almost texted him back. She'd gone so far as to type in three words before she'd deleted them. Granted, the words had been "Leave me alone," but she knew from experience that giving JC any opening would merely present him with reason to believe there would be more.

"I thought he wanted me back," she whispered, embarrassed to her soul to admit that out loud. She still couldn't believe what she'd fallen for. "That he still loved me."

"Oh, E." There was love in the words, but what rang more clear was the disbelief. Bree slid over the cushions to the other end of the sofa and put an arm around Erica's shoulders, and Erica let out a little hiccup of air.

"Why can't I get over him?" she breathed out. "I thought I was. I swear, Bree, I thought I'd moved on from that man. I'd been going out with other guys once in a while, I'd let what he'd done go. Yet . . ." A couple of phone calls and empty promises later, and she'd been right back where she'd never wanted to be. She looked at her baby sister as if someone twelve years younger than her could possibly hold the answers. "What is *wrong* with me?"

"Are you kidding me? Nothing is wrong with *you*."

Erica wrapped both hands around the bowl of her glass as she huddled against her sister, and spoke to herself as much as to Bree. "I think the problem is that I don't get it. That I *never* got it. I have no clue what happened to us."

"He's an ass, is what happened to you. He cheated on you."

"I know that, but"—she eyed her sister—"our marriage was good for *nine* years."

"Seriously?" Bree's eyes bugged out. "How good could it have possibly been? *He slept with another woman.*"

Erica dropped her head to her sister's shoulder. Bree was too young. She didn't get it. She had yet to have the kind of relationship that could frame her entire life. Erica and JC's marriage had honestly been good.

Hadn't it?

Sure, she didn't have the type of polish and glamour he preferred in most things. She was more simple, where his clothes and cars had pizazz. But if that had never been an issue before, why had it suddenly become one?

They'd had something better, anyway. They'd been friends first.

They'd been friends for *years*.

There had been ups and downs, of course. Just like any other couple. They'd never had kids, and some people had thought that weird, but it had worked for them. And anyway, who was to say they never would have had kids? The timing just hadn't been right yet. But she and JC couldn't have been more similar. Their families had known each other for years, both having long histories in town, and she and JC had even ended up teaching at the same school. They couldn't have been more perfect for each other.

Yet in that moment, as she pictured her ex-husband standing beside Lindsey in a crowd full of their friends—a woman who *did* have that shine and polish he sought in every other aspect of his life—Erica couldn't help but wonder if she had always been blind. Had she and JC *not* been on the same page throughout their marriage?

Or had he just gotten tired of her?

Even with the concession that things possibly hadn't been as good as she'd thought, Erica wasn't quite finished feeling sorry for herself. This was her pity party, and no way was she letting go of it so easily.

She swallowed a huge gulp of wine and spoke with a pout. "We were supposed to be *forever*."

"I know you were." Bree patted her arm in a fashion they'd both experienced from their mother. "But wanting something really badly doesn't always make it happen, right? Aren't you the one who always tells me that?"

"Yet it's funny how you seem to get whatever *you* want," Erica mumbled.

Bree pulled back then, her eyes suddenly carrying the weight of more years than she owned. "And is marriage to JC what you want?"

"No."

"Then what is? Sleeping with him whenever he calls?"

"No!" Erica sat up straighter. "Of course not. He cheated on me. He humiliated me."

"Then I don't get it, E. Why in the world are you still hung up on that piece of shit?"

Bree's words seemed to echo off the walls, and Erica sat transfixed. The only thing about her that moved was the blood pounding through her veins, and as if fired out of a starting gate, red-hot anger suddenly burst to life along with it. She'd been divorced for almost two years, yet she sat here practically curled into the fetal position for a man who'd done nothing but prove he didn't want her.

"I don't know," she gritted out in reply. "But I want it to *stop*."

"Then *make* it stop."

"But *how*?"

Both of them stared at each other, each breathing hard as if they'd been in the throes of an argument, and Erica felt herself begin to break. She tried to stop it, but there was no holding it back. Her hands shook. A roar built in her ears.

A crack seemed to split her from the middle of the chest down, and though she gritted her teeth and told herself to pull it together, the next thing she knew, tears poured from her eyes. Bree pulled her back into her arms, and they sat there like that for several minutes, Erica clutching her wineglass to her chest, certain the glass would shatter between her fingers, while Bree gently rocked her back and forth. The first time Erica had cried over her divorce, she'd done so alone. Having a pair of arms around her was nice.

Finally, when the tears began to subside, Bree peered down into Erica's face. "It's time to move on," she whispered. "Why are you so afraid of doing that?"

"Because I might be so boring that he's the only one who'll put up with me."

The words came as a surprise to both of them, and as Erica realized she'd finally put words to her fear, her sister sat back on the couch. Her eyes turned to thin slits.

"Boring?" Bree's voice had gone brittle.

"You know I am. You tell me that all the time."

"But I'm your sister. *I* get to say that. Are you telling me that that douche canoe has also called you boring?"

"Come on, Bree, it's the truth." But Erica couldn't say that she hadn't wanted to kick JC in the gonads every time he'd said it. "I wear khakis," she explained. "I drive a beige car. I'd rather sit at home and read a book on weekends than go out and do things like hike Crow Peak."

"That fucking asshole."

"*Bree,*" Erica admonished. "Quit cussing so much. If Mom were here to hear you . . ."

"Oh, no." Bree stood, her head shaking and her brown eyes glittering. "I'll cuss as much as I want to over this. That little turd doesn't get to get away with that. *He's* the boring one. He always has been. He has to throw money around just to get noticed. And let's talk about his never growing up. For crying out loud . . . his *car,*" she spit out in distaste. "That's a classic case of little-dick syndrome if ever I've seen one."

Erica snorted at her sister's final words, her earlier tears now history. Her ex-husband *did* drive one of the sexiest sports cars she'd ever seen.

And it had a really big motor.

"I'm right, aren't I?" Bree pointed a finger at her in accusation. "The man has a tiny penis. That's why he drives that damned car."

"Hey! I like that car."

"But do you like his dick?"

Tears squeezed from the corners of Erica's eyes. This time from laughter. *"Bree."*

"Tell me it's tiny."

"It's not . . . *tiny.*"

"But it's little."

She couldn't believe they were sitting there talking about her ex's penis, especially only moments after she'd been crying over the idiot.

A light coming on behind the double windows across the street caught Erica's attention before she could figure out how to respond to her sister, and she quickly dipped her head as a wayward thought snaked through her consciousness.

"What?" Bree asked when Erica didn't manage to fully hide her smile.

If they were going to talk about penises . . .

Erica peeked back up. She couldn't help but remember her time with Gabe. "I *have* . . . seen larger."

A bark sounded from outside, and Bree's gaze tracked to where Erica's had just been. Gabe now stood on his porch, those same frayed jeans that he'd had on last Saturday hugging his hips, and his hair once again standing on end. He appeared most every evening at this time with the dog, looking exactly that "relaxed."

Bree gasped as she caught on. "Gabe's is bigger?"

"Stop it."

"Ohmygod." She moved to the window. "How much bigger?"

"I am not going to talk about that with you, and please get away from the window. He can see you. Plus, he's mad at me right now," Erica grumbled. "So I *really* shouldn't be talking about the man's genitals."

Bree's only movement was to pick up her glass of wine before backtracking to the window. "What's he mad at you for?"

Erica made a face. "Because I said that I'd do things a little differently than him."

"What things?"

She shrugged nonchalantly. "Something with his daughter."

Bree's brows shot up. "You told him he was raising his daughter wrong?"

"No! It was about a very specific situation, and I . . . maybe . . . *implied* that he could go a different route."

"You were bossy with him, weren't you? Like you are with everyone else?"

"I was *not* bossy with him. I simply had an alternate opinion."

Bree turned up her glass as she contemplated Erica's story, then finished with a decisive nod. "You were bossy. You always are. And men, especially men like"—she stopped talking as she looked back at Gabe, one finger lifted in his direction.

"What?" Erica sat up straighter. She craned her neck to see.

And then both she and her sister watched as Gabe pulled one arm back, bicep bulging under his T-shirt and a football gripped easily in his wide palm, and powered forward. The ball zoomed across the front yard, the dog barking after it as if he stood a chance of scooping it up between his jaws . . . while both women finished off their wine.

"Men like that don't like women being bossy with them," Bree finished a little breathlessly. Then she shook off her trance and looked at Erica, one finger still pointed at the window. "And I swear to all that's holy, Erica Alexandra, if that man doesn't have a big dick inside that pair of jeans, then that's just a very cruel joke."

Erica howled with laughter.

As if he'd heard, Gabe turned toward her house. Bree flattened against the wall while Erica slumped on the couch, and after a round of giggles between them, Bree dropped to the floor and turtle-crawled across the room. By the time she reached the couch, she'd pulled herself together enough to reach out to Erica. "JC never deserved you." She squeezed Erica's arm. "Not for one second. You're such a brighter light than he could ever be."

Erica put her hand over Bree's. This was why she'd needed her sister to visit her.

"Do me a favor?" Bree asked.

"What's that?"

"Put that man behind you for good."

"I'm trying, Bree. I promise."

"Then help it along. Have a crazy fling, if that's what it takes." She angled her head toward the window. "Enjoy a man with manly size parts for once."

"Seriously, Breedom."

It was Bree's turn to snort.

A comfortable wind blew off the lake Monday afternoon as Gabe and several members of his family sat scattered around his brother's backyard. They were mixed in with Nick's in-laws, miscellaneous kids and spouses, and a handful of local friends. This was the second Labor Day they'd all gotten together at Nick and Harper's house, and someone had already declared it official. They would congregate there every year.

"Beer?" Harper held a bottle out to Gabe.

He looked up from his perch by the fire pit. "Thanks."

She handed another to Cord, who sat next to Gabe, then continued passing drinks out to the group. Once finished, she settled in next to Nick and immediately giggled when Nick pulled her close and whispered in her ear. The two of them still wore their honeymoon glow, and Gabe couldn't help but go back in his mind to *his* honeymoon phase. It seemed like a lifetime ago. He'd been over the moon for Michelle when he'd first met her. Logically, he could state that with certainty. Yet after years of putting up with her self-important ways, there was zero ability for any warm feelings to remain.

The bad parts far outweighed any good, and Gabe could only hope his brother didn't have the same ending in store. Though Harper was a good person—and by all accounts, she was nothing at all like his ex-wife—all the Wilde children had been raised by the same woman. And because of that, it would be a miracle if any of them could truly maintain healthy relationships.

The sun peeked out from behind a cloud, long rays of light beaming down toward the lake, and Gabe's stepmother stood from her lawn chair to peer off in the distance. "The view from here is so beautiful when the sun hits the water," Gloria said to no one in particular.

"I couldn't agree more." Harper's mother rose to join Gloria, and Gabe turned his attention elsewhere. He looked at the house. Erica hadn't shown up yet.

Dani had mentioned that she'd invited his neighbor, and Gabe had bitten his tongue to keep from telling her to rescind the invitation. Erica had pissed him off at the school Friday afternoon. Royally. And he wasn't yet ready to face her again. However, at the same time that she'd made him angry, she'd also planted a seed of confusion. He knew what he was doing with his daughter. He knew that *he* was the best thing for her. And he also knew that *not* helping Jenna to be her best would never be the right solution.

However, with everything he'd tried, Jenna continued to lash out.

He'd taken her math book home after Hannah had let him know that she'd "forgotten" it at school, and then Jenna had spent the remainder of the weekend holed up in her room. Today, she was worse.

Gabe sighed. Too many days, even before letting Erica Bird get in his head, he'd asked himself if he had any idea what he was doing with his daughter.

"I love the changes you guys have made since last year." Dani's words filtered in. "I want a fire pit like this someday." She had her feet near the natural stone surround of the custom fire pit, her body rocked back in a zero-gravity chair, while her six-and-a-half-months-pregnant belly sat like a bowling ball in her lap. A bowl of pretzels was balanced on top of her belly.

"I'll add it to my to-do list," her husband replied. Ben reached out and snagged a pretzel.

Several of the others were gathered around the pit as well, making use of the stone benches built in a circular pattern around the fire, while the older couples relaxed in lawn chairs under the shade trees. The kids ran through the yard, their laughter announcing their locations even when they couldn't be seen. And then there was Jenna. Gabe took a drink of his beer as he eyed his daughter. She sat huddled with Haley on a quilted blanket in the far corner of the backyard. They'd been like that since Haley had shown up.

He thought about this day the year before. Michelle had been with them then.

Not that she'd made it better for Jenna by being there, but it had been the last gathering Jenna's mother had made it to. She hadn't come home with them for Christmas—and then she'd been gone when they'd returned. He wondered if Jenna had been thinking about her mother today. If that might be playing into her sullen mood.

Or was she just being her new normal self?

"I'm more partial to the bricked-in grill, myself." This came from Ben. "Maybe I should add that to the list, too. Upgrade the one you and Haley got me last year."

Talk continued around the group, skipping from last night's football game—another loss, though not quite as humiliating—to the temperature forecast for the coming winter to the trees for the pick-your-own cherry lot that Gabe and his dad planned to set out in the coming weeks. Though Gabe wasn't actively involved in the day-to-day family business anymore, he kept a close eye on things now that he was back in Montana, and given that output had dropped with that year's crop, Gabe had pushed the idea of trying something new. They'd once been on the cutting edge of the cherry farming business, but over the last few years, things had gotten a little stale. If the Wilde Cherry Farm intended to be around for another generation, though, it had to move with the times.

Of course, the unspoken question in his family's minds was whether anyone truly wanted the orchard to exist for another generation. But that was a discussion that none of them had so far been willing to put out there.

Dani opened her eyes at the sound of someone coming out of the house, and Gabe found himself holding his breath. But it was only Jewel, one of Harper's sisters, returning from a diaper change.

"We have a new arrival," Jewel announced, baby snug on her hip, and again, Gabe whipped his attention to the house.

With a squeak, Dani shot out of her chair faster than Gabe would have thought possible and hurried to the woman stepping out the back door. The woman's multicolored dress, sheer in places, seemed to float around her as she walked toward them. Its coloring made Gabe think of a peacock.

"Who *is* that?" Cord spoke at Gabe's side. Cord was the only brother who'd made it in from out of town that year.

"Beats me. I've never seen her."

Their sister hurried the other woman to the group. "Hey, everyone. I want to introduce my new office manager. The timing of her move into town was just perfect, showing up the very day the position became available." Dani beamed. She had a thriving marketing business consisting of both local and national clients, and though she'd hired someone to help out in the office the year before, that person had recently moved on. "I hired Arsula on the spot," Dani continued, "and I couldn't be happier with her first week."

"Arsula?" Cord muttered.

Gabe had the vague notion that his sister might have lost her mind.

"Hello, everyone." Arsula's smile was both polite and hesitant as she looked out over the small crowd. "I hope I'm not intruding, but Dani couldn't stand the thought of me sitting at home alone today."

Gabe smirked. His sister had issues with that.

Harper quickly assured Arsula that she was more than welcome, and someone asked where she'd moved there from.

"Cheyenne. I've lived there all my life, and honestly, I never thought I'd leave. But I had a dream last week that told me to come here." Arsula's smile widened. "So I loaded up my car and hit the road, and the first person I saw as I pulled into town was Dani."

"A dream?" Gabe said. His sister *had* lost her mind.

Arsula turned to him, the move making him realize two things at once. One, he'd spoken out loud. And two, she was a freaking bombshell.

She nodded, her jet-black hair seeming to bounce in slow motion. "I do general office work by day, but my real passion happens in the evenings. I read people's dreams. I'd never heard of Birch Bay before I arrived, but I had a vision that couldn't be ignored. There's someone I need to be here for." She lifted a shoulder in a shrug, and her long hair seemed to shiver with the move. "I don't know who it is yet, but I'm here for them whenever they want to show themselves."

"Yes, ma'am, you are," Cord added under his breath. He pushed off the stone bench and headed for the new arrival.

Gabe looked at his sister as Cord "took" the woman away from her and couldn't help but chuckle at Dani's incredulousness. Their oldest brother was not a man to let a good-looking woman go unshepherded. Annoyance crossed Dani's face as she watched Cord lead Arsula to the patio bar and offer her a drink, but she soon let it go as her lounge chair seemed to produce a louder siren call than that of rescuing her newest employee. She returned to her seat and stretched back out, and, as smooth as a fine whiskey goes down, conversations picked back up.

Gabe took another peek at the house, wondering if Erica had changed her mind about coming.

When he turned back, Dani was watching him. He lifted his brows in question, feeling defensive at being caught keeping an eye out for his neighbor, and his sister's reply was a pointed look at the back door. Damned woman was far too good at reading her brothers. He scowled at her, but it didn't seem to faze her. She simply tucked back into her seat and once again closed her eyes.

Gabe ignored his sister and scanned the yard for Jenna, relief whipping through him when he found her with the other kids. As he watched her smile and then heard her laugh, he silently reiterated that he *did* know what he was doing when it came to taking care of his kid. And he didn't need someone who'd just come into Jenna's life to tell him any differently.

"Well, if it isn't Erica Yarbrough."

Gabe jerked around at his father's words.

His dad—and every other person in his family—stood from their seats and practically ran for the patio. They surrounded Erica and her sister before the two of them could take more than a few steps outside the back door, and they all began talking at once, all offering hugs and saying how good it was to see them. But Gabe merely stared. This wasn't the teacher his daughter saw in class every day.

And it wasn't the woman he'd dated years ago.

This was Erica . . . part two. And she'd taken style cues from her baby sister.

He dropped his gaze to Erica's feet. The handful of times he'd seen her over the past two weeks she'd either had on tennis shoes or some sort of dark loafer that seemed appropriate for teaching. Today her toes and most of her feet showed in a seriously strappy number, and her toenails were hot pink.

He lifted his gaze. That was also no ordinary "Erica" skirt. It had to be her sister's because it rode several inches above the knee, had stars splashed across the front that were as pink as her toes, and looked as if it had literally been stretched over her body. As he stared, he remembered with great clarity how great her rear used to be. His mouth went dry. He wanted her to turn around so he could see what her butt looked like today. How had he not thought to check that out already?

A groan slipped from between his lips, and he found himself thankful to be sitting alone.

"I'd better get to the hot dogs," he mumbled, knowing no one would hear. He didn't need to look at Erica anymore. Especially since the fit of her T-shirt had also imprinted itself on his brain.

Why hadn't she just dressed like normal?

He rose and stalked toward the grill, not taking another look in Erica's direction, and several minutes later Ben joined him. The two of them went back to their college days together where they'd met as roommates, and since neither was especially adept in the kitchen, they'd been assigned to grill duty today. Someone deposited platters of beef and bison patties at their elbows, another brought a tray of hot dogs, and additional food was transferred from inside the house to out. The volume rose while more drinks were handed out, and the party seemed to suddenly be in full swing.

Gabe worked side by side with Ben for fifteen minutes as they got the food going, and all the while Gabe kept his gaze diverted from the center of the crowd. Or he tried to.

"You're going to burn the dogs if you don't quit glaring at her."

Gabe ripped his gaze from Erica. "I was looking at her sister," he lied.

Ben snorted. "Right. Because you always had a thing for underage girls with pink hair."

Gabe frowned. "Bree is of age."

"Yet she's still not who you were looking at."

He ignored his friend and returned his focus to the meat. However, bright laughter coming from the densest part of the gathering kept his ears attuned elsewhere. He should have overridden Dani's invite. Erica and Bree would have been fine on their own.

Because seeing Erica now suddenly made him angry with her all over again. As well as thinking things a single father with a seriously mixed-up kid should not be thinking.

Chapter Six

Later that evening, as the sun headed far to the west, the crowd in the backyard had thinned and the fire roared. Gabe and his siblings remained, as did Harper's, but everyone else had gone home. Erica kept telling herself that she and Bree should leave, too. It was down to family now. Only, the afternoon had been so enjoyable that she couldn't force herself to move.

She rested on a handmade quilt, having inched closer to the fire when the temperature began to drop, and listened to Bree as she laughed at something Cord said. The two sat just outside the main circle of people, and had been talking together for the last thirty minutes. Erica had the thought that she should go over and break it up. Whatever *it* was. But she wouldn't embarrass her sister in front of people that way. Cord was a flirt. He'd made the rounds that day, charming every female in the group—married or not—and Bree had to recognize his actions for what they were.

And if she didn't, Erica would make sure to point it out to her when they got home.

Tilting her chin down, she peered covertly at Gabe, who'd settled in a chair on the opposite side of the fire. He was kicked back, one canvas-sneakered foot on the rim of the fire pit, with Nick on one side of him and Jewel's husband, Bobby, on the other. Gabe seemed engrossed in the three-way conversation, in a fashion similar to what she'd seen the entire afternoon. Every time Erica had caught sight of him, he'd either been fully absorbed in talking with someone else—or he'd been turned away from *her*, looking in the completely opposite direction. Basically, whatever he'd been doing, he'd been making sure that she understood he was ignoring her. And it had seriously begun to get on her nerves.

Yes, she'd overstepped her bounds Friday. She shouldn't have said the things she'd said to him. But she hadn't been wrong! She believed that completely. With eleven years of teaching kids under her belt, she'd learned a thing or two over the years. But more significant than that was that she recognized a heck of a lot in seven-year-old Jenna, and it pointed right back at her.

Rejection. Not knowing exactly where she fit in.

Having her life ripped away from her.

Erica got all of that, and she'd been doing her best over the last couple of weeks to strike a chord with the girl. Little progress had been made, however, and there'd been zero opportunity to add to it that afternoon since Jenna had also steered clear of her.

Her cell phone buzzed in the back pocket of her skirt, and she pulled it out.

This picnic isn't the same without you.

With a sigh, she punched out a quick reply, not in the mood to deal with her ex.

I wasn't a part of it last year, either. Did you forget that?

85

Though she'd promised Bree that she'd get over him once and for all, JC had actually been on her mind more in the last couple of days than normal. She'd spent a lot of years going to the Bird Labor Day picnic, being front and center with the Birds. Everyone in town showed up.

You may not have been a *part* of it, but you were still here. You had on those jeans I always liked so much and a green top. You never left your parents' side. I didn't go over and talk to you because I figured you wouldn't want to talk to me, but I saw you. I knew you were here.

He'd seen her while *he'd* been standing next to Lindsey—and while *they'd* been side by side with his parents.

A lump formed in her throat as she thought back to the year before. Yeah, she'd been at the picnic. It had been easier to make an appearance and to act as if all was right in her world than to be the only one in town who stayed home. But she most certainly hadn't been there with *him*.

Her phone buzzed again, and though she didn't want to look at it, she did.

I've never stopped missing you, E. I love you.

No, he didn't. At least not enough.

Leave me alone. I'm in the middle of a cookout right now, anyway. I've moved on. And we're not doing this again, JC. It's time you move on, too.

Three dots appeared as he began to type once again, but after only a few seconds they disappeared. She watched for another half a minute, but nothing else happened on her screen, and when a chair was plopped down beside her, she looked up. Dani was lowering herself into the seat, so Erica shoved her phone back into her pocket.

"Thanks, honey." Dani smiled up at Ben once she'd settled in place.

"It's what I'm here for." Ben winked and dropped a kiss on his wife's forehead before joining Gabe and the other men on the other side of the fire.

"So," Dani began. She peered down at Erica before tossing a quick glance through the fire, then she leaned to the side and spoke from the corner of her mouth. "My brother seems to be ignoring you today, she whispered conspiratorially. "Any idea what that's about?"

Exhaustion suddenly swept over Erica, her ex forgotten. And mixed in with the exhaustion was a hefty dose of irritation. She was so tired of being ignored by Gabe, and even more fed up with not being given the chance to apologize. And she'd tried! But any time she'd gotten within ten feet of the blasted man, he'd headed in the other direction.

"I said some things to him the other day that I shouldn't have," she confessed.

"Really?" Both of them stared at the men. "Can I ask what?"

Not wanting to risk being overhead, Erica climbed to her knees and propped an elbow on the chair's armrest. Possibly she shouldn't talk about Gabe's daughter behind his back, but Erica had watched the little girl throughout the day, and her worries hadn't lessened. Jenna had ignored her father for hours, she'd sat by herself more than with anyone else, and Erica was pretty sure there'd been tears in the child's eyes when they'd passed in the house earlier in the day.

She needed to talk *about* Jenna to someone, because the child had issues. And she very much doubted that Gabe would listen.

"It was about Jenna," Erica said. "She's fighting so hard, every step of the way, yet I'm not sure she has a clue what she's fighting against. Or why." She glanced at Dani. "I've been assuming it has to do with her parents' divorce. Perhaps also with the upending of her life given that she moved from California back to here. But . . ." Erica paused as her heart crushed a little more at the sight on the other side of the flames. Haley had crawled into her dad's lap, her energy clearly spent, and Jenna now stood alone once more. "I want to help her," Erica added in an urgent whisper. "I want to be a solid wall for her for the time that I'm here. And part of being that means I don't bend on classroom rules. I let the kids make their own successes and their own failures, and some kids have to fail before they can stand up."

"Ah," Dani murmured. "Jenna messed up and Gabe tried to fix it for her."

Erica looked at the other woman. "Does he do that a lot?"

"It's his mission at the moment to make everything right for his daughter."

She nodded, understanding the helicopter parent and how they couldn't tolerate letting their kids trip up even the tiniest amount. But having known Gabe in the past, that wouldn't have been the picture she would've painted of him. "Is there a particular reason why?" Erica asked.

"Guilt is my guess. Regardless of the need for divorce, it can't be easy." They both turned back to the fire, looking beyond it to the strong-willed men sitting as a group, the night sky now dark behind them. The Wilde brothers were all tall, dark, and handsome, and the flicker of the flames did nothing to detract from their looks. However, Gabe stood out from the others. It was as if he had no curved edges at all. And she didn't mean his physical hardness. His nature was unyielding.

And now that she thought about it, she realized she saw the same thing in Jenna. His daughter was mirroring what she got from her dad.

"But does the guilt extend beyond the divorce?" she asked. Parents going through divorce often beat themselves up for not keeping the family together, Erica understood that, but for some reason, she'd lay odds that Gabe's guilt was placed elsewhere.

Dani's jaw worked, likely as she considered what to say or whether to say anything at all, and Erica wouldn't have been surprised if the conversation ended there. But then Dani's eyes left her brother and sought out her niece. Jenna had walked over to the birdbath sitting near the edge of the property, and was now headed back, head down, arms swinging loosely at her sides. Gabe watched his daughter at the same time, and anyone looking could see the abject loneliness in the child.

"Gabe won't really talk about it with me," Dani admitted softly, and Erica turned back to her. "He holds too much in. Thinks he has to handle everything on his own. But Jenna hasn't seen her mother since February. Nor has she talked to her. And don't get me wrong, I am *not* a fan of Michelle's. She wasn't a good mother before, and I'm a firm believer that she never will be. But she *is* still Jenna's mom. And though I'd prefer Jenna never lay eyes on the woman again, I also know that having your mother suddenly ripped from your life is very difficult."

Erica soaked in the information, remembering that Dani and Gabe's mother had died right before Gabe graduated high school. "When did Jenna and Gabe move back to town?"

"The middle of June."

"And Michelle is still in California?"

Dani nodded.

"Then why would Jenna not see her for months before they moved away?"

Worry now seemed to mix with guilt for Dani—probably for talking about her brother—as she locked her gaze with Erica's. "I don't know. But Gabe is handling things. That's all he'll say to me. He's doing what he believes is right, and is determined to see Jenna through this time in her life. And he'll make it work. I don't doubt that. He loves his daughter and would take any pain of hers on himself if he could. But he's struggling. He's winging this single dad thing the best he can, but it's not like he had the best example from either of our parents."

"What do you mean?"

Dani shook her head. "I've said too much already. It's Gabe's life and his business. I'm doing my best to respect that. Yet at the same time, I'm worried about Jenna. She's so different than she used to be."

So much of what Dani had just said seemed to reverberate inside Erica, making her want to work doubly hard to find a way to break through Jenna's barriers. But what had Dani meant about her parents?

Knowing nothing more than that, Erica now found herself worried about Gabe, as well as his daughter.

Dani crooked a finger in a come-here motion, and Erica followed her gaze to Jenna. The girl had made her way back near the fire and looked with longing at her aunt. Her eyes, seeming so dark and lost in the night, shifted briefly to Erica, but the normal hardness didn't appear. Instead, she seemed to be considering Erica in a new light. Not a particularly good light, per se, but not necessarily as if Erica were pure evil, either. Then Jenna lowered her gaze, but made her way to Dani's side.

"Want to sit in my lap, sweetie?" Dani patted the tops of her thighs.

"If you don't care."

Dani shot her niece an are-you-kidding-me look. "Of course I don't care. I always love having my best girl sitting with me."

A tiny smile flickered across Jenna's mouth, and Erica held her breath when that smile was suddenly directed at her. "I got my math homework done, Ms. Bird." Jenna climbed into Dani's lap and rested her head on her aunt's belly. "I even double-checked it like you told us to."

Surprise filled Erica. "That's terrific, Jenna. I'm very proud of you for doing that."

The child's eyes drifted down almost immediately, and Erica forced herself to once again look to the other side of the fire. Gabe now watched *her*. His eyes remained hard, but Erica read the questions in them, as well. At the same time, she wondered if he could read the ones in hers.

Jenna had done her homework. Gabe had taken her book home for her.

Maybe there *was* more than one way to accomplish a task.

Erica had all four windows of her little beige sedan down, wind whipping strands of her hair around her face as she took the curves to her apartment Tuesday afternoon. She'd been expecting the school day to be a rough one after the long weekend, but the kids had surprised her. For the most part, they'd been well-behaved, polite students. Even Jenna. Gabe's daughter had come up front that morning to pass out the reading workbooks without offering a single complaint. Of course, afterward she'd returned to her seat and sunk down low and sullen. As if just then realizing that she'd been pleasant.

Erica chuckled to herself. Even with the tiny setback, they'd taken a nice step forward. It made her hopeful that more would soon follow. The night before had seemed like the first tiny breakthrough, though there'd been no additional talking due to the girl falling asleep on her aunt's lap. But the door had definitely been opened, and there was no way Erica wouldn't work like a pack mule and keep pushing through it.

She took her foot off the gas pedal as she rounded the last bend in the road, anxious to get home to her sister. She and Bree had stayed up talking until late into the night. It was really good to have her sister around, and Erica had spent her lunch break mapping out plans for the weekend, hoping to entice Bree into staying at least that long.

As she pulled into her parking spot, she saw Jenna and Hannah sitting on the small bench on Gabe's front porch. She'd seen the pair coming and going over the last couple of weeks, but this marked the first time the three of them were outside at the same time. So when she stepped out of the car, she waved.

"Hello, ladies. How are you two this afternoon?"

"We're doing great, Ms. Bird," Hannah tossed out. "Just enjoying some lemonade and doing a little homework before Jenna's dad gets home." Both girls had books open on their laps with tall glasses of lemonade on the small tables on either end of the bench. Jenna's dog lay half under the seat and half under Jenna's table. His head was on his paws, but at the sight of Erica, his tail flipped in the air.

Hannah glanced at Jenna, as if waiting for her to speak, and Erica decided to take the moment to force the issue. She didn't move from her spot. Didn't look away from Jenna.

Finally, Jenna's small hand lifted. "Hello, Ms. Bird." The words actually came out polite.

Erica nodded with pleasure. "Hello, Jenna. Good to see you both. Have a great evening."

She grabbed the bags of groceries from the passenger seat and turned for her front door, but before she could step inside, Jenna added, "This is my dog, Mike."

Erica stopped, and once again faced the little girl. She hadn't been formally introduced to the dog yet. "Nice to meet you, Mike." The dog waved his tail in the air once again. Then Erica looked straight at Jenna. "And *you* must be so proud. Mike is a very beautiful and smart dog."

Jenna smile broadly, and Erica shared a knowing glance with Hannah. Progress.

"You have a good evening, too, Mike." Erica turned once again and entered her apartment, and when she stepped inside, the first thing she saw were the pages of a newspaper spread across the bar top. Bree stood behind the paper, one foot off the floor and flattened against the side of her opposite knee as if caught mid yoga pose, while at the same time she held a quart of ice cream in one hand and a spoon in the other. The spoon was hooked in her mouth, her eyes glued to the paper.

She looked up at the interruption, licking the utensil clean. And then her expression bottomed out.

"Khakis?" Bree yelped. She stabbed the spoon into the container. "What happened to the pink skirt? To the other clothes we picked out Sunday afternoon?" She sighed and shook her head. "I swear, I should never have slept in this morning and let you dress yourself."

Erica closed the door and tossed her keys to the countertop. "Those clothes weren't for teaching."

"Well, they could be." Bree moved to the living room, newspaper and ice cream in hand.

"No. They couldn't be," Erica corrected. She kicked off her shoes, dropped the bags of food she intended to use for that night's dinner beside the stove, and grabbed a bottle of water from the fridge. "I might be willing to branch out and wear a hot-pink, too-tight skirt to a causal get-together once in a while, but—"

"It wasn't too tight."

Erica groaned. This was a repeat argument. "Fine. It wasn't too tight. But it was tighter than I'm used to."

"And it looked freaking fantastic on you. Everyone totally saw how hot your ass is in that thing."

"Stop it." Erica held up a palm. She didn't want to argue with her sister tonight. Not over her butt or her clothes or anything else superficial. "We're not talking about my behind right now, got it?" And she was pretty sure Gabe hadn't taken one look at her rear the night before, anyway, so not everyone had seen it.

She pushed the loose strands of hair back toward her braid and followed her sister to the living room. As Bree scooped out more ice cream, her behind now planted on the far end of the couch and the newspaper spread out on the coffee table in front of her, Erica lowered to the other end. She nudged her chin toward the paper. "What are you doing with that? I didn't think millennials knew such things existed."

Bree gave her a mocking smirk. "I had a high school teacher once who was as old as you. She taught me all about these old-timey newspapers."

"Smart-ass." Erica stole both the ice cream and spoon.

"Look at that. My big sister said a bad word."

"I can say bad words." She scooped out a bite of chocolate mint and eyed the paper, trying to figure out what Bree could have been looking at. "Most of the time I simply choose not to have a mouth as naughty as yours."

Bree snatched the spoon away before Erica could put it in her own mouth and began licking along the edge of the ice cream. "Naughty is good." She grinned wickedly and licked again. "You should try it. You might like it."

"Give it a break, Bree."

"Fine." Bree cleared off the bite and handed over the spoon, while Erica reached for the paper. It was open to the classifieds.

"What are you looking for?"

Bree shrugged. "Just checking out what kind of jobs are around here."

Erica heard the words, but none of them made sense. She lowered the paper to her lap. "Jobs?" Did that mean her sister might stick around for a while?

"Yeah. What's the big deal?"

"For you?"

"I do work occasionally, you know? It's how I pay the bills."

What went unsaid was that Bree's art didn't yet cover all her expenses. Which reminded Erica that she'd never paid her sister back for her flight to Montana. She reached for her purse, thinking she might have a check tucked away in an inside pocket. "I totally forgot to pay you for the flight. How much was it?"

"There is no way you're paying me for my flight."

"Sure I am." She found a zipper and tugged, and was rewarded with a wrinkled, but totally viable, check. "How much?"

"Stop it!"

The vehemence in Bree's words had Erica looking up.

"You're not my mother, so put the check away."

"What are you talking about? I never said I was your mother."

"Yet you always try to act like it. You take charge. Even when you don't have to."

Erica opened her mouth to argue, but Bree leaned forward and put a hand over it. "You're twelve years older than me, but that doesn't mean that you need to take care of me. Or of Annalise or Seth. We're all adults. We can all handle our own lives."

Erica had been born right after her parents had graduated high school, then they'd gone to college, gotten jobs, and had waited to plan their second child for *after* they'd both settled into their teaching careers. Seth came along their second summer off from teaching, thus putting him six years behind Erica, while Annalise was eight years back.

"I don't mean to take over," Erica began. What was she supposed to say? It had simply been natural to "boss" them a little. She'd been the older sister.

"But you do. And you do it with a lot of people."

"I'm just trying to help."

"I know. And I love you for it. We all love you." Bree squeezed Erica's hands. "But, E. Honey. You've got to stop. We get to make our own mistakes. It's time to worry about yourself for a while."

Erica didn't know if she *could* stop.

Or if she wanted to worry about herself.

Concern for her siblings had been a major part of her entire life. What was she supposed to do if she didn't have them to focus on?

Same thing she'd done when she'd no longer been married, she supposed.

Which had been nothing.

The thought froze her. Why had she quit participating in things just because she'd gotten divorced? The last two years of her life flashed through her head, and she realized that she hadn't experienced one activity outside of her norm since that moment at the high school football game. It was almost as if she'd been stuck in time. Had she seriously just laid down to die because she no longer had a husband?

It certainly wasn't as if JC had stood still.

She may not have ever been one to stretch her wings overly wide, but she *had* left the house on occasion.

She'd had friends—whom JC seemed to inherit in the divorce—she'd had hobbies. Her prized sunflowers had taken the blue ribbon at the county fair for years. She'd even been known to accompany her husband on a weekend trip on occasion, mostly to prove that she wasn't a total stick in the mud, and had returned from a few of them having had so much fun that she'd declared she would totally try that particular activity again.

But for the last two years, she'd gone to work, and then she'd come home.

Bree leaned over and kissed Erica on the cheek as thoughts continued to roll. "Live a little, big sister. You finally got out of Silver Creek, now see what else you can do."

Erica nodded, her heart already breaking for what was to come at the same time that she silently agreed with Bree's words. She had to change her ways.

And Bree was about to leave. Erica had heard that finality in her sister's tone before.

Bree moved behind the couch and wheeled her suitcase around the end of it, and Erica stood. "You don't have to go."

"I do. You know I never stay in one place too long."

But she'd just been looking at jobs. "I planned to cook dinner for you tonight. I brought home groceries. Stay until tomorrow at least. I'll take you to the airport after school if you still want to go."

"I can't. I'm already booked on a flight out tonight. I've got a car picking me up."

A hole formed in Erica's chest. "Seriously? I wouldn't have minded taking you."

"I know. But I've got this." Bree wrapped Erica in a hard hug, and as they pulled apart, a car rolled to a stop outside the door as if it had been sitting around the corner merely waiting for a sign. Before stepping out, Bree swept her gaze over the interior of the space once more. "At least think about buying it?" she asked.

Erica hugged her sister again. "I'll think about it." Then she forced herself to step away. She knew from experience she wouldn't be able to change Bree's mind. "I'll miss you."

"I'll miss you, too. But I need to go. You have Gabe next door now. I don't want to get in the way of that."

Erica let out a bark of laughter. "That's why you're leaving so soon? Trust me, there's *nothing* to get in the way of there. He's still not even talking to me."

"Yeah, but I watched the way he tried to freeze you out last night." Bree grinned. "He failed, in case you were wondering. So expect a thaw sooner rather than later."

Chapter Seven

"M s. Bird?"

Erica looked up from her desk Thursday afternoon to find the school's secretary—a midforties woman with a shoulder-length bob—standing at her door. The last bell of the day had rung thirty minutes earlier, and though most teachers had already departed the school grounds or were quickly heading that way, Erica had stayed behind to grade a set of spelling tests.

"Yes?" Erica kept her pen poised over the paper she'd been working on, while Louann Michaels twisted her hands together in front of her.

"Jenna Wilde is still here. She hasn't gotten picked up yet."

Worry had Erica dropping the pen. She stood. "What do you mean? Where's Hannah?" She grabbed her cell phone and headed for the door. "Where's Jenna?"

"We haven't heard anything from the young lady who usually picks Jenna up, but we called Jenna's aunt." Mrs. Michaels stepped back as Erica reached her, and together they moved down the hall. "And Jenna is sitting with the nurse right now."

Erica jerked around. "Is she hurt?"

"No. Not at all. It's just . . . well, the nurse and I need to leave. We've each got somewhere we have to be this afternoon, and Principal Rogers is at the superintendent's office for a meeting. We talked to her aunt, but Dani was on the other side of the lake when we got hold of her. She's heading back this way now. And we tried Hannah several more times . . ." Mrs. Michaels's words drifted off, her worry for the younger woman clear.

Erica walked faster, scrolling through her contacts as she went. She pressed "Send" the second she had Gabe's number under her thumb. "Did you call her dad?"

"He didn't answer, either. I'm sure he's at the football field. I thought about just taking Jenna over there on my way out, but she's being quite insistent. She doesn't want to go."

They reached the outer office door at the same time that Gabe's phone kicked over to voice mail, and Erica pushed through the inner door. She found Jenna sitting in one of the two straight-backed chairs tucked in the corner. The second the little girl saw her, she looked the other way.

"What's going on, Jenna?" Erica sat in the empty chair.

"Nothing. I told them I'm fine. I can wait here for Hannah by myself. They didn't need to get you."

"Of course you're fine. That's not why Mrs. Michaels came to find me." Erica nodded to Mrs. Michaels and the school nurse. "You can go ahead. I've got her."

"I hate to just leave." Mrs. Michaels's brow pinched.

"No problem at all," Erica assured her. "I'll stay with Jenna until someone comes for her. She and I will be fine."

Jenna's mouth turned down, but she didn't voice an opinion, and the second the other two ladies disappeared, she edged closer to the other side of her chair. The move wrenched Erica's heart, and she had to clasp her hands together to keep from reaching out to the little girl. The two of them had been doing better since Monday night's cookout. In no way great, but definitely better. Jenna had even been the first to raise her hand with an answer earlier that day, and yesterday she'd asked what she could do to let it be her turn to lead the class to the lunchroom.

Yet fear shrouded the girl at the moment. And because of that fear, she'd instantly retreated.

But Erica refused to let fear define the moment.

"I'm sure Miss Hannah just had car trouble or something," Erica told the little girl. "Maybe she got behind a lot of traffic."

Jenna still didn't look at her. "She has a phone."

"She does." And what Erica didn't voice was *her* fear that the college student might have been the one to cause any potential traffic snarl. Had she gotten involved in an accident on the way back from school? She drove an hour each way.

"Then why hasn't she called?" Jenna whispered.

"I don't know, Jenna, but I'm positive she would have if she could." Erica stared down at her cell, trying to think if there was anything else she could do before Dani showed up, and when Jenna cut a look her way, Erica lifted the phone between them. "We could try your dad again. Or I could drive you over to the football field to see him. We could stay there until your Aunt Dani shows up if you want to."

"I don't want to."

Jenna didn't clarify her reasoning, and Erica decided to let it drop. What she didn't need was to lose ground with the little girl, so dragging her kicking and screaming out to her car wasn't an option. And Erica got the distinct impression that if she tried, there would definitely be kicking and screaming.

She sat farther back in her seat and tried to appear casual. "So then, we wait."

"Then we wait," Jenna repeated remotely. She chewed the corner of her mouth and turned her head to stare straight ahead again instead of at Erica, and after a couple of minutes her feet began to slowly kick in and out.

"Want to wait in my classroom?"

Jenna peeked over at her. "What would we do in there?"

"Well . . . I was grading that spelling test that you and the class took today when Mrs. Michaels came and got me. I could probably use some help with that."

Jenna sucked in a quick breath. "You'd let me grade papers?"

"Sure. I can always use good help." Erica stood and waited for Jenna to join her, and when the other girl climbed from her seat, Erica led them from the room. "You ever graded papers before?"

"Never." Jenna's eyes had gone wide. "But Leslie got to grade some, one time. Her aunt is a teacher, and she let her help with a math test."

"Is that so?" Leslie was also in Erica's classroom, and Erica had noticed that Leslie, Haley, and Jenna had become somewhat of a little pack during free time. "I'm sure Leslie's aunt appreciated the help very much. Grading math papers is super important."

"Is it as important as grading spelling papers?"

Erica hid a smile. "Almost."

Jenna suddenly developed some pep in her step, and she beat Erica to the room, pulling the door open for both of them.

Once they were both settled at the desk, with Jenna in a chair sitting across from Erica, Erica sorted through the stack of papers as if making sure to pull out the most important one. As she landed on a sheet in the middle of the pile, she tugged it slowly out of the stack. "I know I'll never get to this one tonight if I don't have someone to help me."

A smile brightened Jenna's face. "I promise I'll do a good job."

She held out her hand, palms facing up, and when Erica handed over the sheet, a list of the answers, and a very special red pen for marking down the grade, she would have sworn that the meteor-size chip Jenna had been carrying around on her shoulders simply disappeared. Jenna spread everything out in front of her and got busy checking each letter carefully.

Erica watched for several minutes, finding herself thankful for whatever slip had happened that kept Hannah from picking Jenna up— while at the same time, hoping Hannah was safe and sound.

They worked silently for several minutes, Erica handing over another test paper when Jenna had finished with the first one, then out of the blue, Jenna said, "I've seen a prince before."

Erica peeked up, noting that Jenna remained concentrated on the page in front of her, one finger of her left hand moving along the letters of each word on the master list while on the right side she carefully checked each word, one letter at a time.

"And where did you see a prince?" Erica asked. She, also, continued to work.

"At Disneyland. When me and Daddy lived in California, he took me. We did lots of fun stuff. Aunt Dani and Uncle Ben took me to Disneyland one time, too. They came to visit, and Haley came with them. It was *so* much fun." She ended her words with a sigh, as if she'd had the best time of her entire life.

"And you saw a prince there?" Erica didn't miss the comment about Gabe having more time for his daughter before they'd moved back home. "Does that also mean that you saw a princess?"

A smile, unimpeded by sadness or hesitation of any kind, bloomed across Jenna's mouth. She nodded, eyes still alternating from the master list to the test paper. "We saw *all* the princesses. I like Merida the best. Cinderella used to be my favorite, but that was when I was just a kid. Now I like Merida. Or"—she stumbled over her words, her head dipping at the same time—"I *used* to like Merida."

Erica lifted her pen off the page. "I like Merida, too," she said carefully. She didn't take her eyes off Jenna. "I like her red hair."

Jenna glanced up. Her eyes went to Erica's hair. "But your hair is brown."

"I know." Erica touched the tip of her braid. "But that doesn't mean I can't love Merida's hair. Don't you think her hair is pretty?"

Jenna nodded, but the movement was small. Her mouth tightened, making it appear smaller than it was, and anxiety narrowed her gaze. Then she lowered her eyes and went back to grading the paper.

The last minute of conversation left Erica puzzled, but she was at a loss as to what had just transpired. She glanced at the clock in the back of the room, knowing that Dani would be there within minutes, and found herself wishing for more time. Then she followed Jenna's lead, refocusing on the work in front of them, while her mind continued to whirl.

It didn't take long before Jenna looked back up. "My mom said it's stupid to like Merida because of her hair. Because my hair will never be as pretty as hers. Do you think it's stupid?"

Erica's insides pulled tight.

She shook her head, careful to maintain an even keel as she mentally worked on a response. Dani had been right. Jenna's mother obviously wouldn't win mother of the year. "It's never stupid to like something, Jenna. Not if you have your own reasons for liking it. I like Merida's hair because it's red and curly, and because it always gets just a little out of control. It makes me laugh when it drives her crazy, and that makes me like *her* even more."

Jenna stared at her. No smile, not a flicker of emotion. Then she added, "My mom has pretty hair."

Erica gulped. "I'm sure she does. But you do, too. Did you know that?"

Jenna reached for the blonde locks captured high on her head. She pulled the tip of one pigtail in front of her and studied the strands as if she had no idea what it was. Then she lowered her hand back to the table. "Do you know where Miss Hannah is?"

The subject change was abrupt. "I'm afraid not. But I'm sure your Aunt Dani will try her best to find her."

"What about my dad? Is he lost, too?"

Erica shook her head. No words came out for a moment. She simply couldn't get her throat to open. Then she gently reminded Jenna that her dad was at football practice, where he went every day after school. "I know he would have answered the phone if he'd heard it. He may just be so busy he didn't. Would you like me to take you over there?"

Again, Jenna simply looked at her. "He's always busy. And he hates my mother. I haven't seen her in a long time, and I don't even know if her hair is still pretty."

Erica could get whiplash with the subject changes from this child, but the significance of each topic imbedded deep inside her. She felt as if she might be edging out to the thinnest ice in the deepest part of the pond, but she couldn't simply ignore the fact that Jenna was reaching out. The child needed someone to talk to. "And how do *you* feel about your mom, Jenna?"

Jenna blinked at the question. "I don't know. I guess I hate her, too. She was never very nice to me, and anyway, she has a boyfriend now. She likes him way better than me."

It was now Erica's turn to stare. The poor thing.

The door opened, and Erica jumped in surprise, her pulse spiking. Then she forced her gaze from Jenna's to find Dani rushing in. Hannah arrived two steps behind Dani.

"I am *so sorry*, Jenna." Hannah ran to the little girl, dropping to her knees in front of her. "I stayed at school too long, and then I got stuck in traffic." She glanced up at Erica and Dani with a panic-stricken look, then back to Jenna. None of them had moved. Her throat worked and she held up her hand, showing them a phone with a shattered screen. "And I dropped my stupid phone running to the car—" Her voice cracked, and Jenna flung her arms around Hannah's neck.

Jenna clung to the other girl as if she'd never let her go, her body shaking like a leaf.

"I'm sorry, Jenna," Hannah whispered. She stroked Jenna's back. "I'd never leave you."

Jenna didn't speak, but she also didn't turn Hannah loose. Erica looked over the teenager's head to Dani and caught tears in the other woman's eyes, just as she felt the sting in her own.

Finally, the girl released her babysitter and took a tiny step back.

"I wasn't worried," Jenna told Hannah. Her voice sounded far braver than all of them knew she felt. "I knew you'd be here. I told everyone you'd be here, but they made me come back down to Ms. Bird's room."

Hannah rose to her feet, pulling the seven-year-old up with her and letting her ride on her hip. "It looks to me like you were having a lot of fun."

Jenna looked down at the desk. At the paper she'd been working on. And Erica could see that the fight had returned. Jenna wanted to declare that she'd had no fun at all with her teacher. That she hadn't even wanted to be in the classroom to begin with. But then something miraculous occurred. Jenna lifted her eyes directly to Erica's, and her blue gaze softened. The tension seeped from her little body as she snuggled in tighter to Hannah, her head tilting against Hannah's neck, and darned if she didn't give Erica a smile that totally melted her heart.

"I was helping Ms. Bird," she said. "She needed my help to grade the papers."

"Is that right?" Hannah asked. She looked over the work laid out on the desk beside them, and nodded as if in appreciation of the great effort that had been put into the grading. "Do you need to finish what you were working on so you don't leave Ms. Bird in the lurch?"

Jenna lifted her head. "What's 'lurch'?"

Hannah smiled. "So you don't leave her needing someone to finish that page."

"Oh." Jenna quickly scrambled down. She returned to the desk, but stopped before she sat, and looked up at Erica. "Did you need me to finish this one?"

Erica nodded. "I do. Thank you very much. That would be a huge help."

Color bloomed across Jenna's cheeks. "You're welcome."

As Jenna settled back into her chair and pulled the two pieces of paper over to her, Erica forced herself to sit, as well. She didn't want the three of them to all be looking down on the girl. And as she did, she couldn't help but see love literally spilling out of Dani's eyes as the aunt looked on. Erica was pretty sure that she and Dani were thinking along the same lines. Her niece had just shed a layer of the shield she wore so tightly these days. Hopefully it would be only one of many layers to fall over time.

When finished with the paper, Jenna read over the chart to find the correct score for the number of misspelled words, then carefully wrote out the grade at the top of the page. She then stood, and without prompting, moved the chair she'd been sitting in back to its original location before crossing to the whiteboard at the side of the room.

At Dani and Hannah's quizzical expressions, Erica followed and helped Jenna to pull out the small stool provided so the kids could reach up high on the board. Jenna got the stool in just the right place, picked out a black dry-erase marker from the attached tray, and climbed on top of the stool. She reached up high, brows furrowed in concentration, and used the tip of the marker to carefully draw out a perfect little check mark beside her name.

Gabe watched his daughter through his kitchen window as she paced in a tight path in the backyard. She had Mike by her side and looked tiny among the tall pines, while her attention remained focused entirely across the street. She'd been like that for the last ten minutes.

She looked at him then, and nodded, and he gave a returning nod of okay. And then she jumped into action.

"Ms. Bird!"

He could hear her through the closed window.

"Ms. Bird!" Her small hand waved back and forth above her head.

It was only a second before Jenna whooped with excitement and headed for the fence's gate. Gabe leaned forward and watched, hoping she didn't forget the rules—but willing to forgive her if she did. It was rare to catch her in this good of a mood.

But she didn't forget. She stopped inside the gate.

"How are you today, Jenna?"

Gabe couldn't see Erica.

"I'm *amazing*," Jenna gushed to their neighbor. "Did Daddy tell you?" She reached for the gate latch, but snatched her hand back as if she'd been burned. "I'm not supposed to leave the backyard," she explained.

"Then how about I come to you?"

A smile bloomed on his daughter's face, and then a matching one appeared on Gabe's when Erica came into view. His daughter wasn't the only one who'd been anxious to see her teacher.

Erica asked if she could come into the yard, and after Jenna nodded, she unlatched the gate and stepped through. And that's when Gabe finally got his first real look at her for the day. Similar to Monday, she seemed years younger today, and as if she hadn't a care in the world. Her hair swung loose, and the snug jeans she wore stopped at the ankle with a little rip over the knee. They certainly weren't anything she'd wear at school.

"I got to go to the game last night," Jenna announced. "Pops and Gramma took me. *And* it was away. *And* Daddy won."

Pride shone on his daughter's face, and the sight of it swelled Gabe's chest. He so rarely did anything to get that kind of response.

"*And* I got to stay up way past my bedtime. I asked Daddy if I could ride home on the football bus, but he said no. But he did let me say hi to the boys after they won. Because the football players are *so cool*, and because I *love* hanging out with them."

Erica chuckled at his daughter's torrent of words. "And I'll bet they love hanging out with you."

Jenna nodded again. "Chase is my favorite, but I like Caleb almost as much."

Gabe decided to join them. He'd wanted to give Jenna a few moments to herself since she'd been waiting all morning to tell Ms. Bird about last night's game, but he couldn't stand the thought of not getting the opportunity to talk to Erica, as well.

She glanced at him as he stepped onto the patio, but immediately returned her attention to Jenna. "It sounds like a pretty perfect night to me."

"It was," Jenna assured her. "And today is even better. We got to go to the Pancake House for breakfast." Jenna slowed long enough to look at him, her eyes losing a hint of their gleam, but not enough to make him change his course. Then she turned back to Erica and whispered, "Daddy doesn't make very good pancakes."

Erica nodded with complete understanding. "My Daddy doesn't make very good pancakes, either. But he makes the *best* homemade ice cream."

Jenna's animation abruptly stopped. "*Makes* ice cream?"

Gabe smiled over his daughter's head as he met Erica's eyes. Man, it was good to see her. He'd wanted to go over Thursday night after finding out she'd helped when Hannah had been late, but given that their last conversation hadn't been on the best of terms, he'd decided to wait until he could more casually bump into her.

After she finished explaining to his daughter what homemade ice cream was and how to make it, Jenna turned and looked up at him, a serious expression on her face. "Do you think you could make ice cream sometime, Daddy?"

"I could definitely try." His culinary talents may be limited, but he'd for certain pick up an ice cream machine and whatever ingredients were needed in the near future. Anything to keep this less hostile side of his daughter showing up.

Jenna suddenly whirled back to Erica. "I'm going to Leslie's house today and so is Haley. We both like Leslie a lot." Jenna squatted when Mike put a paw to her stomach, and the dog began licking her face. "I love my dog," she announced to no one. Then she fell to her back and Mike pounced on her. Giggling rang out from underneath the dog.

Gabe merely stared at his daughter. The sight of her so happy expanded a place inside him that felt as if it had been closed off for years, and though he had yet to fully understand why, he knew he had the woman standing in front of him to thank for the change.

He tucked his fingers into the front pockets of his jeans and cocked his head. "I heard you helped Jenna out at school a couple of days ago."

Erica dropped her gaze to his daughter. "I did."

"Thank you." He said the words as sincerely as he could, and the emotion in them must have made it through to Erica. She lifted her gaze. "I messed up," he continued. "My phone will always be on me from now on, practice or not. It never even occurred to me that something like that might happen."

He'd felt the lowest sort of low when he'd retrieved his cell and seen so many missed calls.

"She seems to have recovered just fine." Erica looked toward her house, as if plotting her escape route.

"So what do you have going on this weekend?" He wasn't yet ready for her to leave. "Aside from being the target of my daughter's energy, that is." They both watched as Jenna and Mike rose and sprinted across the yard, and Gabe remained amazed at the extent of the change. "How did you do that?" he asked. "One day she practically hates you, and the next, she's driving me crazy wanting to see you, to tell you all about the game." Erica swung her gaze back to his, and he finished with a lame, "It's impressive."

"I didn't really *do* anything," she said. "I've simply treated her consistently from day one. Friendly and engaging her participation during class time, but not letting her get away with misbehavior. And then Thursday while we were waiting for Dani, I let her help me grade papers. She started talking and . . ." Her words trailed off as she once again got sucked into watching the totally different girl now squealing with her dog.

"I'm sorry," she said to him. "I was rude to you last week, and I shouldn't have been."

Gabe swallowed. "And I'm sorry I was rude to you on Monday. My behavior was childish."

Light laughter spilled out of her. "Still. It wasn't my place to say those things."

He appreciated the apology. "And I'm no longer positive you were wrong. I mean, she did her homework assignment over the weekend, and that wouldn't have happened if I hadn't taken her book home to her. But I have no idea if her doing it actually had anything to do with me."

"Kids," she murmured. "You never know what will strike a chord."

"Well, I'm pretty sure you've struck one. I haven't heard her laugh this much in months." She'd been like that since he'd gotten home Thursday night. "And I've yet to have her try and put me in my place in the last thirty-six hours."

"Give it time." Erica gave him a wry smile, and Gabe found that he couldn't take his eyes off her. Her smile was beautiful, her swinging hair and the more casual clothes she wore nothing but attractive. But her eyes told a different story, as they tended to do each time he talked to her.

"How's your day going?" he asked. "Everything okay?"

"Same as any other." Her gaze remained somber despite the happy-go-lucky picture she'd painted, and Gabe knew in that moment he had to dig deeper with her. He had to get her smile into her eyes.

Jenna saw Leslie's mother turn onto the far end of their street then, and she disappeared into the house. She returned just as the car slowed to a stop in front of them, and with suitcase in hand, she hurried to the car. Her dog had come out with her, but Mike was no idiot. He'd understood immediately that the suitcase meant he was being left behind. He dropped down on the porch, looking sad and bereft, and gave a single, grudging thump of his tail.

After a quick word to the adults, Leslie's mother drove back down the street, and Gabe didn't waste a second setting his plan into motion. He put the dog in the backyard—while not so much as glancing at Erica—then headed across the street.

Chapter Eight

Erica watched Gabe walk toward her house. "Where are you going?"

"To put away your groceries."

"To put away my . . ." She frowned at his retreating back. *"Why?"* She hurried to catch up, but his footfalls landed on her small porch before she could make it to the middle of the road. "Why would you do that?" she shouted after him.

"Why wouldn't I?" He disappeared inside her house.

By the time she entered through her own door, Gabe was buried in her refrigerator. "How did you even know I had groceries to put away?"

"I made Jenna wait to call for you until you'd finished unloading them."

"Oh." She hadn't realized anyone had been watching her.

She studied him for a minute, his hands making quick work of redistributing everything currently in her fridge, then she crossed her arms over her chest and pulled out an attitude. "If you're thinking that by helping me I'll cook dinner for you . . ." she began, but she didn't finish the sentence. His shirt had ridden up over the waistband of his jeans, and the thin strip of naked flesh had her forgetting about her groceries.

Gabe peeked over his shoulder. "Is dinner a possibility?"

She tore her gaze from his back. "Not even."

His eyes swept over her as if assessing her motives—as if understanding that she'd had impure thoughts at his expense—then moved to survey the food currently covering every available surface in her kitchen. She'd bought a *lot* of groceries. "It's not like you can eat all this before it goes bad," he told her. "You having a party or something?"

"No, I'm not having a party or something." She picked up the cookbook she'd bought the afternoon before. "I'm just in the mood to try cooking a few new things."

"A few?" He came out of the fridge long enough to scoop up more than she could carry in two trips, then hunkered back down in front of the open door. "I'd say this amount of food could make more than a few meals."

That same strip of skin winked at her again, and a quick shiver lifted the hairs on the back of her neck. She blamed the cool air escaping into the kitchen.

"So who's going to eat all of this after you cook it?"

"There's no guarantee it'll even be edible." She finally forced her feet to move, joining him by working on the nonperishables, while he grunted from inside her fridge.

"Give me a break." His voice had a weird hollowness coming off the inside walls of the appliance. "You were already a great cook back when we were dating," he continued. "You might not have gotten a lot of opportunities, but I do remember a few meals made just for me."

They'd both lived in dorms, but they'd had a friend with an apartment who went home a couple of weekends a month. Erica and Gabe had made a habit of borrowing that apartment on those weekends. She'd liked the intimacy of cooking for a man, while Gabe had enjoyed the ability to take her to bed without having to worry about being interrupted by a roommate.

And honestly, she'd liked that benefit, as well.

"So you liked my cooking back then?" she asked. Her words came out a tad on the sultry side, but she pretended not to notice.

"I liked it a lot." Gabe closed the fridge door and began opening cabinets without looking at her. She didn't have a pantry, so the rest of the food would be stored in the overhead shelving. "But to be fair, I would have liked just about anyone's cooking. Dani had prepared all our meals for years, so I knew how to fix absolutely nothing."

His lack of remembering what else they'd done besides eat in that apartment was a letdown.

"But yes." He grabbed the jars of spices she'd bought and lined each up on the designated shelf. "I liked your cooking." He didn't so much as look at her, but she did catch his half smile and the naughty brow lift. "*And* I liked your desserts."

She chuckled under her breath. More times than not, *she* had been dessert.

They both finished putting away the food, a comfortable smile lining Erica's mouth and an ease about Gabe that she hadn't seen since she'd shown up in town, and as they worked, he told her more about the game from the night before, as well as the fact that his brother had joined him on the sidelines.

"Cord showed up at your game?" she asked.

"Yeah. He played football in school, and I guess he's mortified at the poor job I've been doing."

Erica turned to him, leaning back against the countertop and dropping her hands to the granite on either side of her hips. "Mortified?" She shook her head. "I doubt it. He seemed impressed with the progress you've made." She'd talked to Cord Monday night, and he'd definitely been proud of the role his older brother had stepped into with the school. "Plus, that game didn't sound too bad. The team is clearly improving."

Gabe's brow shot up. "You listened to it?"

"I did." Though she hadn't meant to admit that.

"I knew you still had to like football." He washed his hands in the sink, and while drying them on a dish towel, eyed her with suspicion. "Next week's game is at home. You coming out?"

Erica merely shook her head.

"Why not?"

"I told you. I don't do football anymore. So why would Cord be there last night? Doesn't he live in Billings?"

"He does." Gabe narrowed his eyes and tossed the towel to the countertop. "But we were about an hour in that direction, so he came out. How do you know where my brother lives?"

"Because *he* didn't avoid talking to me Monday night."

"Is that so?" Gabe crossed to stand in front of her. "What else did he tell you?"

She felt exposed in her current position, with arms at her sides and elbows pointing back and away from her body. Gabe's features were a shade too focused on her. "Just things," she said on an exhale. "I like talking to your brother." She gave him a sly smile, unable to refrain from teasing him. She'd once made a habit out of teasing this man. "But then, why wouldn't I? He *is* still the best-looking one of all of you."

A low-pitched rumbled came from Gabe's chest, and she pushed off the counter to move to the other side of the island. It was suddenly too crowded in her kitchen.

And apparently close encounters made her flirty.

The bar top now stood solidly between them, and for some reason, she couldn't let the topic go. "Why was he there? Even being an hour closer to Billings, that's still several hours away from him." She stared at Gabe, feeling as if there were something obvious just out of her reach. "Why would your brother travel so far for a high school football game?"

"Why wouldn't he?" Gabe's jaw suddenly clenched, and this time, it was he who walked away.

He crossed to the dining room and eyed the garage door, and Erica ignored him while he roamed. She straightened a stack of celebrity magazines on the countertop—her guilty pleasure—and found herself wondering what he was really doing there in her space. He'd helped put up the groceries, but why? And what was the purpose of sticking around afterward?

She pulled her cell phone out of her purse and lined it up in the middle of the pile of magazines, plugging it in to recharge, then realigned the laptop sitting next to the magazines so that everything squared up.

Was it merely boredom that had kept him over here?

"What's this?" he asked, and Erica looked over at him. He held up the violin case she'd left on the dining room table. She'd seen the instrument in a used music store one day that week and had made an impulse purchase.

"It's a violin."

"What are you doing with it?"

She suddenly felt silly for buying it. "I plan to learn to play it."

Gabe's expression turned quizzical as he stared at her, and she bit her lip to keep from trying to justify herself. Since Bree had left, she'd found herself roaming the businesses in the small downtown area every afternoon instead of coming straight home from work. She didn't want to be stuck in one spot any longer, so she'd determined to try new things. That said, she had no idea if expanding her cooking repertoire and learning to play the violin truly constituted breaking out of a rut.

As if traveling along with her thoughts, Gabe shifted his gaze to her refrigerator. Then to the cookbook lying beside it. He lifted the violin back up in front of him and examined both sides of the case, as if by studying it hard enough, he'd be able to see through it.

"Cooking, music lessons . . ." he mused. "All this change. Anything else?"

The need to defend herself ballooned inside her. She could do whatever she wanted. She didn't have to answer to him. And she could try out as many new hobbies as struck her fancy.

She clamped her teeth together and told herself to keep quiet.

Then she promptly opened her mouth and spilled her final secret. "An exercise class, if you must know. I stopped by the gym this morning. I'll be offering two-day-a-week classes starting the week after next." They already had Zumba, so she'd suggested hip-hop.

"An exercise class?"

She crossed her arms over her chest. "The director of the facility was very excited about it."

"I'm sure she was."

And possibly, Erica had gone a little overboard with her attempts to venture out. She understood that. But she had to do something to fill her time. She couldn't sit around any longer waiting for her marriage to suddenly reappear.

Gabe put the violin back on the table and crossed to her. "You're staying busy."

"Just trying not to get bored." She fidgeted with the magazines in front of her.

"Lack of boredom is good," he said, as if her explanation made perfect sense. Then he propped an elbow onto the counter beside her and leaned in to peer at her. "What did he do to you, Erica?"

"What?" She jerked her gaze to his. "Where did that come from?"

"You said you moved here because 'life happens, plans change.'" He air quoted her words back to her. "You even claimed to have adapted, but I don't believe it. What happened with the ex?"

Erica shook her head. She was not talking to him about that. Then he reached out a hand and covered hers, and her heart slammed against her rib cage.

"I read something entirely different than 'moved on' in your eyes every time I look at you," he explained. "You're always so pensive. And I can't help but wonder why."

The dinging of a text message broke the tension, and her entire body sagged in relief.

Gabe eyed the phone as if she'd planned the interruption for that very second. "Who's that?"

"I have no idea." But she was thrilled with the timing of it. "Nor do I know why you'd think my past is any of your business." She tugged at her hand to pull it out from under his, and once freed, reached for her phone.

But Gabe snatched it up before she could get to it. And *then* he read her message.

Her eyes went wide. "How dare you."

She went for the phone again, but Gabe held it out of her reach. And when his eyes showed both accusation and concern, her brief appreciation for the diversion turned to humiliation. She had no doubt who the text had come from. Damn JC for not leaving her alone. He'd sent several messages since she'd had that brief exchange with him Monday night, but she'd ignored them all.

"JC is your ex?"

It was as if Gabe could see inside her. As if he understood how tiny she felt. "He is."

He eyed the screen once more, rereading the words to himself before paraphrasing. "He says that he misses you. That he really wants to talk to you." He locked his gaze on hers. "He's even *begging* for you to call." The last was said with a distasteful curl of his top lip.

With a tired sigh, she held out her hand. "Will you just give me my phone, please?"

"If you'll tell me what this is about. Are you still seeing him?"

"No," she ground out. "He's with someone else."

"Married?"

"*No.* They just . . ." She couldn't make herself admit everything. "He left me for her, okay?"

Gabe stared at the face of her phone once again, pushing the button to bring the message back to the screen. Then he slowly brought his gaze back to hers. The air in the room grew thick, and Erica found herself holding her breath as she waited to see what he'd say next. What he thought of her now.

"And do *you* still miss *him*?" he asked.

"I miss being married, yes." She wished she didn't feel the need to explain herself. "I miss having a plan for my life."

"But that doesn't answer my question."

She pulled back in confusion. She hadn't realized that what Gabe had asked and what she'd answered were two separate things. She missed being married. She'd been married to JC.

Did the two things not equate?

"I don't know," she finally replied. Until that moment she'd thought she missed her ex.

"How long have you been divorced?"

"We ended things nearly two years ago."

He twisted his mouth to the side. "That's a while."

She nodded. She could feel the guilt climbing her face.

"So you're *not* over him?"

"I am," she hurried to say. "He cheated on me. We're divorced. I just . . ." She stared at Gabe, wishing she could make someone understand, and wondering if that someone could possibly be him. "He was my high school sweetheart, you know? He was always there for me."

"Ah. You mean that he was always *supposed* to be there for you?"

She felt so stupid. "I don't want to talk about this anymore."

"Fair enough." He handed over the phone. "But will you tell me why you let your ex of two years control you?"

The suggestion was too on point, and it pissed her off. "I don't let him control me."

"Yet you moved from your hometown because of him."

"It's more complicated than that," she tried to argue, but she knew his words rang more true than false. She'd completely allowed JC to control everything about her life since she'd found out he was cheating on her. *He'd* decided when to end it. When to "surprise" her with the truth. *He'd* drawn up the settlement offer. And *he'd* been the one to reach out to her that past summer.

He was the reason she didn't know what her life held next.

Her throat suddenly burned, and she found herself blinking back threatening tears, so she turned away and crossed the room. She stared at the brick wall on the far side of the living room. She did *not* want to cry over JC. Never again.

And she certainly didn't want to do it in front of Gabe.

"I don't know why I allow it," she finally said in response to his question. Her voice came out so thin she didn't know if he'd even heard her. "But I can't get the man out of my mind for some reason, and I hate it. He's there all the darned time."

How in the world had they ended up talking about her ex?

Her hands shook, so she gripped them around her elbows and rolled her eyes toward the ceiling. It was a trick she'd learned to keep the tears at bay. "Can we stop talking about this now?"

"Look at me, Erica."

Gabe's words came out at such a low octave that it felt as if they'd reverberated across the room and stroked down over her body. She shook her head. She would *not* look at him. There would be no benefit to witnessing his pity.

"You should just go." She pitied herself enough for the both of them.

Her husband had not only cheated on her, but he'd done it with a woman who'd once been a very good friend of hers. He'd done it virtually under her nose. *And* he'd gotten the other woman pregnant.

And yet she couldn't figure out how to be done with the asshole once and for all?

She was so stupid.

"Look at me," Gabe repeated. His tone had gentled, but remained firm. He didn't intend to walk away from this, she could tell. She remembered that stubbornness about him. So she forced herself to turn. To face his pity and be done with it.

But what she saw staring at her from the other side of the room wasn't a man feeling sorry for her, but a man she'd once cared for very deeply. A man she'd once thought she might marry.

She'd loved Gabriel Wilde years ago. Even though their split hadn't been the worst thing in the world, she'd loved him. They never would have worked with him adamant about living here, while she'd been just as determined to go home to Silver Creek. But that hadn't stopped them from being good together.

"Now come over here and kiss me."

No other words could have shocked her more. "Excuse me?"

"Kiss me," he repeated.

"I don't—"

Two long strides brought him to her, and he gave her a solid nod, his gaze never leaving hers. "Just a kiss. A temporary reprieve from your mind."

She looked at his lips. "A kiss? To escape my mind?"

"Absolutely. That man is in there, and you want him out, right?"

"Yes . . ." She dragged her gaze off his mouth.

"Then I'm offering to help you with that."

"To help me with . . ." She wrinkled her brow. "How will that help, exactly?"

"It's simple. You kiss me, and you quit thinking about him." The blue of Gabe's eyes darkened, and though up to that point he hadn't strayed from her eyes, he now dipped to her mouth. "We used to be really good at kissing." His breathing grew unsteady. "Excellent, in fact. So it stands to reason that if we kiss, that if we're still as good at kissing as we used to be, then you would think of something other than *him*"—he brought his eyes back to hers—"while kissing *me*."

By the time he'd finished talking, he wasn't the only one breathing raggedly. They *had* once been really good at kissing.

She swallowed. "Kissing wasn't the only thing we did well."

The line of Gabe's jaw hardened, and Erica didn't miss the flare of his nostrils. His eyes turned molten as he stared at her, and she forced herself to shake her head.

"I'm not offering that," she told him.

"Then a kiss?"

She nodded. At this point, she wasn't sure either of them could walk away without one.

"You reach for me," Gabe said, his voice deeper than it had been. "You start it."

His words caught her off guard. "Why do I have to start it?"

"Because you did that first night. *You* kissed me."

She stared at his mouth then. He had a point. She had been the one to instigate their first kiss. But she'd done that because she'd been angry at JC—and because she'd thought Gabe was one seriously sexy man.

Funny how life had repeated itself.

So she didn't give it another thought. Why not kiss the man?

A tiny shuffle of her feet brought them together, and her pulse bounced at the feeling of something hard and solid pressing just below her belly button. She fought the groan that begged to be let out, and with trembling fingers, lifted her hands to his chest. He wore a cotton pullover that was soft under her fingertips, but she didn't care about soft cotton *or* the hard muscles riding underneath. She immediately slid her hands to his back . . . and then she flattened her chest to his.

"Damn," Gabe whispered as her nipples went rock hard. His breath heated her cheek.

"This okay?" she whispered in return. "A little touch *with* the kiss?"

He nodded, the movement tight, and Erica closed her eyes as his hands landed at the small of her back. Maybe this was all she'd been missing. Because other than those couple of times over the summer, there'd been an extended dry spell since a man's hard body had been anywhere near hers.

"This is nice." She nibbled along his jawline, his whiskers from the day before scratching her lips and the taste of him lighting every last one of her fires. And when she inhaled, wanting to imprint his smell on her brain, her breasts burrowed deeper into his chest.

His body shuddered.

"Gabe."

He stared into her eyes then, as needy as she, and she ended the wait for both of them.

His groan reverberated through her as her lips touched his. His fingers buried in her hair. Then without hesitation, he backed her into the brick wall, and when his tongue parted her lips it was *her* turn to moan. Entrance was demanded, and only when the need to breathe reached the edge of necessity did Gabe pull the slightest bit away. He looked down at her, his gaze fierce and his chest heaving with each gasp of air. And then he retook her mouth.

This kiss was slower.

His lips claimed hers leisurely, exhibiting patience in the wait, while at the same time, showing her everything that a kiss could be. The moment stretched into several, and with each stroke of his tongue, each tug of his teeth on her bottom lip, all Erica knew was that she wanted more. That she *needed* more.

That they had to stop now or they weren't going to stop at all.

"Gabe." She could barely get the word out as she sucked in a breath through her teeth, but he must have heard her because his mouth softened. His hands loosened their grip.

He put a foot of space between them.

They stared at each other, each dizzy with lack of oxygen, each on fire from the inside out. And they didn't have to say it out loud to agree. They still knew how to pull off a damned fine kiss.

"You'd better go," she managed. Though him going was the last thing she wanted to happen.

He nodded, and two seconds later her front door closed behind him.

Erica sank to the floor, her entire body vibrating with need, and she dropped her head to the wall behind her. She blew out a harsh breath. *That* was what she'd been missing. Not whatever her ex-husband might be able to give her.

And *that* probably didn't need to happen again.

Because damn. She wasn't sure she'd know what to do with more.

Chapter Nine

I just don't know why I have to do this."

Gabe bit his tongue to keep from snapping at his daughter. She'd certainly lost her pleasantness overnight. By the time he'd picked her and Haley up at Leslie's house that morning, she'd been her sweet lovable self no more. She'd even been ugly to Haley, causing the two of them to snipe at each other all the way to Ben and Dani's house. By the time he'd gotten the other girl home, he'd been ready to beg his sister to take Jenna off his hands, as well. And the plea would have been offered with a large sum of money. Because no one deserved to have to put up with that without some sort of reward.

"*Da-aad,*" Jenna whined, when he didn't answer her.

Gabe grabbed his and his daughter's work gloves off the seat, and looked in the rearview mirror at his kid. He gritted out a phrase he detested. "You have to do this because I said so, Jenna. End of story."

"Good grief." She flopped back, slamming herself into her seat, while at the same time sliding low enough to jab her knees into the back of *his*. "Mom wouldn't treat me like this," she spat out.

That one was a kick in the gut. And a new tactic on her part. "Your *mother* isn't here."

"And whose fault is that?"

He counted to ten as he stepped from the truck, but allowed himself the pleasure of slamming his door. Her mother would treat her worse, and she knew it. And it was *totally* Michelle's fault that she wasn't there. He couldn't fathom where that idea had come from, but he refused to play into his daughter's games.

"Get out of the truck," he barked when Jenna's door remained closed. "Pops is waiting on us."

He could see a group of men gathered at the main barn, with Nick's head rising above the rest, but he couldn't put eyes on his father. He did, however, take note of the four-door Lincoln parked next to his dad's truck. It looked to be a good twenty years old, original copper paint still in excellent shape, and sat up close to the back of the house. Jenna climbed down from the backseat, her bottom lip protruding, and without bothering to say anything else to her, Gabe headed for the house. His daughter followed, but he could hear each drag of her feet.

Basically, she wanted to do nothing that he wanted to do today. But that was too bad. The new cherry trees had come in, and it was time to get them in the ground.

"Dad?" Gabe called out as he climbed the steps to the back deck. But he didn't have to go far to find his father. Doc Hamm appeared at the back door as Gabe hit the top step, with Gabe's dad and Gloria coming out right behind him. Gabe looked from doctor to his father. "Something wrong?"

"Not a thing," his dad answered.

"Good to see you, Gabe." Doc Hamm shook Gabe's hand and nodded to Jenna. He produced a lollipop, which the now-smiling Jenna took, and headed to his car, but he looked over the top of the vehicle before climbing behind the wheel. "Tell Cord hello for me, will you?"

he said to Gabe's dad. "I've been keeping tabs on him. They speak highly of him over in Billings."

"Will do, Doc. Proud of that one myself." His dad waved as the man left, then, ignoring the pointed question on Gabe's face, winked at Jenna and made a motion as if to take her sucker.

"It's mine, Pops," she snapped out.

"*Jenna,*" Gabe growled.

"Well, it is." She stomped off, sucker in mouth, and headed for the workers waiting at the barn.

Gabe forced himself to rein in his anger at his kid, then he gave his dad "the look."

"What?" his dad grumbled. Now *he* sounded as crabby as Jenna.

"The doctor?" Gabe motioned to where the Lincoln had been parked. "Why was he here?"

"Just a checkup."

Gloria murmured something about brownies and disappeared back into the house.

"Doc Hamm makes house calls now?" Gabe asked.

"When you've been around as long as Doc has, you do anything you damned well please."

His dad stomped off, similar to Jenna, and Gabe was left standing alone on the uncovered deck. Why had he bothered with this idea? No one wanted to help get the trees in the ground, apparently, and hell if he was in the mood to do it, either.

Nor was he in the mood to be around his dad lately. He'd been that way since coming back home.

Or hell. Honestly, he'd been that way going on a year now. The closer his marriage had come to taking its final tumble, the more he'd found himself impatient with the role his dad had often assumed in the family. He just didn't get the man anymore—or maybe he never had.

He stepped to the back door and stuck his head in. "Is he okay, Gloria?"

She looked around from the stove, apron tied at her waist. "Your dad?" She nodded. "He's fine. It was like he said. A checkup."

Gabe didn't know whether to believe either of them, but he wasn't sure what else he could do. So he let the door slam behind him and took *his* turn stomping to the barn. But on the way, his mood lightened when he let his mind go elsewhere. Specifically, to Erica's brick wall the afternoon before.

That kiss had blown his mind.

And all for what reason? Because he'd been jealous of her ex-husband? He smirked at himself for that one. He had no right to be jealous of a man who'd been married to a woman he'd long ago broken up with.

But that didn't mean he hadn't been.

Why she was still hung up on someone who'd cheated on her, he didn't know, but when he'd seen the text message, he'd also seen red. He hadn't been joking. The intent of the kiss had been to get her mind off her ex. But it had also been to get it onto *him*. And that was stupid in every sense of the word, because now he just wanted to do it again.

And now he knew that what they'd had years ago had only magnified.

Jenna squealed up ahead as Nick picked her up and put her on his shoulders, and Gabe slowed his steps to watch. At least someone could make his daughter smile today.

He couldn't mess around with a woman right now no matter how much he wanted her. No matter that it was Erica. He had a daughter who alternately hated his guts and acted like the sweetest thing in the world, as well as a wife who—if he were a betting man—had caused last month's delay on the divorce proceedings. He had no idea what her motive could be, but he'd gotten another call from his lawyer the day before. The final hearing had been pushed back yet again.

Probably her motive was merely to fuck with him. That seemed to be a game of hers.

Now he'd have to wait until November before he could put the past behind him and Jenna for good.

He reached the group of men, and when Nick suggested that Jenna hang with him that day, Gabe readily agreed. He wanted Jenna to have fun out there. To feel a part of keeping their family's orchard alive. And he knew, given how their morning had started, that wasn't something she'd be capable of achieving by *his* side.

They broke into pairs, and after all the trees had been hauled out to the prepared field, Gabe found himself working side by side with his dad. They worked well in tandem, this not being the first time they'd set out trees together, but it wasn't long before he noticed Gloria making excuses to appear at their side.

She brought water, needed to talk to his dad about the clothes he wanted to wear to an upcoming wedding, and even had to discuss tomorrow night's dinner with him at one particular moment in time.

With each trip she made, Gabe's mood worsened. Not because he didn't like Gloria. In fact, he'd always thought her to be a great fit for his dad. They'd dated for seven years before marrying, and come December, it would be two years since they'd tied the knot. Yet today, he studied her in a new light. She was hovering. And he didn't like women who stuck their noses where they didn't belong.

His mother had been like that. If she wasn't ignoring them, she'd been controlling them.

So now he found himself wondering if his dad had once again fallen for the same type of woman. It would be just like him. Pick someone who walked all over him—and then stay for the continued humiliation.

Gabe growled under his breath and tried to quit thinking about his past. None of that mattered now, and if his dad *had* gotten sucked in by another woman who only wanted to control him, then that was none of Gabe's business.

He stopped digging at the sound of low laughter, and looked around to find that Gloria had shown up once again. Only, she and his dad had their heads together this time, talking in low tones, and as Gabe watched, more confusion filled him. Because he'd swear that what he was witnessing was real. He'd also swear that he'd never once seen that kind of happiness on his father's face the entire time Gabe had been growing up.

Was he just looking for trouble where there was none?

His dad pressed a kiss to his wife's cheek, and this time the look of utter contentment came from *her*.

Gabe sighed. What the hell did he know about love, anyway? He'd been married to Michelle.

Erica scrolled through the e-mails that had come in that day, twisting up her face every time she ran across one stating how they'd love to have her, but . . .

There was always a but. Securing a teaching position in the middle of a school year wasn't exactly an easy thing to do. Few teachers ever walked out on the job.

She dipped a chip in salsa and popped it in her mouth as she took a break from the e-mails and eyed the dark house across the road. She was perched on a barstool in her kitchen, having chosen the stool with the best direct line of sight out the kitchen window and across the road in front of her house, yet she'd repeatedly told herself that she wasn't sitting there waiting for Gabe. She was sitting *there* because it was a good space to work.

She took in the printouts she'd spread out along the countertop to prove her point. Information on potential schools in the state she could be interested in, schools in other states she *might* be willing to move to. Then there was the scribbled list of jobs that had nothing whatsoever to do with teaching. She didn't want to take another type of job, but at the same time, she wanted to do more than be an on-call substitute for the rest of the school year. She needed a purpose, even if it would be only until the following fall when new jobs would be easier to find.

She pulled up her old school's website, and rolled her eyes at the sight that greeted her. With JC now the principal there, his picture came up front and center. It pleased her that she had no urge to linger over the photo of the man she'd once been married to, but she couldn't shake the anger that still pulsed through her when she scrolled down the list of teachers' names. Her name should be on there, too.

She should be living in Silver Creek.

She absolutely hated the fact that her ex had stripped her entire life from her.

Her phone rang, and when she saw that it was her parents' home number, she pushed the negativity away and decided to answer. It was time to stop playing phone tag and only communicating through texts messages. She missed hearing their voices.

"Hey, Mom."

"It's actually your dad."

"Oh." Erica sat up straighter, unconsciously mimicking the posture of one of his students. Her dad, a no-nonsense high school educator, believed that the brain worked best if not deprived of oxygen. And sitting straight allowed better flow of oxygen. "Then hi, Dad." Her mom was usually the one who made calls. "How are you?"

"I'm great. Missing my oldest daughter, but other than that, I can't complain."

She smiled at his words. "I miss you, too, Dad. Your classes good this year?"

"I've had better."

She chuckled, because he said that every year. Yet by the end of the school year, he would declare his current group of students the best he'd ever encountered.

"How about yours?" he asked. "I usually hear all about your new batch of students by now."

Guilt plagued her once more. She'd hurt them by leaving the way she had. So she went into detail about several of her students, filling him in, not only on their struggles, or lack thereof, with class subjects, but also about whatever she'd learned concerning their parents and their home lives. As a person who'd grown up with teachers for parents, Erica had long ago become accustomed to hearing such conversations at the start of every school year. After she'd begun teaching, she'd made the habit of going over to her parents for dinner one night early in the fall semester, and continuing the tradition.

"Sounds like a good group. You having any real trouble with anyone?"

"Nothing I can't handle."

"That's my girl. What about next month?" he suddenly asked. "Got another job lined up yet?"

"I'm trying, Dad. So where's Mom?" She changed the subject before either of them could become frustrated. She didn't want to risk him pointing out again how she shouldn't have left a secure job, and he wouldn't want to hear her silence as she refused to agree with him.

"She's just coming out of the shower. We found out this week that we're a last-minute addition for this year's Sunset Garden Tour, so we stayed outside working on the flowers until dark."

Her mother had been trying to get selected for that honor for years.

"Good for her. I know she's proud. Be sure to send me pictures on the big day, will you?"

"Sure thing." Her dad paused for a second before adding, "Or you could just come home for it. It's this weekend."

She'd been gone from Silver Creek for less than four weeks, but that was the longest her parents had gone without seeing her since she'd been in college. And with Bree always on the go and Annalise still away at medical school . . .

Erica carefully blew out a breath. She knew her parents missed their kids.

But at least they had Seth—who'd also already granted them two grandchildren.

"I can't come home this weekend, Dad." She rose and headed for the fridge. She didn't really have a good excuse other than that she didn't want to go. "Homework to grade," she mumbled, knowing he would read through her words.

"We could grill out," he offered. "Make some ice cream."

The latter brought a smile to Erica's lips, and as she poured herself a glass of tea, she wished that she *was* back home. Even with JC still trying to get in touch with her, she couldn't help it. She missed the routine she and her parents had created since moving back in with them.

Only, that routine had been a part of her problem.

After her divorce, she'd reclaimed her childhood bedroom instead of finding a place of her own, and she'd allowed herself to once again become part of her parents' world instead of creating a new one for herself.

"Actually, I need to stay here to prepare for a new class I'm starting next week. An exercise class."

"For kids?"

"No. This one is for adults. I'm offering it for free at the local gym."

"Is that so?"

Erica detected a bit of shock in her father's words—as well as the resounding pity she'd picked up on ever since her divorce.

"Well, I'm glad you're getting out some."

"Thanks." The reminder that her parents felt sorry for her for losing JC had her wanting to point out that she had a very full life here. Not only would she be teaching an exercise class, but she had a violin lesson scheduled for the following night, as well. And she'd also seen an ad for a sushi class she was considering signing up for. She'd never been able to fully master sushi, and since JC hated it, she hadn't even tried in years.

She didn't say any of that, though. Because the pitifulness of it was obvious without having to utter it out loud.

"We'll miss you," her dad told her. "But I'll take lots of pictures to share later."

Her mom got on the phone a few minutes later, and after a brief chat while her dad went off to start a late dinner, Erica and her mother hung up. She sat there in the silence of her apartment, staring at her untouched glass of tea and contemplating the emptiness of her life.

Then she eyed another e-mail that had dropped into her inbox. *We'd love to have you but . . .*

She should have poured herself wine instead of tea.

Or something harder.

Her cell beeped with an incoming text message, and with little energy, she leaned over to read the words on the screen.

Any progress on that fling, yet?

A small smile touched her face. Bree hadn't checked in with her since leaving the week before, but Erica wasn't surprised to see a follow-up to the suggestion of sleeping with Gabe. She took a drink, contemplating how she should reply, then quickly typed out a message before she could change her mind.

Only one mind-blowing kiss.

She snickered to herself as she imagined Bree's hysteria at reading the words, and once again looked over at Gabe's house. The two of them hadn't exchanged so much as a word since their kiss. Their paths hadn't even crossed.

And she'd admit, she'd kind of expected him to at least make that happen.

It didn't take long for Bree to respond. Erica's phone rang just as Gabe's truck pulled up across the street. She tapped the answer button and put her phone on speaker as she kept her eyes glued outside. Jenna jumped down from the backseat, her father's foot hitting the ground at the same time as his daughter's, then the little girl lifted a hand and waved at Erica.

Erica waved back. She sat in a small circle of light in her kitchen, and with it now being dark outside, it didn't surprise her that she'd be seen.

Then Gabe looked up.

His eyes landed squarely on hers, and she lifted her glass in a little salute.

"Erica? Are you there?"

Shock yanked her attention from Gabe to her phone. "JC?"

Crap.

She hadn't even checked the caller before answering. "Why are you calling me?"

"I need to talk to you."

Bree's number flashed on the screen. *Now* she was calling. "No." Erica shook her head as if her ex-husband could see her. "We're not talking, JC. Not now or ever. Don't call me again."

"Come on, just for a few minutes? I know I messed up. I—"

His words silenced when Erica jabbed the "End" button. Damn that man for not leaving her alone. Why couldn't he accept that they were over for good? She'd moved away from town in order to prove it. She'd *quit* her job.

Anger had her hands shaking as another text came in. Thankfully, it was only her sister.

Answer the freaking phone! A kiss? What kiss? When? I MUST KNOW ABOUT THIS KISS!

She looked across the road once again, working to catch her breath and get herself back under control, but found that Gabe and Jenna had disappeared inside. She could make out Mike running around the fenced-in backyard, and knew that to mean that Gabe wouldn't be coming back out to walk the dog. At least not anytime soon. Which was just as good. She suddenly found the idea of thinking about any man distasteful.

Picking up her phone, she punched out a message.

Sorry. Yes, a kiss. I'll tell you about it later, I promise. No time now. But don't get too excited. It was a one-time-only thing.

At least, she assumed it was. But at the same time, she kind of hoped that it wasn't.

Chapter Ten

The view off his brother's wraparound deck, though not the usual mountains Gabe saw every morning from Birch Bay, was breathtaking. The city of Billings spilled out in the valley below the house, while the craggy face of the Rimrocks rose up behind them. Gabe leaned forward in his chair, elbows on knees, and breathed in the crisp air loaded heavy with evergreens. "That play you showed me last weekend is going to be gold," he said to Cord, who sat in a matching chair near his.

"That play won me a college championship."

It was the middle of the week, but since the school day had been a half day for teachers only, Gabe had talked his sister-in-law into flying him to Billings.

"We've been working on it every day," Gabe added. "I plan to put it in the lineup this week since the game is at home. If we pull it off, it might help erase the home crowd's memory of those first two games. I want to talk about that other idea I sent you, though. I need your honest opinion." He'd had inspiration for a Hail Mary play that could be used in a tight game, but he wasn't sure it was quite right yet.

Ever since Cord had shown up the previous Friday night, he and Gabe had talked daily. Cord had gotten a firsthand look at what Gabe was working with, and they'd spent hours late into the nights reviewing team video and working through drills that would make the guys stronger. Thanks to all the help, Gabe had seen a virtual one-eighty in a matter of days. The team *and* he had grown in both skill and confidence. Even his assistant coach had stepped up his game.

"I looked at it earlier today," Cord said. He picked up the iPad he'd brought outside with him and pulled up the image from Gabe. "This is good." He drew a slash over two previous lines and marked out different routes for each. "But consider this adjustment. It might be better."

Gabe scooted forward to get a better look. "I see what you mean."

He took the tablet and studied the image before deciding it needed just a bit more tweaking. Then he mapped one final change, twisting the play in a way he hadn't yet considered. Cord's eyes traced the changes, taking in each detail, and when he finally looked up, an intensity burned deep in his gaze.

"Yes." Cord tapped the screen. "*This.* You don't need me anymore, man. You got this."

"Oh, I need you. In fact, I'd darn near commit a felony to get you home to be my offensive coordinator."

"Offensive coordinator?" Cord grabbed two beers from the mini fridge beside him and passed one to Gabe. "If I came home, I'd take *your* job."

Though he knew it was a joke, Gabe hesitated at the words. It wouldn't be as if coming home would be a foreign notion for one of them. Nick had already returned to Birch Bay, and now Gabe. Their family wasn't quite as splintered as it had once seemed.

He studied his brother as he uncapped his beer. "*Would* you consider coming home?"

Cord shot Gabe a look. "Why in the hell would I do that?" He motioned toward the lights beginning to twinkle in the distance. "I have a sweet deal here. Primo partnership, prime location. All the women I could want." He pulled out a thin cigar and lit it up. "I'm good where I am. I'm settled."

"That's what I thought." But still, Gabe couldn't help but wonder about his brother's life. Cord did seem settled. Yet at the same time, there were all those women he'd spoken of. Which didn't reek of settled at all.

Then he thought of his own life. Was *he* settled?

He was trying to be.

He'd moved back home, had a new job, new life, and he'd bought a house that suited both him and Jenna. It wasn't huge, but he and his daughter didn't need a lot. What they needed was a place where they were allowed to be themselves. His bedroom was on the first floor, while hers and a spare were upstairs. The layout would allow both of them to have some separation as Jenna grew older, while still being small enough not to get lost in the space.

Of course, moving back hadn't been his first plan. It had taken a good hard shove for that to happen, but once it had, he'd seen the longtime error of his ways. Having Michelle out of their lives was the best option. It was the *only* option.

Yet that didn't keep him from second-guessing every single move he'd made since stepping foot into his lawyer's office.

"Ever heard from her?"

Gabe took a drink of his beer. "Who?"

"The woman you're thinking of, idiot. Your wife."

"What makes you think I'm thinking about Michelle?"

"That sour-ass look on your face, for one thing." The phone buzzed at Cord's hip, but he ignored it. "And the way you're clenching that beer in your hand, for another."

Gabe stared at the white-knuckled grip he had going on, and forced his fingers to relax. He'd messed up over the summer and shared things with his oldest brother he would've normally kept to himself, but everyone had been in for harvest, and when Gabe found himself alone in the field with Cord, his mouth had suddenly disconnected from his brain. He'd spilled everything.

"Not since February," he forced himself to answer. Seven months, and not a word that hadn't been siphoned through their lawyers. Could he truly hope it would be that easy?

"Yet the divorce got delayed?"

"Paperwork issue."

Cord drew deep on his cigar. "Makes you wonder."

Gabe didn't want to wonder. He simply wanted his ex out of the picture for good.

He rose, crossing to the balcony railing. He tried hard to remain calm, but irritation built. As it always did when he thought about Michelle. He turned back to Cord. "What exactly does it make you wonder?"

The smoke formed a small *O* as Cord exhaled. "If the divorce is really going to happen."

"Of course it's going to happen." Gabe's hand fisted the bottle too tightly again. That made twice in the last month that one of his siblings had suggested such. "Why the fuck *wouldn't* it happen? You know what she's like."

"I do know. I also know that she's the one who left *you*."

Anger swirled. "Yet I'm the one who filed. What's your point?"

The lines on either side of Cord's mouth pulled taut as he snubbed out the cigar, mumbling about how the things were going to kill him, then he rose and joined Gabe. "My point—if I have one—is that we're here for you if you need us. We're all worried about you. We want to see this over and done."

The words made Gabe more nervous than comforted. "So you've all been talking about me behind my back?"

Cord gave him a wry look. "We don't have to talk. You know Dani is worried, and I'm telling you that I am. Dad has probably been wringing his hands for months."

"Dad has more things to be concerned about than *me*."

Cord's brow went up at Gabe's outburst, but he didn't change course. "You've done this all alone, and I can appreciate that. I would have, too. But we all know what she's like." The sound of car doors slamming came from below. "So we're here for you. We're here for Jenna. All you have to do is let us know what you need."

Jenna's voice came from below the deck, followed by Harper's and Haley's. His sister-in-law had made it a girls' afternoon.

"I'm good," Gabe assured him. "I've got this." He didn't need anything.

He could handle his divorce, just like he could handle raising his daughter.

As the girls made their way into the house down below, Cord pulled out his cell and sent a text, and Gabe considered retrieving his and doing the same. All this talk of Michelle had him think of someone else. And something else.

He hadn't spoken to Erica since she'd singed him over the weekend with that kiss, and he suddenly wanted to do just that. He'd been trying to stay away, but he couldn't help himself. She was a breath of fresh air after all the years he'd put in with his ex, and he liked being around her. At the same time, he also knew that seeking her out wasn't the best plan for anyone. Jenna needed his attention, the team needed him focused. No one needed him thinking about a cute little brunette with a to-die-for rear.

Except him.

The apartment across the road remained dark and quiet, and Gabe paced to the far side of his small porch. He looked up at the single room on the top floor before pacing back the other way. His resolution to stay away had lasted exactly two more days. Good idea or not, he didn't care any longer. He wanted Erica awake. And he didn't want to wait until daylight for that to happen.

He punched in another text, hoping the second one would wake her, but after another two minutes of silence, he decided it was time to go another route. He crossed the quiet street, stooping down to pick up a handful of pebbles as he went, and when he reached her place he sent one after the other flying.

Ping. Ping. Ping.

If he broke her bedroom window, it would be a small price to pay if that meant getting Erica down here to see him.

Ping. Ping.

Finally, a soft light came on in the room.

Ping.

And there she was.

He tossed one more pebble, pulling her attention to the spot where he stood just below her, and then he smiled like the fool that he was when she finally looked down. He hadn't succeeding getting her out of his mind for a second.

She lifted the window and peered out into the night. "Gabe?"

"Morning," he said.

She sent a look of doubt toward the east. "I don't think so. What are you doing out there?"

"I thought we could have our Saturday morning after-game chat."

She yawned behind her hand, the light on the far side of the room casting just enough glow to outline her in the window, and Gabe drank in the sight of her mussed hair and bare shoulders. Then she seemed to wake up enough to digest his words. She squinted down at him. "I wasn't aware we have a Saturday morning after-game chat."

"Sure we do."

"Since when?"

"Since last week. Don't you remember? Jenna started it."

He could tell his charm wasn't working on her.

"Come on, E. You won't come to the games, so you can do this for me, right? Don't you want to know how it went?" It had been a big night for him, and he was dying to talk about it.

"I know how it went. Congratulations, by the way. That one sounded like a solid win."

Pride puffed up inside his chest at the knowledge that she'd listened to another game—even though she hadn't once said that her listening had anything to do with him.

"So . . ." He drew the word out. "Saturday morning after-game chat?"

She hid another yawn. "You do know that it's not yet Saturday morning?"

"Sure it is." He held up his phone, face backlit. "Five minutes after midnight. I've been waiting for it to become tomorrow. Now, come on. Come down here and sit outside with me." He cocked his head toward his house. "Haley came home with us after the game, so I have to stay close in case one of them wakes up. We can sit on my porch."

Erica looked down at herself then, so Gabe did the same. She still slept in tanks, and he could very clearly remember how good she used to look in them.

"You want me to put on clothes at midnight," she began, "and come sit in the chilly night air with you?"

"You're welcome to skip the clothes part."

She shot him her down-the-nose haughty teacher look.

"It was worth a shot," he added, only partly teasing.

She merely rolled her eyes at him and closed the window, and he held his breath, hoping that meant she planned to come down. Tank top or not, he wanted to see her. He'd continued telling himself all week that he had to forget that kiss. To forget the way she'd felt in his hands and molded to his body. How hot her mouth had been as she'd met him move for move, and how all she'd had to do was ask and he would have been putty in her very sweet hands.

Yet, he hadn't forgotten one second of it. He couldn't forget.

It still didn't mean he planned to do anything about it. But it also didn't mean he intended to avoid her, either. Erica made him feel good inside, and it had been too long since he'd felt that way.

The door opened in front of him, and pleasure exploded like a firework. "Morning," he greeted her.

She'd put on clothes.

"Good morning," she replied. She'd also grabbed a quilt, an opened bottle of wine, and looked cute as a button inside a too-large Big Sky sweatshirt.

He scanned down over the rest of her, and barely kept himself from asking her to turn around when he saw that she had on black leggings.

He spun on his heel and headed back across the street, too much blood already leaving his brain, and said a silent thanks when he heard her following behind him. A second thanks was given for only having room on his porch for the one bench.

Leading the way to it, he motioned to both ends. "Lady's choice."

"I choose to tell you that you owe me some sleep," she muttered. But snarky or not, she sat on his bench. After choosing an end, she arranged the blanket over her lap, tucking one corner under the edge of one leg, then lifted the opposite corner and motioned to it with her head. "You going to sit out here and freeze, Coach, or are you going to join me under this quilt?"

That was not a question he had to be asked twice.

He settled in next to her, and due to the size of the bench, their thighs touched.

Maybe getting her out there with him hadn't been such a good idea, after all. He already couldn't think straight around her, and now sitting and touching her at the same time?

This was going to be one long night.

"So you listened to the game again?" he asked, when what he really wanted to know was if she'd listened because of him.

"I did. There's not a lot else to do around here on a Friday night."
He looked at her. "You could be *at* the game."

Her reply was a dry chuckle and a sip of her wine.

"Well, it's your loss." He leaned back, stretching his arms and chest out almost comically, as he tried to pull off "tough and sexy." "Because *I* hear the coach is a stud."

Erica eyed him silently, shadows casting most of her face in the dark, but not enough that he couldn't watch her watching him. She took her time with it, too, letting her gaze linger a little here, a little there. Knocking out every intention he had of being funny. The questions that formed in his head during her scrutiny—wondering what crossed her mind when she looked at him, wanting to know if she was thinking about that kiss the same as he—made it difficult to sit still in front of her.

Then finally, she gave a slow nod and took another taste of her wine. "I'd have to agree with that assessment."

His mouth went dry. "You going to share that wine, or keep it all to yourself?"

She held the bottle out in front of her until the glow from the streetlight hit it, then squinted one eye and checked the level of the liquid inside. It was almost full. She turned the bottle up, drank for several long seconds while Gabe sat transfixed, then without a word, she passed it over to him.

She wiped the back of her hand across her mouth. "I can share. It'll warm you up."

"I'm actually pretty hot as it is," he croaked. But he still turned up the bottle. The woman had him tied in knots, and he couldn't tell if she was actively flirting or just being a smart-ass for having been woken up. He cleared his throat, determined to stay on target. Determined not to jump her.

After-game chat.

"A couple of Boise State guys showed up tonight," he told her.

The words meant nothing at first, he could tell by her blank expression, and then he saw understanding dawn. She shifted, turning slightly toward him. "Recruiters?" Anyone who knew anything about football knew that Boise State was a good place to be.

Gabe's chest swelled. "I have this one kid on the team—man, he's a beast. Moved here from Oklahoma last year. He totally deserves a scholarship, and I think we helped him show the recruiters why tonight."

"Congratulations." Erica leaned in as she spoke, her face now inches from his, and he could smell the wine on her breath. "For both the win and the recruiter. I know you must be proud."

"I am." He also wanted to kiss her.

"Cord come to the game tonight?"

Well, that zapped the urge to kiss her. "You got a thing for my brother, E?"

A teasing smile played at her lips. "Not at all, G."

He growled at her quick zing. "I sometimes think you're as feisty as your sister, you know that?"

"You got a thing for my sister?"

He laughed at her naughty smirk. He liked her drinking wine.

He liked her, period.

And he'd like her even better if he were currently kissing her.

Taking the bottle from her, he downed a swallow for courage, then went back to the excuse that first got her lips on his. "You been getting any more texts from your ex?" he asked. "I could kiss you again if you have. Give you something else to focus on."

"*Please.* I kissed you, remember?"

"Huh-uh. You only *started* it."

She looked at his lips then, her throat moving as she swallowed, and her voice shifted, becoming more serious. "Maybe so. But still, it's probably not a good idea, right? Us kissing again?" She sounded hopeful that he'd disagree. "I mean, you're trying to find your place with Jenna. I'm still a mess from my divorce."

146

"Yet that doesn't stop me from wanting to."

The heat of her breaths caressed his chin. "It doesn't stop me from wanting to, either."

His balls tightened at her words, but when she pulled her knees up and wrapped her arms around them, he realized the words hadn't been an offer. Merely a fact.

"So tell me how Jenna's been for you this week," she requested. "Her behavior has continued to improve in the classroom, but that doesn't mean there hasn't been the occasional trying time. All in all, though, I'm pleased."

He smirked. "I'd take *occasional* in a heartbeat."

"She's still giving you fits?"

"Saturday was good," he said. "Of course, she spent that night with Leslie. Sunday was miserable, and Monday and Tuesday had me wanting to put a fist through the wall. We ended up going to her favorite restaurant for dinner Tuesday night to save my walls, and the rest of the week has been hit or miss. It's Jekyll and Hyde over here, any day of the week."

"That's too bad. We've even chatted in the afternoons a couple of times this week. We sit on this very bench. I was hoping that meant improvement for you, as well."

"Afraid not." He pictured Erica and Jenna sitting where they were right now, and a tiny seed of jealousy planted deep. He'd worked so hard to be what Jenna needed, yet no matter what he did, it never seemed to be enough.

Was it just a lack of estrogen on his part?

Or was he simply doing it wrong?

"I don't want to discuss Jenna tonight," he said. Then he took the bottle from Erica. "Let's talk about something else."

Chapter Eleven

Erica watched the way Gabe downed the wine. This was a man with sharks nipping at his heels while he was just trying to stay afloat. So if he wanted a break from life in the middle of the night, who was she to complain. Sometimes she didn't want to talk about things, either. "Not a problem for me," she said. "What other topics are on your mind?"

He looked at her from the corner of his eye. "Me and you?"

She blew out a breath. She couldn't blame him for going there. She *had* just admitted that she still wanted to kiss him. But still . . .

"I really don't know if 'me and you' is a good idea," she told him. "I might be better with a friend right now. Probably better *as* a friend, as well." She twisted up her mouth. "That okay with you?"

Gabe leaned his head back, resting it against the side of his house, and closed his eyes. "Your friendship will always be okay with me."

She liked the way he'd said that.

She shifted to match his position, feet on the ground, head against the house, then she readjusted the blanket, making sure to keep it snug around them both since nights in Montana could get cold. The two of them sat like that for a good fifteen minutes, each in their own thoughts. It was nice being out there. Everything seemed to hover in place around them, just waiting for the world to wake up. And with her eyes closed and the wind quiet, she could make out the sound of the lapping water of the lake.

This spot soothed her, both visually and in spirit, and she couldn't help but think of her sister's plea to buy the fire hall.

They passed the bottle of wine back and forth until it was gone, and Erica realized she'd inched closer to Gabe. She had her head tucked in against him, his body heat warming her, while his arm wrapped snugly around her shoulders.

"So *has* he texted again?" Gabe finally broke the silence.

He meant JC, of course. But before Erica answered, she took a moment to think about her marriage as an unbiased woman might. Bree had asked how it could have possibly been good given that he'd cheated on her, and Erica had been tossing that question around since. Had it been good? Had she and JC truly been compatible?

The thing was, she still felt they'd had a good life. That's why it had been so hard over the summer to hear him say that he wanted her back. Because *she'd* wanted him back.

Or, she'd wanted her life back. She still didn't know if that meant she'd want JC, as well.

"He called the other night," she admitted. "But I didn't talk to him. Then he sent me two dozen roses yesterday." They currently sat on her desk at school with a note reading simply, "I'm sorry."

Gabe whistled through his teeth. "That is one man on a mission."

"Yeah, well"—humiliation once again plagued her; she should have tossed the roses in the trash—"then he shouldn't have slept with my friend."

Gabe's shoulder tensed under her. *"Ouch."*

"Right?" She glanced up, aware that the wine had loosened her tongue, but she didn't care. She needed to talk about this. To get it out of her head, if for only a moment. "*And* I got her the job she had at our school," she added. "JC was a teacher, too. Did I mention that? He's the principal now, but we both taught together for years in the same building. Then Lindsey's marriage fell apart, and she had few current skills due to being a trophy wife, so I helped move her to town. I put her and her kids up for a while—with us, if you can believe that—and I put in a good word for her for a receptionist position at our school."

Disbelief shone down at her. "And he repays you by sleeping with her?"

"I do think he waited until she got a place of her own, but I'm not sure that even matters at this point." She smirked at her own gullibility. "I babysat her kids a few times while she went out with a 'friend.' It was no big deal. JC wasn't home at the time, anyway, and he was usually gone for the entire weekend. Want to guess who that 'friend' was?"

"You're kidding."

"Not even a little. How convenient for her, huh?"

"So maybe that's your issue," Gabe offered. "You're more mad at your friend than you are at your ex? Maybe that's why you can't get over him."

That was an interesting thought. However . . . "Lindsey did not force my husband to put his dick inside her. Nor to do it without protection." She looked directly into Gabe's eyes, letting him see the depth of her hurt. "He also got her pregnant."

His breath whispered across her cheek. "And the hits just keep on coming."

"Yeah. She was showing before I found out about them." She dropped back to his shoulder and decided that she liked that spot. "JC's and my families are very similar," she explained. "Both big names in town, though my family is more about generations of town loyalty and hard work, where his is more money and providing jobs. Our divorce was not a quiet thing, nor his cheating, yet due to who we both are, I've basically had to pretend that all is fine in my new life for the last two years." She closed her eyes and added more softly, "He cheated on me, with my friend, made me the laughingstock, and *I've* been the one to have to 'deal' with it. I hate him. Yet at the same time . . ."

"You still think of him," Gabe finished for her, the puzzlement in his voice not going unnoticed by her.

She didn't get it, either. "It's like I want him back, but at the same time I don't. Why would I?"

"Do you know why he cheated on you? Love? Boredom? Simply an asshole?"

Erica shot him a look. "He told me once that he didn't love her," she shared. "He had to be with her because he'd gotten her pregnant—because his family would have his hide if he didn't—but that he'd rather stay with me."

"So he's just an asshole."

She smiled at that. "Possibly." Then she pictured her ex-friend, and thought about Lindsey's energy and desire for living life. Lindsey was physically beautiful—far different than Erica's more plain-Jane looks—and there wasn't a new experience she wasn't up for. Even that of stealing one's husband. And because of all that, she'd had men eating out of her palm her entire life. Erica shook her head at the truth of the situation and looked at Gabe. "He cheated because Lindsey was more exciting than me. You probably remember her. We were roommates in college."

His brows went high. "*That* Lindsey?"

"The one and only."

"I do remember her. But not just from seeing her at your place. She hooked up with Ben a couple of times."

"No." Erica shook her head. "You must be thinking of someone else. Lindsey dated the same guy all through college. They'd been high school sweethearts and eventually married."

"Ah." Gabe looked away, finding sudden interest in the middle of the street. "I must be mistaken."

She pushed off him then, sitting up and turning back to face him. "Seriously?" She gaped. "Ben?"

Gabe shrugged.

"You've got to be kidding me. She cheated on her boyfriend with your future brother-in-law? How? Her boyfriend was at the same school as us. He was over all the time. How did she date someone else right under his nose and not get caught?"

Funny question since Lindsey had done the exact same thing to her.

Then Gabe turned a knowing look on her, and her sense of feeling like an intelligent woman shattered. "From what I recall," Gabe began, "it wasn't exactly *dating* that they were doing."

"So she's just a slut."

Gabe chuckled. "It was college. Some people were like that."

"But I never had any clue that *she* was. I lived with her for three and a half years, and I always thought that what she and her boyfriend had was perfect. I was so jealous—the whole time—because *my* high school sweetheart had chosen to go to another school, *and* broken up with me. Yet hers still loved her."

Gabe blinked, an odd expression crossing his face. "You're talking about your ex-husband?"

"Right."

"And you were jealous of Lindsey *all through college* because he'd broken up with you?"

And then she realized her mistake. She'd dated *Gabe* for two years during that time. "I mean—"

"You were still thinking about *him* while you and I were together?"

Humiliation washed over her, as well as horror at admitting that out loud. "I'm sorry," she whispered urgently. "I wasn't really thinking about him the whole time. Not while *we* were dating. I had a great time dating you."

He hadn't taken his eyes off her. "I had a good time dating you, too," he said, the words coming out slow. "In *fact*, I would have sworn at one point that I loved you."

She snorted. "Yet you dumped me out of the blue."

"But it wasn't that much of a surprise, was it?" He looked pained. "We'd been heading in that direction since the holidays—when I first suggested you move *here* after graduation. By the time it happened, I felt you were more relieved than broken up about it."

Erica eyed him. He had suggested she move there. While she'd made it clear she saw herself going home. To teach school in the same school system as her parents.

In the same school as JC.

"Still," she muttered, "it was sudden. Like you just woke up one day and your plans had changed."

She stopped talking at the look of guilt that couldn't be missed, and once again felt her IQ drop. She was so naïve.

"You dumped me for someone else," she accused.

"I didn't sleep with her until after you and I broke up." His reply came fast. "I swear."

"Who was it?"

Gabe blew out a breath. "Does it really matter? That was a long time ago, and you were thinking about your ex." He shook his head. "You clearly weren't that into me."

"I loved you, too."

Her words took the steam out of him. Then he gave her a sad smile. "But you didn't love me enough."

He had a point. "Maybe neither of us loved enough. At least, not each other." She glanced down then, looking at her hands where she'd twisted them together in her lap. She tried to tell herself to let it go, but she couldn't. She had to know. "Who was it?" she asked again.

Gabe swallowed. "Michelle."

"Your wife?"

"My ex-wife."

She shot a pointed look at his ring finger. It was bare, but she knew he hadn't signed on the dotted line yet. He'd dumped her for another woman. Just like JC.

Her desirability as a woman crumbled.

"You met her during spring break?" She knew she shouldn't be as insulted as she was. Not when she'd just admitted that her ex had remained at the back of her mind all that time. Yet, she was.

Gabe nodded.

"Can I see a picture of her?"

Surprise crossed his face. "Why? You never saw her at school. She lived in LA. We dated long distance for a couple of years after I met her."

"Can I just see her?" Something told her that Michelle had a level of class that was missing with Erica. Same as Lindsey. Everyone else had always been just one tiny step better than her. Her mother, her sisters, the other cheerleaders in high school. Erica had been cute, yet she'd been the "ugly" cheerleader compared to the rest of them. The boring one. That's why she'd been so excited when the star quarterback had asked *her* out.

"I don't carry pictures of my ex," Gabe told her.

"Then bring her up on Facebook."

"What's the point?" His confusion was palpable. "And I'm not friends with her on Facebook."

"But you can find her, and I can at least see her picture." She motioned to the pocket she'd seen him put his phone in. "Show me."

He dug out his phone. "I don't understand why it matters."

"In the grand scheme of things, it doesn't. But humor me, will you?"

She could see him trying to decipher her thoughts, but she wouldn't expose them. They were *her* thoughts, and she got to keep some things private.

Only, after he'd keyed in Michelle's name and turned his phone around for her to see, Erica knew that her self-doubt shone bright. Even in the dark of the night. Michelle was gorgeous. Completely refined.

She wasn't just better than Erica, she was the gold nugget—with Erica nothing more than a common piece of gravel.

She hated herself for letting that matter.

"You're far more beautiful than she ever was."

Clearly, he'd figured her out. She couldn't bring herself to speak, so she shook her head, trying to let him know it didn't matter that she didn't add up. He didn't have to lie to make her feel better.

She turned back around, leaning against the bench instead of his shoulder, and stared at the road.

"Hey." Gabe touched a finger to her chin and brought her face back to his. He stroked the pad of his thumb over her cheek. "One hundred times more beautiful."

"Stop it." Her voice shook. "It doesn't matter."

"That's not why I broke up with you."

"It doesn't matter," she repeated, her words tight and hard. "It's ancient history."

"Yet I can see that it does. You don't think you measure up for some reason, and I guess I can get it to some extent. Your husband cheating on you; that's got to sting. Probably left a scar. But, Erica, his cheating, I swear to you, it had nothing to do with you."

"It had *everything* to do with me."

Chapter Twelve

G abe heard the heat in the rush of Erica's words. "How do you figure?"

She tried to turn away again, but he didn't let her. This was big for her. Therefore, this was too important to avoid.

"How?" he asked again.

"It doesn't. Never mind. I just—"

"Answer the question."

She glared at him, and he could see her wanting to ignore his demand. To tell him to go to hell. But he refused to back down. He wouldn't let her ignore this, because there was no chance her husband's cheating had been on her.

"How?" he asked more softy.

"I'm *boring*, okay?" she spat out. She stood to face him. "And I always have been." Her quilt slipped to puddle at her feet, and she held her arms out to her sides. "I'm not glitz and glamour. There's absolutely nothing special about me."

"Bullshit." He stood with her. "Nothing about you has ever been boring. Hell, I couldn't take my eyes off you the night we met."

"Yet, you—"

"I never *once* looked at another woman while we were dating. Not the way I looked at you. Not until—" He bit off his words and sent a silent plea for her to understand. For him to be able to explain it in a way that didn't make things worse. "It's hard to describe Michelle. She was so 'Hollywood.' I visited LA with Ben that spring, and everything about the place put stars in my eyes. Michelle came on to me"—he grimaced—"and I was an idiot. I know that. I was mesmerized. But it wasn't her beauty that did it. It was more her *presence*."

"You mean, she wasn't boring."

"Stop it. No." He reached for her hands, but she jerked them away. "Not wanting a big-city life, not needing material things, that doesn't make you boring."

"I need things," she protested.

"You need *people*," he corrected. "You need a purpose. You don't need cars and jewelry in order to have a rich life."

She frowned at his words before grumbling, "Yet you still chose her."

"I was an idiot. I told you that. Young and stupid." He wracked his brain to go back to that time. He hadn't been lying, he'd fallen in love with Erica. He'd known, even then, that they could be something special. But at the same time, it had almost seemed too easy. Their relationship had fit too well with his preplanned life of coming back home and settling down at the farm—minus the part where she refused to come home with him, of course.

And then there had been Michelle. She'd been excitement. Different.

She'd *not* been the plan.

He begged Erica with his eyes, not knowing how better to explain things.

"I was too boring," she said again.

He gulped. He'd never once thought of Erica as boring.

"It's okay, Gabe."

"I swear I never looked at you that way," he whispered. "Not *once*."

"It really is okay. I know what I am. What I've always been. And you followed your heart back then. I have no problem with that."

Before he could say anything else, she added, "I followed mine, too."

He furrowed his brow.

"It hurt, you dumping me." She licked her lips. "But at the same time, I called JC the very next day. We didn't officially get back together until the summer, after we'd both graduated and moved back home. But we married before the summer was over."

Well, wasn't that quick? "Maybe I was too boring for you?" Gabe suggested wryly.

She didn't immediately reply, seeming to think about his question and weigh the reality of it. Then she shook her head. "You were safe. Between us, it was always so . . ."

"Natural," he finished.

She nodded. "It seemed too easy, I think."

He stooped to retrieve her blanket. "We're not so different, you and I." He wrapped it over her shoulders, holding the sides closed together in front of her, and thought about when he'd first met Michelle. She'd blown his mind.

Then she'd turned out to be just like his mother.

He released his grip and dropped back to the bench. "Ask me about my mother sometime, will you?"

He didn't know why he'd said that. He didn't talk to anyone about his mother.

"Never mind," he muttered. His heart raced at the idea of sharing details of his childhood with Erica, but he knew he wouldn't do it. It was too humiliating. He looked up at her. "Suffice it to say that things with her weren't good—though she could weave a hell of a pretty picture. Same as my ex."

Erica remained standing for another minute, studying him carefully as he sat unmoving. Then she settled back in next to him and spread the blanket over them both. She curled into his side. "I'm sorry your marriage didn't work out."

"And I'm sorry yours didn't." He pressed his head to the top of hers.

They both grew quiet once again, and after several minutes, he slipped both arms around her and pulled her in tight. She brought the blanket up over their shoulders and tucked her feet under her on the bench, and they sat there like that, both of them dozing, until bright flashes of sunlight began to peek through the trees.

Without words, they watched the sun rise together. The moment seemed to signal a new beginning of sorts, and when Erica turned her face and let her gaze meet his, he thought he saw hints of peace.

"You'd better get inside," she whispered. "The girls are bound to wake up soon."

He stared down at her. He didn't want to leave her yet.

And he wanted to believe that she didn't want to leave him, either.

Her eyes were almost amber in the early morning light, and the tip of her nose had turned pink from the cold. He swept his fingers across her cheek, noting its chill, and found that he couldn't bring himself to be sorry that he'd kept her outside for hours. "Thanks for spending the night with me."

Then he lowered his mouth.

Erica sucked in a breath at his touch, but just as quickly engaged in the kiss. It moved slowly as first, each exploring, neither ready to push the boundaries. But then she arched her neck. Reaching for more. So Gabe cupped her under the chin and deepened their connection. He'd been wanting to do this all night, and he had no intention of letting go until they both grew faint.

When tiny mewling sounds reached his ears, he scooped Erica into his lap, and they sat like that for several minutes longer. They kissed greedily—yet somehow still leisurely—and when they were finally forced to break apart, Erica watched him from under sex-heavy lids.

He dropped his forehead to hers. Damn, what a kiss. What a woman.

What a way to start the day.

Her breaths puffed against his cheek, and he slid a hand along her rear until he reached the fleshiest part of her bottom. Then he gave her a little squeeze and pressed a soft kiss to her ear. "Did I ever mention how very much I love your ass?" he whispered.

A faint smile curved her lips.

"You showed up at Nick's last week"—he lifted his head and stared at her—"with that damned tight skirt on, and I suddenly had full recollection of what your naked rear used to look like." He squeezed her once more. "It's one of the best sights I've ever seen."

She peered over her shoulder, peeking down at the body part in question, before turning a sassy smirk back to him. "And it still looks pretty much the same today."

He growled and hugged her to him. "You haven't changed at all. You were always such a tease."

"The real problem was that you were always so easy to tease."

He kissed her again, tugging her bottom lip between his teeth as he pulled away. And though she didn't look the least bit put out by the kissing, she pursed her lips. Worry filled her eyes.

"What are we doing, Gabe?"

"We're doing what feels good."

She chuckled at that. "That sounds like something my baby sister would say."

"I always did like that sister." He leaned toward her mouth again, but she drew back.

"I'm serious." And damn, but she even looked it. "What is this? You have a kid—a messed-up kid, I might add. I have a"—she paused and held up both palms—"messed-up *me*."

"You're not so messed up."

But when she didn't reply, continuing to give him her "serious face," he blew out a breath and searched for an answer. He didn't know what they were doing any more than she did. He just knew that he felt as if he deserved this small bit of pleasure. Maybe they both did. Neither of them had experienced great marriages. Couldn't they simply lean on each other as they made their way back?

"We're kissing," he finally answered. "We're flirting, we're hanging out. We're getting to know each other again."

"But why?"

He picked up her hand, gripping her fingers in his, and tucked in his chin so he could look directly into her eyes. "Because that's what we want to do right now. Because I'm not joking when I say it feels good. It also feels *right*."

"But I don't want to hurt Jenna. I'm her teacher."

"I promise you, I won't let you hurt Jenna."

She leaned forward then, until their foreheads touched once more, and he could see her mentally fighting with herself.

"Don't put an end to this before we can even see if it's anything," he pleaded, and she looked him in the eyes.

"Do we want it to be anything?"

"Three weeks ago?" He shook his head. "I would have said no in a heartbeat. I'm just getting rid of a wife who did nothing but make my and Jenna's lives miserable. Not to mention, a relationship is the last thing I expected to want or find. But twelve years ago?" He nodded and brought her fingers to his mouth. "Hell, yes."

"But we're not twenty-one anymore."

He loved that she took things so seriously. "Which makes this even better now," he told her with the same level of sincerity. He kissed her again, capturing her mouth before she could see him coming and pull away. "Stop overthinking it," he whispered against her lips. "Just enjoy. I don't know where this might go, but come over again tomorrow morning and let's keep going. We'll flirt, hang out, and get to know each other a little more." He pulled slightly back and measured his level of persuasion. "Five thirty? Jenna gets up around six thirty most days."

He could see her wanting to say yes.

"I'm usually exercising at that time. I still dance in the mornings."

And he did like the benefits of her exercise. He squeezed her bottom once more, and touched one last kiss to her mouth. "Then come at five. I'll take whatever I can get."

Chapter Thirteen

Their meeting up at five in the morning had become habit by the following Wednesday, and as Erica came out of her apartment, she could make out Gabe already standing on his porch, mug of hot chocolate waiting for her, with the patio heater he'd purchased emitting a low red glow. She skipped across the road, hurrying since the temperature had dropped more than usual the night before, and laughed as she and her blanket were greeted with a hot kiss.

"I missed you." Gabe nuzzled her neck.

"When did you miss me? You've not been anywhere?"

"When I woke up last night and you weren't in my bed."

She shot him a pointed look. "I've not *been* in your bed in twelve years."

"You have in my dreams." He snaked his hands beneath her blanket and slid his warm palms under the back of her shirt. She shivered at his touch. These clandestine meetings had become such a part of her mornings that she'd begun looking forward to them around noon the day before.

"I missed you, too," she whispered when they broke apart. Then the devil danced through her. "But it was while in my shower instead of my bed."

He'd been right before. She liked to tease him.

She chose the end of the bench closest to the heater and took her time making her nest, all the while avoiding the look she knew Gabe had to be sending her way. But she could avoid him no longer when he gripped one hand at the back of the bench and clasped the other across her. Then he leaned in. "You're evil," he whispered.

She lifted her lips, intending to fuse hers with his, but he pulled away with a wink.

"I'm not the evil one," she muttered when he denied her what she wanted.

"Tit for tat."

He slid under the covers with her and pulled her onto his lap, and within seconds they were mired in a conversation about upcoming plans for their respective days. Gabe's workload was heavier than hers, and as he was a first-year teacher, a single dad, *and* a coach, she honestly didn't know how he did it. They'd covered similar topics most days, steering away from more personal conversations, and though that was fine with her, she also sensed a hesitancy in Gabe to share too much.

As the eastern horizon began to grow lighter, she tucked her nose into his neck and breathed him in. "This is nice," she told him. "Flirting, hanging out, and getting to know each other like this."

He dipped his head for a soft kiss. "Very nice."

"I suspect it's close to time for me to go, though." She dug her fingers into the front pocket of his jeans, and pulled out his phone. Each morning they stayed out a little longer. She pressed the button to display the time, and saw that today had been no exception. "I have to go." She held the phone up for him to see. "Calories to burn."

They rose together, and he took her hand in his. "I wish you'd quit closing your blinds every morning so I could see what goes on in these calorie-burning sessions of yours."

"And I wish you weren't such a Peeping Tom," she teased. She took a step toward her house, but he tugged on her hand. He angled his head toward her living room window when she glanced back at him.

"That's the pot calling the kettle black, isn't it? Didn't I catch you doing exactly that the first day I moved in?"

Heat fought with the coolness of her cheeks as embarrassment sparked to life. He hadn't brought that up before, and she'd hoped he'd forgotten it. "That was an entirely different situation," she defended. "It was more like I was checking out my new neighbor."

"And you think I wouldn't be checking you out?"

The heaviness of his voice told her that he'd not only peek through her window, but he'd do his best to get inside the apartment, as well.

She gulped. "I really do have to go, Gabe." No matter how much she'd like to stay.

She could ease off her morning routine a little thanks to the two sessions a week she would now be putting in at the gym, but she'd promised herself she'd keep this thing between them cool. Let them make sure they knew what they were doing before they did anything else.

Wanting to keep the moment light, she patted her butt and tossed out a saucy wink. "I can't keep my rear looking this fine if I don't exercise every morning, Coach."

He laughed and finally released her, but when she reached her front porch, he called out, "You should dance for me, you know? Put me out of my misery."

She looked back at him, seeing the desire in his eyes, and fought to not show him the same from hers. She *wanted* to put him out of his misery. In more ways than one. They'd been amazing in bed together before, and with over a decade of experience since then, she could only imagine what sleeping with Gabe in present day could bring.

But she wasn't quite ready for that yet.

She ducked into the apartment with a wave as her only reply and softly closed the door behind her. Then she looked at the pole mocking her from the middle of the room, and she knew that someday soon she absolutely *would* dance for Gabe.

A Top 40 song blasted from the speakers set up in the corners of the room as Erica shouted above the music, pointing out the next move to the group. Thirty women shuffled to the right with her, feet moving the way she'd shown them, then together, thirty rears poked out. All level of twerking was attempted, followed up by a multitude of giggles, as some got it and others didn't. But the thing that Erica noticed in the wall of mirrors was that everyone tried it. And that thrilled her.

She moved into the final sequence, feeling a bead of sweat drip over the outside corner of her eye as she turned. It was Thursday evening, and only her second time at the gym, but participation had doubled since Monday. A couple of friends from school had shown up tonight after hearing others rave about how much fun the class had been, and Arsula from the Wilde cookout was there, as well. She worked her stuff front and center behind Erica, giving it 110 percent.

When they finished the routine, Erica clapped at the effort each of the women had put in, while from the back of the room someone silenced the music.

"Great job tonight, everyone. Terrific energy!"

Cheers surrounded her. A handful of women came up to thank Erica for offering the class, and after several minutes, most everyone had emptied out of the room. A couple of small groups remained, chatting among themselves. And then Erica caught sight of Maggie Crowder hanging out by the door. Maggie had become a close friend over the last few weeks, with the two of them having lunch together any time the other wasn't on lunchroom duty.

"Hey, Mags," Erica greeted her as she grabbed a hand towel out of her bag.

"Hey. Great class." Maggie was in her late twenties, and had grown up in the area. "But oh my gosh, your stamina is killer. I could barely keep up."

Erica chuckled. "You did great."

She turned up her water bottle as Maggie went into details about which muscle group she expected to hurt the most the next day, then the two of them eased into a casual conversation, doing nothing more than enjoying the opportunity to hang out together outside of school. As they talked, Erica found that she appreciated the simplicity of the moment. It was the type of thing she hadn't experienced since moving to Birch Bay.

When Arsula exited the changing room, Erica called her over. "Do you two know each other?" Erica smiled at the other woman, who had to be at least ten years younger than her. "Arsula moved here from Cheyenne earlier this month," she told Maggie.

Eyelashes as thick and dark as her hair framed smiling eyes as Arsula stuck out her hand. "Pleased to meet you," she said. "Do you teach with Erica?"

"I do. I'm in the classroom next door to her. Third grade."

"Really? My momma taught third grade for years," Arsula shared. "She retired early, though, and she works at the State Museum now."

"I didn't know your mother had been a teacher." Erica had spent some time with Arsula during the cookout, but they'd talked more about Arsula's road trip to Birch Bay and her first week on the job than anything else. "You didn't want to follow in her footsteps?"

"I considered it, but I started being able to read dreams in my late teens, and I decided that would be a better use of my time."

Maggie and Erica both had to know more about Arsula's gift, and soon the three of them were chattering together as if they'd all been best friends for years. The moment seemed big. And it had Erica wanting to extend it. Or at least have a chance to do it again.

"Would the two of you want to come over for dinner sometime?" she suggested during a small lull. And when the other women looked her way, she added, "I've been practicing a few new recipes. I'd be thrilled if you'd let me try some out on you. Plus, I've rented the most fabulous place. I haven't had any guests, and I'm dying to show it off."

"The fire hall." Maggie nodded. "I know the guy who renovated it. Didn't he do an amazing job?"

"Completely," Erica agreed. "So what day works?"

After consultation with the calendars on their phones, they decided on a Wednesday night, almost three weeks away. The long wait was a bit of a letdown, but she couldn't exactly hog everyone's time.

"Then it's a date," she announced before adding, less enthusiastically, "That's the last week of my contract at the school."

"Oh, no." Maggie squeezed Erica's hand. "You aren't really going to leave us, are you?"

"Honestly, I don't know what I'm going to do. But I am looking for a job."

She ignored the panic that always tried to grip her when she thought about her lack of plans, and concentrated on the conversation that quickly kicked back up. After a few more minutes, the impromptu gathering broke up, and they each headed to their own vehicle, and as Erica climbed into her car, she dug her cell out of her bag. She'd felt it buzzing while talking to the girls, and upon retrieving it, she saw that she'd missed four calls. All from her ex-husband.

That was it. The man was getting blocked.

She brought up his number and chose the option to keep him from getting through to her, and while she was at it, she cleared out his most recent text messages. She hadn't read any in the last few days, hoping that if he didn't see the indicator that she'd she viewed them, then maybe he would leave her alone. But the man didn't seem to get a clue.

At this point, it was either block him or sic her baby sister on him.

She smiled at the thought of that. Bree would *love* to handle JC for her. Erica had called her sister after last weekend's violin lesson—which totally had not gone well at all—to finally fill her in on the kiss from Gabe. But she'd also let it slip that JC had been reaching out to her. Given that Bree was already ready to hang the man up by the short hairs, Erica knew it wouldn't take much encouragement for her sister to find a way to retaliate. Bree had always been one who enjoyed fighting the good fight. Whether the fight was hers or not.

In a moment of childishness, Erica Googled a picture and sent it to Bree with the comment:

I might need you to order this for one particular ex if he doesn't leave me alone.

The picture was of a box of extra-small condoms.

Then she started her car, laughing out loud at her actions, and headed for home. Just sending the picture made her feel better. It did nothing to change the way things were, but it left her feeling as if she'd somehow put JC in his place.

Her phone chirped from the passenger seat, but she'd wait until she got home to read it.

She pulled into her parking spot at her house and waved at Gabe, who stood in the front yard while Mike sniffed at a bush.

"Good evening, Coach," she greeted as she climbed out of the car. She'd noted the grin that broke across his face the instant he'd seen her and couldn't hold back the one of her own.

"Good evening, Ms. Bird."

Her words had been light and teasing, but his read somewhat deeper. Which made her recall that a little more than twelve hours earlier, she'd seriously hated separating her lips from his. As she drank him in now, she decided to go inside and start work on a new dance routine. One she just might leave her blinds open for.

Instead of going over to him as she wanted to, she headed for her house. For now, they had the mornings, and that was enough.

But that might very soon change.

As she unlocked her front door, she heard, "See you in the morning, Ms. Bird," come from across the road, and she grinned once more. She looked over her shoulder, and she couldn't help herself. She blew him a kiss.

The wickedness on his features at that small act had her biting her lip. Yes. It was very definitely nearing time for more than an early morning chat.

She closed the door behind her as she entered the apartment and flipped on her overhead lights, and then she took in the pole that seemed to be waiting for her. But before heading to it, she checked the message that had come in from Bree.

Done.

Her throat dried as she stared at the screen.

Done?

Purchased and on its way.

What?

Erica let her bag fall to the floor. Her sister had seriously sent JC a box of extra-small condoms?

She covered her mouth with her hand as her shoulders began to shake with laughter. Of course Bree had sent the condoms. Tears squeezed from her eyes. That's exactly something her sister would do.

And honestly, wasn't that why Erica had sent the picture in the first place? It was time to shut the other man down, and she still wasn't sure she was strong enough to do it on her own.

She pulled her phone back up, but another message came through before she could reply.

Should I send this one to your neighbor?

The text was accompanied by a picture of a box of extra-*large* condoms.

More laughter spilled out. She did love her sister.

She sent one last message, then purposely put her phone away.

No need. They wouldn't get here soon enough.

Chapter Fourteen

The twangy fifties music wove its way through Erica's body as she moved her hips to the bluesy beat. She skimmed the backs of her fingers up her torso, taking in the different textures she touched. The spandex of her workout bottoms, the bare skin of her belly, and the cotton of the cropped tee. She grazed her hands over the outer curves of her breasts, and a soft moan parted her lips.

Bringing her hands to the pole in front of her, she thrust her hips backward, her bottom rocking out before she circled around and pressed the length of her spine to the metal. She went into a squat, trailing her fingers up over her body again and letting herself enjoy every caress, until her hands reached high above her head. Her fingers closed around the pole, its coolness a balm to her overheated body, and she stretched like a cat midpurr. Power rolled through her that morning, and she couldn't wait until Gabe figured out she wouldn't be joining him on his porch.

The music changed, kicking into an even more sensuous groove, and she closed her eyes. She let her body sway, her hips grinding out a motion as old as time, and thought about the man who rarely left her mind these days.

She should have been on his porch by now.

She smiled to herself, sliding her palms back up the pole before grasping it tight and lifting her legs to one side. She curled one calf back while the other stretched out in front of her, and she let her body spin slowly in the air. She'd lain awake the night before, thinking about this morning. Anxious for five o'clock. Gabe had an away game last night, and Erica knew he'd come home alone. Jenna had been excited about staying overnight with her pops and gramma, and Erica had heard Gabe's truck pull up before midnight. One door slammed. One set of footsteps walked in.

Bringing her feet back to the floor, she went into another bump out of her rear. She imagined a mirror hanging on the wall across from her where she could watch the movements of her body. Where she could watch two people making love.

Hands on thighs, face still to the imaginary mirror, she lowered back to a squat, her fingers scraping over her skin and her breaths picking up. She held her back straight, her breasts high, and she quickly opened and closed her thighs, as if offering a single peek into a secret world. Then she was up, eyes once again shut, and roaming her hands over herself. It was no longer about the tease of the dance, but about the needs of one woman. She needed Gabe's hands to replace her own.

His fingers would be strong. Probably callused. She could imagine their coarseness roving over her the way his morning whiskers often scraped against her lips.

A moan slipped out. She wanted those fingers on her this morning.

With hands sweeping in slow circular motions out to her sides, she pulled in her shoulders and dipped forward with the music, going into a shimmy that she knew any man would appreciate. And when the knock finally came, she expelled a whisper of relief. Then she opened her eyes and found Gabe, not at her door, but watching through the blinds she'd left open at her window.

The door opened in front of Gabe, music slithering out to wrap around him, enticing him to step inside, but before he allowed himself that pleasure, he raked his gaze over Erica. She hadn't allowed him to see this much of her yet. Either her body or her need, and he knew he was a fool for not already having her in his arms. But he wanted this moment. He wanted to savor it.

He dragged his eyes along her thighs, taking in their toned strength, then over her slim hips and the tiny shorts. Her T-shirt wasn't much larger, and it seemed that everywhere he looked there was skin.

Being slightly shorter than average, she usually hit at his chin, but the black heels she wore that morning cut that distance by half.

He scanned over her one more time. He couldn't remember making love with her wearing anything like this before, but he didn't doubt for a second that's what was about to happen. He'd known it before he'd stepped to her window.

He'd known it when she hadn't come out her door.

"Nice pole," he tossed out casually. He took a large step, putting him inside her apartment.

"Dancing with it was my sister's idea." She didn't back away. "I told her it was too big."

"I do remember her talking about showing you how to handle something big. I guess it wasn't too big after all."

The pink stains that appeared high on her cheeks had him teasing her with a hot smile, but when her eyes lowered to land directly on his rapidly bulging crotch, he was no longer the one smiling.

"She suggest the heels, too?" he scratched out. Damn, but he felt like he'd never done this before.

She shook her head. "I came up with some things on my own."

He slammed the door behind him. "You didn't show up at my place this morning."

"I came up with that little gem, too."

He chuckled. She was a riot. And hot as hell. He forced his breathing to slow. "So we're doing this?"

"Unless you don't want to."

"I'd have to be a fool not to want to, wouldn't I?" And he could kill himself for the fool that he was. "Only"—he grimaced—"I don't have a condom on me."

Always carry a condom.

Hadn't he learned that one simple rule years ago? Whether it went unused for a decade or not, always carry a damned condom. Because one day, you might just get lucky.

One day, you might have a half-naked woman standing in front of a pole.

"I can run to the store," he offered. Jenna wasn't home. He would run anywhere that would allow him to get his hands on Erica's body. But he soon realized that a store was not a necessity.

Erica's smile turned to pure devilry as her fingers dipped behind the waistband of her shorts. A second later, they came up with three little packets.

"I guess that's that, then," he murmured, his gaze glued to her hand.

"I guess that's that."

He closed the blinds then—with great patience—and without another word, he reached for Erica. Two seconds later, she was up against the pole with her T-shirt above her head.

"Gabe," she whispered. Her body shook against his.

"Don't dance in front of me with a pole, woman," he growled out, "unless you want to be slammed up against it." He shoved the T-shirt higher, and in one smooth move, had it twisted around his fist, imprisoning her wrists against the metal.

Heat burned in her eyes, and the hazel turned full-on green when he hoisted her up by her rear and put his mouth around one lace-covered nipple. It pebbled immediately, adding to the throbbing between his legs, and when her slim thighs clamped around his hips, he pushed forward, grinding in the manner he'd just stood on her porch and watched her do for him.

Her panties turned instantly wet. The heated moisture stroked him through his worn denim, and that was even before he used his teeth to rip the lace from her breast.

Erica sucked in air at the exposure, and her nipple reached for him.

"I remember those," he grunted out. "Very well, in fact." He stared down at her. She had the most perfect breasts. Just a little heavy on the bottom, nipples that were tight and hard but large enough to not get lost in his mouth, and tiny dark areolas that made him want to suck them fully between his teeth. He glanced up at her as he put his mouth back to her nipple, stopping his movements right before he touched her with his tongue.

"Who's evil now?" she whispered.

"I am," he said knowingly. "But I'm going to make up for it before I'm done."

She groaned when he finally put lips to skin, and the way she writhed against him, he thought she might bring both of them to orgasm before he could get his fill of one breast.

When he tugged the lace on the other side out of the way, its fragility also not holding up under the pull of his teeth, her hips began to grind in harder circles. "Hold still," he begged. He pushed harder against her, hoping to pin her in place, as he tried to focus only on her breasts. But his attempts to still her only made her movements grow more out of control.

"We've got three condoms," she breathed out. "Please. I'm *begging*. Let me down so we can both get naked, and then I swear to you that we can take our time with the other two."

He stopped and looked up at her. She had a very excellent point. So he released her wrists and lowered her to the ground, and within thirty seconds there were no clothes left between them and her fingers were shaking as she tried desperately to roll the prophylactic over his length.

He pushed her hands out of the way. "You're only making it worse."

Within seconds he had himself sheathed, and Erica practically leaped back into his arms. With her elbows locked at the back of his neck and his fingers dug into the cheeks of her rear, he finally gave them what both of them needed. He buried himself deep, rocking her against the pole, then pulled out and repeated the move.

She was so hot.

And so wet.

"I'm going to come now," she said, barely getting the words out before her body began to tense in his arms. Her insides clenched around him as she bowed back, and as her breasts angled high, he brought one hand up to run across her skin.

He held her as she broke apart, willing himself to wait, to let her get this first pass out of the way, and the second he sensed her body going into the slightest limp, he cupped his hand around one breast and sucked her deep between his lips. He rocked into her, realigning her with the pole to keep her in place. He alternated the sucking and the rocking, but at the same time making each move slightly harder than the one before it, and within seconds, he wasn't the only one ready to blow. He brought her right back to that point again, too.

"Gabe," she groaned. Her hands gripped at his shoulders as she once again bowed tight. She held onto him while he continued to pump, and he held back for only a few seconds more. He wanted to draw her pleasure out as long as he possibly could, but he had little time left in him.

Finally, he buried his face in her neck. He roared with need as his body found its own release. He filled her, letting her heat and her wetness soak him dry, and when he couldn't hold himself up under his own weight any longer, he pinned her to the pole.

This, he thought.

He lifted his head and gently took her mouth before she could catch her breath. Her lips clung to his as he cherished her, seeming to need the quiet moment as much as him, and when he finally inched away, he whispered against her, *"This."*

Chapter Fifteen

W ell, that answers the other question."

"What question is that?" Erica spoke while trying to catch her breath. She was naked and sweaty, her thighs straddling Gabe's body, and her cheek plastered to the damp hairs sprinkled across his chest. They'd started against the pole, had then moved to the kitchen countertop, she'd spent some time on the dining room table, and finally, they'd wrapped it up when she'd pushed him to her couch and ridden him to the finish line.

He nuzzled the top of her head. "That kissing isn't the only thing we're still good at."

She laughed and pushed up off his chest. "That *was* pretty good, wasn't it?"

"Baby." The curve of his smile matched her own. "Good doesn't begin to cover what just happened here. And I'm not saying that just because it's been a hell of a long time for me."

He dropped his head back against the cushion, his eyes closed in satisfaction, and Erica took the moment to study him in the early morning light. Dark hair, toned body, and a reserved, mysterious air about him that would attract most any female who looked his way. His sculpted cheekbones and wide lips spoke of his unmistakable strength. But in that moment, with his hands lightly cupping the sides of her hips and the words he'd spoken hanging between them, she saw a different side of him. One slightly more vulnerable.

"It's been a while for you?" she asked softly.

He eyed her from under half-closed lids. "Who do you think I've been with? There's not a lot of opportunities with a kid around."

"But doesn't she spend the night with Max and Gloria on occasion? As well as Haley or Leslie?"

"Sure, but honestly"—he shrugged—"I haven't been that interested. Not that I don't love sex, God forbid, but I guess my mind has been on other things."

"Like worrying about your daughter."

"Exactly."

One of his hands slid over the muscles of her thigh, and his thumb began drawing out tiny circles as he seemed to disappear inside his own head. His torso glistened, same as hers, and they had yet to dispose of the last of the protection. But none of that seemed to matter.

When he finally returned to the moment, she said, "How long were you married?"

"Ah." His thumb quit moving. "We're going to talk about her now?"

"I'd like to. If you don't mind."

He thought about the request longer than Erica had expected. "I don't know. Nine years, maybe? The last few ran together."

"And why did you go to California?" She held her breath with that one. The last time she'd asked, he hadn't answered. Yet for some reason, she sensed that he was more willing to share today.

"Because she was going to divorce me if I didn't," he stated simply. "Funny, huh? I moved to save our marriage, yet I'm the one who ended up filing?" He blew out a breath. "It was a last-ditch effort, anyway. We'd been having trouble for years. She wasn't . . ." He let his words trail off for a moment while a look of utter disgust passed over his face. He swallowed, and his fingers tightened slightly on her thigh. "She was neither a good mother nor a good wife. I knew this at that point. Hell, I'd known it for years. But she was Jenna's mother. And I guess I was . . . weak."

"Weak?" She'd never think of Gabe Wilde as a weak man.

He only nodded at that, and she remembered something Dani had told her at the cookout. "Your sister implied that neither of your parents had been the best example."

His free hand landed on one of the heels she still wore on her feet, and he frowned. "My sister needs to keep her mouth shut."

"And then *you* suggested to me that your mother wasn't the best."

He eyed her again. She could see him willing her to stop.

"Your dad, too?" she pushed. Was she on to something? Were there things about Gabe's upbringing that made him feel not good enough? Weak?

She and he might have dated for two years in the past, but it had occurred to her only recently that, in all those months, Gabe had shared very little about his childhood. Just the basics.

"I always liked Max," she said when he remained silent. "I thought he loved you guys. That you were a happy family."

"He does love us. And we are a happy family."

Yet there was more here he wasn't telling her.

"What's wrong with your dad?" she whispered.

Gabe closed his eyes. "Nothing is *wrong* with him, I don't suppose. I'm just not a fan of the way he's always handled his life. He let my mother walk all over him for years. He let her walk all over *us*." His eyes twitched under the closed lids. "And then I grew up to allow the same damned thing with Michelle."

He opened his eyes, and they bore into her. "Can we talk about something else now? Michelle isn't a good person, my mother was even worse, and my dad misplaced his backbone a long time ago. Good enough?"

"I'm sorry." She said the words quickly, then leaned into him and wrapped her arms tight around his chest. "Thanks for sharing that. But please know that I'd *never* see you as weak."

For a moment they stared at each other, each waiting to see what the other would do or say next. But then Gabe's hand stroked up her back, the pressure of his touch firm and solid, and he pressed a kiss to her temple. He may not be in the mood to talk, but she thought he might have appreciated her words.

Comfort surrounded her as she sat there, still straddling his lap. A private space to share things seemed to envelop them. And since she retained a few issues of her own that she needed to work through, she decided to use some of that space. She folded her hands over his chest and parked her chin on top of them. Then she waited until Gabe brought his gaze back to hers.

"JC talked me into sleeping with him again this summer."

The hand at her back quit moving.

"That's why I'm here." She refocused to the base of his throat, suddenly afraid to let him see too much of her while she talked. "I'm not even sure how it started. We hadn't talked in eighteen months. The divorce had been over for a long time, and though we still saw each other at school, we avoided being in the same room together as much as possible."

"It must have been uncomfortable for others when you had to be together."

"Actually, no. I guess we got good at faking it."

His fingers spread wide over her back. "And what about when Lindsey was around? Did you get used to playing nice then, too?"

She shook her head. Not even close. "Lindsey quit her job after it came out they were together."

Her once best friend had never been shy about owning her desire to be a kept woman, no matter that she did have a college education. She went to school purely because her parents paid for it, and because she had to do something until her boyfriend graduated and married her.

So once she had JC tied down, her resignation practically flew from her fingertips.

Erica lifted off Gabe's chest. "I think I just figured something out."

"And what's that?"

"It's not that I'm *more* mad at Lindsey, but I think my anger at her might have played into why I let myself get taken in again by him." Gabe watched her, his eyes hooded, as she continued. "She shouldn't have slept with my husband. She was my friend. Enough said. She shouldn't have done it. But she's the type to want someone to take care of her and her kids more than to have someone to love. I really believe that. So she sleeps with JC. He's got money, he's a name in town. Then the process is sped up by the pregnancy."

"Maybe she planned the pregnancy."

Erica considered his words. "Maybe she did. And honestly, at this point, I'd put nothing past her. But she got JC, he moved me out of the house and her in, and then when he started showing interest in me again . . ." She paused, not liking how her words were going to make her sound. But Gabe got it, anyway.

He sat up straighter on the couch. "You wanted to get back at her," he guessed. "You might be equally mad at both of them, but she came into a marriage where she didn't belong, and you had the opportunity to return the favor."

"Except she and JC aren't married."

Gabe's brows knitted. "After two years and a baby, why has he never married her?"

"I have no idea." At first she'd assumed it had to do with the pregnancy showing. Lindsey wasn't the type to walk down the aisle with a belly. But the baby was over a year and a half old now, and Lindsey had long ago lost all the baby weight.

"So how did this summer come about?" Gabe asked.

"Near the end of the school year I got a text one Friday night. I can't even remember what it was about. But he texted me, and for some reason, I texted back." She gave a half shrug. "A couple of weeks later, I got another one."

"And you replied again?"

"I saw no harm in it. We'd moved on, we were colleagues. We'd been good friends once upon a time. So I texted him back. But then he started stopping by my classroom once in a while, sharing a funny article he found or telling me a joke he'd heard."

"The man was pursuing you."

She nodded. "I didn't see it that way at the time. I was playing nice, and to tell you the truth, after eighteen months, I think I'd lost some of the anger. I was tired of being 'that person,' so talking was easier. And then he'd call once in a while. In late summer, he got word of his promotion, and he said we should celebrate."

"He's clever."

"Or maybe I'm just gullible."

Gabe shook his head. "We all make mistakes. We all want things, even when we know better."

"Possibly." But some people just went stupid.

She lowered her eyes to his chest, needing *not* to see Gabe as she continued her story. "Our celebration ended up at a hotel. I couldn't believe I'd done that. But at the same time, he'd been mine, you know? Why *couldn't* I do that? A couple weeks later, he talked me into meeting him for lunch. He had something he wanted to tell me."

"I imagine he did."

She pulled in a deep breath and kept her eyes glued to Gabe's torso. "He wanted me back," she said softly. "He'd messed up. He'd known it from the beginning, and had decided he was tired of trying to forget me."

"Your ex is full of shit."

She looked up at the growled words, and the fierceness in Gabe's expression suddenly lightened the mood in the room. She gave him a wry smile. "Bree thinks so, too. Of course, she also thinks he suffers from little-dick syndrome."

A look that could only be described as raw masculine pride covered Gabe's face. "He has a little dick?"

"I did not say that." Erica snickered. "I just said that Bree thinks he has that problem."

Talk of another man's genitals apparently did something to Gabe, because she felt him stir against her thigh.

"Is it . . ." He started to ask but didn't finish it. He merely looked at her in anticipation.

"Bigger than *yours*?" she finished for him.

He stirred again, and she gave a little wiggle against him.

"Well?" he prodded. His hands gripped her hips and tugged her up his thighs, the move encouraging more wiggling.

"We used all three condoms," she whispered, as if sharing a secret he wasn't aware of.

"Then stop talking about how I'm more man than your ex is."

She laughed and pushed up off him. "I did not say that."

But as she rose from the couch and stepped over his legs, she looked down at the erection now over half formed, and she caught herself making an "impressed" face.

"I knew it," Gabe crowed. "Mine's bigger." His chest puffed up.

"You boys are ridiculous." She smirked. "I'm going to clean myself up. You might want to do the same."

"But you didn't tell me how it ended," he called after her.

"You mean this summer?" She stepped into the bathroom at the back of the room, leaving the door open as she bent to get a washcloth from one of the vanity drawers. When she stood back up, Gabe was at the door.

"You're going to hotels with him," he said, "being swept off your feet at his charming, little-dick ways, and then what?"

An emotion spread through her that she hadn't felt in a long time. Being with Gabe was pure pleasure. Even talking about JC with him wasn't as bad as when she normally thought about her ex. "He talked me into another hotel," she told him. "A weekend this time—while assuring me that he was breaking up with Lindsey. Just as soon as he found the right time, of course. And as an added bonus, he tossed in a promise that he'd never mess up with *me* again."

"I take it those were lies?"

"Every last one. I overheard him on the phone Sunday morning, giving Lindsey some story about why he hadn't made it home the night before. Telling her he loved her, and that he couldn't wait to see her. His weekend had been utter misery without her."

"He couldn't even leave the hotel room to make that call?"

She shook her head.

"Stupid *and* a little dick."

Laughter burst from her. "Stop it. This isn't funny. The jerk turned *me* into the other woman, instead of the other way around." The humor vanished, and Erica stood there, both of them naked from head to toe, and she found herself glad she'd run into Gabe again. "I never wanted to be that kind of person," she said with all sincerity. "Another person's marriage is none of my business. Another person's relationship applies, as well, but especially when there's a kid involved. But the kicker was that I stood there that morning, listening to this jerk prove his jerkiness to me yet again, and I felt myself beginning to break down. I'd wanted him back. I didn't just get caught up in the moment, I *wanted* it."

Gabe took her hands in his.

"I left Silver Creek because I realized that he wasn't the issue so much as me. I won't have a man who can't be honest with me. And I won't allow myself to be in a position where I'm in the middle of a relationship. Where I have to beg for attention." She shook her head, more determination than she'd ever felt swelling inside her. "So I had to leave. I had to move beyond my ex-husband once and for all."

"And are you beyond him now?"

She paused, her breaths heavier than normal. "I'm close. Being here is good for me. Talking about it is good. But at the same time, I'm terrified that I'm not quite there yet."

"Maybe more sex with a very well-endowed man will do it for you?"

She laughed, the sound as sad as it was happy, and when Gabe's arms closed around her and gently pulled her to his body, she lifted her mouth. "Maybe it will," she whispered against his lips. "I'd certainly be willing to give it a try."

Chapter Sixteen

He had to buy more condoms.

Gabe stared at the video of last night's football game playing out on the TV in his office, seeing nothing but Erica's naked body riding him on her couch. He *definitely* had to buy more condoms. Though he had no idea when they'd get to use them.

"Dad?"

Jenna's face appeared in his office door only seconds after she'd spoken, and he grabbed the remote and paused the game tape. "What's up, kiddo?"

"Can I go outside? One of my friends is here with her mom."

After leaving Erica's that morning, he'd driven over to the farm to get Jenna, and after checking on the new trees—as well as waking his dad from a nap simply to make sure the man was only tired, and there was nothing wrong with him—he and Jenna had headed for the high school. "Is it Mrs. Waters's girl?"

"Yes."

He opened the blinds on the only window in the small room. "Can you play right out there where I can see you?"

"Da-ad. We can't play out there. There's nothing to do."

"Out there" consisted of a small grassy courtyard area between two parts of the building with a concrete drainage ditch running down the middle. "Sure there is." He snatched up a football and tossed it to her. "You can play catch."

A very teenage roll of the eyes was his answer, but both Jenna *and* the football exited the room. Minutes later, she appeared with the girl she'd met the previous Saturday when he'd also come by the high school, and though the football didn't get thrown between the two, Jenna did keep it tucked under one arm. He watched out the window for a couple of minutes, noticing that for the first time his daughter actually smiled more than frowned. Slowly but surely, she really was making progress.

He returned to the paused tape and restarted it, then forced his mind to remain on the game playing out in front of him—and not on the run to the convenience store that he so desperately wanted to make.

Twenty minutes later, another noise sounded at his office door, and he looked up to find Chase. The boys knew that he liked to come into the school on Saturdays when possible, and he'd made it clear that they were always welcome to stop by.

He paused the tape once more. "What's going on, Chase?"

"Hey, Coach." The boy seemed nervous as he shot a quick look behind him. "You got a minute?"

"Sure." Gabe turned off the TV. "Take a seat." He motioned to the vinyl armchair on the other side of his desk, and at the same time, took a quick peek out the window. The girls were still out there, and Jenna was now tossing the football in the air.

"I've just got a few minutes," the boy said. "Mom's waiting on me."

"Everything okay?"

"Yeah." Chase nodded and lowered to the chair. "Actually it's pretty good. I got a callback from Boise."

"Yeah?"

"As well as Oregon." The words rushed out, and then Chase's ears turned pink. "*And* Montana."

The kid's wildest dreams were coming true, and the poor thing looked scared to death.

Gabe sat up straighter in his chair. "This is a good thing, Chase. This is what you want."

"I know. I just . . ." Chase stared at his lap. "They want me to visit the campuses."

Gabe couldn't help the smile. Being a teen could be rough when you suddenly had choices you'd worried would never be presented. "And you *want* to visit them, right?"

"I do." Chase peeked up. "Very much."

"Good deal. Explore your options before deciding. There's no hurry."

"I know." His breaths came harder. "But my mom. She . . ."

Gabe was aware that Chase's mother was raising two boys alone, and understanding began to dawn. "I could go with you," he offered. "If you wanted. If your mom has to work." It might eat into whatever time he could pull together to be with Erica, but this was important. This was the type of man he wanted to be.

"My mom says she can work it out with her boss. It'll be tricky, but she thinks she can do it. It's just . . . the money." His words grew thin. "She doesn't know how we can afford it."

"Ah." Gabe nodded. The boy looked pained, but this, too, could be handled. There was always a way. "I'll tell you what. You and your mom work out the details, and Coach Mann and I will put our heads together on this."

"Yeah?"

He stood. "Absolutely." He reached across the desk. "Congratulations, Chase. You've got three great schools looking at you. We'll make sure *you* get to look at them, too. We won't let this opportunity pass you by."

Relief put a smile on Chase's face, and soon Gabe once more sat alone in his office. But instead of turning the video back on, he just sat there. Chase would get a scholarship, Gabe had no doubt. The team continued to improve, and with three schools now looking at him, there would be zero chance he'd get passed by.

He leaned back, true contentment settling inside him for the first time since coming home. His team was doing well, his daughter might still hate him—but she'd been outside for thirty minutes now with a football in her hand—and he'd just spent the morning in the arms of a woman he cared for and respected. And who he was pretty sure thought he wasn't so bad, either.

Life was looking up.

When his phone rang, the display showing a private caller, he thought nothing about answering it. It could be any number of students or players he'd shared his number with. Except, it turned out to be none of them.

"Hello, Gabe."

His blood froze. "Michelle."

He forced himself to breathe normally, ordering himself to come up with something else to say, but all he could do was face the window and stare at his daughter. She was still out there, walking around in the grass, the football once again tucked under her arm. But her friend was nowhere to be found.

"Why are you calling?" he finally scratched out.

"I just wanted to talk to you. I've missed you. I miss Jenna."

"Bullshit." She never *just* wanted to do anything. And she'd never missed either one of them.

"Come on, don't be like that." A tiny mewling sound hit his ear. "I know I messed up, but I've changed, I swear."

"Good for you." He'd heard the story before. "Maybe it'll help with your new relationship."

"But I want to have a relationship with my daughter, too." Her words and pleading tone gave voice to the fleeting thought that she had to be performing for someone. Her boyfriend, most likely. But why?

And why now?

"I'm busy, Michelle. I'm *working*. Something you know little about, I'm aware, but it's what people who don't have yachts and buckets of money do every day. And we already addressed your relationship with your daughter. You no longer have one. Now, if there's nothing else?"

"But there is." The soft kitten routine disappeared. "I want to *see* my daughter, Gabe."

"No."

"I have rights. You can't keep me from her. The separation agreement granted me visitation."

"Which you proved yourself too irresponsible for."

"I don't know what you're talking about."

He pulled the phone back and stared at it. What in the hell was she up to? She knew exactly what he was talking about.

Forcing his grip to relax before he damaged his phone, he racked his brain to try to figure this out. There was no way she wanted to see Jenna. Not because she cared.

And there was no way he'd let his daughter be a pawn in whatever game this was.

He closed his eyes and silently cursed that the damned papers hadn't been signed already. That he'd never forced the issue and gotten her visitation revoked. He hadn't attempted to prove a single thing; he'd simply told her she was out of the picture. And it had worked. Until now.

"As I said," he began again, trying his best to remain calm, "you squandered your rights."

"Not according to my lawyer."

He opened his eyes. "Michelle—"

"I want to see her, Gabe. And I want her to come here."

Fear cut off his air. The last thing Jenna needed was to go back to California. She was just starting to have a normal day now and then. Nor did she need to see her mother.

"That's not going to happen."

"I've changed," she repeated. "I regret the way things ended, and I want to see our daughter."

She wouldn't push for this, would she? Because legally, she could.

He closed his eyes again. "As I stated before, you lost your visitation rights. You lost your daughter. Now, if you have anything else to say on the matter, you can say it through our lawyers."

He hung up before she could reply, his hands shaking at the confrontation, and cupped his fingers over his mouth. He should have called the cops that night. Well, before they'd been called on him.

"Was that Mom?"

He looked up, his stomach turning over at the sight of his daughter standing just inside his door. Pain contorted her features. "Jenna," he began. He stood. But he had no idea what else to say.

"Did she want to talk to me?"

He shook his head. "No, baby. She was—"

He cut off his words when tears appeared in his daughter's eyes, and circled his desk to go to her. Damn Michelle for doing this.

"Honey." He stooped and took her hands. "Your mother left us. You know that. She—"

"But she just called." Wide eyes stared back at him, and he could see her wanting to trust the words coming out of his mouth. But at the same time, he saw the distrust. "Why didn't you let me talk to her?" she whispered.

Because the last time the two of them had talked, Jenna hadn't come out of her room for two days.

Crossing his fingers on what he was about to do, he opened his mouth and directly lied to his only child. "She didn't actually ask about you, sweetheart. She didn't want to talk to you."

"This *pizza*." Erica moaned in pleasure before leaning back in her seat in the teacher's lounge. "I've never had any so good."

"Tell me about it," Maggie added. "I need to date the owner, if for no other reason than for free pizza."

"Except he's about eighty years old," another teacher at the table tossed in.

"There is that," Maggie muttered. "Not that I'm too proud." She grabbed another piece of the shared lunch that had been delivered by their favorite pizzeria, checking her watch as she took a bite. "Ten minutes before we've got to get back to the kids."

"Enough time for one more slice."

While Maggie and the other teacher ate their pizza and began talking about that morning's headline news—a local man who'd been arrested the night before for literally being caught with his pants down— Erica pulled out her phone and scrolled through her social media account. She'd admired pictures on the site from the Silver Creek Sunset Garden Tour the week before, and since then she'd been keeping up with the happenings around her hometown a bit more. When she'd moved away, she'd purposefully ignored all communication from home, not wanting to see anything going on in Silver Creek. But at the brief reminder of everything she'd been missing, she couldn't help but want to see more.

Using her finger, she moved past random updates from friends about how their mornings started, skipped over pictures of what people had eaten for dinner the night before, then stopped the page and tapped on an article about the town's football team. Silver Creek hadn't lost a game that season.

"Your class last night earned me extra pizza today," Maggie informed her, and Erica smiled without looking up.

"Wait until Thursday. I added a new sequence into the routine this morning."

Erica still exercised each morning before coming to work, but she also still sat with Gabe on his porch every day, too. They'd not been "together" since the weekend, and they really hadn't talked that much about what they'd done. But Erica was hopeful it would happen again. Preferably soon.

She saw a post from her older sister, who was in school at Chapel Hill, then clicked over to Bree's page to see that her youngest sibling was currently somewhere in Mexico. That tiny flame of irritation that liked to rear its head concerning Bree never having to "follow the rules" lit up, but Erica squelched it. Some people were simply different. She needed to accept that.

Erica had talked to Bree Sunday afternoon, confirming that, yes, condoms had indeed been used with her neighbor, but she hadn't spoken with Annalise in over a month. Maybe she'd give her other sister a call later that week.

Probably she should call her brother at some point, too. It hadn't occurred to her until now that since she no longer lived in the same town as him, that meant they rarely talked.

A few clicks later, and she was scrolling through the latest pictures of Seth's two boys.

"Are you hearing anything we're saying over there?" Maggie leaned onto the table and stuck her face in front of Erica's.

"Huh?" She looked up.

"We were asking if you'd given any thought to staying on here."

"I can't stay on here, you know that. Mrs. Watts will be back in less than three weeks."

"We meant as a substitute."

Her new colleagues wore pleading expressions, and Erica shook her head, feeling her own sadness at the fact that she'd soon have to give up this lunchtime camaraderie. She'd miss seeing these women every day. "I want something *more*," she said. "And you would, too. And I *need* something more. The bills don't pay themselves."

"But we need you here."

Maggie's whine was only partially fake, Erica knew, but that didn't mean the feelings behind it were.

"How about a compromise?" she offered. "If nothing else gets offered, I'll stay. I do have the apartment rented until the end of the year, after all." But she couldn't give up hope that an opportunity would come up, either. Her dad would be calling that night. He'd been reaching out to his contacts in the field, trying to find something for her.

The idea of her dad's contacts *not* coming through suddenly had her wondering if it would be so bad to just stay. That way, not only would she get to continue her budding friendships, but she could have more time with Gabe, as well.

And wasn't it interesting that the thought of that didn't strike her as being as scary as it probably should have? She *wanted* to spend more time with Gabe. As well as with his daughter. For the most part, Jenna continued to do better in school, but Erica still saw so much pain in the little girl's eyes. They'd talked at her house a few times now—Hannah and Jenna came over for cookies occasionally before Gabe got home— yet Erica didn't feel she'd made any real headway with the hurt piled high inside the girl.

"Time's up," Maggie announced while Erica was still mired in thoughts of Gabe. "Back to work."

The three of them rose as one, and as Erica picked up her trash to dispose of it, a new post on her phone caught her attention. She lifted her hand back up slowly, and though telling herself not to do it, she clicked on the picture of her once best friend.

Silver Creek's JC Bird to marry longtime girlfriend next month.

Her stomach twisted in knots. He was getting married. Finally.

While at the same time, the asshole had tried to call her yet again the night before. He'd used his office phone since he could no longer get through with his cell.

What a jerk. Hot tears suddenly stung her eyes, and before her friends could see them, Erica made a quick excuse and dashed from the room. She disappeared into the storage area of her own classroom, and once there, leaned back against a set of shelves. She rolled her eyes to the ceiling.

Why the tears?

She shook her head. She wasn't sad. Not over this. She honestly didn't want JC back. She could finally say that with certainty.

But what had all the calling and the texting been about if he was just going to turn around and announce his engagement? Without realizing it had happened, Erica had let those calls make her wonder if maybe she *hadn't* been quite as boring as she'd always thought herself to be.

If maybe he *had* truly wanted her back.

Chapter Seventeen

U ncle Cord." Jenna and Cord sat in the leather recliner positioned with the best view of Gabe's sixty-five-inch TV. She'd curled into her uncle's lap the minute they'd gotten in from the football game, and Cord had been entertaining her ever since.

"Yes, Jenna?"

"Would you read me the sheep story again?"

Gabe looked up from his notes from that night's game to watch the interaction on the other side of the room.

"Sure I would, kiddo."

His brother dug through the small stack of books on the end table, finding the one Jenna had loved since she'd learned that kids could ride sheep in rodeos, while Jenna settled her head over her uncle's heart. Cord looked at her before opening the book, a rare hint of tenderness touching his features, and Gabe would swear there was something quite similar to longing mixed in with the tenderness, as well.

Within ten minutes of beginning to read, Jenna had fallen asleep. The three of them had gotten in from the game way past Jenna's bedtime, but given that Cord rarely showed up for visits in his hometown, Gabe had allowed his daughter to stay up.

With the steady sound of breathing now coming from Jenna, Cord lay the small paperback on the end table and shot Gabe a smug look. "Your kid likes me more every time I see her."

Gabe made a face. "What female doesn't?"

Erica hadn't been mistaken when she'd pointed out that Cord was the best looking one of them. At six two, his brother was the tallest, the most successful, and also the all-around hardest. It was that hardness that drew women like flies.

His brother returned his gaze to the sleeping Jenna, and Gabe teased, "You about ready to have kids of your own?"

"Not bloody likely."

"Then what's that I see going on over there?" Gabe motioned, not to Jenna, but to his brother's face. "You look like you could sit in my recliner cuddling my kid all night."

Cord's shoulders shrugged under his shirt. "Your kid is cuddly."

Gabe snorted. "Come around when she's in one of her moods. You'll change your tune then."

"She still struggling with everything?"

Gabe eyed his daughter. "She's better some days. Her teacher has helped a lot, but she certainly still has her moments." He thought about the call that had come in the weekend before, and about how the mention of her mother had Jenna clamming up until he'd talked her into a trip to the ice cream parlor Saturday evening. Then he overruled his default need to keep everything to himself, and shared the latest with his brother. "Michelle called."

His words had Cord's expression icing over. "What did she want?"

He didn't want to say it. He glanced out the window instead, where he could make out the darkened first floor of Erica's apartment. He should have talked to Erica about it. Asked if it had affected Jenna's behavior at school that week.

Instead, since no more calls had come in, he'd pushed it aside. Pretended it didn't matter.

"Claimed she wanted to see Jenna," he finally admitted. The sick feeling that had shown up with Michelle's words returned.

"What for?"

"I have no idea."

Jenna's eyelids suddenly fluttered, and Gabe held his breath, thinking they'd woken her, but she never did more than fidget. Once she'd settled back down, Gabe blew out a breath and looked back at his brother.

"I said no."

"That's good. Don't mess things up now."

"That was my theory."

"You did the right thing getting her away from that," Cord added. "She's going to get past this." He looked at Jenna once again, and his tone softened. "I've been worrying about her, but she's doing fine. She's getting what she needs here."

Though his brother had recently admitted to worrying over the situation, the admission still amazed Gabe. Cord rarely showed concern over anyone but one of his patients. Nor did he make a habit of doling out compliments.

Both things made Gabe uncomfortable enough that he pushed his notes aside, deciding they were finished talking about his past for the night. But he did have another topic they could discuss. He leaned forward in his seat. "Want to worry about someone else for a change?"

"Who?"

"Dad." He'd stopped by their dad's again that week, and though there'd been no more signs of Doc Hamm coming around, Gabe couldn't squelch the feeling that something was off. "I'm concerned that he's sick. Or maybe it's just the farm; it might be too much for him." Their dad had been forced to come out of retirement when Gabe moved to California. "But then again, he retired early to begin with. So it's not like he's *that* old."

They sat with only one floor lamp burning in the room, but Gabe could make out the concern crowding his brother's eyes.

"What makes you think there's a problem?" Cord asked. "He said anything?"

"No. And *that's* part of it. I've asked him a couple of times, but he claims all is fine."

"Then I don't understand."

Gabe stood to pace. "They left Nick's house early at the cookout this year—"

"So did Harper's parents," Cord pointed out.

"Yes, but"—he played with the blinds on the window, making sure to leave them open so he could see across the street. Then he turned back to Cord. "Did you notice that Gloria got the car for him when they went to leave? They'd parked at the community lot, and though it was only a block away, she made him wait at the house until she came back with the car. Then I caught Doc Hamm at the farm."

Cord moved as if to get up himself, before remembering he had a sleeping child in his arms. "What did Hamm say?"

"Like he'd tell me anything about dad's health. He said he was there for a checkup. Dad repeated it, claiming everything was fine, and Gloria echoed the sentiment. But I'm telling you, there's something going on."

Cord nodded, and Gabe could see the wheels turning.

"But then," Gabe continued. "Maybe I'm imagining things, or maybe it's Gloria who's the problem."

His brother's brows shot up. "How is Gloria a problem?"

"She hovers," Gabe tossed out.

"And this is somehow making Dad sick?'

WHe didn't even want to think it.

"There is no way that Gloria is like her." Cord followed Gabe's train of thought, and Gabe looked back at him. None of them liked calling their mother "Mom," because she'd never once been motherly.

"Something's going on," Gabe said again. "It's a gut feeling."

"Then I'll check on him before I leave."

Gabe nodded, comforted with the knowledge, then he once again faced the window. He looked for signs of life from the other house. Erica's bedroom light had been on when they'd first gotten home from the game, but other than that he'd seen nothing.

"You seeing her yet?" Cord spoke from behind him.

His entire family had each asked him that question within the last six weeks. He'd denied any involvement each time.

"I am," he said now. "As often as she'll let me."

"That's a change."

Gabe had once declared that if he ever got rid of his wife, he'd never have another. And granted, what he was doing with Erica didn't necessarily have to be heading toward a wifelike thing.

But at the same time, it didn't mean it couldn't.

"I'd forgotten how much I liked her," Gabe admitted. Erica had come home with him a few times during college, and she'd immediately fit in. Even Cord had latched onto her, for once treating her more as a sister than a conquest.

"And how does she feel about you?"

Gabe studied the dark night in thought. She hadn't actually said how she felt about him. They'd continued meeting every morning over the last week, but that's as far as it had gone. Jenna had been at the house every day, so it wasn't like he could sneak over to her place again, and neither one of them had suggested doing anything public such as going out to dinner.

It was nice, this little encapsulated world they'd built, but Gabe was ready for more. Her timeline of only two remaining weeks at the school meant her job search had picked up, and looming thoughts had begun to echo in Gabe's head. He wouldn't be ready for her to leave in two weeks.

"Beats the hell out of me," he finally answered. But he wanted to broach the topic.

He pulled his phone out and considered texting her. She could at least turn on her light and give him a smile.

But did he want to wake her up? He'd get to see her first thing in the morning.

"Go on over," Cord said. And when Gabe looked at him, he pointed a look at Jenna. "I'll keep an eye on this one. Stay all night if you want to."

Fire flared at the suggestion. All night wrapped around Erica? "I'd hate to . . ."

The words were bogus. He wouldn't hate to.

He studied his brother. Cord had never been one to want kids, but he'd always been loved by his nieces. "You don't mind?" he asked.

"It would be my pleasure. Erica's a good one."

Gabe nodded. She was. "You don't think she's like Michelle?"

How fucking needy could he be? Asking for validation from his younger brother.

But damn, what if he did the same thing again?

What if their dad had?

"She's a good one," Cord reiterated. "I thought so the first time I met her, and that was only confirmed at the cookout." He nudged his chin toward the door. "Go on. I've got this."

"I'll have my phone on." Gabe moved to his daughter's side and kissed her cheek, then looked at Cord. "Call if she needs me. For anything."

Then he left his house and grabbed a handful of pebbles. The instant the light came on inside Erica's bedroom, he felt a heaviness lift from his heart. He was going to fall in love with this woman. And he might just enjoy the journey.

Erica raised her window.

"Cord is at my house." He didn't wait for her to speak. "Tell me I can stay the night."

Her smile matched the one in his heart. "You can stay the night."

Erica slid her hand across the mattress and then groaned when she found nothing but an empty sheet.

"I'm right here." Gabe's voice came from the opposite side of the room. She rolled to her back and cracked open her eyes. He had jeans on and was buttoning his shirt.

She groaned again. "You have to go already?"

"Afraid so."

"But the sun's not even up yet." She knew she was whining, but she'd really liked having Gabe in her bed last night.

He crossed the room, picking up his socks on the way, and sat beside her. "Cord has to get going right after breakfast, and Jenna and I promised to take him out for pancakes."

She made a face and let her eyes fall closed again. "You really should learn to cook pancakes," she grumbled. "Then you could stay longer. It's not like they're hard to make."

He chuckled and leaned down, grazing his lips on the spot just below her ear. His touch lit goose bumps down her body, and she reached out a hand, resting her fingers against his hip. "But Jenna loves telling people that I can't make them," he whispered.

She peeked up at him. "*Can* you make them?"

He waggled his brows. "One of the few things I make well, actually." He shrugged and tossed her words back at her. "Because it's not like they're hard to make."

She frowned at him. "You're weird."

"I know." He kissed her eyelids. "But you like weird, right?"

"I do, actually." She curled to her side and watched as he stooped to pull on a sock, and fought the urge to brush his hair back off his forehead. She did let herself trail a finger along the seam at the side of his jeans, though. It was a nice compromise.

She'd been pleased to see him the night before, and neither of them had taken the time for idle chitchat, but in the predawn morning light, questions came to mind. And they didn't all have to do with whether he'd enjoyed the night before as much as she had. He'd only been able to spend the night with her because Cord had been there, and she very much suspected his brother hadn't driven half a day *solely* to act as an overnight babysitter.

"Cord came for the game?"

Gabe glanced at her. "Yeah. And since I have an extra room, he spent the night."

"Why'd he come?"

He furrowed his brow. "What kind of question is that? He came for the game."

"To help you?" She'd listened to it on the radio. The announcers were now saying Birch Bay had a real chance to make the state playoffs, and though she had faith in Gabe, she also knew that Cord had a lot more experience playing. So when Gabe didn't answer her question, she persisted. "Are you worried you're not a good enough coach, Gabe?"

"Why would you say that?" His tone was too casual, and he didn't look up as he pulled on his other sock.

"Is that why your brother keeps showing up?"

"It's only two games, Erica."

"Yet I got the impression when he and I talked that he rarely comes home. And now, twice in one month—plus driving three hours for the other game."

Gabe let the words hang between them for only a second, then in a quick move he had her pinned on her back, her arms above her head. "What's the deal with you and my brother, anyway?" he growled with a smile. "Something I should be worried about?" She heard the teasing in his voice, so she went along with it. For the moment.

But she very much intended to bring them back to the subject at hand.

She wiggled underneath him as if attempting to escape, laughing as they battled for control, but when his fighting turned dirty by dipping his mouth and tugging the sheet down over her chest, her movements stopped. Her breaths deepened as his gaze burned on her naked breasts, then his tongue flicked over a nipple before he blew softly over the spot he'd just wet. She moaned, that quickly going from zero to needy. However, she doubted he planned to take his pants back off. Therefore, she forced herself to continue their game.

"Why would you be worried about me and your brother?" she asked throatily. She bit her lip, and shot him her most over-the-top, sexy look. "Did he say something about me? Because I could say *plenty* about him."

Gabe laughed at her seductress voice, his shoulders shaking with the sound as he held himself above her. Then he leaned down and pressed quick kisses to both of her nipples, before pushing himself up and going in search of his shoes.

"He didn't say anything that I'm about to repeat to you, I'll tell you that"—Gabe talked from his position on the floor as he reached under her bed—"but I will say that he likes you." He popped up on his knees and narrowed his eyes at her. "But don't even *think* about trying to entice him to run off with you. He knows you're mine."

"Little ol' me?" She gave him her most innocent batting of her eyes. "Why, I'd never do such a thing as that." Then she smiled like the devil. "Even if he is cuter."

Gabe dropped back to the mattress, hitting the surface hard enough to make her bounce. "Don't have to rub it in, smart-ass. I know he's . . . *cuter*." He said the last word with disgust. "I've been aware of that my whole life." He rubbed a thumb over her bottom lip, fondness beginning to fill his eyes. "But I also know you wouldn't run off with him."

She smiled at him, ready to drop the charade and admit he knew her well, but the smile fell away when he added, "Mostly because *he* wouldn't have *you*."

"Why *wouldn't* he have me?" she yelped.

Gabe captured her lips with his, his hand kneading her breast at the same time, and the kiss lasted long enough that she almost forgot what they'd been teasing each other about. But when he pulled away, she caught the flicker of seriousness in his eyes. "Because he respects *me* too much."

She nodded, her teasing gone. "I can grant him that one. You deserve respect. But I'm just saying that if I wanted him . . ." She lifted her brow, and Gabe laughed again.

"Tell you what," he said, "let me share with him the magic you're capable of with that smart mouth of yours, and trust me, his respect for me would be thrown out the window." His eyes heated. "He'd be beating down your door."

"Like that's what I want." Her voice grew heavy at the reminder of the things she'd done with her mouth the night before. "Another man looking only to get laid."

Gabe went quiet, studying her as if seeing a side to her he had yet to discover, and she realized that her words could be taken as if she were reading more into *them* than just two people getting laid.

Which she was.

"If I don't prove myself capable by winning state," he said, returning to her original question, "then this will likely be the only opportunity I get to do so. So yeah, I'm worried I'm not good enough."

She nodded. Understanding the importance. "And Jenna?"

"What about Jenna?"

Erica had always been good at reading people, so she tossed out her theory. "Are you worried that if you don't win that Jenna won't think you're good enough, either?"

It took a few seconds for him to answer. "I want to make my daughter proud."

"I think she already is."

"Maybe," he acknowledged. "But I'd rather not risk it."

He took her hand in his then, and as first light began inching its way through her bedroom window, the lines of Gabe's face grew taut. "I don't want to risk you, either." He kissed the backs of her fingers. "I want to tell my family about us, Erica. Tell them we're dating."

Nerves now held her on the bed instead of Gabe's bodyweight. "*Is* that what we're doing? You're not even divorced yet."

"You know that isn't a factor."

"But . . ." She swallowed. "There's Jenna to think about."

"I've thought about her." He squeezed her fingers. "I want her to know, too. This is serious for me, Erica. I don't want to hide that from my daughter. You and I are together, and I want to shout it to the world."

"But you could change your mind," she whispered. Fear engulfed her, while at the same time, she wanted to grasp the golden ring and hang on. Gabe was a good guy. She knew that. She'd always known that.

But he was also slightly unavailable.

"You've been married to her for a long time." Her voice shook. The idea of him going back to his wife wasn't unheard of. It happened for some people.

"And I've been over her for a long time." He braced a hand on the other side of her and leaned in so she couldn't miss his intensity. "Let's do this, E. Let's give us a chance."

She wanted to do just that. "My contract"—she licked her lips— "it's up in two weeks."

"And I know they'd love to have you stay on, wherever they can use you." His eyes turned even more serious. "I get that's not what you want forever, but could you consider it for now? For us?"

She stared into his eyes. She hadn't realized he'd been thinking about this. "Nobody else has offered me a job yet."

"Then say yes."

"But . . ."

"Say yes for the length of the semester," he suggested. "Say yes, and give *us* a try until the end of the year. Can you agree to that much?" His eyes connected with hers, and she could see the anticipation in them. She felt it, too.

"And what happens after the end of the semester?" she whispered.

The gentle way the corners of his mouth lifted had her holding her breath. "Hopefully *everything.*"

He kissed her then, and she felt his desire for them to be more by the way he cherished her with his touch. She had that same desire.

She sucked in a quick breath when they pulled apart, and mentally crossed her fingers. "Let's try it out with Jenna first." The whole idea terrified her. She hadn't come to Birch Bay for this. But at the same time, *this* could be the best thing to ever happen to her. "You and Jenna come over for lunch tomorrow. And if that goes well . . ."

"It'll go well."

"I hope so." She cupped his cheek, her own smile now as tender as his. "Do you like sushi? I took a class this week." She'd replaced the violin lessons with that. Musical talent had proven not to be her strong suit. "I'd love to try out what I learned. I could fix something else for Jenna if you don't think she'd eat it."

"We love sushi. Both of us. One good thing California gave us."

She let out a breath. "Then come prepared to eat."

When he rose and headed for the stairs, she dropped back to the bed, aware that her smile was dreamy. But she didn't care. He made her dreamy.

He made her hope.

Before disappearing from sight, he looked back, and a curious expression crossed his face. "Any chance you've still got that cheerleading outfit lying around?"

She should have known. "And if I do?"

"Then we could put a wager on how Jenna will take us being together. If she loves the idea"—he boldly stroked his gaze over her body—"then you have to put it on for me."

"And if she hates it?"

He grinned in the wicked way that only men could competently pull off. "Then you still put it on, but *I* get to take it off of you."

Chapter Eighteen

Gabe lifted his hand to Erica's door at exactly noon, the hour she'd told him and Jenna to be there, and tried his best to contain his excitement. He hadn't talked with Jenna about Erica yet—the two of them had agreed to do it together after they ate. But Jenna was as excited as he to be there.

Erica pulled the door open, and Jenna immediately thrust out the slender box. "This is for you."

"A present?" She took the package, eyeing the red-and-gold paper topped with a fat gold bow, then wrinkled her nose down at Jenna. "I'm almost positive it's not my birthday. How about you?" She stepped back and let the two of them in. "Is it your birthday, Jenna?"

His daughter giggled. "No. I had my birthday already. It was in August."

"Hmmm." She slid a look at Gabe. "Is it your daddy's birthday?"

"No!" Jenna laughed again. "It's not a birthday present. It's just a present." She glanced up at him, before returning her gaze to Erica. "It's a present just because." She repeated his earlier words. Then she bit her bottom lip in anticipation, the corners of her mouth lifting at the same time. The outcome was a look more tender than any Gabe had seen on his child's face in a very long time.

"Well, thank you for my present." Erica bowed her head at Jenna, and when she lifted it, her smile snagged Gabe. "It's always exciting to get presents just because."

Jenna immediately climbed onto one of the barstools and leaned her elbows on the counter. "Will you open it now?"

"Absolutely."

While Erica dug into the package of personalized chopsticks Gabe had sought out and purchased for her the day before, he made his way to the other side of the room. He'd been in Erica's place twice since their first kiss—both times with nothing more than sex on his mind—but each time he'd noticed more indicators of her personal touch dotted throughout the place. Candles lined up down the middle of the dining room table, a bright scarf thrown over a lamp. The scarf cast a muted glow in a little space in the back of the room. A space that if he were to guess, he'd say she'd turned into a reading nook.

But the significant change was the large paneled mirror now hanging in the exact spot they'd first kissed. It created a windowpane effect on the brick wall, only looking *into* the room instead of outside of it, and was lined up perfectly with the fireman's pole. As he traced his gaze between the two objects, he was suddenly eager to make love to her up against the pole for a second time. Just to watch.

"Pretty, isn't it?"

He had to rein in his desire.

Glancing over his shoulder, he found Erica now standing within inches of him while Jenna remained in the kitchen, carefully pouring sauces into dipping bowls. Shimmery little lights had been turned on in the dining area. They covered the walls and the space overhead, and provided a backdrop that glowed behind his daughter.

"Very," he told her. "I like where you put it. I like the touches of yourself you've added to the place."

Her eyes went to the mirror before tracking directly to the pole, and a sly smile flitted across her lips, but she didn't comment on the mirror's location. Instead, she picked up a frame that held a picture of her family and turned it to face him. "How about this for touches of myself? Bree sent it. She made it for me."

The frame was small, but it wasn't about the picture inside it so much as the frame, itself. It was a piece of art. Instead of merely wood or metal, it was made up of a mixture of items that could be found around any house. A button, the tip of a blue crayon, a broken piece of a shade. There were so many random objects outlining the photo of her family that he could spend hours discovering them all. It should be gaudy, but it was exquisite in its delicacy.

He looked back at Erica. "Your sister is talented."

"Yes, she is." She put the picture back on the end table. "And some-day, someone is going to recognize that." Vulnerability shone bright, and her words turned wistful. "Then my little sister may forget to *ever* find her way home again."

"There's no chance she won't come back to see you."

Her eyes flicked to his. "You think?"

"Absolutely. You're both too much alike."

"Right." She motioned to the frame. "The woman who made that has pink hair and is a world traveler." She looked at him. "I've barely ever left the state of Montana, and my hair color is the same bland brown I was born with."

"I love your hair," Jenna spoke up from the kitchen.

Gabe winked at Erica.

"But it's not as pretty as Merida's," Jenna added in the cute but blunt way children used. When Gabe and Erica both turned to her, she looked up from her task, unrepentant in her opinion. She shrugged her shoulders. "Sorry."

"You know what? I like her hair better, too," Erica agreed.

Gabe simply marveled at the change in his daughter.

"The dips are ready," Jenna announced, and Erica motioned for him to go ahead of her. Since it was her place, he did as requested. Only, as he slipped by, he moved in close enough that the backs of his fingers brushed across the backs of Erica's. When hers fluttered against his in return, his confidence in the outcome of the day soared. Jenna would be okay with the two of them being together. She had to be.

"This looks amazing," he announced when he reached the kitchen. "How can I help?"

"We need to take all the dips to the table," Jenna informed him before preceding to show him what bowls went beside which plate.

Erica followed with two platters of sushi rolls, and Gabe's mouth instantly watered.

"Wow," he muttered. "That must have been some class."

"It was, actually. So good that I signed up for another this morning." She broke eye contact as she added, "It's not until next month, though."

At her words, he almost leaned over and kissed her on the mouth. Erica's contract would be up by next month. She'd just said that she really did plan to stay.

The three of them took their seats—Erica across from Gabe, and Jenna on the end between them—and Gabe found himself truly enjoying a meal with his daughter. It had been too long since that had happened. She laughed, was personable, and darned if she didn't seem to bubble over with happiness. Erica was so good for her that he couldn't help but believe that he and Erica being together would only continue to improve things.

As the meal wound down and Jenna and Erica talked softly between themselves, discussing the ingredients used in each type of roll, Gabe let himself relax back into his seat and soak in the moment. He wouldn't trade this for anything.

"And what about this one?" Erica asked. She used her new chopsticks to dip a roll into one of the sauces she'd made, and held it out for Jenna. "Do you like this ginger sauce that *I* made better"—she narrowed her gaze, teasing with her eyes—"or the tempura sauce I bought from the store?"

Jenna snickered as she attempted to pull a serious face. She ate the sushi, dipping it into each sauce, one at a time, then stated her decision matter-of-factly. "I like the store-bought one the best."

His daughter howled with laughter at the mock outrage on Erica's face before admitting that she was joking. "I like yours the best, Ms. Bird. It's a hundred times better." She grew quiet for a moment as she picked at a few pieces of rice that had spilled onto her plate, then she tilted her head and stared up at Erica. "Did you know that my momma taught me to like sushi rolls? And she also likes ginger sauce."

Gabe tried not to tense, but his relaxed state immediately dissipated. Jenna had brought her mother into the conversation several times over the last week.

"And when did she teach you to like sushi?" Erica asked.

"When we lived in California. Momma loved going to Japanese restaurants, and they had a lot of them, so we went all the time. We had so much fun."

"Did you have a favorite type of sushi roll? Maybe I can make it for you next time."

"I liked two of them the best. The same ones as my momma. We liked the—"

"Can we talk about something else?" Gabe bit out.

Both females whipped their heads around at his outburst, but he didn't back down. Jenna's growing need to paint Michelle in a happy light wasn't healthy. "Surely there's some other topic—"

"You *never* let me talk about her," Jenna suddenly shouted.

"Jenna."

"And you won't let me see her, either! And I know she wanted to. I heard you tell Uncle Cord."

214

Dismay settled in his gut. She'd heard that? The look in Erica's eyes let him know what she currently thought of him, too.

"Maybe we should go." He pushed back from the table, but Erica shot a finger out toward him.

"Stay," she gritted out. Then she leaned toward his daughter, and somehow, her demeanor flipped. She motioned to the other side of the room, an easy smile on her face. "Did you know that pole over there comes out upstairs in my bedroom?" she said to Jenna. "And that you can actually slide down it?"

Jenna turned to take in the pole, and without waiting to see if she'd ask, Erica added, "Would you like to try it out?"

Instead of agreeing, Jenna looked back at him. The anger in her eyes had turned to full-fledged hatred, and he found himself at a loss as to what to say next. What could he possibly say? His carelessness had set them back months. He should never have said anything to Cord.

"I'd like to talk to your dad for a minute, Jenna. Could you please play while we do that?"

Gabe watched as Jenna finally got up from her seat. She didn't so much as glance his way as she headed for the stairs, and the second her feet sounded overhead, he forced himself to turn back to the other side of the table. Erica had not lost her disgust with him.

"You don't understand," he said.

"Then explain it to me."

Where did he even begin? "Her mother cares about no one but herself. She never has."

Jenna slipped down the pole, and without asking, headed back up the stairs.

Gabe returned his attention to Erica and lowered his voice. "Especially not Jenna."

"And why is that?"

He shook his head. "Because that's who she is. There is no 'why,' she just *is*."

"Yet surely she loves her daughter. And clearly she wants to *see* her daughter."

Jenna came spiraling down the pole again, this time with a hint more animation, and Gabe bit down on the inside of his cheek until she left the room, then he leaned over the table. "Let this one go, Erica. It's out of your jurisdiction."

Erica stuck out her chin, the action almost identical to one of his daughter's favorite moves. "My *jurisdiction* is not only all the kids in my class, but the child of the man I'm *supposedly* dating," she hissed. "And I'm not about to apologize for worrying about your daughter's well-being. Why isn't she seeing her mother? Why isn't she talking to her? Why has it been *months* since she's seen her?"

He sat back at the last question. Clearly, Erica had been talking to someone other than him.

"Jenna tell you that?" he asked. "Or was it my brother?" And then he got it. *"Dani."*

His sister talked to Jenna a lot. It wouldn't surprise him to find out that she'd been using those conversations to mine for information.

"Leave your sister out of this. She's as worried about Jenna as I am."

"Yet neither of you need to bother."

"Why hasn't Jenna talked to her mother in months?" she asked again.

"Why hasn't her mother talked to *her*?" he shot back. "I never told her not to call."

Some of the steam seemed to leave her. "Does that mean you *did* tell her not to see her?"

Exasperation rose when he saw that she didn't plan to back down on this, and he shoved back his chair. *"Outside."*

Erica followed, waiting to join him on the porch until Jenna had slid down another time. He could hear her inside, explaining that she and he needed to have a grown-up conversation, and that Jenna was welcome to keep sliding all she wanted.

Then she stepped outside, softly closed the door, and looked down her nose at him.

"Do not judge me," he said. "You don't know anything about what Jenna's life was like before."

"Well, I would if you'd tell me." She drew in a breath, making an obvious effort to get herself under control. "I may not have all the details, but I know something about what that child is going through, Gabe. She's hurting. Surely you can see that. She's improving, yes, but her issues are still there. She feels rejected, she's alone. She has to be wondering if her mother doesn't love her anymore. And I'd venture a guess that she's blaming herself for all of it."

He swallowed.

"What happened? Why would you make her mother stay away?"

"Michelle was never a good mother to begin with, I told you that."

"Yes, and that's all you've told me. Not a good mother. Not a good wife. She walked all over you." She repeated the words he'd once said to her. "Are you sure your issue with Michelle isn't more about you and your hurt feelings than about protecting your daughter?"

Fury rolled through him.

"Given the fact that I've never known you to be an unreasonable man," she continued before he could get in another word, "I suspect there's more to the story. But what I can't figure out is what. How can any mother possibly be that bad?"

"Be glad you *don't* understand how a mother can be that bad." His words were menacing, but he didn't try to temper them. Instead, he let his frustration mount. "Go back to Dani and ask for details about growing up a child of a narcissistic mother, why don't you? About how your own flesh and blood will manipulate you any and every time an ounce of attention might be placed on you instead of on her. About how she'll pit you against your siblings, ensuring that she's the center of your world—while at the same time, the center of your world is sucking the very life out of you. Talk to her," he roared. "Then you might start to get a clue. It's not pretty. Not every mother gives a shit about her kids, and that's just the facts. My mother hated all of us. And trust me when I say it can have lifelong effects on a person. So no." He shook his head, his rage in full steam. "I will not have that happening to my daughter. Not on my watch. And I won't apologize for it, either."

A bit of Erica's anger had evaporated as his increased, and she looked from him to her front door then back to him. "Narcissistic?" she asked. "Michelle is, too?"

"At least she isn't as bad as my mother. I'll give her that much."

"Okay." Erica nodded, and Gabe could see the wheels turning in her head, still trying to "fix" the situation. Still determined it could be made right. "It was a bad environment for Jenna to live in. I get that. But that still doesn't mean she shouldn't see her mother on occasion. How did you get a judge to grant that?" She pulled in a sharp breath before adding, "Or are you simply ignoring court orders?"

Gabe stared in through the wide window framing Erica's living room, wondering how the afternoon had gone downhill so quickly. This was not the conversation he'd wanted to have. He *never* wanted to talk about his marriage. How he'd stood around for years ignoring the fact that being around Michelle was damaging his daughter. How he'd almost let that go too far.

But when he brought his gaze back to Erica's, he recognized that if he wanted *them* to go beyond this moment, then it was a conversation he had to have.

He muttered a curse, and called upon a patience he wasn't sure he'd ever had.

"I brought up divorce late last summer," he started slowly. "Right before school started. We'd been fighting, all three of us were tense every minute of the day. I was tired of it. Jenna hid in her room most days, her mother had nothing to do with her, or if she did, more times than not it left her in tears. Divorce seemed like the path we needed to take. Only, Michelle convinced me otherwise."

He dragged a hand down over his face at his gullibility.

"She spent the next few months showing how she could change. It wasn't perfect, but I could see her trying. We started doing more things together—like going out for sushi every week. And she started paying more attention to Jenna." He stared at the sky so he wouldn't have to see her when he admitted the real kicker. "She even convinced me to try for another baby."

He still couldn't believe he'd fallen for that one, but thank goodness it hadn't happened.

"Then Christmas came." He looked back at Erica. "Everything had been going great for months, but Michelle didn't want to come to Montana with us. She wanted to go see her mom. Or so she said. But she promised Jenna they'd do something special when we returned. Just the two of them. Only . . ."

Only, his wife was a selfish, self-centered bitch.

He sighed, his own anger beginning to lift, and finished in a monotone. "When we got home after the holidays, Michelle was gone. No good-bye to Jenna, no note, no call. Just gone. Her clothes, her jewelry. She'd moved out."

"Why?"

"Because she could." His ex's irrationality had never made sense to him, but if she could hurt either him or Jenna, then Michelle seemed to do it. "She doesn't care, Erica. I'm not making that up. She thinks of no one but herself. I found out that she'd spent the holidays and the week after on her boyfriend's new yacht, and I did what I should have done years ago. I filed for divorce."

He could see that she was starting to get the gist of his ex-wife.

She wet her lips. "So Michelle just disappeared? She gave you custody? No visitation?"

"Oh, no. Things are never that simple with my wife. Michelle came back from her trip bearing gifts for Jenna—mad, I might add, when she found out that I'd filed and she no longer had a place to live—and promptly turned back into the doting mother."

"So Jenna *did* go to see her?"

"Until late February. That's when I found out that one of the teens in the apartment building where Michelle had rented was doing most of the *visiting* with my daughter. Typically, Michelle stayed gone until late in the night, leaving Jenna in the care of a fourteen-year-old. Only, this time, Michelle didn't return, and the teen went home."

"What?"

He nodded. "Midnight came, and it was time for her to be home. Jenna was in bed, so she didn't see the harm."

"Your daughter was left in the apartment all alone?"

"At six years old, yes."

"What happened?"

"She woke up sometime during the night, and when she couldn't find anyone else there she called me."

"But she was okay?"

"Scared, but yes. She was fine. She's been able to fend for herself for a long time."

He saw the additional questions at the statement, but he didn't go into the fact that he'd once been a bad parent, too. Not bad in the way that Michelle was, but bad in that he'd sat back and let his sister see to his kid more than he had. Dani had lived at the farm with them before he and Michelle had moved away. She'd come home from college years earlier when their mother had died, and had stuck around to finish raising their brothers. So when Jenna had come along, it had been easier to let Dani do her thing than to be in the house and around Michelle every day. He'd spent his days on the farm or out running errands. Exactly as his dad had once done.

"Why hadn't Michelle come back that night?"

He could see Erica's chest rising and falling with her breaths. "That's the million-dollar question, isn't it? Or more like, the million-dollar *ring*."

Confusion darted through her eyes before she got it. "The boyfriend?"

"Right in one. They'd gotten engaged that evening, and she simply *couldn't* run home and leave him after that."

"I didn't realize she'd cheated on you, too." Her words came out strangely calm.

"Neither did I until I got home from Christmas, but that was the least of my concerns, wouldn't you say? In fact, I wouldn't be surprised to find out that he wasn't her first." The sad thing was, discovering his wife had cheated had barely fazed him at that point. They'd not only had a bad marriage for years, but since the day he'd announced he was returning to school, she'd made fun of him for his new career choice. It wasn't high-class enough for her. "I stayed until she returned the next morning, and then we had a real argument."

"Did it scare Jenna?"

"It scared everyone. Someone across the hall ended up calling the police, and the minute they knocked on the door, Michelle tried out a new routine. That of scared ex-wife."

Horror crossed her face. "She said you'd hit her?"

"She claimed utter terror that I would—since she could produce no physical proof that I *had*."

"But you told them what you were arguing about? That she'd left Jenna there alone?"

Humiliation burned through him as he shook his head. "No." He tried not to picture that day in his head, but the images wouldn't go away. "They had cuffs slapped on me before I could begin to tell my side of the story. Jenna was curled up in the corner, crying her eyes out at that point, and Michelle went over and huddled on the floor with her. I looked guilty as sin."

"So they took you to jail?"

He leaned back against the pillar of her porch, ready to get the story over with. "They took me to the police car outside, but before they could pull away, Michelle came out. I have no idea what she said to them, but knowing her and how she hates to cause a public scene, she didn't want it getting out that I'd been hauled to the police station. The next thing I know, I'm uncuffed and out of the car. Michelle is smiling as if she's Mother Teresa and just done the world a favor, and once again, my daughter is upstairs, left alone in the apartment.

"I got Jenna," he continued. "And I swore to Michelle that if she ever so much as tried to see our daughter again, I'd go to the judge and claim abandonment. And as I said, she doesn't like public scenes."

"So she just disappeared?"

"She just disappeared." He watched Jenna through the window. She'd quit sliding, and had sat on the couch. She picked up a magazine lying open on one of the cushions, but didn't look at it. She just sat there. "After I calmed down, I had my lawyer let Michelle know that I'd be open to her talking to Jenna on the phone. I even offered supervised visitation." He looked back at Erica. "I'm not evil. It would have been better to wean Jenna off her mother more slowly before we moved away. But at the same time, I'm not sorry for the way it happened. Michelle plays mental games, and Jenna doesn't need that in her life."

"Gabe." The word was little more than a whisper, and he could tell she wanted to reach out to him. But he stood his ground.

"Don't feel sorry for me, Erica. I chose her, remember? I dumped you for her."

"You were a stupid kid."

He chuckled dryly. "I was a stupid adult."

"Maybe so, but I'm still sorry."

They both looked at Jenna again. "Have you talked to her about it?" she asked. "About her mom at all?"

Gabe shook his head. She'd lived it. He saw no need to keep rehashing it.

"What about . . ." Erica paused, and from the look in her eyes, he could already guess that he wouldn't like how her question would end.

"Have you ever considered letting *Jenna* make the decision to see her mother or not? I mean, if Michelle is calling again."

Anger swelled once again. "Did you not hear what I just told you? Michelle can't be trusted to care for our daughter. So no, I have *not* considered giving Jenna any say in the matter. I handled it. I'm still handling it. And I wouldn't change anything about how it happened."

"But does making one mistake mean Jenna can't even talk with her? It's her mother, Gabe. You could take Jenna for visits? A girl needs—"

"One mistake?" His words came out deadly calm. "You're not hearing what I've been telling you. Michelle's mistakes started years ago. This wasn't *one mistake*. And even if it had been, she made her decision when she first left without a word. You don't know what you're talking about with this one, Erica. I've already told you that. You might be a great teacher, but you're out of your element with this one."

"But Jenna didn't get to make any decisions for herself," Erica argued back. "She had no say in anything. You moved her back here, turned her world upside down, and now she's trying to figure out where she fits in. Don't you get how shattering that can be?"

"She is not you."

Shock had her taking a step back. "I never said she was."

"Yet you're seeing parallels all over the place. Only, the difference is that you merely pretended to be fine after your ex ripped your world apart, whereas my daughter *is* fine. Or she will be."

She pulled in several breaths until he heard them even out. "Jenna needs to deal with reality, Gabe. You can't make up for all the bad things in her life by buying her candy or taking her to her favorite restaurants. You can't shield her from it, either. Let her call her mother, at least. She needs to be able to process this change in her own way."

"She needs to forget certain things ever happened," he snapped out.

"Forget her mother exists?" She didn't back down. "Have you forgotten yours?"

He glared at her. The lady knew how to hit below the belt. There was no forgetting the woman who'd raised him. "Back off this one, Erica. Jenna's mother doesn't really want to talk to her, no matter what she recently claimed. She's up to something. I promise you that. Michelle doesn't care about Jenna—about anyone—unless there's some benefit in it for her."

She crossed her arms over her chest. "Then let your daughter figure that out on her own."

"My daughter is only seven. It's my job to protect her from such things."

He reached for the doorknob, disgust filling him to the point that he needed to be away from her. *Now.* Thank goodness they hadn't brought up the idea to Jenna of them being together. He couldn't have someone in his daughter's life who couldn't see straight enough to keep from hurting her.

He yanked open the door. "Time to go, Jenna."

"I think you're making a mistake," Erica said quietly behind him.

"And I'm telling you that I'm not."

Erica stood at the window in her bedroom looking out over the front of her house. Gabe had been gone for several hours. He and Jenna had climbed into his truck after they'd left her place, and she hadn't seen anything from them since. She'd spent the time replaying their fight in her head, unable to fathom the kind of mother he'd talked about. It was a known fact that such people existed. But thankfully, she hadn't had direct dealings with anyone like that in her personal life.

Yet Gabe had spent his childhood with a mother who couldn't be pleased. Dani had, too.

As had all of the Wilde children.

She would have never guessed that when she'd known them before. Anytime she'd visited, they'd all seemed well adjusted. Sure, they'd each had their quirks, some with more anger than others, some getting in trouble here and there. But the other boys had all been teenagers at the time. Teens ran synonymous with issues. Yet hearing Gabe's story, she now wondered about her ability to read people. As well as her capability to understand them.

She still thought she was right about Jenna. That's why she hadn't backed down. Someone needed to have that child's back.

But could she really understand what Jenna was going through?

Jenna's mother was a narcissist. Which, by definition, meant that Jenna came low on her mother's priority list. But still . . . she was her mother. Didn't that count for something? Even Dani had stated how difficult it was to have your mother suddenly not there.

She leaned her forehead against the window as she continued to let the questions churn, but in the end, she maintained belief that Jenna needed the chance to be around her mother. If only to figure out on her own that *not* being around her was a better plan. She needed to *not* be silenced.

Walking away from the window, Erica grabbed her phone and paced to the other side of the room. She was tired of looking out at the empty house and wondering what all of it meant. There was Jenna and her issues, Michelle and hers, and then there was Gabe and *her*. Had her refusal to back down during their argument sealed the deal on any possible future for them?

Even if it had, she'd do it again if she had to. For Jenna.

She settled in at the floor where the pole came up through it, dropping her legs over the edge to dangle from the ceiling below, then leaned forward and put a shoulder against the metal. She'd likely overstepped her bounds again, but she wasn't yet ready for her and Gabe to end.

Scrolling through her contacts, she paused over Maggie's name, but in the end, Erica wasn't sure she was ready to share this part of her life with her new friend. She and Gabe were still new themselves. Possibly they were over. So it was best to keep it to herself.

Yet, she needed to talk to someone.

Locating Bree's number, Erica punched the FaceTime button before she changed her mind. On the third ring, her sister answered, her face flushed.

"What are you doing?" Erica asked.

"Jogging." Bree bent over at the waist, and Erica saw a view of her red face against a blue sky backdrop.

"I didn't know you ever exercised."

Bree had one of those metabolisms that people would pay their life's savings for. "I don't," her sister confirmed. "I met this guy today, and he suggested we meet up for jogging before going to breakfast in the morning. I needed to see if I could do it before I agreed."

"And are you going to agree?"

She shook her head, finally beginning to catch her breath. "No man is worth this. I'll just stay home and have ice cream for breakfast instead."

That sounded about right. "You still in Mexico?"

"Drove back over the border two days ago. I got some great inspiration while down there, though. I'm in Texas now, but I probably won't stay for too long." She straightened. "So what's up with you? Still knocking boots with your neighbor? Need me to send condoms?"

Erica gave her a wan smile. "Condom levels are good, but thanks."

Though she'd called to talk about the situation with Gabe, she now found herself reluctant to bring it up. Maybe it would be enough to simply spend time talking to her sister.

"How about the other box I sent?" Bree asked. "Get any thanks from him? I did mention that I signed your name to it, didn't I?"

Erica's face fell. "You didn't?"

The last thing she needed was JC thinking she'd sent him the box of condoms.

"Bree," she warned. She should have never sent her sister that picture.

Bree rolled her eyes. "Geez. Quit stressing. I'm kidding. I sent it anonymously, though he totally deserved to know it came from you." The look in her eyes changed then, and concern masked her face. "Did you hear?"

"That he's getting married?" Erica nodded. "I saw it on Facebook."

"You're okay, right?"

Erica allowed herself a moment to think about her answer before giving it, and in that moment, she was pleased to find out that yes, she was okay. Completely. "I'm good. It's time he finally married her."

"Then what's with the sad face?"

She looked away from the phone, her gaze once again landing on the window, and beyond it to the other house. Her heart was breaking inside her chest. "I had a fight with Gabe," she squeezed out.

"Ah. I'm sorry."

Erica brought her gaze back.

"Want me to send him something, too? Something for erectile dysfunction, maybe?"

She shook her head, letting out a sad chuckle as she did. "I love that you've always got my back, you know? You make being a big sister easy."

"Oh, man. You're not going to get all sappy on me, are you?" Bree tried to pull off sarcasm, but Erica didn't miss the worry in her eyes.

"I won't get sappy." She looked at his house again. "I'm just sad. I really like him."

"Want to tell me about the argument?"

"No. I just"—she shrugged—"I don't know. I just wanted to call."

"I get it. And if I weren't at the very bottom of the country right now, I'd come over and let you *not* talk about it in person."

She gave her sister a small smile. "Thank you."

"Was it bad, though? Can I at least ask that much?"

"I think it might have been."

Bree went quiet for a moment as she stared at Erica, and the directness of her gaze seemed to shake something loose. There was really no need to sit around moping, because they'd never even officially been dating. It was what it was, she supposed. And that was likely a couple of good rolls in the hay and nothing else.

At least it had helped her see the light with JC.

"Don't worry about it," she told her sister. "I shouldn't have even bothered you. I've only got two more weeks that I have to be here, so if things don't improve by then—" She clipped off her words because her voice had begun to shake.

"Come see me," Bree said.

"What?" Erica shook her head. "It's Sunday afternoon. I can't come see you. I have school tomorrow."

"I mean in two weeks. If things don't improve."

Erica stared at the screen, at the complete love and compassion on her baby sister's face. This girl might have the biggest case of wanderlust Erica had ever seen, but she also had the largest heart.

Could she just go to Texas, though? She'd love to hang out with her sister for a while. Maybe she could even catch a flight to North Carolina before coming back home, as well. Have dinner with Annalise.

The reality, though, was that she *should* be working. And if she and Gabe didn't work out, she should probably go home. The idea of returning to her parents' house, however, had zero appeal. If she ended up going back to Silver Creek, she would at least find her own place to rent.

"What would we do?" she asked, not yet willing to give up the idea.

"We'd see the country. A road trip. And we'll do it right. We'll take at least a month."

"A month?" Erica was shaking her head before she'd even realized she'd moved. "I can't be gone for a month, Bree. You know that." Hopefully her dad's contacts would come through with something before then.

"You can *do* anything you want to."

"I know that," she defended. But she couldn't do a month. Her parents really wouldn't understand her then. Quitting her job was one thing, but roaming the country for a month?

There *was* a certain appeal to the idea, though.

She nibbled at the corner of her mouth as she pictured the tourist sights she could see. Something more than the national parks she'd once visited with her parents. But the appeal of just going where the wind took her quickly disappeared. She was no Bree. Plus, she wasn't quite ready to give up on the potential of what she was building here. Maybe a few days apart from Gabe would change things.

"A lot can happen in two weeks," she told her sister. Possibly she could find some way to work things out with Gabe.

And if she didn't, chances were high that her heart might just get broken.

Chapter Nineteen

Saturday morning rolled around, and as Gabe and Jenna sat across from each other at their favorite booth at the Pancake House, Gabe continued to stew over the argument he'd had with Erica the weekend before. They hadn't talked all week, and though it had taken everything he had not to pound on her door that very morning and demand they have their Saturday morning after-game talk, he hadn't let himself. First of all, her blinds had been closed.

And second, nothing had changed.

He couldn't let Erica into his daughter's life with any sort of permanence, because at some point, either Erica would wear him down or she'd simply go behind his back. And she was wrong about this one. She couldn't be right about everything.

He eyed his daughter, who sat clutching a doll that had arrived earlier that week.

A doll from her mother.

He frowned. If he'd been home when the thing had arrived, he'd have tossed it in the trash. But Hannah hadn't known any better, so she'd let Jenna rip into the box. And Jenna hadn't put it down since.

Aside from getting the doll, nothing much had changed that week. He hadn't been able to get Jenna to talk to him, and right now, instead of eating the breakfast on the plate in front of her, she was using a fork to push a bite of pancake around in the syrup. When she tired of playing in the syrup, she reached for the salt shaker, and in a quick motion, she had the top off and the bottle tilted, with salt now pouring freely into a tiny white pyramid on the table.

Gabe held in a sigh. "What are you doing? You know better than that."

She ignored him and continued pouring.

"*Jenna*. Stop it. This behavior has gone on long enough."

Again, no response. His entire week had been this routine played on repeat. She'd completely ignore him, while at the same time doing anything she could to get a rise out of him.

When she unscrewed the lid of the pepper shaker and lifted her head to stare at him, daring him to make her stop, Gabe snapped. He slapped a hand down over hers before she could pour out the pepper, sending the glass shaker rattling across the scratched surface of the table until it tumbled to the floor. Glass shattered, and fury steamed out of his daughter's ears.

"Stop being mean to me," she said, her voice way too loud for a public place.

"I'm not being mean to you, Jenna. I'm trying to get you to behave."

She smacked the empty salt shaker and sent it flying in the direction the pepper had gone, and when one of the waitresses rushed over, worry coloring her features, tears suddenly appeared in his daughter's eyes.

"I'm sorry," she sobbed. "My daddy was yelling at me, and I didn't know what else to do to get him to stop."

Giant hiccupping sobs were the only sounds filling the room as all eyes turned to him.

"We're leaving," he told the waitress as he reached for his wallet. But before he could pull out enough bills to cover their meal, the woman squatted in front of Jenna and wiped at her tears.

"Are you okay, sweetie?" The waitress cast an evil glare his way. "He's not hurting you, is he?"

"Oh, for crying out loud." He tossed down a twenty and reached over to lift his daughter from the bench so they could make their escape. She immediately wailed as if he were beating her. "Stop it, Jenna." He moved quickly toward the door, wanting to get out of there and put an end to the madness. "This isn't a joke, nor is it even mildly funny."

She wailed louder.

Two customers blocked his exit, and Gabe could do nothing but stare at them in shock. They weren't going to let him walk out of there with his own child. He looked down at her, still in his arms, and saw the surprise on her face as well. But at least she'd stopped crying.

"I called the police," the waitress informed the customers as she hurried up behind Gabe, and with those four words, Gabe understood that his bad week had just gotten worse.

He and Jenna moved to an unoccupied booth, and as they waited for the police to arrive, he noted that Jenna never uttered a single word. No more tears, either. She'd pulled her shoulders in on herself, and she neither looked at nor spoke to anyone. No matter how many well-meaning customers tried to rouse her out of it.

When the officers showed up, Jenna's entire body began to shake, and finally Gabe got it.

He moved to the bench to sit beside his daughter and pulled her into his lap, no longer caring about anything or anyone else in the restaurant. Not even the officers. And when Jenna buried her face into his chest and real tears began to fall for the first time in months, all he could do was hold her.

The police had shown up that other day, too. And now, with officers standing in front of them once again, blue lights flashing outside, and every customer hovering around whispering to each other—as if they were nosy neighbors outside a Hollywood apartment complex—he had zero doubt that his daughter was reliving her biggest nightmare.

"You're fine," he whispered in her ear, soothing her as best he could. "You're always going to be fine. I've got you, and I'll never let anything happen to you."

"I miss my mom," she sobbed, and at her words, Gabe froze.

She missed her mom?

Her mother was the reason she was having a flashback in the first place.

Her mother was the reason both their lives were in complete upheaval.

Yet . . . she *missed* her mom?

"She's the best mom in the whole wide world," Jenna whispered to herself, her words wobbly with her tears.

And at that, Gabe set personal feelings aside and dealt with the officers. He recognized a deputy who'd been around for years, and explained the situation. The divorce, Jenna being in therapy to help her with all the changes, and even the past incident with the police. All of it. It shamed him to reveal so much personal information, but he had to get his daughter out of there as soon as possible.

Since Gabe had never been in any trouble, and due to the officer having known the Wilde family for years, he and Jenna were soon free to go. He assured both the eavesdropping customers and restaurant staff that he and his daughter had just had a bad week and that they were going through a rough time, then he walked out of the restaurant with Jenna's hand in his. He moved on wooden legs to his truck and helped Jenna into the backseat, then he closed her door and turned his back to the vehicle.

She missed her mom.

Her mother had been the best in the world.

He put his hand over his mouth as if to hold back any potential scream. What had happened to his daughter? She knew what her mother was like. She used to seek him out when Michelle wouldn't say a word to her for the entire day. Or when Michelle would blame Jenna for every last thing that had ever gone wrong in her life.

She'd come to him and climb into his lap and beg him to let them run away, just him and her, and never, ever have to see her mother again because Michelle was so mean. Michelle hated both of them—and she'd never made any bones about telling them—and Jenna had become the world's best at slipping into her own mind and ignoring her mother's fits, because that's the only way to survive in a house where her mother lived.

Yet after only nine months away, her mother had been the best mother in the world.

And then he got it—and he almost vomited in the parking lot. Dani had been a lot older when she'd gone through this, but she'd done the exact same thing. Their mother had died when his sister had been eighteen. Carol Wilde's issues had never been addressed while she'd been living, neither by a professional nor any of the kids, and least of all, not by their dad. And though life at home had been one situation after another of not knowing who their mother would mentally beat down from one day to the next, they'd been the perfect Wilde family whenever in public.

Because of this, they'd all remained confused, feeling not only as if their mother didn't love them but certain it was their own fault, and desperately wanting that love at the same time.

Carol Wilde had died after years of screwing with everyone's head, but as the only girl in the family, Dani had taken the brunt of the abuse, because in their mother's head, she'd seen her own daughter as competition. After Carol's death, however, Dani became fixated on proving she was good enough. If she'd just do enough, care enough, their dead mother would finally be proud enough.

Due to this, over time, Dani had begun to place their mother on a figurative pedestal. This had gone on for so long she'd literally rewritten what their lives had been like. Dani had turned their mother into something she absolutely had never been in order to assuage her own guilt at not being enough.

And now, his daughter was doing the same thing.

Only Jenna's mother wasn't dead, thus Jenna would have many more years to carry the guilt.

Gabe opened his door and climbed behind the wheel, and then *he* began to shake. His hands trembled so violently he wasn't sure he'd be able to hold the wheel steady enough to drive them away from there. So he didn't even try.

He looked in his rearview mirror at his daughter, and then he asked a question he'd hoped never to voice.

"Should we call your mother?"

Her eyes went wide. She'd stopped crying before he'd gotten her into the truck, but the evidence remained. Tear tracks lined her soft cheeks. Her eyes were swollen and red. "Can we?" she asked. Her voice shook with timidity.

He nodded. He suspected they had to. "We'll go home right now and do it. How does that sound?"

Her nod was slow in coming, but he got the feeling it was more a lack of belief in him actually making the call than it was in concern over talking with her mother. Gabe started the truck and pointed it toward home, and as he neared their house, his daughter spoke from the backseat.

"Thank you, Daddy. I've been missing her so much."

Chapter Twenty

I can't believe you all got me all of this."

Dani's face beamed as she stepped from one shower gift to the next, touching each, even picking a few up and holding them to her face as if she could already smell her own baby wearing them. She and Ben had chosen not to find out the baby's gender, so while most of the presents were gender neutral, there were some pinks and blues tossed in, as well.

Dani seemed to favor the pink, though, as she'd been carrying around a tiny pink blanket for the last few minutes, and every time she came to a girlie onesie or a pink stuffed animal, her smile took on a more whimsical glow.

She moved from guest to guest now, hugging each and thanking them for coming.

"Arsula." Dani squeezed her receptionist in a huge hug. "Thank you so much for being here today. And thanks for the dream catcher." Dani held the hoop of the dream catcher up in front of her, its white and teal feathers dangling down below. "It's so perfect. It'll be the first thing we put up."

Erica watched the action quietly. She was glad she'd come.

Gloria had thrown the baby shower, inviting Erica since Dani and she had become friends, and it had been a true extravaganza. Food had lined the Wildes' dining room table, while presents had been piled high in the middle of the living room. The house was made over in crepe paper and decorative booties and bells, and the view from the room overlooked the lake. As guests had arrived earlier, they'd marveled upon catching their first glance out the set of floor-to-ceiling windows.

Jenna was there, as well, along with Haley, but the two girls had quickly bored of the grown-up stuff and disappeared up the stairs. Their footsteps and laughter had often been heard as they'd played, but now that the party was coming to an end, both children had made their way back downstairs.

Haley moved to stand with Dani, and Erica found herself watching Jenna as the other voices in the room grew in volume. Jenna and she were currently the only two not actively involved in a conversation, so Erica took it upon herself to end that for both of them. She crossed to Gabe's child, trying not to let herself wonder about Gabe himself, and scrunched her nose up playfully when the blonde peered up at her.

Jenna grinned wide and bounced from the chair to throw her arms around Erica's neck. "I was *so glad* Gramma invited you, Ms. Bird. I told her she had to. Haley did, too." Then the little girl blushed. "We also told her that you're the best teacher ever, and we *so* wish you didn't have to stop being our teacher."

Erica's heart filled with joy. "Thank you for making sure I got invited. I love parties. And thank you for telling your gramma that you like having me as a teacher."

She lowered to the chair beside Jenna's, intending to sit next to the little girl, but Jenna climbed onto Erica's lap. There was definitely something different going on with Gabe's daughter today.

"And we love having you as our teacher," Jenna gushed. "But why can't you stay?"

"Because Mrs. Watts had her own baby just like your Aunt Dani soon will, and it's now time for her to come back to school." They'd talked about this as a class over the last week, as she tried to ensure the transition went smoothly.

Slight concern filled Jenna's eyes. "Do you think Mrs. Watts will be as nice as you?"

"I suspect she will be. It would be hard not to be nice when she's got students as terrific as you."

The little girl beamed. "I love second grade. It's been the best ever. I love my dad, too."

The words caught Erica off guard. Not that she didn't believe the sentiment, but because since she'd been in Birch Bay, Jenna hadn't once expressed it out loud.

"How is your dad?" Erica asked hesitantly. She hadn't intended to ask. She hadn't heard from him at all in the last week, and it would be easier to get through the afternoon—as well as her final week of school—by having nothing to do with him.

But since Jenna had brought him up . . .

"He's great." Her smile remained bright. "His football team won again Friday night, and he says that if they win this week and next week, then they'll be playing for a really big trophy and will be the best in the whole state." She sighed. "I hope they win."

"Does it matter to you if they don't?"

Had she been wrong in thinking that Gabe's prowess as a coach wasn't what would win Jenna over?

"What do you mean?" Jenna asked.

"I guess I'm asking if it'll make you super happy if he wins the big trophy. Will it make you love him even more?"

She held her breath at the leading question.

"It'll make me so happy because it'll make my daddy happy. And I want him to be happy." Her words softened, and Jenna suddenly patted Erica's cheek. "I want you to be happy, too," she whispered, her face now close to Erica's. "I'm sorry he argued with you and that you guys aren't talking now."

The words floored Erica. "You know we're not talking?"

She'd considered marching across the street several times during the last week and telling the stubborn jerk of a man to quit being angry with her. They'd simply had an argument. It didn't have to be the end of them. But she hadn't done it because she feared nothing had changed.

"I do, but I don't think he likes not talking to you, because he's been so grumpy all week." Jenna grimaced. "But that might have been my fault, too. I've been kind of bad."

"Why were you bad?"

"I don't know. I was just so angry." Her face brightened. "But I'm not angry now, because my momma is coming to see me tomorrow."

"Your . . ." Erica had no words.

What had happened across the road during the past week?

Jenna's pigtails bounced. "We called her last night and talked to her for a long time. Daddy talked to her first, but then I did, too, and she was so happy to talk to me. Daddy said he'd buy her an airplane ticket if she'd come see us, and she said she'd get on one today." Jenna clapped her hands together. "She'll be here tonight."

Tonight.

Michelle Wilde would be in town tonight.

The knowledge should have made Erica happy. It's what Jenna needed. Yet instead, it put a cloud of dread inside her. Not for Jenna's sake, but for hers and Gabe's. She'd been fine that last week. Even accepting that she might have killed all hope for the two of them by insisting Gabe was wrong.

But deep down, she supposed she'd thought they might still work through it.

With his wife coming to town, though, it suddenly *felt* done. He could change his mind about Michelle. About their divorce. Michelle might have learned from her mistakes. Would she change for *him*?

"I can't wait to see her again," Jenna sighed, and Erica realized she hadn't replied to the announcement.

"I'm sure you can't, sweetheart. I hope it's a terrific visit."

"Do you want to meet her?"

Again, Erica was taken aback.

"She's going to be staying with us, so I could bring her over to meet you."

"I, ummm, maybe that should be your daddy's call, Jenna." The last thing Erica wanted was to meet Gabe's wife.

"Then you probably won't meet her." A frown turned the corners of Jenna's mouth down. "Not unless he stops being grumpy with you."

"You're probably right." She scrunched her nose up at the little girl again. "But that's okay. I'm going to be really busy this week, anyway, getting everything ready for your new teacher to come back. So you just focus on having fun with your mother and don't worry about me, okay?"

"Okay."

Haley yelled for Jenna then, her voice coming from upstairs once more, and the girl climbed from Erica's lap. "I'm going to tell my daddy he's wrong for not talking to you."

And then she was gone.

Erica was left sitting alone, realizing that most of the guests had either left or moved to the deck out back, so she rose to do the same. Only before she made it through the living room, the women outside parted as if God himself had shown up, and Erica looked up to find a dark-haired, six-foot, seriously hot Gabe Wilde striding through the middle of them. He caught her eye before hitting the back door, and when he entered the house, Erica forgot to breathe. He looked so fierce.

"Are you here for Jenna?" she asked when he stopped in front of her. "She just went—"

"I need to talk to you first."

She nodded in agreement, her heart pounding, then she turned and followed him down the hall. Once they were sufficiently hidden away from the remaining crowd, he just looked at her. He didn't say anything at first, but in his eyes she recognized the same blend of hope and sorrow that she knew to also be in hers.

"I'm sorry," she whispered, needing to go first. "I'm sorry we fought. That we disagree."

"I'm sorry I've not seen you all week."

Relief washed through her. "What went on this last week, Gabe? Jenna is so different today. And she says her mother is coming."

"Michelle will be here sometime late tonight." He reached out and took her hands. "Jenna had a blowup yesterday. At the Pancake House, of all places. It ended only when the cops came."

"The police?" Her eyes rounded. "What happened?"

"Basically, a huge fit." His face remained grim. "She played the my-daddy-is-mean-to-me card for sympathy, and it backfired when everyone in the place came to her defense. But when the cops showed"—hurt filled Gabe's eyes as he squeezed her hands—"she had a flashback to that morning in LA, and the result of that ended up being me calling Michelle. I finally get that her not seeing her mother has caused more damage than good. She was building Michelle up into something she's never been. I watched the same thing happen with my sister, but the similarities never hit me until yesterday."

"So, what does all this mean?" Fear mixed with hope. "You're bringing Michelle here to prove Jenna wrong?" That didn't sound very fatherly.

"I'm bringing Michelle here because she's Jenna's mother. I don't trust her judgement, and honestly, I still think she's up to something. I just have no idea what. I'd truly like to believe she simply misses her daughter, but that'll have to be proven to me. Jenna is excited, though, and that's what matters right now. Possibly she and her mother *can* have some sort of relationship going forward, even if it's not a perfect one. I can go to California with Jenna in the summers, or I could bring Michelle here." Sincerity rolled off him. "Michelle hated Montana when we lived here, so I don't see her ever coming back. Whatever the case, though, I'll do what it takes for Jenna to be happy. This is the first step. We'll see what happens, then Jenna and I will go from there."

Erica's eyebrows raised. "Jenna and you? Does that mean you're going to let Jenna be a part of the decision?"

"I am." He pressed his lips together before continuing. "It occurred to me that I was seven once, too. And my mother controlled every decision in my life, both then and in the years to come." He twined his fingers through hers. "I *hated* her for that. I never wanted to tell you that part of me. It made me feel weak the way she overpowered me. I didn't want you seeing me that way."

"But it's understandable, Gabe. She was your mother. You were a kid."

"Not the whole time. I was seventeen when she died."

"You were a *kid*."

"I wasn't when I married Michelle. Yet I allowed her to do the same. Control me, either through words or threats." Hatred filled his eyes. "She may have gotten away with it with *me*, but I won't let her do that to Jenna. And I'm telling you that I fear that outcome. It's why I let everything ride when Michelle simply went silent. Why I prefer she stay out of Jenna's life. But if I'm there when Jenna is with her, if I'm keeping an eye on things"—he squeezed her hands again, and this time tugged her a step closer—"Jenna and I will figure this out together, and we'll be stronger for it. I believe that. Now tell me that you and I are okay, too." He tugged her closer still. "I need for us to be okay."

She didn't bother swiping at the tears in her eyes. "We're okay."

A shaky breath escaped Gabe as he pulled her into his arms. "I've missed you so much."

"I've missed you, too." She peered up at him, allowing her joy in the moment to show. "Jenna tells me you've been grumpy this week."

He snorted. "Jenna hasn't exactly been a piece of cake herself."

"She told me that, too." Erica touched his cheek. "She's so different today, Gabe. I almost couldn't believe it."

"She's herself again." He pressed a kiss to her forehead. "And I've never been more grateful for anything." He pulled back and looked down at her. "We're really okay, you and I? We can try this thing?"

"You're sure you and Michelle . . ."

"You know she's nothing to me."

"I just don't want to be in the middle of anything," she murmured. "The other woman."

"You're *not* the other woman. You weren't even with your ex. He was *your* husband."

"Not two months ago, he wasn't."

Gabe stroked his thumbs over her palms. "But he wasn't hers, either. I've got a final court date in four weeks, Erica. My marriage ended a long time ago, and my lawyer assures me the date won't be moved again. This divorce is happening. No matter what comes from Michelle's visit."

She found herself far more relieved to hear the words than she'd expected.

"Now tell me we can go out on a date," he continued. "And when. Dinner? Football? This week's game isn't at home, but it's close and we're playing our biggest rival." He reeled her in another inch and whispered, "Come with me. Be there for me."

She wanted to be there for him. "How long is Michelle staying?"

"I don't know. We decided to play it by ear." His eyes pleaded with her. "Does it matter?"

"I'd hate to confuse Jenna. Maybe it's best if I stay away until her mother is gone. Let Jenna focus on Michelle this week, okay?" She hated the thought, but she knew it was the right thing to do. "She needs this time."

Gabe started to argue, but he stopped before saying anything. She could sense his acceptance.

"It's not fair," he said. "I want time with you."

"I want that, too."

"Then next week's game." There was a determination in his words she'd not seen yet. "No excuses. It's homecoming next week. Be my date. I want to go public, Erica. I won't take no for an answer."

And she wouldn't give him a no.

It was time to move past her own issues. "JC and Lindsey's affair came out at a football game," she told him bluntly. "Someone noticed that she was pregnant and asked when she was due, and suddenly everyone surrounded her, gushing over her." She licked her lips before continuing. "And JC chose that moment to rise from where he sat beside me, and to stand with her."

Understanding filled Gabe's eyes.

"Between congratulations, there were side eyes thrown my way. No one mentioned that JC was married to me. And no one seemed the least surprised to see him standing there with her. Except me." Her voice broke. "I was humiliated. It was clear I was the only person in that crowd shocked to discover that my husband had gotten another woman pregnant." She swallowed her grief. "And I've been unable to stomach the thought of sitting in another crowd like that since. It was as if JC took that away from me, too. My life, my home, our friends . . . my love of football."

Gabe pulled her against him and held her tight. She didn't cry for what was or for what had happened. She didn't even come close. Tears for her ex-husband had finally dried.

And she'd never been so relieved to be held in a man's arms as she was in that moment.

After a few minutes, Gabe pressed a kiss to the top of her head and peered down at her. He smoothed the backs of his fingers over her cheeks. "I'm very sorry your ex is a complete ass, you have to know that. And your aversion to attending games now makes complete sense." He touched her under the chin. "But you do know that I'm not him, right?"

She nodded. "I do know."

"Then say yes, baby. Be my date for homecoming. Be *with* me."

"Yes," she said without hesitation. It was time to be with Gabe. She let that bad memory finally ebb away.

Triumph burned bright at her quick acceptance, and Gabe's eyes immediately lowered to her lips. His breaths quickened, and she could tell he now had more than talking on his mind.

"Don't you dare," she whispered. She put her fingers over his mouth to stop him. "I'm here at a baby shower."

"The shower's over." Only they could both still hear other women talking outside. "I want to see you this week," Gabe said. He nipped at her fingers. "Mornings? My place?"

"Your wife will be there," she hissed out.

"I don't care," he replied in a matching hiss. "I miss you, Erica. I'm tired of being away from you."

"But it's not right." She shook her head. "Not this week. I think Jenna already suspects about us, anyway, so we don't need to add to her anxiety. We can wait."

"Fine," he growled out, his frustration evident. "But damn, woman. You can be so stubborn."

"And the reward for patience can be so great," she responded naughtily. She gave him a gentle smile and leaned into him. "Call me when she books her flight home. We'll talk to Jenna together, then the three of us will go out."

"Deal."

Before she could stop him, his mouth descended, and she sighed into him. She'd missed this so much. They kissed far too long to be doing so with other people around, and when he finally released her, tenderness shone down at her. Possibly even more than tenderness. So she let the same shine back at him. She wanted this to work between them.

"I'll see you soon," he promised. He kissed the tips of her fingers, then headed up the stairs in search of his daughter. She was left standing in the hallway all by herself, replaying the last few minutes. She touched her fingers to her lips and couldn't hold back the smile. She had a date for homecoming. She'd need a new dress.

Turning on her heel, she intended to search out the hostess and the mom-to-be and thank them for inviting her. But the mom-to-be had already found her. Dani stood at the end of the hall, a wide grin covering her face.

"I take that things have changed between you and my brother?" Dani practically bounced on her toes—while embarrassment flooded Erica.

"We've . . ." She stopped. She couldn't come up with a single thing to say but the truth. So she hung her head. "We've been seeing each other. But no one knows." She looked toward the stairs. "We haven't told Jenna yet."

"I can keep the secret." Laughter suddenly bubbled from Dani, and the other woman rushed down the hall. She pulled Erica into a hug, her bulging stomach pushing in ahead of her, and squeezed her tight. "I couldn't be happier for either of you." She kissed Erica on the cheek. "I always thought you were great for him, and after getting to know you better now, I'm certain you're perfect for my niece, as well."

"This is all still pretty new," Erica began, but Dani butted in. "It's pretty *awesome*."

Erica let out a nervous breath as warmth filled her. She grinned, the vibrancy of her smile matching Dani's, and gave her friend a solid nod. "It's pretty awesome."

And she very much hoped that it remained that way.

Chapter Twenty-One

To girls' night." Arsula held her wineglass out in front of her. "May this be the beginning of many more to come."

Erica leaned forward over the outdoor bistro table, as did Maggie and Arsula, and the three women clinked their glasses together. The sun hadn't yet set, but the night chill had already crept in. She'd purchased a portable heater to warm the area, making for a cozy space for the small group, and they'd already eaten their way through the three different appetizers Erica had tried out for the evening. Their main course needed a few more minutes in the oven, so they'd temporarily taken the party outside.

She'd quickly come to regret that decision, however, because not two minutes after settling among the trees, voices had drifted from the other side of the road. Gabe, Michelle, and Jenna had decided to have a go at making homemade ice cream together that night, and he'd set up the vintage machine he'd bought on his back deck. She'd been listening to their muted conversation and laughter for the last ten minutes.

"May Erica decide to stay in Birch Bay forever," Maggie added, holding up her glass again, "and may the wine continue to flow free."

"Hear, hear." Arsula's agreement came with a lazy smile and half-lidded eyes. The younger woman definitely couldn't hold her wine.

"You might have to spend the night if *your* wine keeps flowing," Erica told her.

"I'll be fine." Her speech was just the tiniest bit slurred. "Serve me bread with dinner, and it'll soak it right up."

"If you say so." Erica wasn't convinced, though, and had already decided to give up her bed for the evening if she needed to. It wasn't as if there'd be a man in it with her or anything.

Her pettiness irritated her. It was the middle of the week. It's not as if Gabe could have spent time in her bed even if Michelle hadn't been at his house. And really, his absence the last few days was of her own making. She'd told him to focus on Michelle and Jenna, so that's what he'd been doing. His late-night texts had even slowed.

Sunday night after the baby shower, they'd shared thirty minutes of clandestine texting after everyone else had gone to bed. Then Monday it had been twenty minutes.

Last night, he'd sent her a quick "sorry, it's been a long day" kind of message, and they'd texted for only a couple of minutes, and something told Erica not to expect him to even think about sending a text that night. He was having a good time entertaining his wife.

Erica downed over half her wine in one gulp, and when she lowered the glass, the sound of high-pitched laughter affected her like fingernails on a chalkboard. She wanted the other woman gone. She was tired of getting up every morning and seeing the rented BMW parked in the spot where Gabe's truck should be, and exhausted from listening to her put on airs. Anyone who heard that laugh should be able to tell that it was fake.

But the way Gabe returned the laughter led Erica to believe that he didn't have a clue.

Maggie leaned forward, tipping the open bottle over Erica's glass, and emptying it of its contents. "Everything okay?"

"Great." Erica forced a smile. "Just enjoying the company."

That part was true. She was thrilled to have her friends over, and had enjoyed every minute of it so far. It's possible too much wine was making the rounds for a school night, but at the sound of even more laughter—this time a high-pitched yip bursting out as if someone had given Michelle a quick pinch—Erica decided that she didn't care. Soberness be damned. It was girls' night. She turned up her glass.

And maybe if she drank enough she'd drunk-text Gabe later tonight and entice him over.

She thunked her glass back on the table. Drunk texting was not an option. She had to be patient. Just as she'd convinced Gabe to be.

"What's that noise?" Maggie looked around at the beeping sound, her smile now lazy and similar to Arsula's.

That noise was the oven timer.

"Dinner's ready." Erica rose from the table, grateful to be going back inside, and led the small group into the house.

Tonight she'd decided on a Greek theme. She'd made Greek orzo with beef, and had a Greek salad waiting in the fridge. She'd enjoyed her different attempts over the last few weeks, and had determined that *this* would be her new thing. She didn't need music lessons or other random hobbies such as the painting class she'd briefly considered signing up for. Instead, she simply needed to get lost in the kitchen once in a while. She planned to make girls' night a more regular event, just as they'd hoped.

"Oh my stars," Arsula murmured from in front of the kitchen window. She'd leaned over the sink and was peering outside, and at her comment, Maggie hurried over.

"What is it?" Maggie asked.

"Those two." Arsula nodded toward the window. "They're *gorgeous* together."

Erica didn't have to join the women to know who they were talking about. Gabe and Michelle made a striking pair. She'd picked up on that herself.

"They've always been a gorgeous couple," Maggie added. "That's his wife. I used to see them around town together once in a while. I knew they'd moved away, but I hadn't realized they'd broken up. They always seemed so perfect together."

They still did. At least on the outside.

"Any idea what she's doing back?" Maggie looked to Erica with her question. "Do you know if they're getting back together? Because if not . . ."

"What?" Erica asked. Did Maggie somehow know about her and Gabe?

"Him across the street from you? Every day? And not married?" Maggie peeked back outside. "Honey, I'd be all over that."

"Yeah, well . . ." Erica swallowed against the knot of words stuck in her throat. She wanted to share her secret with her friends. She wanted to ask their opinion, or just have someone other than her twenty-one-year-old sister to talk to about him. But could she dare?

Yes, she told herself. Soon. And possibly even before she and Gabe made it public.

But tonight was about the three of them getting together. Not about asking if they thought all the laughter coming from the other side of the street meant anything.

"I had a dream about him last week," Arsula announced. She'd left the other woman to gawk alone, and pulled the salad from the fridge.

"A dream?" The urge filled Erica to ask if Arsula had "seen" anything about Gabe in her dream, but at the same time, what if she'd seen something Erica didn't want to hear? Changing the subject might be better. "I would have thought you'd be more likely to dream about Cord. You and he seemed to hit it off at the cookout."

"Yum." Maggie's dreamy look was back. "I remember Cord." She suddenly remembered the wine in her hand, and took a large swig. "There was always something about Cord."

Erica grinned as she transferred their dinner from the baking dish to a serving bowl. "There's still something about Cord."

"Not for me," Arsula stated matter-of-factly. "He has too many problems."

Erica cocked her head. "What kind of problems? Did he say something?" From what she'd deciphered concerning Gabe's brother, the man was a vault when it came to personal subjects. Even more so than his older brother.

"Nothing obvious, but I pick up on things. It comes with my ability," Arsula explained. Neither Erica nor Maggie had taken Arsula's "ability" too seriously thus far. "He has a charming way about him, but he'd be too much for most women. Too difficult to get past his walls."

"Maybe that's why he's still single," Erica guessed. And maybe that's why Gabe was so good at erecting *his* walls. But then, she supposed growing up like he had—like all of them had—instilled that kind of natural protection inside a person.

"I don't mind walls," Maggie murmured. She swayed just a bit as she found her seat and lowered into it. "I'd scale his walls in a hot minute."

Erica smiled as she pictured her friend doing just that. She liked Cord, no matter what Arsula thought, and suspected he'd be very worthwhile if a good wall-scaling session was what a person were after. Because closed off or not, Cord was a good guy. Just like his older brother. "Too bad you just missed him, then," Erica teased.

"What?" Maggie gaped at her.

"A couple of weeks ago." Erica set a glass of ice water in front of the other woman as Arsula took her seat. "He came in for a football game and spent the night with Gabe."

Maggie looked back toward the window, and when she faced Erica once more, her look cried of desperation. "Any idea if he might show up again? I have a friend who went out with him once." She licked her lips. "If he's coming back to town, I might be so rude as to invite myself over to see you."

Concern filled Arsula's eyes. "Wait for someone else, Mags. Cord's not for you."

"Yeah, well, no one has been for me in a long time," Maggie added wryly.

"Have you had any dreams recently?" Arsula suggested. "Maybe there's something in one about a relationship that you didn't realize. Tell me anything you can remember, and I'll see."

"I haven't had any dreams." Maggie looked crestfallen, as if Arsula had taken away her last drop of wine, and Erica decided they'd been talking about the Wilde boys for far too long.

"I had a dream," she tossed out.

All eyes turned to her, and as she passed the food around the table, she felt suddenly silly for bringing it up.

"It's nothing, really," she prefaced. "It was just a little strange, is all."

Arsula reached across the table and put a hand on Erica's. "Tell us."

The directness of the other woman's gaze gave her pause. Up until that moment, she'd thought her new friend to be half joking every time something was mentioned about reading people's dreams. She assumed it to be more of a novelty act than anything real. But the intensity being directed at her now told her otherwise, and she found herself wanting to see what Arsula might say.

"I was in a skating rink," Erica began. Which had struck her as incredibly strange because she hadn't been anywhere near a skating rink in years. "I had on this flowing dress. It was white at first, then it changed to a brighter color. I can't remember what color, though. Just bright."

"I thought people didn't dream in color," Maggie interrupted.

"Shh." Arsula didn't look away from Erica as she admonished the other woman. She nodded for Erica to continue.

"I was laughing." Erica closed her eyes as she worked to recall the details. It had been a couple of nights since she'd had it. "Having the best time, and feeling more free than I have in years." She wrinkled her brow as she tried to remember. "Then I was floating up off the ice. Flying, but not really. More like just rising higher and looking down to where I'd been skating."

She opened her eyes to make sure Arsula wasn't looking at her as if she were crazy, and Arsula once again nodded encouragingly.

"And then I had a bowl of rice in my hands." Erica made a face at the weirdest part of her dream. "I'm hovering, still wearing my bright, happy dress, but now stirring rice in a bowl almost too large for my arms to hold." She laughed as she finished, the sound tight with nerves.

"We're *eating* rice," Maggie whispered urgently, as if Erica serving them rice must be some sort of sign.

"And I assume that's why I dreamed about it," Erica concurred. "Because I was a little nervous about this dinner."

"It's about a job," Arsula stated.

Erica and Maggie turned back to Arsula.

"The rink signifies circles," Arsula continued. "That you are or have been going in circles."

Erica listened more carefully now. Because yeah. The last two years of her life had been nothing but circles.

"And then you rose above it." Arsula's fingers lightly squeezed Erica's arm. "You're putting the circles behind you and rising above it. Success is heading your way."

"And the rice?" Erica asked anxiously. She certainly hoped she was finally putting those circles behind her. It kind of felt as if she was.

"The rice can be a number of things." The other woman looked across the table, taking in Maggie, as well. "Rice in dreams signifies success and warm friendships."

"Awwww," Maggie murmured.

"It can also imply fertility."

Erica clamped her hands over her stomach. "No." She shook her head. "Not fertile. Not me."

But the idea of a baby had her heart clenching.

A baby with Gabe?

"*Cooking* rice, though"—Arsula regained everyone's attention—"is a sign that new responsibilities lie ahead. Ones that will provide great joy."

Erica blinked at her. "What kind of joy?"

"A new job is my guess. Have you heard anything you haven't shared with us?"

"No." Not even more e-mails telling her they'd love to have her, but.

And then her phone rang from the other side of the room.

Every one of their eyes went round, and they all stared at the kitchen island sitting in the middle of the oversize room. Erica's phone lay plugged in on her stack of magazines, its ringtone blasting in the now-quiet room.

"Answer it," Maggie urged. "It could be about a job."

"It's eight o'clock at night. Who would be calling me about a job?"

But she had to know.

No one said another word as Erica crossed the room. She suspected the ringing would stop before she even got to it, but that didn't turn out to be the case. And when she picked up her phone, the display showed that it was a number from Silver Creek.

Worry suddenly had her hurrying to answer. Who would be trying to get in touch with her late at night from her hometown if there wasn't something wrong?

"Hello?" she practically yelled into the phone.

"Ms. Bird?" a man's voice spoke.

"Yes."

Was the man from a hospital? The police?

A morgue?

"This is Superintendent Miller from the Silver Creek school system. I'm sorry to be calling you so late, Ms. Bird, but the board just let out of an emergency meeting. Do you have a minute to speak with me?"

She dropped onto one of the barstools. "I do." And then she looked straight at Arsula.

When she got off the phone, she explained that she'd just been offered her old job back, tenure reinstated. The teacher they'd hired to replace her hadn't worked out, and though they admitted that they didn't understand why Erica had left at the last minute in the first place, they'd do whatever it took to get her back.

They *needed* her back. At her ex-husband's school.

Maggie's jaw hit the floor. "Your dream really was about a job."

"I'm not just some hack," Arsula muttered, but no one paid her any attention.

"What are you going to do?" Maggie asked.

She had a job if she wanted one. A permanent, full-time job.

Or she could stay here for Gabe. Who seemed to be having the time of his life with his wife.

She returned to the table on shaky legs, snagging another bottle of wine on the way. Then she took in her new friends and felt fresh tears begin to fall. "I have absolutely no idea."

Chapter Twenty-Two

"Let me see what you've got so far." Erica spoke to one of the small groups of students working together in her classroom as she pulled a seat over to their table. The kids were creating a movie storyboard today. It would be their last assignment from her before Mrs. Watts returned the following week.

They were to come up with and describe what their main characters looked like, outline the problem the characters would have to solve within the movie and how they'd go about solving it, then draw out the scenes, one to each page. Erica intended to bind each movie script together before she left for the day and leave them for their returning teacher as a welcome-back present. This was a sharp group of students, and she'd been looking forward to seeing their ideas all week.

She'd been making her way around the room for several minutes, checking on each three-person team, and tickled to see that many of the ideas involved teachers who'd just had a baby, while others involved a friend leaving town on her last day. Just as she began to study the plans of the team in front of her, she picked up on Jenna's voice from the grouping behind her.

"I heard Daddy say that he could see she was really trying," Jenna said. "They thought I was sleeping, but I was still awake. I think that means that he doesn't hate her as much anymore."

"Does that mean you don't hate her, either?" Leslie asked.

"I probably never should have hated her. She took me shopping last night and bought me three new dresses and the most beautiful coat I've ever seen. She loves me again."

"Did she quit loving you before?" This came from Haley, and Jenna paused before answering. Erica's heart raced as she listened.

"I don't know," Jenna finally said. Her voice lost its edge of enthusiasm. "Sometimes I think so, but then I'm not sure."

"Why would a momma quit loving her daughter?" Leslie asked.

"I don't know."

Jenna's answer was simple, yet a truckload of heaviness seemed to fall with the three words. All three girls fell silent, as if none knew exactly how to wade deeper into the conversation, until Leslie landed on a different route.

"What are you doing with your mom tonight?" she asked.

"We're going to the football game. We're gonna ride with Gramma and Pops, and we won't get to sit with Daddy because he'll be coaching, but he said we could come down to the bench before the game. We'll get there early so we can check everything out, and we might even get to go in the locker room, too."

"Man," Leslie whispered. "I'd love to go into the locker room. We're coming to the game tonight, too. You think he'd let me see the locker room?"

"Maybe another night. I think tonight he just wants it to be me and Momma."

The three girls continued talking, Jenna telling them more fun stories from the week with her mother, and Erica couldn't bring herself to ask them to quieten down. It was all she could do to focus on the task at hand and check over the work of the three whose table she sat at.

Jenna, Gabe, and Michelle seemed to be hitting it off quite nicely. She should have known. All indicators had certainly pointed that way.

Which meant what when it came to *her* and Gabe? She'd been right that he'd forget to text Wednesday night, but he had sent her a message the night before. They'd talked for about ten minutes, but something in the messages had felt off. Not quite as flirty. Not as fun. She'd lain awake for hours afterward, trying to decipher what that meant, but overhearing Jenna now, she felt as if she'd been given her answer.

It meant she had to get out of the way. She had to give Gabe and his family a chance to reconcile if that's what was meant to be. Because a child needed two parents, if at all possible. Her years in teaching had shown her that.

And she needed to *not* be the other woman in the middle of someone else's relationship.

"What about this, Ms. Bird?" Nikki asked. The group had flipped through the big book of ideas Erica had passed out, and come up with additional characteristics for their protagonist.

Erica read over them, her heart breaking into tiny pieces as she did, because she knew what she had to do. And that meant that she wouldn't just be losing her classroom of students she'd come to love over the last two weeks when she walked out of the school for the last time that day. She'd quite likely be losing the man she loved, too.

Mark Mann, Gabe's assistant coach, stood next to a scratched, burgundy file cabinet topped with a stack of papers ten inches high, with a box of game tapes perched on top of the papers. His elbow was propped on the only cleared space on the metal top, and the pencil in his hand beat out a rapid staccato against the side of the cabinet.

"We can't let him play tonight," Mark was saying to Gabe. "You know that. The kid failed three tests today."

Gabe cringed. "I know." Their best wide receiver had been having issues in school for the last few weeks, but today had done him in. And they *needed* him in the game tonight. They needed this win. "He say anything to you about what went wrong?"

"'Didn't study' was all he said."

That was pretty much all Gabe had been able to get out of him as well. He'd brought Kevin in several times over the last few weeks, trying to let the kid know that he was more than just a coach. He was also an ear if the boy needed someone to talk to. But so far, little talk had happened.

"So who do you want to play?" Mark asked. "I think we go with Vinny."

"Vinny hasn't caught a pass all week."

"But until this week, he was catching everything put up."

"True. So what's been his problem this week?" They had to make this decision, and soon. They had a bus to board.

"His girl broke up with him over the weekend."

Ah, Christ. How had he missed that? "And you think that suddenly won't be a problem tonight?"

"Not if my sources are right." Mark angled his head with a knowing look. "Word is that she planned to be waiting on him after school."

Gabe lifted a brow.

"*And* she's going to get back with him."

"So he'll be able to catch again," Gabe said, understanding all too well the male brain. He'd had plenty of weeks where he hadn't been able to "catch" throughout his life. One specifically, a couple of weeks ago when he'd been on the outs with Erica. He'd barely been able to think straight all week for missing her.

This week hadn't been much better, but at least he knew she'd be there waiting for him after Michelle left. If she *ever* left.

At the thought of his wife, he realized what was going on with Vinny's girlfriend. "She's just getting back with him so Vinny will be able to catch tonight, isn't she?" The girlfriend was a cheerleader, and she wanted to go to the state championship as well as the rest of them.

"That would be my guess."

Gabe shook his head. Some days he wondered why he'd chosen this path. Teenagers could drive a man to drink.

But then he saw Chase peeking through his door, and he remembered exactly why he did this. Because of kids like Chase. Gabe motioned for the boy to come in. Chase had become a regular over the last few weeks. He'd shared some details about his parents' divorce that Gabe suspected the kid's mother didn't even know about, and then they'd had multiple discussions about what was right and wrong for a man to be doing when he was in a committed relationship.

They'd also delved into lengthy conversations on Chase's college plans and the schools showing interest in him. The team had put together an online fundraising account to help get Chase a visit to each school, and now it was down to the decision. The boy had to choose.

"Hey, Coach," Chase said as he came in. Then he nodded to the other man. "Coach Mann."

"You make that decision yet?" Mark asked him.

Gabe held his breath. He would have at least greeted the kid first, but now that the question was out, he wanted to hear the answer. He understood the pressure of selecting a school, though his experience had come secondhand. He'd gone on visits with Cord back when Cord had been considering his possibilities. In the end, his brother had chosen Boise State, and Gabe couldn't help but hope Chase did the same.

"I talked to Oregon again last night," Chase told them.

Mark leaned forward from the cabinet, as anxious to hear as Gabe.

"But my mom and I talked afterward . . . and we decided definitely Boise," the player finished in a rush. Then a wide smile broke across his freckled face.

Gabe stood. "It's done? It's Boise?"

"It's done." Chase reached out a hand. "Thanks, Coach. I wouldn't be here without you."

Gabe shook the boy's hand, and a lump formed in his throat. He didn't necessarily believe the words were true, but he did know he'd been an influence over the last weeks. "Congratulations, Chase." He slapped the kid on the back and pulled him in. "You're going to kill it with Boise."

Chase shook Mark's hand, and then Gabe realized that someone else had stepped to his door. Mark and Chase followed his gaze to Michelle's. She flashed a hundred-watt smile around the room before landing on Gabe, and Gabe found himself anxious about what the look might mean. They'd had a surprisingly good week, and even he had to admit that she'd been so amiable that he'd had less harsh feelings toward her than he had in years. But that didn't mean he'd completely bought into her act.

"Men." He nodded toward the door without looking at the other two in the room. "I'll see you on the bus. Coach Mann, make the call, will you? Let the player know before we pull away."

"Will do, Coach." Mark touched a finger to his forehead as he passed Michelle, as if he wore a cowboy hat and were leaving on his horse, then Chase walked silently out behind him.

Only after the room had emptied of testosterone did his wife step inside. She kept a smile on her face as she picked her way across the floor, but Gabe could see she thought the small, cluttered space was beneath her.

"Where's Jenna?" He rose.

"She's with Hannah."

Things might have been going well that week, but he'd kept his daughter's babysitter on hand. He wasn't ready to leave Jenna alone with her mother anytime soon.

When Michelle made it to the other side of the desk, she lowered to the chair and set her purse at her feet, then turned her smile back up to him. Only this time, the curve of her lips was tinged with an edge of hardness.

"Have a seat, Gabe."

He sat, then wanted to kick himself for doing as she'd said. "What can I do for you, Michelle?"

He didn't want to believe that the last week had all been lies. For his daughter's sake, he truly did not want to entertain that option. But the cold eyes now peering back at him told a different story. And it was a story he'd heard several times before.

"I need a new car," she finally said.

Had all of this been about a car? He kept his expression neutral. "And?"

"And I want you to buy it for me."

"I'm not buying you a car." Even if he were sitting on a stash of money, he wouldn't do that for her. "What's wrong with your old one?" Last he'd seen, she'd had a shiny new Mercedes.

"I need a better one."

He frowned. She'd always had expensive taste. "Then get your boyfriend to buy you another one."

He glanced at the clock over the door, knowing he had only a few minutes before he had to get to the bus, then fidgeted with a pencil as he wondered if his refusal would send her packing before he got home from the game.

But she didn't seem to be going anywhere anytime soon. Instead, she scooted back in her chair, straightened her spine, and crossed her legs at the knees. Her lips pursed just slightly before she said, "You're not hearing me, Gabe. I want *you* to buy me a new car."

"And you're not hearing me. I am *not* buying you a car. Plus, even if I were willing, where do you think I'd get the money? I'm a school teacher now, remember? You certainly lamented the fact that I'd be making little to nothing often enough."

"Yet you are part owner of an orchard."

He snapped the pencil in two. She couldn't be . . .

No.

A weight settled in his chest. He couldn't believe this was where the conversation had gone. "And you're suggesting what?" he asked, forcing a calmness that he didn't feel. "That I should sell my part of the orchard?"

She stared at him, unblinking, her eyelashes so thick they made him think of the pinup girl calendar one of his brothers had as a kid. "It is a profitable orchard," she finally responded. "Not to mention, it comes with a house and sits on lakefront property."

"You're full of shit." Anger enflamed him. "No way am I selling."

Not for her.

Not for anyone, unless he did it for himself.

He forced his muscles to relax, to remain seated in his chair when what he really wanted to do was storm to the other side of his desk and drag her from his office. They had to get through this conversation, and that would be more easily accomplished if he didn't lose control. If he remained *in* control. But then her gaze landed on the framed photo he had of Jenna on his desk, and the contents of his stomach pitched. And he suddenly knew exactly what would come out of his ex's mouth next.

Crossing her hands in her lap, she smiled once again. The look was pure evil. "Then I'm filing for custody."

He was on his feet. "You'll lose. You left our daughter alone, have you forgotten that? I'll claim abandonment."

Her level of calm doused him with icy fear. "Prove it."

Fuck.

Double fuck.

He'd known she'd go there. He'd never once mentioned her actions to the police.

"Plus," Michelle continued, now taking on a woe-is-me look, "you haven't let me see our daughter in months."

"I haven't . . ." He stared at her. What the hell? "You haven't *asked* to see her in months."

She bent forward and reached into her bag then, and pulled out a small object, and after she set it on his desk, she pushed "Play."

"I want to see my daughter, Gabe."

"No."

He gulped as she clicked off the tiny recorder. Then he dropped back to his seat. So that had been the reason for the earlier call.

"I've phoned you every week since you kicked me out of the house," she said now. "And I have a cop friend who'll testify to that very thing on my behalf. He'll say that he heard multiple of those very calls personally. *And* that he was there the day you kicked me out."

"But I didn't kick you out." Gabe spoke through gritted teeth as panic placed a stranglehold around his throat. "So all of this—your coming here, pretending to care about our daughter—this was for money?" She made him sick. "*Why?* Why would you do that to Jenna?"

"A girl's gotta eat."

"And if you have custody—" He quit talking as the answer to his own question clicked into place. *Of course.*

"Then my daughter has to eat." She enunciated the words very clearly. This was about child support. The very thing that *she* hadn't been paying to him.

Could he use *that* in his favor to fight her on this? With his temporary custody, she'd been ordered to pay child support, though not a single dollar had filtered his way. Would her lack of sending money prove that she didn't care?

"Don't do this, Michelle." It would be better not to have to fight at all. "You know she's happier with me. And you know you don't want her."

"What I know is that you called me last week because you'd lost control. You finally let me see my daughter only after the police were called on you. *Again.*"

Damn.

He could already picture his daughter sailing away on a yacht with Michelle and whatever flavor of the day she'd sunk her claws into. And then he suddenly understood the situation. "He dumped you," he said. "That's what this is about. Your rich boyfriend dumped you."

"My rich boyfriend isn't a factor in this." But her lip had curled at his words.

"Did he take back your car, too?"

His taunt didn't even get a rise out of her. She remained calm, legs crossed, hands once again placed in her lap. "Your part of the orchard for my promise to leave your daughter alone."

His cell beeped then, jerking his attention from the evilness sitting calmly across from him, and he took a much-needed break from looking at Michelle to stare at the screen of his phone. It was a text from Hannah, and when he pulled it up, he saw a picture of Jenna smiling broadly while modeling a pink coat.

Jenna loves the new coat her mother got her. She can't wait to wear it to the football game tonight.

Buying her things was how Michelle had convinced Jenna she cared last fall. The idea that she was using his daughter in her scheme had him wanting to lunge across the desk and squeeze his fingers around her throat. But he couldn't very well kill the mother of his child. That would certainly be frowned upon. He could kick her to the curb, though.

But as he started to tell Michelle it was time for her to take her leave, he looked at the picture of Jenna again, and he knew he couldn't do that to his daughter. Not without some sort of explanation, and not without her being a part of it. He'd learned his lesson the first time.

But what if she wanted to go with her mom instead of stay with him?

He couldn't allow that, either.

His mouth went dry as thoughts whipped through his head. He could cancel the divorce. If he did that he . . .

No. He couldn't cancel the divorce. Doing that would only put him and Jenna back where they'd started.

In a quick move, he stood once again, this time sending his chair crashing to the ground behind him. He needed Michelle out of his office. He had a game to play. And then he had his life to figure out.

"I can't do this right now." He needed to talk to Erica. She was always rational. She'd help him figure this out.

"That's fine." Michelle stood as well, only in a much more orderly fashion. She picked up her purse and slipped the strap over her arm, then once again presented a smile. "I think I'll skip your little game tonight, though. If it's all the same with you. Jenna can go with your parents."

He hadn't even though about that.

"But I am going to want your decision soon."

She walked out of his office then, and his body recoiled as if one of his linebackers had landed a blow to his stomach. He collapsed back to the chair, his mind still whirling a mile a minute. He had to tell Hannah to get Jenna out of there. To take her to his dad's. And he had to get to the bus. The team should have already been on the road.

He picked up his phone. But first, he had to talk to Erica. This week without her had about done him in, but he needed her now. He didn't give a crap about his agreement to stay away.

He dialed, and as he listened to it ring through the headset, he became aware of a phone ringing just outside his office. Looking up, he was presented with a sight a million times better than the one Michelle had made as she'd stood in that doorway earlier.

"Erica."

He was on his feet and had her in his arms in two seconds flat. Only, as he held her, her arms remained stiff at her sides.

He drew back. "What's wrong?"

She held up a piece of paper, her face strangely blank. "I got a job offer."

The words didn't compute.

"You got a what?"

"A job," she whispered. She bit her top lip as she shoved the paper toward him once again. "And I'm going to take it."

Anger swallowed him. "What are you talking about?" He snatched the paper from her hands. "We just discussed this last weekend. We're giving us a try, remember?" He could not deal with another issue right then. He needed her here. Standing by him. And he sure as hell didn't need her running away.

"I know we did." She lowered her gaze. "But this offer came in the middle of the week. I've been thinking about it ever since."

"And what? You couldn't be bothered to talk to me about it?" He ducked down to get into her line of sight and didn't move until she looked at him. "Why not?" The question came out hard, but he found he'd moved well beyond pissed.

"You were busy, Gabe."

"I was right next door."

"With your *wife*."

He had to force himself to breathe more calmly, deciding to put Michelle and everything else behind him for the moment. They clearly had to deal with this first, and time was sorely limited. Yet fear swelled inside him. Something told him that if he didn't get Erica to change her mind right now, she'd be gone before he got back tonight.

"Yes," he said calmly, trying not to crush the paper in his hands. "I've been busy with my *ex*-wife this week. But wasn't that the plan? What you wanted?"

"It's what was best for Jenna," she argued. "Not what I wanted."

"Then what's changed? If it was best for Jenna five days ago, then it's still best for her now, right?"

Her jaw clenched, but she held back any words.

"Erica. Honey." He glanced at the clock above the door. "I've had far too much shit going on this afternoon to read your mind. Tell me what happened to change things this week. Let's work this out now, then I'll come over first thing in the morning and we'll finish talking through everything." He lifted her chin when she tried to look down again. "Okay?"

She shook her head. "It's too late. I've already decided."

"And yet five days ago you'd decided something else." His voice inched higher. "What happened to change your mind?"

"*You* happened, okay?" She spoke through clenched teeth, but her words were little more than a whisper. "*Michelle* happened."

"I don't know what you mean by that."

"You're good together, Gabe. I've overheard it all week. I've watched it. I've listened to Jenna be thrilled that her mom is back in her life. And"—her voice cracked—"and she needs that," she finished in a tight whisper.

"And *I* need *you*." Panic now had his brain trying to shut down. "Michelle is nothing, baby. She—"

"I *can't*," she hissed.

He refused to believe that, but he was taken aback at her anger. "You should have called me when you got the offer, Erica. Texted me. Something."

"I should have texted you?" She took a step back. "I guess I thought you'd be too busy to reply."

"Of course not. I would always text you back. Hell, I'd have come over."

And then he realized where she was going with this.

"Erica," he began, trying to rein in his anger. "I had a *lot* going on this week. You know that. That's why the conversations got shorter. This is a big game tonight; practices have been intense. Not to mention, we're at the end of the semester. We've had finals, and you know I have five classes. I've had a lot to do." He looked at the clock again. "And yes, Michelle has been at my house."

"All week," she muttered quietly.

He nodded. "All week." The urge to share what had gone down in his office before she showed up had left him. "What's the point of having Jenna's mother in town if she's never around to see Jenna?"

He'd worried about that when Michelle had suggested staying with them. About Erica not being able to handle another woman in his home all week. But he'd thought she'd be fine with it.

Or maybe he'd just hoped she would be.

But even he had to admit that all the laughing and carrying on Michelle had been doing could come across as a little too much to someone on the outside looking in. Michelle had certainly put on a good show—especially now that he realized none of it had been real.

He clenched his hands, feeling as if the battle had already been lost.

"I'll come over after I get back tonight," he told her. He'd explain about Michelle then. "We'll talk. We'll be okay."

He had to get on that bus.

Without saying another word, Erica tugged the paper from where he'd wadded it in one hand, and after smoothing it back out, she once again held it out to him. This time, he finally let himself look down at it. And that's when he saw it. The location of the job. The part of the story that he'd been missing all along. This wasn't about Michelle at all.

"You're going back?" he accused.

She nodded her head.

"To him?" He couldn't believe how much the thought hurt.

"I'm going back to teaching at his school," she corrected. "He's getting married next month. He's not a factor here."

Gabe didn't believe that at all. "And if you told him *you'd* take him back?" he asked. Gabe was fully aware how fast the other man would change his matrimonial plans if Erica so much as hinted at a reconciliation. Hell, once she was in town, plans might change, anyway. "How long do you think it would take for him to cancel the wedding if you asked him to?"

"I wouldn't do that." She looked away from him once again, and he thought he saw the shimmer of tears in her eyes. Only, he didn't know who the tears were for.

"Don't leave before I get back tonight," he gritted out. "Let's talk about this."

The intercom in the small room crackled to life. "Coach Wilde?"

"Yes?"

"The team bus reports that they're waiting on you," the school receptionist said.

He looked at the piece of paper in his hand. "Tell them I'm on my way."

The intercom went quiet, and he crumbled the paper into a ball. "Don't leave before I get back," he repeated. And then he walked out of his office and away from Erica before he could watch her do the same to him.

Chapter Twenty-Three

The air was crisp and cool the following morning as Gabe sat on his porch bench alone, the sun still over an hour from coming up. He'd been out there for two hours now, willing himself to go back inside.

She'd left before he'd gotten back.

He still couldn't quite believe it. Erica's little car had been nowhere to be found when he'd returned late last night from the game, and as he'd carried Jenna in and tucked her into bed, she'd mumbled that Ms. Bird had come over to tell her good-bye before she and Pops had headed out to the game. His body felt hollow at the loss.

Of course, the other woman in his life had *not* left before he'd returned.

Michelle had been holed up in her room, though. But she'd conveniently left an official-looking document on his kitchen table detailing exactly what she'd outlined in his office. Her riding off into the sunset for his piece of his family.

Though the orchard was owned by him and his five siblings, she hadn't been mistaken in her assumption. His portion would bring a pretty penny. A heck of a lot more than a car. But that's if Dani and his brothers even wanted to buy him out. Or could get the money to.

Hell, maybe it was time to bring up the idea of selling, again. Did any of them even want to keep it at this point?

The screen door squeaked as it opened behind him, and Mike's nose pushed out first. Jenna followed, a blanket dragging on the ground behind her, and climbed into his lap.

"What are you doing up so early, kiddo?"

"I wanted to sit out here with you."

He reached down and lit the patio heater and covered her with her blanket, not wanting his daughter to get too cold. Then he wrapped his arms around her and snuggled her into his chest. Leaning his head against the wall behind him, he peered down through the pre-morning light. "And how did you know I was out here?" he asked.

"Because this is where you talk to Ms. Bird."

So much for keeping secrets. "You knew about that?"

She nodded against his chest, her eyelids drooping. "I wake up early sometimes, and hear you talking." She smiled shyly up at him. "I saw you kiss her one time, too."

"Ah." Well, he hadn't meant for his seven-year-old to see that. He just hoped it hadn't been one of their more amorous kisses.

"It's okay, Daddy. I don't mind that you kissed Ms. Bird. I wanted you to do it some more because then she might have wanted to be your girlfriend."

Seems he should have had a talk with his daughter a long time ago. "You did, huh?" He pushed a lock of her hair behind her ear. "And why would you want her to be my girlfriend?"

She closed her eyes on a yawn. "Because she makes you laugh and smile and not be grumpy anymore. And she makes me laugh, too," she added drowsily. "And because she's a really, really nice person, and she never ever yells at me when there's no reason."

Gabe didn't take his eyes off his daughter as he stroked his hand over her hair. He wasn't the one who'd made a habit of yelling at her when there was no reason. Had she recalled that fact about her mother after spending the week with her?

He had to figure out a way to break the news to Jenna that Michelle would have to leave today. And then he had to figure out what in the world he was going to do about the situation. He could lose Jenna if he didn't come up with the money. There was no guarantee he'd win in a custody battle, and given that the cops had now been called on him twice, he'd go so far as to guess that winning would be out of the question.

What then? He'd quit his job and move back to California?

He'd have to. Anything to make sure Jenna wasn't raised solely by her mother.

"When's Momma going to leave?" Jenna murmured against his chest.

He thanked the heavens for the seemingly simple question. "Are you ready for her to go?"

Jenna yawned again and patted him on the stomach as if she were petting her dog. "It's been fun with her here, but I like it better when it's just me and you," she murmured. "Or me and you and Ms. Bird would be okay, too. But not me and you and her."

Her. She'd referred to her mother in a fashion similar to the way he and his siblings talked about theirs.

"Plus, she's only nice when you're in the same room, and yesterday, she wouldn't even go to the football game with me. She said football was stupid." She looked up at him. "Football isn't stupid, is it, Daddy?"

He shook his head. "Not at all, kiddo."

Thank goodness Jenna was making this part easy on him.

"I'll talk to her as soon as she gets up, okay? I'll tell her it's time to go."

"Okay. Or I can tell her if you want me to. When you tell her she's probably going to get mad."

Jenna didn't know the half of it. He looked down at his daughter, thinking about the difference a week had made. She'd been herself again the past seven days. Nice and sweet. No obvious chip riding high on her shoulder. But at the same time, she had no idea that every day her mother had been there, it had been a lie. He didn't know how she would take it. Or if he should even tell her.

Again, he turned his gaze to the silent house sitting on the other side of the street. Erica had left him when he'd needed her the most. That hurt. It left a hole that he didn't yet know how to close, but he couldn't think about that now. At that moment, he had to protect his daughter. And if that meant talking to his siblings about selling his part of the farm, then that's what he intended to do.

"Do you want to tell her together?" he asked. The idea went against everything he felt was right, but at this point, he didn't want to leave his daughter out of anything.

She nodded, her mood flattening as she seemed to intuitively grasp the severity of the situation, and when they eventually heard a noise coming from inside the house, they called in the dog and walked through the front door together. They found Michelle in the kitchen, having just come down the stairs, bags packed, and wearing a pantsuit that probably cost a month of his salary. She also carried the doll she'd sent to Jenna before arriving in Montana.

"You're leaving?" Jenna asked.

"I am. But did your daddy tell you the good news?"

"Michelle, no." He didn't want to bring up custody. Not yet.

However, his opinion didn't seem to matter. "Your daddy wants you to come live with me."

"No, I don't."

"Daddy?" Worried eyes turned up to his.

"I don't, Jenna." He squatted beside his daughter and breathed a sigh of relief when she stepped into him. "I want you to stay with me forever," he explained.

"That's not what you said—"

"Shut up, Michelle. And quit lying to our daughter." He turned back to Jenna, already seeing the fear and uncertainty reenter her eyes, and he fought to show her the kind of calmness that he certainly didn't feel.

"I don't want to go with her," Jenna whispered. She wrapped an arm tight around his neck, and he could feel her heart pounding wildly inside her chest. "I want to stay with you," she added urgently.

"And you will. Always. Your mother is leaving now. Just like you and I talked about."

When he looked up at Michelle, the gleam of satisfaction shone back at him. "So I can expect a check?" she asked.

Whatever it took. "You can expect a check."

"Excellent. Then I won't be needing this." Jenna's mother tossed the doll she held into the trash can, and then she walked out of the house without looking back. He and Jenna didn't move as a car door slammed outside and the rental started up. And only when the sound of tires crunched over the gravel did he look back at the trash can. Jenna stared at the doll as well. But before he could come up with the best action to take, she walked over and shoved the doll deeper into the can. Then she faced him.

The blue of her eyes had dulled. "I'm going to throw away everything else she bought me, too. Because I hate her, Dad. And I'll hate her forever. And I'm *never* going to see her again."

Gabe held his arms out for his daughter as tears began to roll over her cheeks, and she rushed into them. Then they both sat on the kitchen floor. They held on to each other as she cried, and it broke Gabe's heart to know that both of them had lost something very important that morning. Jenna now fully understood the type of hatred Gabe held for Michelle.

And he'd discovered that there were simply some hurts he couldn't save his daughter from.

Mike eventually came over and began licking Jenna's tears away, and when the dog had Jenna smiling once again, Gabe wrapped his arms around the both of them. "How about you and I do something fun today?" he suggested. "Just you and me?"

"Can we? You don't have to work?"

He'd been so busy since moving back home that he hadn't always made time for his daughter. But he wouldn't be too busy today. In fact, he wouldn't be too busy for the rest of his life. Not for Jenna.

"I don't have to work."

As he continued sitting there, her warm little body snuggled up tight to his on one side and her dog on the other, he suddenly got that winning the state championship would do nothing to better his relationship with his daughter. Nor would having more estrogen. She simply needed *him*. And he now knew without a doubt that he could be that man for her. He may not have had the best role models in the world, but somewhere along the way he'd picked up enough skills to be the father his daughter needed.

Chapter Twenty-Four

Her mother's squeal was the first thing Erica heard as she turned the car into the driveway of her childhood home. Ellen Yarbrough stood in the middle of her front flower garden, one hand now over her mouth and the other stretched high above her head. She waved madly while Erica's dad rushed around the corner looking panicked.

When he saw that the shout had come from excitement and not fear, Phillip Yarbrough plucked off his garden gloves and moved to stand with her mother. He nodded in approval as Erica parked the car and opened her door.

"You're home." Her mother hurried to her side. "Oh, Phillip, our daughter has come home."

The welcome seemed a bit too much, but Erica didn't voice the thought out loud, she merely accepted their hugs. She'd gotten out of Birch Bay Friday night, knowing she needed to be gone before Gabe returned from the game, but she hadn't been quite ready to return to Silver Creek. Her meeting with the district superintendent wasn't until Monday, so instead of heading south, she'd told her friends good-bye and driven north toward Glacier. It had been too late in the day to enter the park, so she'd spent the night at the base of the mountain and had given Saturday to a leisurely drive through the national park. Once she'd come out the other side, she'd finally pointed the car south, but she'd stopped yet again. This time in Great Falls. She'd spent the night still ninety minutes from her family, and only after playing tourist for most of the next morning had she finally been ready to go home.

"We thought you might have shown up yesterday," her dad told her. Which totally shocked her. She hadn't told them she'd left Birch Bay.

"What made you think I was coming home at all?"

Her mom hugged her again. "Charles told us. You got your old job back."

She should have known the superintendent would tell her parents about the call. They'd all been friends since their college years. "I've been *offered* my job back," she corrected. "I haven't accepted it yet."

"But you will." Her mom patted her cheek and smiled at her. "It's so good to have you home."

"We're proud of you, honey." Her dad was passing out hugs today, too. "Pop your trunk, and I'll get your things."

"There's no need," she told them. "I'm staying at a hotel."

At that, both her parents seemed dumbfounded. Her mother had turned for the house to lead them all inside, but she now stood with one foot on the ground, the other lifted toward the first porch step, seeming frozen in motion.

"Why would you do that?" her dad asked. "Your mother got your room ready for you."

"I want my own space, Dad." She bit down on the inside of her lip to give her courage. "And if I decide to stay in town, then I'll be renting a place of my own, too."

"Phillip?" Her mother said the one word, as if Erica's dad had the answers to the questions she couldn't formulate. Then she seemed unable to say anything else.

"Let's not worry about it now, okay?" Erica said. "I wanted to come back and see you both, and then I thought I'd head over to Seth's and see him, Angie, and the boys. Now show me these gardens that got so much attention on the Sunset Garden Tour."

Both her parents remained perplexed that their oldest daughter hadn't returned as the same person she'd been when she'd left, but neither voiced their confusion. Instead, they led Erica through the yard, same as they'd probably done for the crowds during the weekend of the tour.

"A few things have faded by now, of course," her mom pointed out, "but overall, it still looks good. We've not had any snow yet, so your dad and I have continued to putter out here until the weather no longer allows it."

"Your mom wants to add in sunflowers next year. We thought you might help."

She might. She'd been intrigued by sunflowers since she'd been a kid. She loved the way the heads always looked toward the sun. "I have a book on them," she told her mom. "I'll lend it to you if you want."

Before any of them could say anything more, the purr of a high-horsepower sports car drove up the road and turned into her parents' driveway.

"What's he doing here?" her mother whispered, and Erica could see from the look on her mother's face that she continued to wish Erica and JC had not gotten divorced.

Well, she had news for her mother. Divorce hadn't been her favorite moment in her life, either. But it *was* her life now. And she intended to send her ex on his way as swiftly as he'd shown up.

"I have *no* idea," she responded calmly. Then, with long strides, she made it to the car before JC could open his door.

He grinned up at her as she stood there, his teeth gleaming from a recent polishing.

"What are you doing here, JC?"

"I heard you were back in town."

"And?" She'd tried to figure him out. She had. Why in the world had he ever wanted her back? Why would he show up there now?

"Come on, baby." Somehow his smile got even brighter. "I just wanted to see you. I've missed you."

"How are Lindsey and the baby?" She crossed her arms over her chest. "How are the wedding plans?"

Finally, his smile dropped. He unfolded his legs and stood from the car, then took her by the elbow to lead her away. Clearly her parents had moved within hearing distance.

She shrugged out of his hold when they got far enough away, and he leaned in. "Fatherhood isn't for me," he whispered urgently. "That's another reason it was always better with you. We didn't have kids. We didn't want kids."

She actually had wanted kids.

But as she stood there, she became aware of her gratitude that she'd never had any with him. He was kind of pathetic.

"Then I guess you shouldn't have knocked someone up."

"Say the word, E, and I swear, I'll cancel the wedding. It's not about her or the baby anymore. It never should have been. I want *you*. That's why I've been trying to get in touch with you. My dad wanted us to announce, and Lindsey had all these plans already in place, but I wanted *you*." He licked his lips, desperation in his every move. "Say the word, and I'll make the call."

She just stared at him. What nerve.

What a jackass.

"You're a real piece of work, James Christopher the third. What would your daddy think if he even knew you said the words 'cancel the wedding'?"

JC's tone lost its desperation then, and he seemed real for the first time. There was pain in his eyes. "I don't care what he'd think," he said softly. He reached for her, but she jerked her arm away. "I messed up with you, and I know that."

"You sure did." She took another step back.

"And I've regretted it every day. Please, E, give me another chance."

Another chance wasn't even a blip on her radar. Instead, she asked a question she couldn't believe she'd never voiced, but before she did, she looked up at him, making sure she had his eye. "Why did you cheat on me, JC? What made you do it?"

"Come on. Let's not talk about that. That's the past." He shot her another pleading look. "Let's talk about the future."

"*Your* future is with Lindsey."

And it *had* been good between them, she decided. At least at one point in their relationship. She hadn't been wrong about that. But the problem was that that point had been a very long time ago. And then she'd grown up.

She'd outgrown her husband—while he'd stayed a spoiled little rich boy.

It had never been about her being too boring for him. It had been about him being unable to move beyond the past. Since high school, they'd always been JC and Erica, doing the same things, going the same places. Their lives as a couple had defined who she was. Just as before that she'd been Mr. and Mrs. Yarbrough's oldest daughter.

When did she just get to be Erica?

She looked behind her to where her parents remained. At her mother's hopeful expression, and at her dad's slightly annoyed one. Her dad, at least, had been fully supportive of her divorcing the man who'd cheated on her. He might have experienced disappointed that she hadn't been able to hold on to him, but he'd never been less than encouraging for her to kick him to the curb.

Then she looked back to the man she should have ejected from her life years ago.

She got to start being just Erica today.

"Time for you to go." She moved to the driver's door and opened it. "Good luck with your life, JC. I'll be living my own now."

"Erica."

She shook her head and motioned for him to get in. "I'm not the woman you once married. I'm not the girl you dated in high school."

"I know. You're better." Urgency filled the words, and she felt her dad step up beside her.

"Yes, I am. And I'm way too good for you."

As JC finally climbed into his car and started it, she heard a whimper come from her mother, and Erica immediately turned.

"Why would you want me with someone who cheated on me?" she barked out. "Someone who made me the town joke?"

"We just want you to be happy."

Erica's eyes widened at her mother's comment. "And what? You think living with a man who could treat me that way would make me *happy*? Seriously, Mom?"

"Ellen," her dad interrupted when her mother started to speak again. "That's enough."

But her mother couldn't let it go. She tried to explain herself. "Silver Creek is a small town, Erica. That's the concern. There's not a lot of good men to choose from. I hate what he did to you, you know that. I've stood by you all this time. But he wants you back now, baby. Shouldn't you at least consider it? He's got a good family."

Erica stared in shock and had the sudden realization that her mother's opinion could so easily have been her own. Once upon a time. But thank goodness she'd moved on.

"Silver Creek is *one* town, Mom. And there are a lot more out there to choose from." Another decision became clear in that moment, and without letting herself think about it any longer, she took in both of her parents. "I won't be going to that appointment tomorrow."

"What?" her mother asked.

"Why not?" her dad added.

"Because there's no need. I won't be taking the job."

"But we talked to Charles for you." Her mother stopped talking at the wild-eyed expression Erica assumed had landed on her face.

"You did what?"

"Now don't get mad," her dad jumped in. "We knew your contract was ending, and when it didn't work out with your replacement here, we simply reminded Charles what an asset you are to the county. Two-time teacher of the year, Erica. You can't just give that up."

"I won't give it up, Dad. I love teaching. I just don't want to teach here."

"But what will you do?" Her mom looked truly confused, as if there were no other places to live or work in the world, and Erica decided that she would do something she should have done a long time ago. She'd enjoy a little downtime. She'd spend some of that settlement money her ex-husband had so graciously given to her, and there wouldn't be one ounce of guilt over not clocking in every morning.

She pulled her phone out to send a text to her baby sister. Maybe she had a little of Bree's wildness in her after all.

And maybe she liked it.

Road trip? Where are you? I'll come to you.

The reply was quick and simple.

Woohoo!

Then another text followed.

Wait. Does this mean it's truly over with Gabe?

Erica swallowed.

It's over with everyone.

The impromptu dinner had gone well, with Dani and Nick having both agreed to be at the family home the following evening, and as Gloria bustled around the kitchen scooping banana pudding into bowls, the four adult Wildes silently stared at each other in anticipation. Gabe hadn't informed them why he'd requested a family meeting, but he'd asked that Cord, Nate, and Jaden be included, as well. They were waiting for Nate to call in now. Nate was Nick's twin, and he lived in Alaska. He was the hardest to get ahold of, but the minute they got him on the phone, they'd conference in Jaden and Cord.

"This is a new recipe I've been waiting to try," Gloria informed them as she sat a tray of bowls on the table.

"It looks delish, Gramma." Haley pushed up from her seat to lean over the table, checking out each bowl as if one might be better than the others.

"Thanks for doing this," Gabe told the older woman. "You didn't have to."

"Oh, goodness. A houseful of guests, and you didn't think I'd cook?"

"Well, I appreciate it."

Gabe's cell rang, and the tension in the room mounted. As he answered, Dani rose and suggested to the girls that they take their desserts into another room. She followed to turn on a video for them to watch, and by the time she returned, Gabe had all three brothers on the line.

"So what's this about?" Dani asked as she sat back down. She had less than three weeks to go of her pregnancy, and she looked every inch of it.

"It's about the orchard," Gabe told them. He pulled in a deep breath, knowing they'd had a similar conversation a little over two years ago, and at the time, it had been agreed to continue with the status quo.

Keep the orchard in the family, their dad would come out of retirement to run it, and no one would talk about whether there was a better alternative or not.

"I need out," Gabe told them now.

Spoons clattered to the dishes as everyone at the table stopped eating. "What do you mean out?" Nick asked.

"And what are you thinking that does to us?" added Nate.

"Why?" This came from Dani. She watched him as shrewdly as he knew Cord would if their oldest brother were in the house with them, and Gabe knew it was time to bring his entire family into the past nine months of his life.

With the kids safely out of the room, he informed them that Michelle intended to fight him for custody. "Though it's actually more like blackmail."

He told them about her leaving after the holidays, prompting him to finally file for divorce, about the night he'd found Jenna home alone, and about the police being called the following morning.

"And I'm sure you know the police were brought out to the Pancake House a few weeks ago."

"But nothing came from that," Gloria inserted.

"No. Nothing did. Other than Jenna breaking down over her mother, and me finally asking the woman to come back into our lives. Only, she showed up with an agenda." He let his gaze roam over the log beams of the walls and out the back windows toward the trees and the lake beyond. He'd spent the majority of his life in this place. "It's either sell my share of the farm and give her the profits . . . or she takes me to court for custody."

"She can't do that," his dad spoke up. "Jenna needs to stay here with you."

"I know that, Dad. That's why I'm willing to sell. So either everyone buys me out, or . . ."

"Or what?" Jaden asked from the phone. Jaden was the youngest of the clan, only twenty-four, and currently finishing up his master's in psychology in Seattle. He planned to move back to town and open his own practice the following year.

"Or we sell the whole thing to someone else and we all profit." The words felt like sandpaper coming out of Gabe's mouth. This home and the orchard around it had meant a lot to him over the years, both good and bad, and the truth was that none of them would be who they were today if the farm hadn't been a part of their lives.

"Or I give you enough money to fight her," Ben added. "I can buy a hell of a legal team." This wasn't the first time Gabe's friend had made the offer.

"I *could* fight it," Gabe agreed, "but she has a record of calls to the police on her side. Not to mention, she recorded me saying she couldn't see Jenna."

"She can't use that recording," Jaden interrupted. "That was made without your consent."

"But that doesn't mean she wouldn't use the *cop* she has lined up ready to lie on her behalf. I've no doubt she's filled his head with untruths about me—likely along with filling his bed to make sure he sees things her way. Either way, it would be a tough sell for me to prove otherwise."

"I'm not selling," Dani abruptly announced. She'd been the loudest objector two years before, too. Though now that he thought about it, Gabe and his brother had never really stated how they'd felt about the idea. Dani had been adamant, so it hadn't gone to a vote.

"But I have to do something," Gabe told her.

"Then I'll give you the money." Gloria spoke up, and everyone turned to her in shock. She typically remained quiet during family meetings, but at that moment she stood from her seat, temper rising, and pointed a finger at Gabe. "I've been around this family longer than that child has been alive, and I've seen what that woman you were married to is like. How she demeans and crushes Jenna's spirit. No." She shook her head, her anger continuing to build. "She's not getting her claws into that child again. I won't allow it. *I'll* give you the money."

"Gloria," Gabe's dad said. Concern masked his face. "That's *your* money."

"And this is *my* family." She looked at Gabe. "I have retirement money I've never dipped into. I'll give it to you. Every penny of it."

"You can't do that," Gabe started. But that *could* be the answer to the problem. As a loan, of course.

But this was coming from the very woman Gabe had recently thought might be more like his mother than not.

"I can give it to whomever I want," Gloria informed him. She went to a lower cabinet and whipped out a purse, then she dug out a checkbook and looked up. "How much?"

"Wait a minute." Nick spoke up from the table. "We have something else on our side."

"What's that?" asked Cord.

"Reality," Nick stressed. "There are things she's done over the years—"

"Things we'd all testify to in court," Nate added. His tone was harsh.

"Things that would paint her in a very unattractive light," finished Jaden.

Gabe watched as a glimmer of hope began to shine from his brother and sister at the table, while at the same time, he heard it coming through from the rest of his siblings through the phone. Could they really fight Michelle on this? Because the idea of giving up a piece of them, of their livelihood, to *her* rated right up there as one of the most abhorrent things Gabe could imagine.

But he hadn't thought he had a choice.

"She's always been very careful out in public," he warned. "The whole town was shocked to find out I'd come home having filed for divorce."

"Then we'll share some secrets," Cord replied. "We're not about to let her paint our next chapter for us."

"Agreed." Dani gave Gabe a tight smile from across the table, pride flashing through her eyes as she stared at him, and he couldn't help but concur with what he saw. They'd come a hell of a long way in the past two years. They were truly learning how to be a family again. "We've worked too hard to be where we are," she added. "There's no need to stop fighting for us now."

Everyone began tossing out ideas then, of things they remembered over the years and who could testify about which of them. Gloria even brought up a key piece of evidence they could use against her. Phone records. If Michelle intended to get on the stand claiming she'd tried to get visitation for months, then all Gabe's attorneys would have to do was provide his phone records showing there had been no calls.

"That's terrific," Gabe told her, and wanted to kick himself for not thinking about it.

"We just need to catch her in her lies," Jaden added from the phone. "Expose irrefutable misinformation, and she'll lose her cool. That's what people like her do."

As his five siblings continued talking, Gabe's dad reached over and put a hand over the back of Gabe's. "Are you sure about this, son?" he asked softly. "The safer bet would be the money. We don't want to lose Jenna."

Gabe looked into his Dad's eyes then, and he saw the man he'd grown up with. The one who'd been known for rolling over and letting their mother walk all over him. And he thought about how very much like his father he was. But at the same time, he *wasn't* like his father. Because he refused to provide that same example for his daughter. He wanted to win, both for himself and for Jenna. And he wouldn't go down without a fight. He never should have considered any other option to begin with.

"I'm sure, Dad." He didn't know exactly where the conviction came from, but with his family support around him, Gabe knew that he could do this for his daughter. For his family.

And he would do it for Gloria, too. The woman was who nothing at all like his mother.

They all put their heads together, and before the night was over, he had his lawyer on the phone and a plan in the works. Ben called in reinforcements, adding to Gabe's legal team, and a course of action was outlined. By the time they walked into that courtroom in a few weeks, Gabe's ex-wife wouldn't know what hit her.

Chapter Twenty-Five

Warm sand sifted through Erica's toes as she dug her feet into the Santa Monica sand and stared out at the horizon. She and Bree had been on the road for three weeks now, and though they'd had a blast hitting all corners of the country, over the last few days she'd found herself more than ready to head home.

Only, the home she kept picturing wasn't Silver Creek. She missed Birch Bay.

Lowering her gaze, she propped her chin on her knees and let her eyes linger on the maroon color of her toenails. She and Bree had splurged on several spa treatments in San Diego the previous day, before heading up the coast. And though views along the drive had been breathtaking, she'd been unable to focus on any of it due to the fact that Gabe should have been in court the day before finalizing his divorce. Unless he'd changed his mind, of course. She hadn't spoken to anyone from Birch Bay since she'd driven out of there that Friday night, so she rightly didn't know where things stood.

"I brought you a slushie," Bree said.

A blue drink appeared at eye level, and after taking the cup from her sister, Erica looked up. Her sister had turned herself into a bleached blonde the day before. Add to that the maxi dress swirling around her legs and the headband and John Denver sunglasses, and Bree would fit in nicely had it been several decades earlier.

"Do you ever run out of energy?" Erica asked as her sister didn't merely sit on the ground beside her but bounced down into place.

"Rarely." Bree slurped her drink. "So where should we head next?"

"I have no idea."

Bree lifted her cell phone and held it out in front of her. She took a couple of selfies before lowering her hand and looking over at Erica. "Are we just taking one more week, or do you want to go longer?"

Erica considered telling her sister that she was ready to cut the trip short right then and there, but at the same time, she had no idea what she'd do once they finished traveling. Therefore, she kept her mouth shut. Instead, she dug into the straw bag she'd picked up from a shop on the boardwalk earlier in the day and pulled out her own phone. But not for selfies.

"No more than one week," she finally answered. She turned on her cell, having had it off since the previous weekend, and watched as it booted up. "I have no idea how you live like this all the time," she muttered as she waited. "How is it all fun and adventure to you? How do you not need permanence?"

"I need permanence," Bree argued. "Or I will someday."

Erica glanced at her. "Do you really believe that?"

"Absolutely. And I might even settle in Montana when that day happens."

"And I'll believe that when I see it." The phone was up, and Erica ignored her sister and loaded Facebook. She'd taken to only turning her cell on once a week since she'd headed out of town. She hadn't wanted to think about the fact that Gabe wasn't calling her, and she'd certainly not wanted to break down and be the one to call *him*. She'd gotten out of the way for one reason only, and that's because it had been the right thing to do. Calling him would have negated that.

"Anything good happening back home?" Bree asked as she pulled two hot dogs out of her cross-body purse and passed one over to Erica.

"A wedding." Erica turned the screen so Bree could see pictures of the Bird nuptials, then together, the two of them poked fun at everything they saw. It was childish and immature, but at the same time, it was also fun.

When Bree brought up Instagram and started posting on there, Erica shut down her own social media to check her e-mail. She may not have talked to anyone from Birch Bay since leaving, but she had been sending postcards to Maggie and Arsula. And last weekend she'd e-mailed them. The football team had made it past the first postseason game, and while seeking out the scores, Erica had found a picture of Cord standing on the sidelines during that game. She'd been unable to resist sending that photo to Maggie and taunting her new friend with all his manly Wilde hotness.

She smiled now as she saw a return message from Mags.

I was there. OMG . . . HOT!!! But the man disappeared before I could make my way down to him. I must get better at this stalking thing.

Maggie didn't say anything about Gabe in the e-mail because Erica had never mentioned to her friend that she'd fallen for the man. But at this point, she'd grown desperate to hear something about him. Even if it was that he and Michelle *had* gotten back together.

She scrolled through the rest of her e-mails, passing over the majority of them, but paused on one that had come in the middle of the week. "Hmmm."

Bree looked up from her keypad. "Hmmm what?" she said around a bite of hot dog.

"I have an e-mail from Gabe's sister."

Opening it, Erica went weepy at the picture that immediately displayed. "Dani had her baby."

She and Bree admired the pink-bowed newborn for several seconds before Erica pulled the phone back and read through the rest of the message. There was an update on Haley and Jenna, a recipe Dani had gotten from Gloria that she suspected Erica might like, and she found out that Dani and Ben had won a Halloween costume contest only hours before she'd gone into labor.

"Sounds like everyone is doing well," she said as she closed the e-mail.

"Any mention of Gabe?"

Erica shook her head. Over the first few days of their trip, she'd filled her sister in on what had happened with Gabe, and then they hadn't talked about him since. That hadn't kept her from missing him, though.

"Any missed messages from him?" Bree prodded hopefully.

Erica glanced at the icon for text messages. "Nope."

But then, she hadn't called or texted *him*, either.

Regardless of the silence—and her lack of knowing anything that had gone on in his life over the past few weeks—she found that she wasn't ready to give up on him quite yet. Not if he was divorced, anyway. And maybe he wasn't finished with her?

"I just wish I knew if he went through with it," she mumbled. "His court date was supposed to be this week."

Her sister dropped back to the sand then and stared up at the sky, and sensing something wasn't right with the situation, Erica looked over at her. "What?" she asked when Bree didn't meet her eyes.

Bree grimaced in response, and Erica's radar went on alert.

"What?" she asked again.

"It's just that"—Bree swallowed—"I could *probably* find that out for you. If you want me to."

Erica went still. "And how could you do that?"

Bree still didn't look at her. "I could ask Cord."

"Cord *Wilde*?" Erica turned in the sand until she directly faced her sister. "You're in touch with Cord? Since when?"

293

"Since I got his number when I met him." Bree closed her eyes and muttered, "We've been texting."

As Bree's words set in, Erica's eyes narrowed. She jabbed her finger into her sister's side until Bree opened her eyes, and when their gazes finally met, Erica said, "You and Cord have been texting for two months?"

"Nothing is going on, E. So stop mothering me."

"I'm not mothering. I'm just"—she sighed before finishing—"I'm not. I swear." But she knew that she was. "Okay, fine," she protested when Bree simply stared at her. "I am, but I can't help it. It's who I am, okay? Cut me some slack."

"You cut me some slack. Whatever man I might be talking to has nothing to do with you."

"But Cord isn't the man for you."

"And how do you know that?"

"Because he's ten years older, Bree. And because he's probably slept with twenty-five times as many people as you have."

"You don't know how many people I've slept with."

"I know I don't. But I do know that you're still just a kid compared to him." She eyed her baby sister as she remained lying in the sand, her hair splayed out around her head. Honestly, Erica had been doing really good trying not to butt in to Bree's life over the last few weeks. But she hadn't known she'd been texting with Cord!

But since she had been, did that mean she'd heard something about Gabe that she hadn't shared?

"Just be careful, will you?" Erica grumbled. She smacked sand off her capris. "Don't do anything you shouldn't. I wouldn't want to see you hurt."

Bree rolled her eyes at the words. "We've not *done* anything. I haven't even seen him since the cookout. We just text once in a while."

"Good. Keep it that way."

"I'm not a kid, you know." Bree might have pulled her statement off better if she hadn't made a face and stuck out her tongue, but after her bit of rebellion, she went to work texting, so Erica left her alone.

Erica held her breath as messages flew back and forth, and after what seemed like a good fifteen minutes, Bree finally sat up.

"Well?"

Her sister nodded. "Judge ordered it yesterday. And, E . . ." Bree paused, her eyes wide and round. "Michelle signed away her parental rights."

"What? People can do that?"

"Apparently so." She held up her phone. "Cord says she tried to blackmail Gabe—custody or a payout—and they all came together to make her life a living hell instead. They brought in the cavalry, prepared to prove her unfit, but she bailed. She didn't want the bad publicity."

Gabe was free.

And Jenna could finally be happy.

Erica stared down at her phone again, her heart hammering as she fought with herself on whether to send him a message or not. But what should she say? Congratulations on the dissolution of your marriage? Would he send *her* a message now that it was over?

In the end, she brought up last night's high school football scores, instead. Then she let out a whoosh of air at what she saw. She turned to Bree. "They're going to the state championship."

"The football team?"

Erica nodded.

"Which team?"

When they'd checked the scores from the games the weekend before, they'd discovered that both Birch Bay and Silver Creek had won in the first round. Winning their respective games this week meant they would be down to only one opponent—each other—since round three would determine the champions.

Erica smiled. "Both of them. And they're playing at Silver Creek."

A broad grin broke out on her sister's face, and she immediately hopped to her feet. "Then that's where we're heading next. We're going to Silver Creek."

Erica agreed. "We're going to Silver Creek."

Chapter Twenty-Six

The stands were completely packed when Erica and Bree showed up for the Montana High School State Football Championship, but Erica didn't worry about finding a seat. If it came down to standing or sitting, she'd stand—right in front of the stands, with the visiting team's coach.

She giggled to herself at the thought. She'd been running on high since the weekend before, anxious to get back to Montana. She'd neither called Gabe to let him know she'd be there tonight, nor informed anyone other than their parents that she and Bree even planned to be in the area. She'd merely wanted to show up and see if she couldn't be the center of attention again, but this time because *she* planned to cause a spectacle that would hopefully change her life—and not because one would happen to her.

Only, before she and Bree had made it all the way back to their home state, they'd made two more stops on their road trip, this time in Colorado and Wyoming. They'd hiked in Estes Park before going white-water rafting in Wind River Canyon. The views had been spectacular with each, and for a Montana girl who'd grown up with some of the most beautiful scenery in the world, she'd determined that she could have spent a week riding the water between those rock walls. It had thrilled her to find an outdoor activity that she actually loved, and she couldn't wait to try to drag Gabe and Jenna off to do it with her.

"There he is," Bree announced in a hushed tone. As if anyone could hear them in the pregame crowd. Bree pointed, and Erica followed her gaze to the front of the stands. Only to see that her sister had pointed out Cord.

"That is *not* the brother I'm here to see."

"But it's the brother I'm after."

Infectious laughter spilled from Bree, and all Erica could do was shake her head. Bree would be Bree, no matter what. And Erica would not be telling her sister that it was quite possible Maggie had made the trek to Silver Creek as well, and that she would also have her sights set on the man. As would potentially every single woman in the stands. Some things her sister would have to learn on her own.

"There's Mom and Dad." Erica motioned to their parents sitting about two-thirds of the way up the stands. Seth's two boys sat with them, and between the four of them, there seemed to be enough blankets packed in to cover everyone in the stands. She waved when they saw her, but she didn't pause in her pursuit to find the right seat. She'd see her family later that weekend, anyway. Annalise would be in for the weekend, and Erica and Bree had promised to stick around for a rare family dinner.

Finally, Erica's gaze landed on the person she'd been hoping to find. And there even looked to be space for two additional people.

"Come on." She grabbed her sister's hand and dragged her up the bleachers, and when she got to the fifteenth riser, Erica got the exact reaction she'd been hoping for.

"Ms. Bird!" Jenna threw herself into Erica's arms. "You came," she whispered into Erica's ear. "I knew you would."

"You did?" Erica looked at the child she'd been missing almost as much as the man. "And how did you know I'd be here?"

"Because my daddy and I have been missing you *so much*."

Love flooded Erica. She squeezed Jenna to her chest again and nodded a hello at Nick, Harper, Max, and Gloria, then looked back down at the little girl. "I've been missing you so much, too."

She'd shown up tonight certain in her feelings for Gabe, and she hadn't for a moment let herself entertain the thought that he would have moved on without her. He'd never said he loved her, but some things a girl just knew. Or they hoped they knew.

Because surely her feelings hadn't all been one-sided.

He may or may not be in love with her yet, but she intended to stick close to his side until he fell. And then she intended to move in even tighter.

When the crowd around them started making noises about the two of them sitting down, Erica realized that Bree had already taken a seat, and that someone else had wedged in nearby, shrinking the remaining space. This meant that Erica would either have to sit somewhere else or take Jenna's seat and let the girl sit in her lap.

She looked at Gabe's daughter. "You up for sharing a seat with me tonight?"

"I'm up for anything, Ms. Bird. As long as you promise to stay and talk to my daddy. He'll be grumpy again if he finds out you were here and didn't talk to him."

"Then I promise to stay and talk to your daddy."

Gabe's family chuckled—since they'd all apparently been tuned in to the conversation—and made enough room for Erica to squeeze in between Bree and Harper. She looked around once more, making sure she hadn't missed anyone, then leaned across Bree to ask, "Ben and Haley stay home with Dani and the new baby?"

"They did," Gloria answered. Her cheeks lit up like lights on a Christmas tree. "That little girl is so precious."

"'Bout ready for a grandson, though," Gabe's dad added before turning his gaze to Nick and Harper. "Seems to me someone else could be putting some effort into that."

As Gabe's brother tried to dodge the comment, Erica turned back to Jenna. It was great to see her doing so well. "How's school?" she asked.

Jenna smiled instantly. "I love my new teacher."

"Are you working very hard to be a good student?"

"I am. Just like you taught me."

"Good." Erica hugged Jenna to her. "Then you've made my day."

Erica looked out over the little girl's head, her eyes scanning the field, but Gabe was nowhere to be seen. When a hand landed on her knee, she glanced over to find Gabe's dad peering across the space at her.

"It's good to see you here tonight," he told her. "Gabe is going to be thrilled."

She laid her hand on his. "I wouldn't have missed this for the world."

One minute twenty-five seconds remained in the first half, Birch Bay was on the offensive, behind by two. Cheerleaders climbed into pyramids at each end of the stands as corresponding bands played their school songs, and the crowd roared louder than any game Gabe had previously coached. But none of that bothered him because tonight he was focused. Win or lose, this was his battle to fight.

He called for the play. It was the Hail Mary he and Cord had developed earlier in the season, and a move originally planned for the end of a game. So when the quarterback sought him out from inside the huddle, Gabe gave a nod. It might not be Hail Mary time, but he didn't want his boys going into halftime down by *any*.

Time ticked down and the players got into position, but the guys continued to stall as they kept an eye on the play clock. They needed to run the play at exactly the right second so Silver Creek wouldn't get the chance to retaliate. As Gabe watched along with the rest of the crowd, he heard his brother make a "hmmm" sound to his left.

"What?"

"Nothing." Cord's reply came quick. "Sorry."

Gave shot him a look. "You think I made the wrong call?"

"It's not about the call." Cord nodded at the field, as if telling Gabe to get his head back into it, and Gabe glanced at the play clock again. Almost time.

"Then what's it about?"

"Erica."

The center snapped the ball, but Gabe missed the moment. Because he'd turned to stare at his brother. "Is she here?"

"I just laid eyes on her."

Gabe forced himself to return his gaze to the field instead of the stands. The quarterback faked, then handed off the ball. "Where is she?"

"Sitting with Jenna."

Adrenaline burned inside Gabe as Chase wove through the defense, his long strides eating up the distance and pulling him out in front of everyone else. And though there was still thirty-five yards to go—and still a chance any mishap could happen—Gabe could wait no longer. If Erica was there sitting with his daughter, it had to mean she *wasn't* there sitting with her ex. He faced the stands.

Everyone was on their feet, screaming and cheering, and there wasn't a snowball's chance in hell he could pick out Erica's sweet face in the sea of colors. Yet somehow he did.

Her hair was shorter than it had been before, and Jenna bounced up and down on the riser in front of her. But even though every other pair of eyes seemed to be watching the play in action, Gabe would bet his last dollar that Erica had hers directly on him.

"Hey, Coach," Cord murmured as the noise level increased.

"Yeah?"

"We scored. Thought you might want to know."

Gabe dropped his head, but only for the second needed to reorient himself, then he rejoined the game. His boys set up for the extra point, and they took that with them into the locker room, as well. Half the game was over, and he'd gotten them into great position to finish it out.

He had to get to the locker room with the team, but first he turned back to the stands. The crowd had thinned as people headed for the concession stand, and there was no sign of his family. Yet Erica remained, her eyes still on him, and he would swear they spoke to each other across the distance. It was too scary to think she might have said what he'd just said, but his heart insisted otherwise.

She smiled then, the look tender, and blew him a kiss. And as he turned and jogged to the locker room, he knew that no matter the outcome of the game, absolutely everything in his life was finally going to be fine.

Chapter Twenty-Seven

"Tough loss," Cord said. His words drew Gabe's attention from the end zone, where his team had just lost by one play.

"Yeah," Gabe agreed. He'd really thought they were going to pull it off.

"Better luck next year," someone else offered. A hand slapped Gabe on the back as the man passed, and Gabe had the thought that he certainly hoped there was a next year. He may no longer be coaching to prove himself to anyone, but he sure enjoyed the game.

As the boys made their way through the opposing team's players, congratulations being tossed out by those whose spirits hadn't been completely crushed, Gabe turned his attention to a single woman standing in the middle of the Birch Bay crowd. Her eyes were glued to his, her smile a mile wide, and it no longer mattered that they'd lost. Because Gabe had every intention of kissing the very last breath out of her in the next few minutes.

He took off, ignoring whomever called out behind him, and tried to remain cool and collected. But he soon gave that up. He jogged to the fence separating the field from the bleachers, which forced him to stop twenty feet in front of Erica.

The majority of the remaining fans, no matter which side they cheered for, stopped what they were doing to watch, and the attention only fired the need in Gabe. Murmurs wound through the crowd when he crooked his finger at the woman he loved, and her feet began to move. He picked up on a couple of whispered "Ms. Birds" throughout the crowd as she made her way to him, and he just smiled.

That's right. He was seeking out Ms. Bird. Right there at a football game, in front of God and everyone.

And it was *not* because he intended to humiliate her.

Two more steps, and there she was, nothing separating them but four feet of chain link. He shouldn't have made her come to him; he should have scaled the fence.

"Hi." Her smile had turned tender again.

"Hi," he replied. He'd wanted to call her so many times since she left. "My divorce is final."

"So I heard."

She looked so good.

And he loved her so much.

"Then will you please come home with me? I miss you more than any one person should ever have to put up with." He leaned in an inch. "I *need* you more than one person should have to put up with."

"But do you *love* me more than one person should have to put up with?"

Her words gave him pause, but he quickly recovered. Surely she wouldn't ask about love if she didn't feel it, too. He nodded, letting the teasing drop from his eyes. "I do," he whispered. "More than I'll ever be able to show you."

He took in every detail of her face as she stared back at him, drinking her in as if it had been a year instead of a month since he'd last seen her. Then finally, he reached across the top of the fence and allowed himself to touch her. He took her hands in his, but when her fingers didn't squeeze his in return, worry crept along his spine. "And do you love me?" he asked bluntly.

Why hadn't she said it?

She stared at him, her smile slipping away, and fear gnawed hard. But he ignored it. He wouldn't consider alternate outcomes. She was here. She had to care.

And anyway, if she rejected him tonight, he'd simply try again tomorrow. That had been his plan all along. He'd had to get through his divorce, then this championship game, and then he'd intended to hunt her down and drag her back to where she belonged—whether she'd been with her idiotic ex or not.

She belonged with *him*. And with Jenna.

They belonged together.

"Erica." He tightened his fingers on hers, refusing to believe in anything other than them. "Say something, baby. We have an audience." He thought about the night her world had first fallen apart. It had been with an audience of football fans, as well. In these very stands.

And then she nodded. "I suspect I just might," she said softly.

He blew out a breath. "You suspect? Any chance I might hear it from you anytime soon?" He'd beg to hear those words from her.

"You might."

Suddenly she smiled again, her eyes taking on a hot glow, but this time the smile was that naughty curve of her lips she liked to use when she was trying to get him riled up. He'd been had.

He tugged her until her knees bumped the fence. "You're a tease, Erica Bird."

"That's only because you haven't kissed me yet, Gabriel Wilde." Her gaze lowered to his mouth. "I need to make sure we didn't forget how to do that before I say three little words I might live to regret."

"Oh, you won't regret them." He cupped the back of her neck. "I can promise you that."

He didn't know if the remaining crowd went quiet when his lips touched Erica's, but he certainly heard no sounds coming from any of them. Instead, he picked up on Erica's soft murmurs as he did his best to not only provide the woman of his dreams with the best kiss of her life but also to show her without words how very much she meant to him.

It hadn't been easy, her not being there with him that past month, but he'd come to appreciate the fact that she'd had to step away while he got his life sorted out. She'd needed the chance to get her head on straight, as well. Doing anything else wouldn't have been fair to either of them.

When their mouths finally separated, the crowd once again roared, but this time, it was for them. Football had been forgotten.

"Way to go, Ms. Bird."

"Kiss her again, Coach."

"Get a room!"

Others laughed at the last one, and Gabe dropped his forehead to Erica's, his nose touching hers. "I love you, Ms. Bird. We may have taken the long route to get here from our college days, but what I feel for you now can't be questioned. This is real. You and I fit, and our time apart only solidified that for me. So will you *please* come home to me? To us? Jenna and I need you in our lives."

She touched his cheek. "And I love you, Coach Wilde." Her lips curved with her words. "Long route or not, I'm just glad that I found you again, because I happen to think that we fit, too. So yes. Since you asked so nicely, I *will* come home to you. To Jenna. I don't want a life without either of you in it."

Epilogue

"D id you want your present?"

Gabe sat upright at the question from the woman beside him, the sheet falling to his lap and exposing both of their bare chests. "You got me a present? I didn't know we needed presents."

It had been one month since the championship game, meaning thirty days that the two of them had officially been dating. There had already been three snows in Birch Bay, Thanksgiving had come and gone, and Erica had hosted two dinner parties at the fire hall—which she'd subsequently purchased. She was also back at the school again, substituting as needed and filling the rest of her time tutoring. And she'd already been offered a full-time position for the following year.

At the same time, he'd had his coaching contract extended.

She leaned over the edge of the mattress, the curve of her back capturing his attention as she pulled a wrapped box out from under the bed. Then she sat back up and presented it to him as if serving up a gourmet dinner for a very special guest. "We don't *need* presents," she told him. She eyed the box now in his hands and added, "Except . . . *you* might need this one."

That was all he needed to hear. He ripped the wrapping off in two quick moves, and grunted when he found the box taped shut on all four sides.

"You're an evil woman, Erica Yarbrough."

She gave him the smile he loved so much. She'd told him she wanted to go by her maiden name again and had the paperwork already waiting to be signed off on. However, his plans were to turn Yarbrough into Wilde just as soon as he could talk her into it.

"And I think you might like evil," she taunted.

"I think you might be right." With his thumbs, he popped the tape, two sides at a time, and then he lifted the top of the box. And what little blood that had managed to make it back to his brain in the last fifteen minutes once again headed south.

Sitting inside the pale-yellow tissue paper was a tiny little sleeveless vest and a super short skirt. They were black, white, and yellow, with the words "Silver Creek" stitched across the front of the vest. It was her old cheer uniform.

"It still fits," she whispered into his ear.

"Then you have exactly one minute to get it on."

She squealed when he reached for her, but instead of grabbing up the uniform, she leaned into his chest. "I love you, Gabe. And I love your daughter. I'm in no hurry to move beyond what we currently are, but I want you to know that I'm here for you from now on. And I'll be here for you for forever."

He kissed her gently on the lips. It may have taken a number of years for them to make their way back to each other, but Gabe had no doubt they were where they belonged. That life was as it should be.

"I love you, too," he told her, his heart open for her to see. "But for the record, I *am* in a hurry. My daughter needs a mother who can actually love her—and my father seems to think that he needs a grandson."

He held his breath as he waited for her response.

"Kids?" Warmth colored her cheeks. She nodded. "I think I'd like kids."

"I know I would with you."

He kissed her again, and when they finally came up for air, he dangled the uniform from one finger. "One minute, Yarbrough."

"Fine. But you have to go downstairs and wait for me."

He looked down at his nakedness. "Why?"

She pressed her lips to his. "Trust me."

So he did as she'd asked, not bothering with clothes but grabbing a condom just in case. He headed down the stairs, and not two minutes later she yelled for him. Only, she didn't yell from the top of the stairs.

He crossed the room, his erection already growing at what he suspected was to come, then he looked directly up when he got to the pole. Ten feet above him, there was a pair of naked thighs wrapped about the pole, the outline of a skirt, and bare-naked butt cheeks heading his way.

He laughed as she slid into his arms, then he trapped the woman he loved up against the very place it had started.

Acknowledgments

This book was like birthing a baby. A very large, stubborn, and resistant baby. And I fear that baby would still be dug in tight if not for quite a few people in my life who had to listen to my woes time and again. Not to mention try to help me solve the puzzle of just what Gabe and Erica's story was supposed to be. I'd like to apologize to all those people for needing them so much in order to get this book finished, but at the same time, I also know that no apology is truly necessary. Because that's what friends are for. With that said, I *will* add that I'm so completely grateful for your friendships.

Now, I shall attempt to name all those people (but please forgive me if I miss someone!):

Anne Marie Becker, June Love, Lizzie Shane, Autumn Jordan, Darynda Jones, Emma Leigh Reed, Terri Osburn, Isabelle Osburn, my husband, probably even my son, my mother (this one is for making her continually worry that I'd never get this book finished), my agent, Nalini Akolekar (to whom I suspect I added a few gray hairs), and my editor, Chris Werner (whom I might have given his first gray hair).

Additionally, I want to give a shout out to Bette Hansen and Gina Meier for helping me with some last-minute naming issues when I couldn't come up with anything myself. Bette and Gina are a couple of my super readers, *all* of whom I'm so thankful for.

And last, this book would never have gotten fully baked at all if not for my developmental editor, Krista Stroever. I'm so sorry you had to put so much effort into helping with this one—and I'm doubly apologetic that you had to spend your birthday rereading this book!—but I'm also quite pleased with the result. Thank you for all your help.

About the Author

As a child, award-winning author Kim Law cultivated a love for chocolate, anything purple, and creative writing. She penned her debut work, *The Gigantic Talking Raisin*, in sixth grade and got hooked on the delights of creating stories. Before settling into the writing life, however, she earned a degree in mathematics and worked for years as a computer programmer. Now she's living out her lifelong dream of writing romance novels. She's won the Romance Writers of America (RWA) Golden Heart Award, been a finalist for the prestigious RITA Award, and served in various positions for her local RWA chapter. A native of Kentucky, Kim lives with her husband and an assortment of animals in Middle Tennessee.